Palgrave Studies in the Enlightenment, Romanticism and Cultures of Print

Palgrave Studies in the Enlightenment, Romanticism and Cultures of Print will feature work that does not fit comfortably within established boundaries – whether between periods or between disciplines. Uniquely, it will combine efforts to engage the power and materiality of print with explorations of gender, race, and class. By attending as well to intersections of literature with the visual arts, medicine, law, and science, the series will enable a large-scale rethinking of the origins of modernity.

Titles include:

Melanie Bigold
WOMEN OF LETTERS, MANUSCRIPT CIRCULATION, AND PRINT AFTERLIVES IN THE EIGHTEENTH CENTURY
Elizabeth Rowe, Catharine Cockburn, and Elizabeth Carter

Ildiko Csengei
SYMPATHY, SENSIBILITY AND THE LITERATURE OF FEELING IN THE EIGHTEENTH CENTURY

Noah Comet
ROMANTIC HELLENISM AND WOMEN WRITERS

Alexander Dick
ROMANTICISM AND THE GOLD STANDARD
Money, Literature, and Economic Debate in Britain 1790–1830

Elizabeth Eger
BLUESTOCKINGS
Women of Reason from Enlightenment to Romanticism

Ina Ferris and Paul Keen (*editors*)
BOOKISH HISTORIES
Books, Literature, and Commercial Modernity, 1700–1900

John Gardner
POETRY AND POPULAR PROTEST
Peterloo, Cato Street and the Queen Caroline Controversy

George C. Grinnell
THE AGE OF HYPOCHONDRIA
Interpreting Romantic Health and Illness

Anthony S. Jarrells
BRITAIN'S BLOODLESS REVOLUTIONS
1688 and the Romantic Reform of Literature

Emrys Jones
FRIENDSHIP AND ALLEGIANCE IN EIGHTEENTH-CENTURY LITERATURE
The Politics of Private Virtue in the Age of Walpole

Jacqueline M. Labbe
WRITING ROMANTICISM
Charlotte Smith and William Wordsworth, 1784–1807

Michelle Levy
FAMILY AUTHORSHIP AND ROMANTIC PRINT CULTURE

April London
LITERARY HISTORY WRITING, 1770–1820

Robert Miles
ROMANTIC MISFITS

Robert Morrison and Daniel Sanjiv Roberts (*editors*)
ROMANTICISM AND *BLACKWOOD'S MAGAZINE*
'An Unprecedented Phenomenon'

Catherine Packham
EIGHTEENTH-CENTURY VITALISM
Bodies, Culture, Politics

Nicola Parsons
READING GOSSIP IN EARLY EIGHTEENTH-CENTURY ENGLAND

Jessica Richard
THE ROMANCE OF GAMBLING IN THE EIGHTEENTH-CENTURY BRITISH NOVEL

Andrew Rudd
SYMPATHY AND INDIA IN BRITISH LITERATURE, 1770–1830

Sharon Ruston
CREATING ROMANTICISM
Case Studies in the Literature, Science and Medicine of the 1790s

Erik Simpson
LITERARY MINSTRELSY, 1770–1830
Minstrels and Improvisers in British, Irish and American Literature

Anne H. Stevens
BRITISH HISTORICAL FICTION BEFORE SCOTT

David Stewart
ROMANTIC MAGAZINES AND METROPOLITAN LITERARY CULTURE

Rebecca Tierney-Hynes
NOVEL MINDS
Philosophers and Romance Readers, 1680–1740

P. Westover
NECROMANTICISM
Travelling to Meet the Dead, 1750–1860

Esther Wohlgemut
ROMANTIC COSMOPOLITANISM

Palgrave Studies in the Enlightenment, Romanticism and Cultures of Print
Series Standing Order ISBN 978–1–403–93408–6 hardback 978–1–403–93409–3 paperback
(*outside North America only*)

You can receive future titles in this series as they are published by placing a standing order. Please contact your bookseller or, in case of difficulty, write to us at the address below with your name and address, the title of the series and the ISBN quoted above.

Customer Services Department, Macmillan Distribution Ltd, Houndmills, Basingstoke, Hampshire RG21 6XS, England

---

Also by Sharon Ruston

SHELLEY AND VITALITY

ROMANTICISM: An Introduction

THE INFLUENCE AND ANXIETY OF THE BRITISH ROMANTICS: Spectres of Romanticism (*ed.*)

LITERATURE AND SCIENCE (*ed.*)

TEACHING ROMANTICISM (*ed. with David Higgins*)

Creating Romanticism

Case Studies in the Literature, Science and Medicine of the 1790s

Sharon Ruston
Chair in Nineteenth-Century Literature and Culture,
University of Salford, UK

palgrave
macmillan

First published 2013 by
PALGRAVE MACMILLAN

Palgrave Macmillan in the UK is an imprint of Macmillan Publishers Limited, registered in England, company number 785998, of Houndmills, Basingstoke, Hampshire RG21 6XS.

Palgrave Macmillan in the US is a division of St Martin's Press LLC, 175 Fifth Avenue, New York, NY 10010.

Palgrave Macmillan is the global academic imprint of the above companies and has companies and representatives throughout the world.

Palgrave® and Macmillan® are registered trademarks in the United States, the United Kingdom, Europe and other countries.

ISBN 978–1–137–26428–2

This book is printed on paper suitable for recycling and made from fully managed and sustained forest sources. Logging, pulping and manufacturing processes are expected to conform to the environmental regulations of the country of origin.

A catalogue record for this book is available from the British Library.

A catalog record for this book is available from the Library of Congress.

Typeset by MPS Limited, Chennai, India.

This book is for Jerome de Groot, whom I love very much

Contents

Acknowledgements

This book has taken me a long time to write and its debts are many. I'd like to thank the following for their generosity in sharing their expertise and helping me with queries: David Amigoni, Stephen Bending, Brycchan Carey, Monika Class, Alex Dracobly, David Duff, Cian Duffy, Tim Fulford, James Grande, Jan Golinski, David Higgins, Maurice Hindle, Frank James, Anne Janowitz, Chris Jones, Vivien Jones, David Knight, Simon Kövesi, David McClay, Clare McManus, Robert Mitchell, Lynda Pratt, Richard de Ritter, George Rousseau, Aris Sarafianos, Phil Shaw, Jane Spencer, Stephanie Snow, Alannah Tomkins, Neil Vickers, Ian Watts, Sarah M. Zimmerman. I am grateful to the anonymous reader for such a positive endorsement of this book. I would also like to thank my PhD students, Wahida Amin, Jessica Evans, Alison Morgan, and Jen Morgan for many stimulating conversations, as well as the entire LitSciMed group who made thinking about all of this so much fun. I am particularly grateful to Simon Bainbridge and Peter Kitson who continue in their roles as mentors despite the fact that I'm supposed to be a grown-up now. Alison Morgan, Bernadette Ruston, Gavin Ruston, and Matthew Sangster helped me in the preparation of the manuscript when help was most needed. Thanks too to my colleagues in English at the University of Salford who have stuck together during the most awful times.

I would like to thank my friends for their support and encouragement, reminding me that there is much more to life and doing their best to distract me from the writing of this book, particularly thanks to Dominique Aspey, Richard Ball, Helen Burness, Sue Chaplin, Bal Chima, Richard Clemens, Jen Cockin, Ben Crouch, Lou Curtis, Tim Derby, Jon Dickson, Christian Dixon, Sunil Duggal, Phil East, Lucy Hill, Parveen Khan, Jelena Lee, Sean McKenzie, Daniel Murphy, Al Raven, Julie Sheppard, James Stanley, Kath Taylor, Dale Watson, and Richard Willock. Thanks also to my family, George, Bernadette, and Gavin Ruston. This book is dedicated to Jerome, whom I love very much; thank you for keeping me sane during the writing of it.

The librarians and archivists in the British Library, National Library of Scotland, Royal Institution, New York Public Library, Bodleian Library, and American Philosophical Society have been hugely helpful. I need to thank the Research Institute for the Humanities at Keele University and the British Academy for financial support. Thanks to the Bodleian Libraries, University of Oxford for permission to quote from Oxford, Bodleian Library, MS. Abinger c. 8, fol. 72. The Humphry Davy manuscripts are published here by courtesy of the Royal Institution of Great Britain. The Carl H. Pforzheimer Collection of Shelley and His Circle, the New York Public Library, Astor, Lenox and Tilden Foundations granted me permission to quote from Pforzheimer Misc. MS 4039. Thanks to the American Philosophical Society for permission to quote from the William Temple papers.

I am grateful to Pickering and Chatto for allowing me to reproduce 'Authority and Imposture: William Godwin and the Animal Magnetists', in *Liberating Medicine, 1720–1835*, ed. by Tristanne Connolly and Steve Clark (Pickering and Chatto, 2009), pp. 153–64, in Chapter 2. Chapter 1 contains a small amount of material previously published in *Literature and Science* (D.S. Brewer, 2008) and is reproduced by permission of the English Association and the publisher, Boydell & Brewer.

List of Abbreviations and Manuscripts

Biographia	Coleridge, S.T. (1993) *Biographia Literaria*, J. Engell and W. Jackson Bate (eds) (Princeton: Princeton University Press)
Coleridge Letters	Coleridge, S.T. (1956–71) *The Collected Letters of Samuel Taylor Coleridge*, E.L. Griggs (ed.), 5 vols (Oxford: Clarendon Press)
Collected Works	Davy, H. (1839) *The Collected Works of Humphry Davy*, John Davy (ed.), 9 vols (London: Smith, Elder, and Co.)
Davy Letters	Davy's letters are in the process of being transcribed and annotated for a print edition. They are currently available here: <http://www.davy-letters.org.uk/>. I shall also give a printed source if there is one or an archive reference if not.
Godwin Diary	Godwin, W. (2010) *The Diary of William Godwin*, V. Myers, D. O'Shaughnessy and M. Philp (eds) (Oxford: Oxford Digital Library) <http://godwindiary.bodleian.ox.ac.uk>
Novels and Memoirs	Godwin, W. (1992) *Collected Novels and Memoirs*, M. Philp (ed.), 8 vols (London: Pickering and Chatto)
Philosophy	Smellie, W. (1790) *The Philosophy of Natural History* (Edinburgh: Charles Elliot, et al.)
Political Writings	Godwin, W. (1993) *Political and Philosophical Writings*, M. Philp (ed.), 7 vols (London: Pickering and Chatto)
Prose Works	Wordsworth, W. (1974) *Prose Works*, W.J.B. Owen and J.W. Smyser (eds), 3 vols (Oxford: Clarendon Press)
Southey Letters	Southey, R. (2009–11) *The Collected Letters of Robert Southey*, I. Packer and L. Pratt (eds), 8 Parts, A Romantic Circles Electronic Edition, Part One: 1791–1797 and Part Two: 1798–1803 <http://www.rc.umd.edu/editions/southey_letters/>

Works	Wollstonecraft, M. (1989) *The Works of Mary Wollstonecraft*, J. Todd and M. Butler (eds), 7 vols (London: William Pickering)

The Bodleian Libraries, University of Oxford
Oxford, Bodleian Library, MS. Abinger c. 8, fol. 72 Letter from Anthony Carlisle to William Godwin

Carl H. Pforzheimer Collection of Shelley and His Circle, the New York Public Library, Astor, Lenox and Tilden Foundations
Pforzheimer Misc. MS 4039 Joseph Johnson's Letterbook of 1795–1810

Royal Institution of Great Britain
RI MS HD 13c Davy's Personal Notebook
RI MS HD 13f Davy's Personal Notebook
RI MS HD 13h Davy's Personal Notebook
RI MS HD 20b Davy's Personal Notebook
RI MS HD 20c Davy's Personal Notebook

American Philosophical Society
William Temple Franklin Papers, American Philosophical Society, CVI, 94 Letter from Benjamin Vaughan to William Temple Franklin.

Introduction

In a notebook kept around the time that he worked on his safety lamp (circa 1815), the invention that would be praised for the countless lives it saved in British mines, Humphry Davy writes the following:

> Those brilliant and poetical works in which enthusiasm takes place of reason, and in which the human intellect exhausts itself, as it were, in imagination and feeling, resemble monstrous flowers, brilliant and odorous, but affording no materials of re-production
>
> (*Collected Works*, I, 212)[1]

He is writing of a particular kind of poetry here perhaps, rather than poetry in general, but there is further evidence in the notebooks for Davy's coming to distinguish between poetry and science in these ways.[2] For example, comparing Shakespeare to Bacon and Milton to Newton around 1805, Davy writes: 'The object of poetry, whatever may be said by poets, is more to amuse than to instruct; the object of science more to instruct than amuse' (*Collected Works*, I, 147). It is important to keep in mind the fact that, notwithstanding such views, Davy himself wrote poetry throughout his life, but it does seem that he valued chemistry more highly for these reasons.

These quotations introduce many of the topics of this book: Davy sets up an opposition between intellect, reason, and instruction, on the side of science, against imagination, feeling, enthusiasm, beauty, amusement, and sensual pleasure on the side of poetry.[3] In the 1790s, the decade with which much of this book is concerned, these oppositions were not rigidly in place: in Davy's writings we find, for example, a conviction that brilliance, beauty, and imagination were to be seen in chemistry, which he regards as a sublime science. Much of the literary writing considered in this book (admittedly, not all of it poetry) is informed by a sophisticated understanding of scientific and medical ideas; it exhibits both intellect and reason, and often there is a distinct aim to instruct the reader. The question of the reproductive qualities of literature is considered in Chapter 3. Taken as a whole, this book contends that science and medicine should be recognized as playing a part in the creation of what we now, anachronistically, call 'Romanticism'.[4] It recognizes, as do the writers themselves, that scientific and medical writing as much as any other kind of writing is a product of its historical moment and shows that this writing is employed knowingly for political purposes.

My previous book, *Shelley and Vitality*, investigated Percy Shelley's uses of biology, or the science of life (Ruston 2005). Two important areas worthy of further research emerged from my work on this book. First, that many other poets and novelists of the Romantic period, some of whom are far less well known than Shelley for their interest in the natural or physical sciences, shared his interest in and use of such scientific knowledge. Second, that the surgeons debating these ideas were motivated by contemporary politics and religion as well as by science, and that their arguments used the rhetorical techniques and devices common to all texts just as they suffered the same possibilities and problems of interpretation. Using specific case studies, in this new book I look at the ways in which a range of writers of the Romantic era participated in contemporary debates, expressing scientific knowledge within a recognizably Romantic aesthetic. My emphasis on the traditional themes and concerns of the period allows me to explore Romantic-era culture by a method of cross-section.

It is testament to the extensive work that has been published in this area in the past twenty years that the claim that Romantic writers were not necessarily anti-science no longer seems far-fetched.[5] It is now sometimes the case that scientific and medical contexts are included in general textbook readers of Romanticism (see Bainbridge 2008). Literature and science constitute an exciting sub-field within the larger discipline of Romantic-period literature, although it is as yet nowhere near as established and accepted as it is in Victorian literary studies, for which the work of Gillian Beer is largely responsible.[6] Within the History of Science, the Romantic era (broadly 1780 to 1820) is awarded particular significance: the turn of the nineteenth century has been described as witnessing a 'second scientific revolution', which, according to Paul Wood, 'marked the shift from natural philosophy to "science" in our current sense of the term' (Wood 2004, 6). It is generally agreed that this historical period saw the beginning of a new era of scientific specialization with the creation of many societies crucial to the development of disciplines that we still have today; and, connected to this, that it witnessed the beginnings of the professionalization of science, indicated by a move from provincial to institutionalized science.[7]

Despite my use of 'Romanticism' in the title of the book, I follow critics who view Romantic writing as a product of its historical times, marked by revolution and repression, rather than as a single, unified movement (see Ruston 2007). Even so, most would agree that there are a number of keywords, issues, or themes, that are of general importance to the period and in each chapter I examine a specific aspect of these: nature and the natural, the imagination, literary creation and creativity, and the sublime.[8] Some of these concepts have fallen out of favour over the past thirty years, but there has also been recent work undertaken to recover these ideas in their original historical and political contexts and I hope that this book will add to this project with relevant scientific and medical history.[9] I show in each individual case study how understandings of these key concepts were informed by, challenged by, or emerged in opposition to scientific material and knowledge. My larger claim, then, is that what became known as 'Romanticism' was created by scientific as well as literary and philosophical ideas. I deal in the main with British scientific, medical, and literary writings, leaving *naturphilosophie* aside as a markedly different tradition.

I recognize that I am in danger of re-inscribing difference – of a 'two cultures' kind – with my insistence in labelling types of knowledge as either 'scientific' or 'literary': in reality it is clear that there was a public sphere in which both poets and men of science participated. That said, many of the literary writers here seem conscious themselves that they are engaging with material of a different nature: for example, Mary Wollstonecraft is keen to note that she has 'conversed, as man with man, with medical men, on anatomical subjects' and S.T. Coleridge is eager to show off his knowledge of chemical nomenclature (*Works*, v, 193, n. 3). Ralph O'Connor has persuasively argued that discussion of the relationship between science and literature has been framed incorrectly: it is 'not that science writing and literature enjoyed a fruitful relationship, but that scientific writing *was* literature' (O'Connor 2007, 13). Instead we should be looking at writing in terms of intended audience, whether popular or specialized. The bridging of the gap is also shown in the fact that many of the writers discussed in this book deliberately and knowingly intervene in debates that we would now consider to be scientific and medical, such as Wollstonecraft on whether animals have reason, William Godwin on animal magnetism, Edmund Burke discussing a regimen for health, or Coleridge on the nature of life. Such interventions show in relief the cultural and political dimensions of 'scientific' knowledge at this time. I also subject the scientific and medical writing featured here to the same analysis as other kinds of writing. The book is not intended to be thought of as comprehensive, either in terms of the authors addressed or the scientific topics or disciplines discussed, but I hope that it does have a broad enough range to be considered as a general introduction to the topic of Romantic literature and science and to show how pervasive scientific and medical knowledge was in the literary culture of the time.

Each chapter approaches the issue from what I hope is a new angle, often using material that might be regarded as 'paratext' in conjunction with better-known primary texts (see Genette 1997). For example, I look at Wollstonecraft's reviews in the *Analytical Review*, Godwin's diary, a number of prefaces, introductions, works of literary criticism, and other texts of this nature, and many of Davy's unpublished letters and manuscript poems. The use of prefaces and other such texts is another way in which the book considers how 'Romanticism' was created, since these often attempt to define a new sense of the literary taste by which authors wished their work to be judged. Authors such as Wollstonecraft, Godwin, Burke, and Wordsworth set out with deliberate intention to forge new sensibilities for the times in which they lived.

The case studies, or chapters, can be read on their own and they have been written as discrete units; that said, I have also always picked up the previous chapter's subject briefly at the beginning of a new one, hoping to show lines of continuity throughout the period. I begin and end with Davy, the man who is both a chemist and a poet; he fits comfortably within the Romantic aesthetic and should, I think, be thought of as more central to the period. His presence is felt in many of the chapters and his influence on the figures discussed has not yet been fully realized. Where earlier chapters consider what happens to science when it is used and appropriated by others for their own uses, the final chapter on Davy explores his appropriation and adaptation of the sublime. This concept is itself recognized as having developed with the aid of scientific and medical ideas.

The work of Michel Foucault has made us more aware of the power relations discussed in literary and historical texts.[10] Chapters 1 and 2 are particularly concerned with the ways in which scientific and medical experiments are motivated by political objectives; in turn, the writers of other kinds of texts often use the 'facts' put forward by scientific studies for their own political purposes. Both of these chapters discuss dubious attempts on the part of medical men or quack doctors to assert a professional authority and dupe the most vulnerable in society. The internalization of such beliefs in medical authority can be seen in Chapter 4 when a patient is convinced he has been cured after Davy puts a thermometer in his mouth. In the early chapters, literary and philosophical writing reveals explicitly the political and cultural values given to scientific fact and, on the other hand, expressly discusses the ethical dimensions of contemporary medical research. As Charlotte Sleigh has argued in her excellent book, 'literature is now, as much as it ever was, ground on which we can negotiate the criteria for judging science' (Sleigh 2011, 24). The examples given below rarely demonstrate any straightforward influence of science on literature; instead we see a sophisticated understanding of scientific knowledge, a complex engagement with it, as well as critique and challenge. At the same time, the book generally shows the persistence of Enlightenment ideals into the Romantic era: in particular, the search for 'laws' to explain human behaviour as well as natural phenomena can be seen in all chapters, as can evidence of the continuing influence of Newton and mechanical philosophy.

It is my contention that the terms that formulate still-current debates about the respective values attributed to literature and science were shaped in the Romantic period, and it is Wordsworth who looms largest in the debate; his extended discussion of the differences between the poet and the man of science added to the 'Preface' to *Lyrical Ballads* in 1802 has traditionally been read as evidence of the Romantics' disapproval and distrust of science. Below, I look again at Wordsworth's 'Preface' and the dialogue between him and Davy on the respective value and benefits of poetry and chemistry. Ian Reid has explored the way that Wordsworth's writings 'served eventually to forge a normative curriculum and pedagogy for [the study of] English' (Reid 2004, x). Gowan Dawson and Sally Shuttleworth have argued that this passage in Wordsworth's 'Preface' has been 'enormously influential in discussions of the relations between science and Victorian poetry' (Dawson and Shuttleworth 2003, 1). Its influence has extended beyond this, because, in Dawson and Shuttleworth's words, 'its insistence on a sharp divide between the subjective and the objective [...] pitted the metaphysical and imaginative values of poetry against the dispiriting, but increasingly authoritative, creeds of science and industry' (Dawson and Shuttleworth 2003, 1). These are the very terms in which divisions between science and literature continue to be framed today (see Ruston 2008a, 1–13).

Wordsworth's 'Preface' also opens debates that will be further discussed in the individual chapters of this book. It has been seen as the most obvious example of a wider endeavour in the period: according to Martin Wallen, 'The Romantics all saw themselves as the corrective to their misdirected age; throughout their works they proclaim themselves the embodiment of the new, healthy, natural culture and society' (Wallen 2004, 5). Certainly the Romantics' emphasis on the natural above the man-made or artificial can be seen, in this regard, as a return to 'first principles' or 'simple truths', in the words of Wollstonecraft, who, as I discuss in Chapter 1 of this book, used the evidence of the natural world gained from her reading of natural history books to argue for a proper understanding of gender (*Works*, v, 89).

Wordsworth's 'Preface' broaches issues of legitimacy, value, and authority which preoccupy both Chapters 1 and 2, whether science is used to support political motive in Wollstonecraft's arguments about gender, or to attack perceived charlatans (both medical and aristocratic) and their willing victims in Godwin's writing. The imagination is a major concern for Wordsworth and this appears to be the ground upon which he initially distinguishes between literary and scientific endeavours. Godwin's writing on animal magnetism similarly leads him to consider the deceiving powers of the imagination and to contemplate the spectacle and display of medical power. Mesmerism was one medical treatment that seemed explicitly to involve the imagination of the patient. Godwin's writings on mesmerism and his close friendships with medical and scientific men are the subject of Chapter 2.

Wordsworth's 'Preface' is also clearly fascinated with ideas of literary creativity, and offers a medical diagnosis of taste. These are the topics of Chapter 3, which also discusses contemporary medical attempts to account for literary genius. In this chapter I am interested in the ways that literary creativity is described. Mary Shelley's *Frankenstein* is used to explore the ideas of 'monstrous' creation and I examine the 'science' of teratology, or the study of monsters, to explore Shelley's understanding of her own literary invention.

Chapter 4 picks up the discussion of Davy again, examining his use of literary metaphors and techniques, particularly his fascination with the sublime, which can be seen in his poetry and scientific writings. This chapter also looks again at Edmund Burke, Joseph Priestley, and Immanuel Kant's descriptions of the sublime experience, finding in them the signs of contemporary scientific and medical thought. Davy's poetry is explored and its application of the sublime analysed before examining his appropriation of the term for chemistry itself.

'Poetry' and 'science' in the Romantic era

Wordsworth's 'Preface' to the *Lyrical Ballads* has been seen as having created the division between poetry and science during the Romantic period. Richard Yeo, for example, in his 1993 book *Defining Science*, argues that the oppositions Wordsworth sets up between the two form the framework of later discussions, specifically that William Whewell's 'early discussion of science' was framed by these oppositions (Yeo 1993, 67). In this section, I look again at the precise terms used in the framing of this division. In a footnote to the 'Preface', Wordsworth argues that rather than opposing poetry and prose 'the more philosophical' distinction is between 'Poetry and Science' (*Prose Works*, I, 134n). In 1802 and all further editions he expands this footnote to offer further explanation as to what he means by 'Science'; writing that the more philosophical contradistinction is between 'Poetry and Matter of Fact, or Science' (*Prose Works*, I, 135). What Wordsworth means by this association between 'Matter of Fact' and 'Science', may be seen in his poem 'Memorials of a Tour in Italy, 1837', where he complains of:

> lifeless fact to fact
> Minutely linked with diligence uninspired,
> Unrectified, unguided, unsustained,
> By godlike insight
> (Quoted in Wyatt 1995, 190)

John Wyatt describes the 'Preface' as the '*locus classicus* for the study of the differentiation between science and the humanities'; its importance extending beyond its historical moment: '[it] has been taken to be the schismatic moment for the two cultures' (Wyatt 1995, 6, 7). He too regards the real distinction being made here as between '"fact" in opposition to affairs of poetic or imaginative activity' (Wyatt 1995, 7). According to Eliza May Hamilton, William Rowan Hamilton's sister, Wordsworth only objected to a particular kind of unimaginative scientific endeavour, not science per se:

> all science which was a bare collection of facts for their own sake, or to be applied merely to the material uses of life, he thought it degraded instead of raising the species. All science which waged war with and wished to extinguish Imagination and the mind of man, and to leave it nothing of any kind but the naked knowledge of facts,

> was he thought much worse than useless [...] and of dangerous and debasing tendency.
>
> (Quoted in Wyatt 1995, 192)

Even this suggests that there might be another kind of science possible, one that is imaginative. In general, it seems that Wordsworth is most opposed to the loss of the imagination, and a further passage, discussed below, in his *Convention of Cintra* confirms this.

Yeo credits William Whewell with coining the term 'scientist' in 1833 (Yeo 1993, 5). Just as in coining this term Whewell was attempting to 'defend and affirm [science's] moral, intellectual, and cultural value', Wordsworth was trying to do the same for a new kind of poetry (Yeo 1993, 9). What is understood by the term 'science' in the Romantic period is difficult to define, with Yeo acknowledging that there was almost a return in the early 1800s to its former meaning: 'systematic knowledge of any subject, including ethics, architecture, language, and politics' (Yeo 1993, 9). Wyatt sees the older definition existing simultaneously with 'the special, more limited range of meaning it has in our day', and gives examples of the Wordsworth circle using the same word in both ways (Wyatt 1995, 5). While such terms are beginning to be used, therefore, with greater precision, it is clear that at the time that Wordsworth used the word science its meaning was in no way certain, fixed, singular, or universal. Noah Heringman makes the point that 'Wordsworth's poetry [...], like Banks's natural history [...] is inextricably a part of the long episodic process of specialization leading to the formation of modern disciplines' (Heringman 2003, 3). Comparisons have been made with the terms 'literature' and 'Romantic', which also need to be used carefully and with due consideration for their different contemporary meanings. Ralph O'Connor draws a direct link between efforts that resulted in the coinage of the word 'scientist' and a move to 'redefine "literature" in terms of a new concept of the "creative imagination", excluding non-fiction' (O'Connor 2007, 14). Though this shift is situated in the late nineteenth century, it was motivated partly by reading the poets of the early part of the century, for whom had been coined the 'new collective label, "the Romantics"' (O'Connor, 2007, 14). There is evidence that for the Victorians, the term 'poetry' came to refer specifically to the poetry of these Romantics.[11] For Jon Klancher (1987) the narrowing of the meaning of 'literature' was the work of the 'Romantics' themselves.[12] Reid is persuasive on the specific importance of Wordsworth to our present-day understanding of 'such notions as literature, creativity, expressiveness, or personal development' (Reid

2004, 13). Wordsworth's opposition between 'Matter of Fact, or Science' and imaginative poetry supports the idea that he was intent on narrowing the definition of literature and poetry, and tried to achieve this by contrasting it with other, more factual, forms of writing.

Heringman writes that recent critical attempts aim to 'redeploy categories of literary history, such as "Romanticism," within the broad new context of cultural history emerging from the work of literary scholars and historians of science' (Heringman 2003, 6). My book also attempts to redefine what 'Romanticism' means within this new context. Many of the authors in this book would not be regarded as Romantics but as Enlightenment figures. However, since the efforts to redefine what Romantic means in political and historical terms, we now expect to see such writers as Mary Wollstonecraft or William Godwin on university courses and in critical accounts of the period (see also Heringman, 2003, 6). The 1790s have been viewed repeatedly as an important decade in which the philosophies of the earlier period were used to forge new sensibilities (see Keen 1999 and Manly 2004). R.S. White, specifically arguing that the language of natural rights in the 1790s evolved from the earlier concept of natural law, writes: 'Among the results [of this process] were new and more egalitarian ways of thinking about society, far-reaching political reforms, and the birth of new forms of literature and the movement we call romanticism' (White 2005, 1). As this makes clear, I do not see that there was such a break between Enlightenment and Romantic literary endeavours; indeed there is much evidence in this book that Enlightenment ideas continue. Alan Bewell has argued that Wordsworth is an Enlightenment figure, and that *The Recluse* is an encyclopaedic, anthropological poem of moral philosophy examining human origins according to earlier Enlightenment models (Bewell 1989b). Likewise, this book continues to rethink the relationship between the Enlightenment and Romanticism, finding much that suggests that the latter emerges from the former.

O'Connor reads Wordsworth's distinction between poetry and science as a division between two kinds of language: 'fact versus feeling, objective versus subjective', while admitting that this 'cannot easily be sustained on closer examination' of the texts themselves (O'Connor 2007, 25).[13] Lorraine Daston and Peter Galison begin the history of the term 'objectivity' and its association with science in the Romantic period.[14] In turn if we look at the *OED*'s recorded first uses of 'subjectivity', Southey and Coleridge feature highly in examples given.[15] The Romantic preoccupation with the self then, understood within a philosophical framework of Berkeley's insistence 'nothing is but as it is perceived', had an important part to play in the emerging representations of science as objective, detached, impartial, and impersonal that were pervasive from the 1860s. In the early nineteenth century while these definitions were taking shape there was a much more fluid and contested understanding of the domain and character of literature and science. For example, both poets and men of science made claims to truth. The qualified apothecary Keats asserted 'the truth of Imagination' for example.[16] O'Connor traces the opposition between science's 'truths' and literature's 'fictions' to the seventeenth century, citing this as the reason why 'several poets of the period were promoting their own claims to philosophical or spiritual truth against the myopia of mere fact-gatherers'. This in turn has been misread, he argues, by 'many of their Victorian (and later) admirers [...] as hostility towards science in general' (O'Connor 2007, 14).

Richard Holmes's book *The Age of Wonder* counters popular understanding of the Romantics' hostility towards science on different grounds: he unites poets and men of science in the period by their sense of wonder at nature and their new vision of the world and their place within it. Holmes typifies the 'second scientific revolution', which led to what he labels 'Romantic science', as characterized by a 'new imaginative intensity and excitement [...] It was driven by a common ideal of intense, even reckless, personal commitment to discovery' (Holmes 2008, xvi). The new poetry and science of the period he finds represented in the metaphor 'of the exploratory voyage, often lonely and perilous', while he discusses other analogous tropes that he finds mirrored in the poetry and science of the period (Holmes 2008, xvi). My book will not offer the kind of biographical narrative seen in Holmes but instead will examine the scientific ideas and discourse found in tropes considered particularly resonant with Romantic literary thought.

Catherine E. Ross and others have made the point that poetry and science were published for the same middle-class audience. Using the case of Wordsworth and Davy she argues that poetry and science 'addressed virtually the same polymathic public, and vied for the same jurisdiction (that of philosopher and sage)' (Ross 2003, 24). We need to remember however that there was 'No single, unified "reading public"' in the Romantic period, and that Wordsworth was, with others, '*creating* the taste' he wished his work to be judged by (Klancher 1987, 3). Research into periodicals, one of the most important media forms in this period, sees scientific and literary essays, reviews, and extracts jostling for attention.[17] There are many ways in which science and literature collide, overlap, and influence each other during the Romantic era: far more than has yet been recognized despite the burgeoning critical work now being done in this area. This book contributes to that endeavour and shows how some Romantic authors and texts not thought of in this way in fact participated in scientific and medical debates.

Wordsworth's experiments

The *Lyrical Ballads* has been viewed traditionally as a text hostile to science, and yet it is possible to see this text as scientific in its methods. Wordsworth states very clearly in the 1798 'Advertisement' to the original edition: 'The majority of the following poems are to be considered as experiments' (*Prose Works*, I, 116). As with a scientific experiment an objective is clearly set out.[18] These poems were composed with an express aim: 'to ascertain how far the language of conversation in the middle and lower classes of society is adapted to the purposes of poetic pleasure' (*Prose Works*, I, 116).[19] Wordsworth does not want the reader to judge his poems against the criteria of whether or not they are 'Poetry' because this is a 'word of very disputed meaning', reminding us that, as much as science, poetry was perceived as difficult to define, and that one of Wordsworth's aims is to offer a new definition (*Prose Works*, I, 116). Instead readers are to test the poems against different criteria: they should 'ask themselves if [the volume] contains a natural delineation of human passions, human characters, and human incidents' (*Prose Works*, I, 116).

The 1800 'Preface' rehearses points made in the 1798 'Advertisement'. The volume is to be considered as an

> experiment, which, I hoped, might be of some use to ascertain, how far, by fitting to metrical arrangement a selection of the real language of men in a state of vivid sensation, that sort of pleasure and that quantity of pleasure may be imparted, which a Poet may rationally endeavour to impart.
>
> (*Prose Works*, I, 119)

His 'principle object' was to 'make the incidents of common life interesting by tracing in them, truly though not ostentatiously, the primary laws of our nature: chiefly as far as regards the manner in which we associate ideas in a state of excitement' (*Prose Works*, I, 122–4). This too can be seen as scientific in its objective and method; Wordsworth hopes by accurate observation to delineate a certain aspect of human life and in so doing to trace something far larger, 'the primary laws of our nature', those transcendent and constant laws by which cause and effect take place. Newton's 'laws of motion' are exactly these kinds of laws. In *OED* definitions, the scientific or philosophical use of the phrase 'law of nature' is illustrated with Samuel Johnson's 1755 definition of '*Law*' as 'an established and constant mode or process; a fixed correspondence of cause and effect'. Thomas Reid in 1764 writes, 'The laws of nature are nothing else but the most general facts relating to the operations of nature' and in 1794 James Hutton, the geologist, notes 'We [...] name those rules of action the laws of nature' (*OED*). The action here, 'tracing [...] the primary laws of nature', might also be connected to the method or the experimental nature of Wordsworth's project; one definition of 'trace' in the *OED* is 'To discover, find out, or ascertain by investigation; to find out step by step; to search out', and interestingly, the same quotation from Dryden ('Happy the Man, who, studying Nature's Laws, Thro' known Effects can trace the secret Cause') appears in the definition of both the noun 'law' and the verb 'trace' (*OED*).

Wordsworth chooses as the subject of his experiment 'Low and rustic life' because, using a metaphor drawn from the natural world, 'in that situation the essential passions of the heart find a better soil in which they can attain their maturity' (*Prose Works*, I, 124). In other words, this class of people provides a better environment in which 'essential passions' can grow. The 'elementary feelings exist in a state of greater simplicity' in this class and thus may be 'more accurately contemplated', making clear Wordsworth's intention to observe accurately and communicate 'forcibly' those feelings (*Prose Works*, I, 124). The heart, then, provides the soil for the feelings and 'the manners of rural life germinate' from these feelings (*Prose Works*, I, 124).[20] This language further identifies a close connection between this class of society and the nature with which they live; indeed the organic term 'germinate' suggests that these people are like plants in the way they grow and develop.[21] These metaphors are, presumably, suggested by the fact that 'in that situation [low and rustic life] the passions of men are incorporated with the beautiful and permanent forms of nature' (*Prose Works*, I, 124). Editors Owen and Smyser argue that 'incorporated' here means 'associated, closely connected' and in Wordsworth's poetry we see this when the feelings of the poet or narrator are mirrored in the landscape around him. In other words, in rustic life men are more closely connected to the natural world; they are in fact more natural themselves. In Rousseau's terms, they are closer to a natural state than urban men. Their language too, Wordsworth believes, is 'far more philosophical', in the sense of accurate, since, 'arising out of repeated experience and regular feelings,

[it] is [...] more permanent' than that used by 'Poets' (*Prose Works*, I, 124). The effort to be accurate in his portrayal of emotion, by focusing on people who are more accurate in their expression of it, is part of an attempt to discover permanent and transcendent truths, or the laws upon which nature operates. In this again, Wordsworth's project is not so very different from that of the natural philosopher of his day.[22]

Wordsworth's insistence on the spontaneity of the feelings he wishes to delineate is another indication of the naturalness he wishes to capture: 'For all good poetry is the spontaneous overflow of powerful feelings' (*Prose Works*, I, 126). It is of vital importance that these powerful feelings be naturally and instinctively produced, rather than artificially created, even if this emotion is to be recollected at a later, more tranquil moment. The 'man' who can achieve this in his poetry is one 'who being possessed of more than usual organic sensibility' does not separate himself 'from the sympathies of men' and now writes for a world of his own creation but one who is attached to (and can feel as and for) his fellow man (*Prose Works*, I, 126, 124).[23] Later, in the 1802 'Preface', Wordsworth argues that a poet's qualities differ only in 'degree' and not in 'kind' from his fellow man (*Prose Works*, I, 142). The 'passions and thoughts and feelings' of a poet are the 'general passions and thoughts and feelings of men' (*Prose Works*, I, 142). They are connected to 'our moral sentiments and animal sensations' and in poets and all men are caused by the same multitude of events and occurrences in the natural world and in our individual, private lives (*Prose Works*, I, 142). Arguably alluding to a method more usually associated with science, Wordsworth writes in both versions of the 'Preface' that we shall 'discover' things 'by the repetition and continuance of' certain acts (*Prose Works*, I, 126). In the 1802 'Preface' he writes that since the poet shares the same 'sensations and objects' as all men, his language must also share with 'all men who feel vividly and see clearly' the power of expression: 'It might be *proved* that it is impossible' for this not to be the case he argues (*Prose Works*, I, 142).[24]

It is possible therefore to see the *Lyrical Ballads* as proceeding in what we might describe as a scientific manner, that Wordsworth's project in the collection can be seen as systematic in its methods.[25] Ross has also noted that in his poetics Wordsworth 'emphasized experiment, expertise, reason, and "system"' (2003, 24). Even the '*style*' that Wordsworth adopts in the *Lyrical Ballads* might be seen as more scientific, in the sense of writing more accurately or precisely, in what Wordsworth calls a more 'philosophical language' (*Prose Works*, I, 130, 124). Thomas Sprat famously approved of the Royal Society's care that 'Their manner of

Discourse' avoided the 'luxury and redundance of *Speech*' the corrupting affects of which were to be found in 'most other *Arts* and *Professions*' (Sprat 1667, 111). Wordsworth similarly intends not to use 'personifications', 'abstract ideas', and 'poetic diction' wherever possible, those forms that might be considered as belonging particularly to a poetic style (*Prose Works*, I, 130). The reason for this is that he wishes 'to imitate, and, as far as is possible, to adopt the very language of men, and I do not find that such personifications make any regular or natural part of that language' (*Prose Works*, I, 130). Again he speaks of a return to nature and to what is natural in man; unnecessary tropes such as personification are a product of the corrupting effect of civilization. Instead Wordsworth desires to strip language back to its primitive and simplest forms, in order that it might be most effective in its communication.

Wordsworth the physician

Another scientific language that has been noted in Wordsworth's 'Preface' is a medical one: the physical body is of great importance in this text. In his 1800 'Preface' to the *Lyrical Ballads*, Wordsworth declares 'I wish to keep my Reader in the company of flesh and blood, persuaded that by so doing I shall interest him' (*Prose Works*, I, 130). Presumably by the phrase 'flesh and blood' he means that the characters he creates will seem real to the reader, they will evince recognizable human qualities (the Ghost in *Hamlet* says that details of his punishment are not for the ears of 'flesh and blood' (Shakespeare 1994, I.5.22)). James Robert Allard has drawn attention to this statement, arguing that it signifies what he terms a 'body consciousness' (Allard 2007, 12). The other common meaning for the phrase is to describe family, or specifically children, as in 'my own flesh and blood'. It has been much commented upon that Wordsworth is often in these poems more concerned with mad, diseased, foreign, and wounded bodies than with healthy or normative bodies: Paul Youngquist describes the way that such deviant bodies both disturb and intensify the authority of what he terms the 'proper body' (Youngquist 2003, xv).

References to the body, real and metaphorical, continue even during Wordsworth's discussion of the merits of metre against prose.[26] When stating unequivocally that 'there neither is nor can be any essential difference' between the language of prose and metrical composition, Wordsworth imagines them as being biologically the same:

> They both speak by and to the same organs; the bodies in which both of them are clothed may be said to be of the same substance,

> their affections are kindred and almost identical, not necessarily differing even in degree; * Poetry sheds no tears "such as Angels weep," but natural and human tears; she can boast of no celestial Ichor that distinguishes her vital juices from those of prose; the same human blood circulates through the veins of them both.
>
> (*Prose Works*, I, 134)

Wordsworth gives way to personification here, but more than that, poetry and prose are given bodies. This sustained metaphor may owe something to his earlier reference to 'Poetry' and 'Painting' as 'Sisters' (commonly known as the 'sister arts') and this passage is an attempt to discover the 'bonds of connection' that 'typify the affinity' between prose and metre. Like sisters, they share 'almost identical' affections, but the point is not really their 'kindred' bodies but their equal humanness. Both poetry and prose, ultimately, are of the same species, 'the same human blood circulates through the veins of them both'. Wordsworth imagines that the 'vital juices' that animate both poetry and prose are the same, and, presumably at least one of these 'vital juices' is blood, which animates the human frame, rather than any superior 'celestial Ichor' that might do the same for one of Milton's angels. In his fragmentary and unpublished 'Essay on Morals' (supposed to have been written in 1798) Wordsworth uses a similar image: 'Now, I know no book or system of moral philosophy written with sufficient power to melt into our affection, to incorporate itself with the blood & vital juices of our minds' (*Prose Works*, I, 103).

Wordsworth not only embodies metre and prose, he also considers the effect they have upon bodies. He turns to the body of the reader, and considers how literary creations might endanger the health or heal the reader's, and by extension, the nation's body. The nation is sick, according to Wordsworth in his 'Preface'. Using, but denying, the language and medical theory of John Brown, a Scottish physician who argued that illness was the result of either too much or too little excitability, and who posited the use of depressants and stimulants as treatment, Wordsworth claims that 'the human mind is capable of excitement without the application of gross and violent stimulants' (*Prose Works*, I, 128).[27]

Wordsworth would have learned about Brown's ideas via Coleridge, who in turn was introduced to them by Thomas Beddoes.[28] Brown's theory was more influential in Italy and Germany than in Britain, but significantly, Thomas Beddoes and Erasmus Darwin were among its converts.[29] Beddoes was a radical who in 1788 had been forced to resign from the readership he had held at Oxford because of his open support of the French Revolution and criticism of the British government. He publicized Brown's work and wrote an introduction for a newly translated edition of *The Elements of Medicine* in 1795, which included Beddoes's own 'Observations on the Character and Writings of John Brown, M.D.' The evidence of Brown's personal life did not help win over supporters for his system, and Beddoes did not shy away from describing Brown's alcoholism, opium addiction, and periods of penury in his biography.[30]

When Beddoes set up the Pneumatic Institute in Clifton, Bristol, the treatment given there was influenced by Brown's vitalist theory of 'excitability'. Beddoes reduced Brown's theory of life to a number of principles: 'I. To every animated being is allotted a certain portion only of the quality or principle, on which the phenomena of life depend. This principle is denominated EXCITABILITY' (Brown 1795, I, cxxvii). Brown divided diseases into those caused by an excess of excitement – the sthenic – and those caused by an insufficient degree of excitement – the asthenic – and advised that they be treated accordingly. Wallen writes that by placing health and disease at either end of a continuum, like the two poles of electricity, Brown posited the notion that health was not a singular, whole state linked to one's moral condition, but an entirely material condition which had gradations that could be measured and quantified (Wallen 2004, 6).[31] Apparently he had a thermometer, which, according to Stephanie Snow, purported to tell 'the exact degree of under- or over-stimulation of the body, and thus the dose of therapy required' (Snow 2006, 13). These ideas underpinned the diagnosis and method used at Beddoes's Pneumatic Institute, to which Southey, among others, turned for treatment.[32] Coleridge wrote to Beddoes about Wordsworth's ill health in July 1800, though neither this letter nor Beddoes's reply is extant. In any case it seems that Wordsworth did not take Beddoes's advice.[33] In a letter of 9 October 1800 to Davy, Coleridge suggests that Wordsworth's health has not improved stating that he had 'not done common justice to Dr Beddoes's kind Prescription' (*Coleridge Letters*, I, 632). Clearly Wordsworth disapproves of medicines; Coleridge continues with: 'I saw his countenance darken, and all his Hopes vanish, when he saw the *Prescription*—his *scepticism* concerning medicines—nay, it is not enough *scepticism*!' (*Coleridge Letters*, I, 632). Coleridge would come to describe Brunonianism as the 'Doctrine of Death' and it may be that Wordsworth similarly rejected it on the grounds of its materialism and denial of mind and body dualism (cited in Wallen 2004, 103).[34]

Despite this, in a letter written on 2 December 1800 to Davy, Coleridge describes his life in Brunonian terms as alternating between stimulus and depression: 'one while cheerful, stirring, feeling in resistance nothing but a joy & a stimulus; another while drowsy, self-distrusting, prone to rest' (*Coleridge Letters*, I, 649). The same medical language is found in Coleridge's critique of Charles Maturin's *Bertram* in *Biographia Literaria*, accusing it of leaving the reader 'craving alone for the grossest and most outrageous stimulants' (*Biographia*, II, 229). Such statements, as Gavin Budge has noted, clearly allude to John Brown's theories (Budge 2007b, 173). Ford suggests Brown's theories may have been responsible for Coleridge's taking up opium, this being one of the most usual of the stimulants prescribed in Brown's regimen, and certainly by 1807 Coleridge had repudiated Brown's system (Ford 1998, 29). Neil Vickers confirms that in his first forays into opium consumption Coleridge was 'guided by contemporary medical opinion' and that he followed doctors 'whose writings he consulted and applied scrupulously and thoughtfully' (Vickers 2004, chapters 3 to 6; 3). The incessant escalation of stimulation, in Budge's words, is 'represented by Coleridge as a botched Brunonian therapy', encouraging 'a self-reinforcing spiral of addiction' (Budge 2007a, 173).

The stimulants Wordsworth describes in his 'Preface' are specifically of a literary nature, such as 'frantic novels, sickly and stupid German Tragedies, and deluges of idle and extravagant stories in verse' (*Prose Works*, I, 128). Wordsworth believes it is not necessary to apply such stimulants, themselves described as unhealthy (producing fever, illness or torpor), and that it is the job of a writer to instead excite the mind (in the sense of rouse up, awaken, quicken, even enliven perhaps) by other less 'gross and violent' means. The problem is larger in 'the present day' than at former times, and this Wordsworth ascribes in part to the fact that so many live in cities, 'where the uniformity of their occupations produces a craving for extraordinary incident which the rapid communication of intelligence hourly gratifies' (*Prose Works*, I, 128). To paraphrase in modern words, our lifestyle is responsible for the state of our minds; Wordsworth ascribes both a physical cause (the 'uniformity' of occupations) and a physical effect or symptom ('a craving for extraordinary incident') to the illness he perceives. The increased ability to communicate news – presumably of the 'great national events which are daily taking place' such as the war with France – 'gratifies' these cravings (*Prose Works*, I, 128). He describes this craving as a 'degrading thirst after outrageous stimulation', again imagining it in physical terms as a symptom (*Prose*

Works, I, 150). The end result is 'to blunt the discriminating powers of the mind' and yet he does think that the mind has the ability to heal itself (*Prose Works*, I, 128). He is sure that the human mind has 'certain inherent and indestructible qualities', as does nature, and that poetry of the kind he is suggesting can help to heal (*Prose Works*, I, 130). His medical language is appropriate given the fact that he hopes a new kind of poetry can restore health to a nation of men vitiated by modern life.

The word 'vitiated' is used in a remarkably similar paragraph describing the effect that 'Manufacturing and Commerce' have had in Spain, in Wordsworth's *The Convention of Cintra*, which, 'by unnaturally clustering the people together—enfeebled their bodies, inflamed their passions, by intemperance, vitiated from childhood their moral affections, and destroyed their imaginations' (*Prose Works*, I, 332). In contemporary scientific accounts air that had been 'vitiated' by either combustion or respiration could be 'restored' by vegetation, thus implying a divinely ordained economy in the world (Golinski 1992, 77–8). It was also common to measure air and newly discovered gases in terms of their 'goodness', meaning their ability to be respired, but again with a suggestive association of moral worth (see Priestley 1775, 388–9). It seems likely that Wordsworth was alive to these possibilities, which combine both physical and moral meaning. The imagination may be vitiated, but it can also be restored.[35]

While Wordsworth held that poetry could 'restore' and heal the individual and the body politic, it appears that the act of writing poetry at least did not achieve this for him. Andrew Bennett has argued that contrary to the idea of 'a Wordsworthian writing "cure"', 'writing for Wordsworth is not so much the cure as the disease' (Bennett 2007, 7). He quotes Wordsworth, writing in 1843: 'Poetic excitement when accompanied by protracted labour in composition has throughout my life brought on more or less bodily derangement' to undermine 'the notion that writing for Wordsworth is curative' (Bennett 2007, 8). Traditionally Wordsworth's poetry has been considered as a healing or restorative force, but Bennett counters this view, using evidence from Wordsworth's own ill health, which the poet himself associated with the act of writing. John Stuart Mill famously found in Wordsworth's writing 'a medicine for my state of mind', and cited Wordsworth as a prescription for the depressing effects of utilitarianism.[36]

Robert Burns was described by his biographer, the physician James Currie, as having suffered from a nervous illness of the nature described by Wordsworth. Daniel Sanjiv Roberts notes that by 29 September 1800 Wordsworth 'had transcribed various fragments from Burns using the second volume of Currie's edition' into his Commonplace Book (Roberts 2003, 120).[37] Indeed Nigel Leask suggests that the passages discussed above from Wordsworth's 'Preface' may have been influenced by Wordsworth's reaction to Currie's influential 'Life of Burns' (1800) and his 1788 review in the *Analytical Review* of Thomas Reid's *Essays on the Active Powers of Man* (Leask 2007). Currie found in Burns the archetype of Hume's deterministic associationism, at least as Thomas Reid represented it, his nervous condition resulting in the flitting of an alternate 'over-energetic sensibility' that betrays the lack of a controlling and regulating moral will (Leask 2007, 69). The treatment, according to Currie, is self-discipline. Eschewing such measures Burns's alcoholism is regarded by Currie as one form of his misapplication of the 'stimulant regime'. For Roberts, 'Currie's picture of the melancholy Burns thus serves to remind us how far he had strayed from the healthy vision of poetic sensibility suggested by the "Preface" to *Lyrical Ballads*' (Roberts 2003, 124).

In a later passage of the 1800 'Preface' a kind of medical diagnosis and treatment are offered by Wordsworth, again relating to the subject of the proper degree of 'excitement' or stimulation that should be offered by poetry. He describes the purpose of poetry as being, ultimately, 'to produce excitement in coexistence with an overbalance of pleasure' (*Prose Works*, I, 146). The reader's mind can become disordered when in a state of excitement: 'excitement is an unusual and irregular state of the mind; ideas and feelings do not in that state succeed each other in accustomed order' (*Prose Works*, I, 146). There is a danger, where the words 'by which this excitement is produced are in themselves powerful, or the images and feelings have an undue proportion of pain connected with them' that 'the excitement may be carried beyond its proper bounds' (*Prose Works*, I, 146). In such a case, the regulating effect of metre can mitigate the potential danger and restore the balance needed: 'the co-presence of something regular, something to which the mind has been accustomed when in an unexcited or a less excited state, cannot but have great efficacy in tempering and restraining the passion by an intertexture of ordinary feeling' (*Prose Works*, I, 146). Metre is by definition regular, the regular pattern of beats might here be imagined to calm the beating of the heart in a state of excitement.[38] In this passage Wordsworth sounds like a doctor, prescribing a treatment, something to temper the stimulant and balance the reader's emotional response to the text.

Wordsworth describes the successful tempering of passion in 'Tintern Abbey', in a passage that imagines this as a distinctly bodily experience:

> sensations sweet,
> Felt in the blood, and felt along the heart,
> And passing even into my purer mind
> With tranquil restoration
> (Wordsworth 1992, 117, ll. 28–31)[39]

Richard Matlak has suggested that Wordsworth's reading in the spring of 1798 Erasmus Darwin's *Zoonomia*, a medical treatise, provided the evidence for such images (Matlak 1990, 79). Matlak looks particularly at Darwin's chapter 'Of Propensity to Motion, Repetition and Imitation', in which Darwin argues that pleasure can result from repetition in language, both from repetition in sounds ('the rhimes and alliterations of modern versification') and in whole words (Darwin 1794–96, I, 251). In this chapter, Darwin presumes that the enjoyment taken in hearing a drum beat tells us that 'this pleasurable sensation must be owing to the repetition of the divisions of the sounds at certain intervals of time, or musical bars' (Darwin 1794–96, I, 251). He goes on to apply musical notation to poetry, when he categorizes the 'grave or heroic verses of the Greek and Latin poets' as written in 'common time', 'the French heroic verses, and Mr Anstie's humorous verses in his bath [*sic*] Guide' (in common time but 'one bar shorter'), and Pope's translation of Homer (in 'triple time') (Darwin 1794–96, I, 252).[40] Clearly this link had already been made and was available to Wordsworth in his discussion of the bodily experience of reading poetry.

Wordsworth's 'Poet' and the 'Man of science'

Roger Sharrock noticed in 1962 that there were striking similarities between Wordsworth's revised edition of the 'Preface' and Humphry Davy's 1802 *Discourse, Introductory to a Course of Lectures* (Sharrock 1962; see also Hindle 2012). More generally in this book, I argue for Davy's centrality to Romantic-period culture, both literary and scientific. Wordsworth knew Davy through Coleridge; they did not meet until 1804 when Davy visited the Wordsworths in Grasmere, but Davy had met Southey and Coleridge between July and 19 December 1799 while working at Thomas Beddoes's Pneumatic Institute in Bristol and they were both very enthusiastic about him.[41] Coleridge wrote to Davy on 16 July 1800, ending his letter with the request 'Will you be so kind as just to look over the sheets of the lyrical [*sic*] Ballads?' (*Coleridge Letters*, I, 606).[42] Wordsworth then wrote to Davy on 29 July 1800 asking him to proofread the second volume of the *Lyrical Ballads*, sending him the first manuscript sheet of poems and asking him specifically to correct in those 'any thing you find amiss in the punctuation a business at which I am ashamed to say I am no adept', and to 'loo[k over] the proofsheets of the 2nd V[olume] before they are finally struck off'.[43] Sharrock suggests that Davy may have undertaken this favour partly in repayment for Coleridge having negotiated with Longman on Davy's behalf for the publication of Davy's *Researches Chemical and Philosophical; chiefly concerning nitrous oxide, or dephlogisticated air, and its respiration* (Sharrock 1962, 64).[44] Wordsworth was ill in the autumn of 1800; he was slow in sending poems for the second edition; eventually the volume appeared on or around 26 January 1801.[45] Whether Davy's fault or not, when this edition of the *Lyrical Ballads* was printed it contained many errors.[46] Davy left Bristol for the Royal Institution in London, arriving on 11 March 1801.

The influence of Coleridge's conversations, poems, and letters and Wordsworth's 'Preface' and poems can be clearly seen in Davy's own poetry and letters written during this time. Davy wrote poetry throughout his life and left hundreds of poems in manuscript in his surviving notebooks and letters. Chapter 4 of this book considers one aspect of Davy's poetry particularly, his fascination with the sublime. There are many textual echoes between Wordsworth's poetry and 'Preface' in 1800 and Davy's 1802 lecture, but there are also echoes between the 1802 lecture and Wordsworth's changes to the 'Preface' in 1802, demonstrating what Gillian Beer has called two-way traffic.[47] Catherine E. Ross has found that Davy's influence extends beyond this to Wordsworth's 1805 *Prelude*: she argues that it is in this text that Wordsworth identifies a 'cognate relationship' of 'personal and professional kinship' between the poet and the man of science (Ross 2003, 24).

Reading the 'Preface' as a favour to Wordsworth and Coleridge, Davy would have discovered Wordsworth's statement that the philosophical opposite of poetry was science. Davy took up science's defence in his *Discourse, Introductory to a Course of Lectures*, a lecture that he gave at the Royal Institution (when Coleridge was present) and which was published in 1802. There is a remarkably similar passage to Wordsworth's medical diagnosis of the depravity of literary taste among his contemporaries in Davy's 1802 *Discourse*, but here it is not poetry that can heal but science:

> In common society, to men collected in great cities, who are wearied by the constant recurrence of similar artificial pursuits and objects,

> and who are in need of sources of permanent attachment, the cultivation of chemistry, and the physical sciences, may be eminently beneficial.
>
> (Davy 1802, 25)[48]

In this Davy may be reacting to something that had become very apparent in 1801, the year that had elapsed between publication of Wordsworth's 'Preface' and his own *Discourse*, namely that Coleridge and Wordsworth did not think that chemistry was as capable as poetry of producing 'deep passion' in a man.

According to Coleridge in a letter dated 3 February 1801, a plan was proposed that Wordsworth and Dorothy take a house near Coleridge in which a chemical laboratory would be built (*Coleridge Letters*, II, 670–2; see also Sharrock 1962, 60). Coleridge asked Davy for advice about this project: which books to buy, which apparatus, the cost of it all, and whether Davy would personally supervise the making of it (*Coleridge Letters*, II, 671). Reasons for the project included that

> [Wordsworth] because he feels it more & more necessary for him to have some intellectual pursuit less closely connected with deep passion, than Poetry, & is of course desirous too not to be so wholly ignorant of knowledges so exceedingly important.
>
> (*Coleridge Letters*, II, 671)

The second reason quoted here perhaps seems a little tagged on and may have been a sop to Davy's pride following the first reason, that chemistry is 'less closely connected with deep passion, than Poetry'. As we have seen Wordsworth himself linked his 'persistent health problems – headaches, bowel complaints, chest pains, irritability, sore eyes, fatigue, insomnia, and so on' with 'the "work of composition"' (Bennett 2007, 145). In response, in his 1802 *Discourse, Introductory to a Course of Lectures*, Davy argues that chemical pursuits as much as poetry can be healing or restorative.

Davy went further even than this; according to him scientific pursuits, especially chemistry:

> may destroy diseases of the imagination, owing to too deep a sensibility; and it may attach the affections to objects, permanent, important, and intimately related to the human species. Even to persons of powerful minds, who are connected with society by literary, political, or moral relations, an acquaintance with the science that represents

> the operations of nature cannot be wholly useless. It must strengthen their habits of minute discrimination; and, by obliging them to use a language representing simple facts, may tend to destroy the influence of terms connected only with feeling.
>
> (Davy 1802, 25–6; see also Sharrock 1962, 67)

In this Davy echoes Wordsworth's phrasing; where in the 'Preface' Wordsworth had warned against blunting the 'discriminating powers of the mind' here Davy talks of strengthening these powers, the 'habits of minute discrimination'. Perhaps thinking of Wordsworth's own nervous illnesses, Davy speaks about the 'diseases of the imagination' to which those who suffer from 'too deep a sensibility' are subject. Davy even suggests here that the study of chemistry encourages the use of a language that is more closely associated with 'simple facts'.

Davy characterizes the chemist as having:

> powers which may be almost called creative; which have enabled him to modify and change the beings surrounding him, and by his experiments to interrogate nature with power, not simply as a scholar, passive and seeking only to understand her operations, but rather as a master, active with his own instruments.
>
> (Davy 1802, 16)

There was nothing in this of the passive or anatomizing mind described by Wordsworth. This was not mere 'Matter of Fact', but imaginative and creative. For Davy (as for Wordsworth) nature had 'active powers' and the chemist (as the poet was for Wordsworth) was capable of 'exhibiting to men that system of knowledge which relates so intimately to their own physical and moral constitution' (Davy 1802, 7, 17). Davy reached a high pitch of bombastic rhetoric in his *Discourse*; he argued that chemistry could change the world: 'We look for a time that we may reasonably expect, for a bright day of which we already behold the dawn' (Davy 1802, 22).

Duncan Wu's catalogue *Wordsworth's Reading* tells us a little more about the access that Wordsworth had to Davy's published work (Wu 1995, 71–2). Wordsworth may already have read of Davy's nitrous oxide experiments in his 1800 *Researches Chemical and Philosophical*, since he ordered that from Longman's and paid for it on 26 January 1801, the day, coincidentally, that the second edition of the *Lyrical Ballads* was published (Wu 1995, 71). A copy of Davy's *A Syllabus of a Course of Lectures on Chemistry Delivered at the Royal Institution of Great*

Britain (1802) was retained at Rydal Mount; this may have been a signed copy that Coleridge had and which he gave to John Monkhouse on 16 December 1809, or Wordsworth's own copy (Wu 1995, 72).[49] While it may be coincidence that Davy's phrase 'too deep a sensibility' is very similar to Wordsworth's use of 'too deep for tears' in his poem 'Intimations of Immortality', it certainly does not seem to be a coincidence that in the revisions to his 'Preface' published in 1802 after Davy's *Discourse*, Wordsworth inserts a lengthy new section on the differences between 'the Poet' and the 'Man of science' (Wordsworth 1992, 77, l. 208; *Prose Works*, I, 140–1). Responding directly to Davy's confidence that science would change the human condition, this passage discusses the various merits of poets and men of science, acknowledging Davy's claims for science and further explicating Wordsworth's concept of the differences between them.[50]

In the passage added to the 1802 revised 'Preface', Wordsworth determines to speak 'upon general grounds', and his discussion of the difference between a 'Poet' and a 'Man of science' are to be regarded, again, within the context of his efforts to define poetry. He even begins this discussion by asking 'what is meant by the word Poet? What is a Poet?' (*Prose Works*, I, 138). In presenting his own sense of what poetry is and must be, Wordsworth is aware that he is changing our understanding of which poets in the past and in his present are judged to be great. His redefinition of poetry means that the canon will be revised, and in so doing we will change: 'our moral feelings influencing and influenced by these judgments will, I believe, be corrected and purified' (*Prose Works*, I, 137). As Percy Shelley will later also profess, the 'Poet' in Wordsworth's account is a man who is different physiologically, intellectually, and emotionally from other men; specifically, he is a man 'endowed with more lively sensibility' than others (*Prose Works*, I, 138; see also Ruston 2005, 132–8). In the 1802 revised 'Preface' both the poet and the man of science study nature, but the poet, in Wordsworth's formulation, 'converses with general nature' while the man of science converses 'with those particular parts of nature which are the objects of his studies' (*Prose Works*, I, 140). Both, though, experience affection akin to one another and both experience pleasure in the knowledge gained (*Prose Works*, I, 141).

There is a difference in the way that knowledge is gained, however, since for the poet, knowledge is a 'necessary part of our existence', whereas for the man of science knowledge 'is a personal and individual acquisition, slow to come to us, and by no habitual and direct sympathy connecting us with our fellow-beings' (*Prose Works*, I, 141). In other words science offers atomized knowledge that is individual to its recipient rather than the collective and connecting knowledge of a poet. Wordsworth imagines the 'Man of science' to be a solitary figure, for whom 'truth is a remote and unknown benefactor' he seeks; in contrast, truth for the 'Poet' is always visibly present and he is joined to his fellow humans by 'singing a song' in which they all join (*Prose Works*, I, 141). Then follows a series of oppositions set up between poets and men of science, from which the poet emerges as the general 'upholder and preserver' of all human nature, binding 'together by passion and knowledge the vast empire of human society, as it is spread over the whole earth, and over all time', able, in other words, to transcend boundaries of culture, geography and class (*Prose Works*, I, 141).

Perhaps responding directly to Davy's confidence that science would change the human condition, Wordsworth writes:

> Poetry is the first and last of all knowledge—it is as immortal as the heart of man. If the labours of Men of science should ever create any material revolution, direct or indirect, in our condition, and in the impressions which we habitually receive, the Poet will sleep then no more than at present; he will be ready to follow the steps of the Man of science, not only in those general indirect effects, but he will be at his side, carrying sensation into the midst of the objects of the science itself. The remotest discoveries of the Chemist, the Botanist, or Mineralogist, will be as proper objects of the Poet's art as any upon which it can be employed, if the time should ever come when these things shall be familiar to us, and the relations under which they are contemplated by the followers of these respective sciences shall be manifestly and palpably material to us as enjoying and suffering beings. If the time should ever come when what is now called science, thus familiarised to man, shall be ready to put on, as it were, a form of flesh and blood, the Poet will lend his divine spirit to aid the transmigration, and will welcome the Being thus produced, as a dear and genuine inmate of the household of man.
>
> (*Prose Works*, I, 141)

This passage has traditionally been received as a negative comment upon science: one biographer declares that Wordsworth shows 'a lack of imagination about the scientist's task' (Moorman 1957, I, 583). It has been more common recently though to see that while Wordsworth feels science might not yet have provided appropriate subject matter (the 'proper objects') for poetry, he does here allow for this to be the case in the future. The phrase 'flesh and blood' appears again to describe this advanced state of knowledge. It is fascinating that for Wordsworth, it is poetry that can help give 'flesh and blood' to the knowledge that science reveals to us. Another way to put this is that poetry will give this knowledge life, will enable scientific ideas and theories to exist in our world and be a part of our everyday lives. In his 'Essay Supplementary to the Preface' (1815), Wordsworth writes that poetry has to provide 'sensuous incarnation' for 'transcendent' meaning; in other words, poetry brings ideas into being (*Prose Works*, III, 65). In his *Essay upon Epitaphs* he voices disbelief that words 'be not [...] an incarnation of the thought but only a clothing for it' (*Prose Works*, II, 84; see also Kelley 1988, 5, 195, 199). The passage in the 1802 'Preface' might seem to prefigure the creation of the Creature in *Frankenstein*, but this is a description of the right way to do it, to produce a 'Being' that is welcomed rather than rejected by society.

A few lines earlier Wordsworth had imagined poetry as the 'impassioned expression', which editors Owen and Smyser see as giving 'meaning and unity' to the 'countenance' of science (*Prose Works*, I, 141, 181). The question of what Wordsworth might be imagining when he speaks of a 'material revolution' which the labour of natural philosophers could effect in our condition is confidently answered by Sharrock, who sees this as an acknowledgement of Davy's 'astonishing prophecy of the transformation of human life by technology [...] which has taken place in the century and a half since Davy spoke' (Sharrock 1962, 71–2). In his *Discourse* Davy had argued:

> Science has done much for man, but it is capable of doing still more; its sources of improvement are not yet exhausted; the benefits that it has conferred ought to excite our hopes of its capability of conferring new benefits; and, in considering the progressiveness of our nature, we may reasonably look forwards to a state of greater cultivation and happiness than that which we at present enjoy.
>
> (Davy 1802, 17)

It seems that Wordsworth shares this expectation that the work of science could change the way that people think of their world – perhaps in just the same way as poetry can.

Poetry's aid to science, providing the 'divine spirit' needed to make the whole being, is in keeping with the role Wordsworth sees for it at the side of the 'Man of science', 'carrying sensation into the midst of the objects of science itself'. The objects of science are presumably natural objects, and when science is at this point in its advancement, poetry will use its abilities to convey sensation and passion to the nature that scientific knowledge has transformed.[51] Wordsworth has argued earlier that the poet has this ability, that he can bring the natural world to life and even 'create' passions where he does not find them in nature. Davy had also argued that the chemist had 'active powers', which 'enabled him to modify and change the beings surrounding him' (Davy 1802, 16). Poetry and science have far more in common in Wordsworth's 1802 'Preface' than they did in 1800 and this is the result of his engagement with Davy's ideas.

I hope in this introduction to have shown how a debate key to the formation of central tenets of Romantic-period writing and which can be seen as key to the separation of the arts and sciences was itself imbued with scientific language and ideas. Wordsworth's protestations in 1800 that poetry was to be regarded as the opposite of science were challenged by Davy, and Davy's optimism for chemistry filtered into a vision of a future where the poet and the man of science worked side by side for the good of humankind. Wordsworth's project with the poems of the *Lyrical Ballads* has much in common with scientific methods and objectives. The case study method adopted in this book allows a focused attention upon key critical debates but, taken as a whole, the book reveals just how pervasive were the interactions between literary, scientific, and medical ideas. The next chapter examines a writer not usually thought of for her interest in natural history and yet this interest is seen to have influenced one of the most important works published in the 1790s, *Vindication of the Rights of Woman*. This text, though a product of the Enlightenment, was written in a language of rights that influences much Romantic-period writing in Britain. Revealing the science at the heart of Wollstonecraft's feminist project also reveals the science at the heart of the creation of Romanticism.

1
Mary Wollstonecraft and Nature

During the period of the composition of *Vindication of the Rights of Woman*, Mary Wollstonecraft read and reviewed a number of works of natural history for the *Analytical Review*.[1] Examining the remit of these works, and Wollstonecraft's response to them, it is possible to see *Vindication* as offering a kind of natural history of woman. The books that Wollstonecraft read and reviewed compared 'man' to animals and plants, and men and women to each other; the authors felt qualified to discuss the 'natural' distinctions between men and women and consequently to advise women on what behaviour and conduct was 'natural' to them. From such texts, Wollstonecraft learned that natural knowledge could be put to political use and she follows this model in *Vindication*. She determines to prove that women should be regarded as part of the 'human species' rather than the 'mere animals' they seem to some (*Works*, v, 73, 76). This chapter explores the links between natural history and natural rights in this critical moment when the concept of what was 'natural' was debated.[2] Wollstonecraft emerges as an astute reader of natural history texts, who challenges as well as utilizes natural knowledge for her own political ends.

I begin with a discussion of contemporary physiological and anatomical accounts of women's bodies. The second section considers the *Analytical Review*, its proprietor, Joseph Johnson, and the circle of scientific and medical men whom Wollstonecraft knew during the years before 1792. Wollstonecraft's particular interest in education, as evinced in her own publications as well as in these reviews, goes some way to explaining her interest in natural history and the lessons that she would take from it for *Vindication*. Natural history, as a scientific discipline, was concerned with description and education, rather than experiment, and would be superseded by the more investigative discipline of biology in the nineteenth century. Noah Heringman considers natural history in this period to be 'a literary practice' (Heringman 2003, 3; see also Jardine et al. 1996). Natural historians certainly felt themselves qualified to discuss moral as well as physical traits in humans and this chapter looks at the connections between natural history and conduct books, many of which were written by the same authors. Wollstonecraft is clearly aware of the cultural application of this knowledge, especially for issues of gender. In many cases the audience for works of natural history such as William Smellie's, which Wollstonecraft reviewed, was children and women. In such works, ideological opinion, masked as natural knowledge, is presented as authoritative.

The third section explores in depth Wollstonecraft's review of Smellie's work, the ideas with which she agreed and those with which she took issue, and the way that these ideas are appropriated in support of her thesis in *Vindication*. This chapter considers how women are regarded within natural histories of 'man', the concepts of instinct and reason, and the relation between the mind and the body. Debates on these topics help Wollstonecraft to formulate her argument in *Vindication*.

Unsurprisingly, the reviews that Wollstonecraft wrote for *Analytical Review*, during the period 1788–92, often focus on areas that reappear in *Vindication*. She reviewed Thomas Bewick's and Ralph Beilby's *A General History of Quadrupeds* (in July 1790); William Smellie's *Philosophy of Natural History*; John Rotheram's answer to Smellie, *The Sexes of the Plants Vindicated* (both October 1790); *A New System of the Natural History of Quadrupeds, Birds, Fishes and Insects*; and an abridged version of the Compte de Buffon's *Natural History* (both January 1792).[3] In many of her reviews Wollstonecraft is primarily interested in how animal species, plants, and human races can change or develop from what she calls, in *Vindication*, a 'natural state' (*Works*, V, 75). Following Smellie, her preferred term is 'improve', which can be used to describe both physical and moral changes.[4] In another review, Wollstonecraft deplores satires of Africa 'written by men who wish to insinuate, contrary to all experience, that it is the nature of man to degenerate rather than improve' (*Works*, VII, 479). The evidence in the books she reads supports her theory that the women of her society have changed (for the worse) but also that they are still capable of change (for the better). When Wollstonecraft looks around her she sees women who are not necessarily equal to the men of her society, and she is often harsh in her treatment of women in *Vindication*, particularly of those in the upper classes because she feels they have degenerated. She believes that environmental conditions have altered the peoples whom travel writers encounter and, similarly, that natural history shows that species of animals are capable of change and development. The fourth and fifth sections of this chapter look specifically at her writings on botany and race theory, which explore such changes. Plants can be cultivated to such a degree that they become weak and artificial, providing new metaphors for the state in which Wollstonecraft finds woman. Such ideas also allow Wollstonecraft a more optimistic vision of women's future potential as the equal of man. As is well known, education was the means by which the 'revolution in female manners' would be effected (*Works*, v, 114).

Wollstonecraft's Rousseau-influenced aim is to study woman (using a singular generic noun, as though speaking of a species) in her 'natural state' and to point out the way in which this state has been corrupted and has degenerated because of education, socialization, decadence, luxury, and the treatment of women by men (*Works*, v, 75). Women must, 'return to nature and equality' according to Wollstonecraft (*Works*, v, 90). One cause of the 'barren blooming' of women she attributes to 'a false system of education, gathered from the books written on the subject by men, who [consider] females rather as women than human creatures' (*Works*, v, 73). That women are first and foremost human is a crucial point for Wollstonecraft. In her 'Preface' to *Vindication* Wollstonecraft tells her reader that she calls 'with the firm tone of humanity' and that she writes because she has 'an affection for the whole human race' (*Works*, v, 65). The question of the genre of *Vindication* as – in part at least – advice literature is further illuminated by the examination of other works written in this genre by medical practitioners. Wollstonecraft sees in works of natural history a model for how natural knowledge can be used to bolster an ideological position, and she follows this model in *Vindication*.

In order to prove that certain characteristics are natural to women, Wollstonecraft used her knowledge of natural history and medicine and in so doing reveals her sense that such knowledge offers a certain authority: 'In the present state of society it appears necessary to go back to first principles in search of the most simple truths, and to dispute with some prevailing prejudice every inch of ground' (*Works*, v, 81). As Virginia Sapiro argued, for Wollstonecraft, 'nature provides the ground rules within which human societies function' (Sapiro 1992, 43). She examines animals and plants both to draw analogies with and to point out differences between them and humans (often specifically women) in her efforts to establish these 'first principles' and 'simple truths' that reveal the 'law of nature' (*Works*, v, 74). She is quick to distinguish between what is really natural, and what has been naturalized. What she sees in the women around her, in the way that they have changed and degenerated, she finds mirrored in the domestication of animals, the cultivation of plants, and the differences of race. In this chapter, the position of scientific knowledge in Wollstonecraft's political project is recognized and its importance in the development of her ideas is traced and followed.

Her reviews of natural history books often focus on issues that are key to the arguments of *Vindication*, such as issues regarding education for children, for example, that girls and boys should not be educated differently, and that girls should also be allowed physical exercise; that species of animals and plants were capable, through domestication or cultivation, of degeneration, becoming physically weaker and prone to disease; that races differed because of external causes, such as climate and education; that the mind and the body were inextricably linked, and that to improve one you must improve the other; as well as a whole host of medical and scientific information that resurfaces in *Vindication*. While she may not always have been able to choose the books that she reviewed, the sections that she picks out for comment often have a bearing on those subjects with which she was most concerned. As her knowledge widened and deepened we can also see it being brought to bear upon establishing few but crucial facts, specifically that women in her society are only the way that they are because of the way they have been educated, and that like domestic animals their true natures have been perverted, but also – and crucially – that they can regain their 'natural state'. It is not simply the case that she finds in scientific texts metaphors for her political points; she also finds evidence to prove her political agenda and knowingly uses it for political effect.

Her review of Smellie's *Philosophy of Natural History* is one of the longest that she wrote for the *Analytical Review*, a fact that, as Anne Chandler has written, 'shows her basic respect for his work and her keen interest in the subject itself' (Chandler 2005, 14). She strongly objects to his idea that reason is simply an extension of instinct and his suggestion (with examples) that animals might be capable of reason. Wollstonecraft's religious sensibilities are offended by these ideas because, for her, intellect is what separates us from animals and assures our superiority to them. Reason, coupled with passion, is the means by which humans can improve and reach towards virtue (see Sapiro 1992). It is important to Wollstonecraft that virtue is not an instinct, but is instead something that can be learned and worked towards. Her invocation of the soul and the afterlife at this point is also politically canny: employing tactics like those used by anti-slavery writers who similarly supplemented natural rights with religious arguments to win over their audience. For her, animals are only capable of imitation; they do not have the power to 'improve', which is the power of reason. Smellie confuses this imitation with reason when he describes the tricks that domesticated animals can do. In *Vindication*, domesticated animals symbolize women in Wollstonecraft's society, women who have become 'artificial' rather than natural beings.

1.1 'I am then going to be the first of a new genus': scientific and medical notions of 'woman'[5]

The question of what was 'natural' or 'unnatural' in women was debated through the 1790s and beyond, and scientific knowledge of plants and animals was used to bolster or challenge political opinions concerning women's bodies, intellectual abilities, future existence, and sexuality. After Samuel Thomas von Soemmerring noted that women's skulls were heavier than men's in proportion to their total body weight, the Edinburgh anatomist John Barclay argued that this was evidence of their infantilism because children's skulls are similarly proportioned (see Schiebinger 1989, 207). The childishness of women, which Wollstonecraft railed at in *Vindication*, was by the time of Barclay's 1822 book *The Anatomy of the Bones of the Human Body* in part being explained by their bodies.[6] The Marquis de Condorcet wrote that a 'natural difference' needed to be found to justify any social or political exclusion in this age of natural rights (quoted in Schiebinger 1989, 215).

Wollstonecraft herself was attacked on the grounds of her so-called unnatural behaviour. Horace Walpole in a letter to Hannah More famously described her as 'that hyena in petticoats' (Walpole 1961, XXXI, 397). The hyena was, in Thomas Laqueur's words, 'long thought to be hermaphroditic' (Laqueur 1990, 19). However, Thomas Pennant in his 1781 *History of Quadrupeds* had dismissed the 'wild' opinion of the ancients that the hyena changed sex and 'imitated the human voice'; instead he characterized them as 'cruel, fierce, and untameable animals' (Pennant 1781, I, 251). Wollstonecraft's effort in *Vindication* is to prove that the mind has no sex, that characteristics such as reason and virtue should not be considered 'manly', but human. She wishes 'to prove that the prevailing notion respecting a sexual character', or that women and men have different natures, is 'subversive of morality' (*Works*, V, 67). This 'prevailing notion' had become commonplace; Londa Schiebinger tells us that after the 1750s, 'The seemingly superior build of the male body (and mind) was cited more and more often in political documents to justify men's social dominance' (Schiebinger 1989, 216). Wollstonecraft had to confront such ideas and argue from within these parameters.

To do so, natural history becomes an important weapon for Wollstonecraft's text and argument. In her most famous statement: 'It is time to effect a revolution in female manners', she writes that it is time that women are recognized as 'part of the human species' (*Works*, v, 114). In this passage many of the arguments in *Vindication* to which natural history is key are rehearsed. She calls for 'unchangeable morals' to be distinguished from 'local manners', reiterating her call throughout *Vindication* that universals might be distinguished from specifics, that, for example, reason should be seen as characteristic of all humans (*Works*, v, 114). To argue that women deserve the same rights as men, Wollstonecraft needs to prove that they can be equal in terms of their intellect and moral being. She endeavours, therefore, to argue that women have reason, that they have souls, and that any evidence to the contrary is just an effect of the way they have been educated. Reason, after all, is 'the dignified distinction which raises men above the brute creation' (*Works*, v, 74). Wollstonecraft writes: 'In what does man's pre-eminence over the brute creation consist? The answer is as clear as that a half is less than the whole; in Reason' (*Works*, v, 81).

Her use of natural history to prove such points is complex. In a society where some regard women as 'the link which unites man with brutes', Wollstonecraft has to prove that women are not 'mere animals' and instead are capable of the reason that distinguishes humans from animals (*Works*, v, 104, 76). Wollstonecraft is adamant that there is a distinction between human and animals. While the word 'brute' in *Vindication* can simply mean animal, it also is used on occasion to indicate an animal-like insensibility. Wollstonecraft asks: 'Is one half of the human species, like the poor African slaves, to be subject to prejudices that brutalize them [...]?' (*Works*, v, 215). To 'brutalize' here is to become brutal or to lower oneself to the level of brutes. Similarly Jemima in *Maria, or the Wrongs of Woman* speaks of the lower classes being 'brutalized [...] by the low cunning of trade, and the despicable shifts of poverty' (*Works*, I, 110). Just as humans can 'improve' so can they degenerate: husbands are described in *Maria* as woman's 'embruted mate' (*Works*, I, 145).

Vindication was dedicated to Charles Maurice de Talleyrand-Périgord, and responded to Talleyrand's report on public education presented to the National Assembly in France, which Wollstonecraft felt had failed to realize the potential of the French Revolution's assertion of rights for all.

Similarly, a question remained over whether the French Declaration of the Rights of Man actually concerned 'men' rather than 'man', whether the word 'man' meant human beings or specifically men (and, thus, not women). In scientific writing the term 'man' was often used to refer to the entire human species and yet, simultaneously, there were also telling distinctions made between the sexes. Woman's place in the 'natural history of man', as it is often called, is difficult to discern. As Marilyn Butler points out, Wollstonecraft's decision to call her book *A Vindication of the Rights of Woman* rather than 'of women', challenges this tradition (*Works*, I, 10). Catherine Macaulay, in her *Letters of Education*, similarly had to ensure that when she used the masculine pronoun in speaking about man's education, her reader understood that she was talking about the education of both girls and boys (Macaulay Graham 1790, 142).[7] Wollstonecraft and Macaulay were clearly at pains to be precise about whom they were including in the language that they used, and both make the point that other writers on education, seemingly writing about the education of all children, were actually referring primarily to boys.

Key critics writing about how our modern ideas of gender have developed have seen the end of the eighteenth century as a watershed. Laqueur asserts that ideas of sex changed from what he calls the 'one sex' to the 'two sex' model at this point:

> By around 1800, writers of all sorts were determined to base what they insisted were fundamental differences between the male and female sexes, and thus between man and woman, on discoverable biological distinctions and to express these in a radically different rhetoric.
>
> (Laqueur 1990, 8, 5)

No longer content with understanding women as inferior men, their genitalia the same but formed on the inside rather than the outside, as Aristotle had argued, the physician and naturalist now found women to be completely biologically and anatomically different to men, in terms of their bodies, morals, intellectual abilities, skulls, and skeletons. Schiebinger has examined the many and varied efforts to describe the new 'distinctively female body' (Schiebinger 1989, 189). Wollstonecraft struggles against an attempt to prove women to be essentially different (and thus inferior) to men.

For Laqueur, as for Schiebinger, science is neither a neutral nor an objective study. Laqueur points out that until the mid-eighteenth century 'no one was much interested in looking for evidence of two distinct sexes, at the anatomical differences between men and women, until such differences became politically important' (Laqueur 1990, 10). Cynthia Eagle Russett identifies Wollstonecraft's view of both gender and race as an Enlightenment way of thinking, which 'stress[ed] the commonalities shared by all human beings' (Russett 1991, 6). In 1819 the surgeon William Lawrence was convinced of the difference between male and female minds: 'the mind gradually strengthens; slowly advances, with the body, through childhood to puberty, and becomes adult when the developement [*sic*] of the frame is complete: it is, moreover, male or female, according to the sex of the body' (Lawrence 1819a, 108). By 1834, in William Whewell's now famous review of Mary Somerville in which he coins the term 'scientist', he also states firmly: 'Notwithstanding the dreams of theorists, there is a sex in minds' (Whewell 1834, 65). The debates rumbled on, and later in the century, Darwin's ideas of sexual selection would be used to explain both 'physical and behavioural differences between the sexes' (Russett 1991, 11–12). Wollstonecraft believes there is a connection between the mind and the body, and that both must grow strong together, but is adamant that the mind does not have a sex.

Vindication is not restricted to the moral and mental aspects of female education, but also discusses the body and health. Aristotle's teachings about sex and reproduction were still current at the end of the eighteenth century; Vivien Jones shows that *Aristotle's Complete Master-piece* (reprinted many times throughout the eighteenth century and into the nineteenth) represents the sex education that the reading public would have had access to (see Jones 2005). This text offers a very explicit sense of the difference between the sexes, for example in the way that the 'active principle' of the male seed needs to be inserted into the 'passive' female womb (Aristotle 1799, 32). Jones identifies a paradox within Wollstonecraft who seems at times to urge women to ignore their bodies (Jones 2005, 141). This is borne out in *Mary: A Fiction*, when the protagonist 'had such power over her appetites and whims, that without any great effort she conquered them so entirely, that when her understanding or affections had an object, she almost forgot she had a body which required nourishment' (*Works*, I, 17). On the other hand, Richard Sha's *Perverse Romanticism* is at pains to show a vein of Romantic writing that does not equate sexual desire with brutish or animalistic behaviour, and he counts Wollstonecraft among this group, for whom sexual liberation is part of their political aims (Sha 2009a). In *Vindication*, in accordance with John Locke's teachings, the body must not be overlooked in favour of, or given more attention than, the mind (Locke 1989, 83). Both need to be strengthened together and Wollstonecraft might also have encountered this idea in her reading of medical texts.[8]

Conduct books were an important source of information on women's bodies at this time, and these often slid between offering medical advice and advice on conduct and behaviour. Wollstonecraft herself intended to write such a book, which would cover pregnancy to the second year of a child's life and was to be called 'Letters on the Management of Infants' (*Works*, IV, 457–9). Though little of this book is extant, she does note that it is 'our deviation from simplicity' that is at fault in the rearing of children, commenting 'I know that some able physicians have recommended the method I have pursued' (*Works*, IV, 459). It is, of course, a terrible irony that Wollstonecraft's death was directly connected to childbirth, after having employed a female midwife, Mrs Blenkensop. In *Vindication*, she regrets that 'the word midwife [...] will soon give place to *accoucheur*', and argues that medicine is one profession women could do well in: 'Women might certainly study the art of healing, and be physicians as well as nurses' (*Works*, V, 218). The continued influence of Aristotle shows that popular knowledge of such subjects was woefully inadequate. It is important for my purpose to note that these are areas that Wollstonecraft felt qualified to discuss and that *Vindication* needs to be recognized not solely as offering moral advice but, in keeping with the genre of such books, to be discussed further below, as coupling this with advice on issues of health and well-being.

1.2 Joseph Johnson, the *Analytical Review*, and natural history

From 1786 Wollstonecraft was part of the circle surrounding the publisher Joseph Johnson, which had specific interests in scientific and medical publications, and particularly popular books on these subjects. In *Vindication* Wollstonecraft writes: 'I have conversed, as man with man, with medical men, on anatomical subjects' (*Works*, V, 193, n.3). Wollstonecraft was explicit in *Vindication* that women 'should be taught the elements of anatomy and medicine' in order that they may be competent nurses for others as well as for themselves (*Works*, V, 249). Many of the 'medical men' she knew would in all likelihood have been dissenters, given her known associations during these years and the fact that dissenting academies, such as those in Hoxton and Warrington, schooled their pupils in science and medicine; Johnson had particular associations with these networks.[9] I here focus on a physician Johnson knew, John Gregory, who also wrote moral and religious advice literature. Wollstonecraft witnessed in Gregory's work the political uses to which a knowledge of natural history could be put.

Marilyn Butler notes that Wollstonecraft's publications before 1790 'had a broadly educational function' and that '[a]s a reviewer Wollstonecraft pursued the same educational specialism' (*Works*, I, 8, 9). This fascination with education can be seen throughout much of Wollstonecraft's career, in her books for children and books of moral and educational instruction.[10] *Vindication* can be seen as primarily concerned with education, and as participating in the advice literature genre.[11] In this, it is not so different from the natural history works considered in this chapter.

Writing for the *Analytical Review* brought Wollstonecraft into closer contact with medical and scientific men. The 1788 *Prospectus of the Analytical Review* had promoted the importance of science to the journal: 'it being one part of our design to establish a repository for genuine information in every department of Literature and Science' and promised to publish, among other things, 'chemical and medical discoveries' (Anon. 1788a, iii–iv). The *Prospectus* states that the first volume, published in June 1788, would include reviews of *Pharmacopoeia* of the London College, with the *Philosophical Transactions of the Royal College of London* and of the Royal Society of Edinburgh and a number of scientific works (Anon. 1788a, iv).[12] The first issue (May 1788) organized material into fifteen sections, including sections on 'Natural History', 'Botany', 'Chemistry', 'Medicine, Anatomy, Surgery, &c.', and 'Mathematical Sciences' (Anon. 1788b). There were twenty-six review articles in these sections compared to forty-two appearing under other headings; clearly science and medicine were key to the journal's core business. Of the seven books listed as being published in 'Botany and Natural History' at the back of *Analytical Review* for July 1790 three were reviewed by Wollstonecraft (on Smellie, Rotheram, and Bewick).

The journal's political affiliations were also clear. Luisa Calè points out that '*The Anti-Jacobin* was founded with the explicit aim to destroy *The Analytical Review*' (Calè 2000; see also Chandler 2005). The inclusion of scientific books for review reminds us that what we would now categorize as science was not regarded as part of a distinct culture, though this chapter argues that for Wollstonecraft scientific knowledge had a special status, being recognized as offering some degree of authority on a subject. This practice also reflects Johnson's own particular interest in science and medicine, which I briefly collate here. He was the first, for example, to publish an English translation of the chemist Lavoisier's works (Tyson 1979, p. xiii). He was the proprietor of the *London Medical Journal* from 1783 to 1790, from which date he began another journal with the same editor, James Foatt Simmons, *Medical Facts and Observations* (Tyson 1979, 78–9, 106). These publications were so popular that from 1792 Johnson also published *Transactions of a Society for the Improvement of Medical and Chirurgical Knowledge*, which contained the work of eminent surgeons involved in this society, including, in the first volume, George Fordyce, John Hunter, Matthew Baillie, and Everard Home (Anon. 1792). Many of his scientific contacts were made through his friendship with Joseph Priestley and accordingly Johnson published the work of Lunar Society members, including Erasmus Darwin, Richard Lovell Edgeworth, Samuel Galton Jr, Joseph Priestley, Jonathan Stokes, and James Watt (Tyson 1979, 22). Hunter and Fordyce published their first major works with Johnson; he also published work by the President of the Manchester Philosophical and Literary Society, Thomas Percival, and the collected political essays of Benjamin Franklin (Tyson 1979, 45, 37, 51). Tyson points out that the medical books that Johnson published often had appeal to the lay reader as well as the practitioner, describing Fordyce's *Elements of the Practice of Physic* as 'the kind of practical "how-to" book that Johnson delighted in publishing' (Tyson 1979, 46). In this respect, the natural history books that Wollstonecraft and others reviewed for the journal suited Johnson's own interests well. Johnson is also the natural publisher for *Vindication* – even without the personal interest he took in Wollstonecraft – because of the links her work makes between physical, moral, and political issues.

We might ask why Wollstonecraft was chosen over other *Analytical* reviewers to review natural history books? Sapiro has speculated that Wollstonecraft's 'writing during this period suggests she was working in Grub Street style, accepting any writing to support herself [...] even some natural history', but I think there is much more to it than this (Sapiro 1992, 19). Other reviewers for the journal included a number of medical and scientific men, such as John Aikin, James Currie, and Thomas Christie, who were perhaps more obvious choices. I think the answer to this question lies in the fact that natural history was often considered to be within the remit of education rather than experiment, and moreover, was considered particularly of use and benefit in the education of children. In *Vindication* Wollstonecraft argues that natural history is a subject that should be taught to both boys and girls (*Works*, v, 240). More broadly, it is clear that for Wollstonecraft and other children's authors referring to animals is a good way to broach certain important topics and to draw comparisons with the reader's own life.

In *Thoughts* it is clear that Wollstonecraft thinks that teaching children to care for animals can help them learn how to respect and be gentle with other children:

> Animals are the first objects which catch [children's] attention; and I think little stories about them would not only amuse but instruct at the same time, and have the best effect in forming the temper and cultivating the dispositions of the heart. There are many little books which have this tendency.
>
> (*Works*, IV, 10)

She particularly approves of Dorothy Kilner's, *The Life and Perambulation of a Mouse* (1783), which in its preface tells us '*that the Author's design in writing it was no less to* instruct *and* improve, *than it was to* amuse *and* divert *you*' (Kilner 1790, preface, n.p.).[13] Animals have a particular part to play in Wollstonecraft's texts, though they are often considered in their relation to humans rather than for their own sake. She does not think them capable of reason, but domesticated animals come to represent the 'artificial' being that woman has become in her society.

It is an interesting and perhaps not enough remarked upon fact that a number of writers of advice literature were medical practitioners, among them Aikin and Percival. Often the instruction offered is a subtle blend of moral, religious, and medical advice. Medical practitioners clearly felt they were qualified to advise women and young people on matters other than the purely medical. In these writers, as with the writers of children's books, Wollstonecraft finds a model in the use of scientific or natural knowledge for political purposes, though usually their political purpose is very different to her own.[14] Though not a physician himself, James Fordyce (1720 96), to whose *Sermons to Young Women* (1765) Wollstonecraft objects in *Vindication*, did have a much younger brother, George Fordyce (1736–1802), who was both a physician and a friend of Wollstonecraft, and who was also published by Johnson.[15] While there is not much evidence of George Fordyce's scientific influence on James Fordyce's *Sermons*, the language Wollstonecraft uses in her criticism of the *Sermons* alludes to the potential for such conduct books to enforce a definition of what is 'natural' upon young women: 'I should not allow girls to peruse them, unless I designed to hunt every spark of nature out of their composition, melting every human quality into female meekness and artificial grace' (*Works*, V, 162). Wollstonecraft is clear that it is because they have been 'Educated in the enervating style recommended' by such writers as James Fordyce that women now 'appear a defect in nature' (*Works*, v, 185). This introduces a topic key to this chapter: women can be educated in such a manner as to shape them into 'artificial' creatures, unnaturally meek and graceful. We see this again in her comparison between women and domesticated (or 'artificial') animals.

John Gregory was another such writer and Wollstonecraft certainly read and engaged seriously with Gregory's books. He was a physician who also wrote natural history and advice literature. Gregory's *A Comparative View of the State and Faculties of Man, with those of the Animal World* (1765) claims that we can learn much about human behaviour and society from the study of animals (Gregory 1765, 9). Wollstonecraft used a quotation from *Comparative View* to open the main body of *The Female Reader*, which alludes to this idea: 'As the two sexes have very different parts to act in life nature has marked their character very differently' (*Works*, IV, 67). This suggests that her use of Gregory's *Comparative View* was complex: at least, at this point in time, she could quote him in a seemingly approving way.[16] Both Gregory's natural history work, *Comparative View*, and his conduct book, *A Father's Legacy to his Daughters*, appear in *The Female Reader* and Wollstonecraft quotes Gregory at length in a section called 'Men and Animals Compared' (*Works*, IV, 287–8). In her reading of Gregory's *Comparative View*, Wollstonecraft encountered a scientific understanding of the relations between humans and animals. In *A Father's Legacy*, she sees these ideas applied to advice given to women on their conduct and behaviour.[17]

Gregory's *Comparative View* sets out to establish precisely which instincts 'are natural to mankind', a subject that Wollstonecraft interrogates in her review of Smellie's *Philosophy of Natural History*, which bears particular interest for her when she writes *Vindication* (Gregory 1765, 15). On the question of whether animals have reason or merely instinct, the issue Wollstonecraft will take up in her review of Smellie in 1790, Gregory is at pains to point out that while humans have instinct as well as reason, animals possess more instinct and less reason than humans. He is convinced of the hierarchy of the 'Chain of Being':

> The advantages, which the Brute Animals have over us, are possessed by those of our own Species, who are just above them, guided in a manner entirely by Instinct, equally strangers to the noble attainments their Natures are capable of and to the many miseries attendant on their more enlightned [*sic*] Brethren of mankind.
>
> (Gregory 1765, 14–15)

In other words, animals are strangers both to the idea that they could improve and to the miseries that humankind experiences. Gregory believes that it is nature rather than education that determines which characteristics (both physical characteristics and personality traits) are transmitted from one generation to the next. Indeed he considers human nature as a constant to be discovered and revealed rather than something capable of the improvement that both Wollstonecraft and Godwin can see.

In *Comparative View* some opinions are voiced that Wollstonecraft would not, presumably, have disagreed with; for example, Gregory is against the wearing of stays, otherwise known as corsets, and writes that 'Nature has shewn her resentment of this practice in the most striking manner, by rendering above half the Women of fashion deformed in some degree or other' (Gregory 1765, 31). In *Vindication*, Wollstonecraft remarks that women's shapes have been altered by such practices. Many of his objections to the 'contrivances of modern luxury' Wollstonecraft would also have agreed with, along with endorsements of such activities as the daily cold bath (Gregory 1765, p. 33). He blames the 'debility and morbid sensibility of the nervous System' upon the 'softness and effeminacy of modern manners' (Gregory 1765, p. 34). At other times, though, Gregory's words may have jarred with Wollstonecraft. Though he writes of 'Mankind' throughout, there are telling sections where his language betrays a clear distinction between 'them' and 'us', such as the passage on the 'universal aversion, which all Men have to Infidelity in the fair sex', which makes it clear that he believes he is writing for a male audience and that when he discusses 'men' he may be writing specifically of men (Gregory 1765, p. 166).

In his conduct book, *A Father's Legacy*, it is with the 'propriety of conduct peculiar to your sex' that Gregory is most concerned – writing as a man to women – and it is in his preferment of 'that modest reserve, that retiring delicacy, which avoids the public eye, and is disconcerted even at the gaze of admiration' that Wollstonecraft finds most to offend (Gregory 1774, 7, 26). According to Wollstonecraft, Gregory is one of those writers who has 'contributed to render women more artificial, weak characters, than they would otherwise have been; and, consequently, more useless members of society' (*Works*, v, 91). The word 'artificial' here means 'opposed to natural' and the word is used for the same reasons to describe domesticated animals (*OED*). In 1819, for example, William Lawrence in an entry for Rees's *Cyclopædia* regards animals that become 'completely domesticated' as having been 'rendered artificial'.[18] Gregory's text reveals a medical man who thinks himself qualified to speak on matters of female behaviour and morals. Gregory's advice to his daughters does include physical matters; he urges them, for example, not to indulge in the 'luxury of eating' (Gregory 1774, 39). The fruit of such advice can perhaps be seen in the society Wollstonecraft describes in *Vindication*; she mentions a 'weak woman of fashion' who would 'boast of her want of appetite' (*Works*, v, 112). Gregory advises women to look after their health because 'Bad health seldom fails to have an influence on the spirits and temper' (Gregory 1774, 49). If a woman is lucky enough to enjoy good health, she should 'enjoy it in grateful silence' because 'when a woman speaks of her great strength, her extraordinary appetite, her ability to bear excessive fatigue, we recoil at the description' (Gregory 1774, 50–1). In other words, health should not be maintained for its own sake but because no one wants to hear a woman complain about her ill health. Equally, men do not want to hear a woman boast of her good health and physical strength. Since we see Gregory, a medical man, presuming to offer advice outside of his area of expertise, it is perhaps less surprising that Wollstonecraft, an educationalist, feels qualified to write, 'as man with man, with medical men, on anatomical subjects' in *Vindication* (*Works*, v, 193, n.3).

Wollstonecraft's anger with Gregory's *A Father's Legacy* in *Vindication* is palpable. While she may have found some common ground between her ideas and his *Comparative View*, *A Father's Legacy* moves unjustifiably from medical to moral advice. She is for example, in *Vindication*, simply 'unable to comprehend' what Gregory or Rousseau mean when they claim that 'The love of dress is natural to [women]' (*Works*, v, 97; Gregory, 1774, 55). The issue is whether such things are 'innate' as we would now describe it and this idea Wollstonecraft thinks laughable (*Works*, v, 97).[19] Such sentiments go to the heart of Wollstonecraft's project in *Vindication*. She has been moved to write because it seems from the evidence of women in her society 'that either nature has made a great difference between man and man, or that the civilization which has hitherto taken place in the world has been very partial' (*Works*, v, 73). Her objective then can be seen as a natural history one. Just as Gregory sets about comparing men to animals, Wollstonecraft determines to compare humans with each other (by which she largely means to compare men to women). Why is it that there is such a difference between men and women? Has nature really made this clearly visible distinction between them, or is civilized society responsible? The fact that Gregory's conduct book is written by a man who is supposedly an expert in what is natural to mankind – as witnessed by *Comparative View*'s consideration of the characteristics that both link and divide mankind from other animals – is surely important here. This gives him a degree of authority with which to pronounce on the 'natural' behaviour of women.

In *Vindication*, Wollstonecraft is strident in her opposition to the suggestion of both Gregory and Rousseau that a love of dress is natural to women: 'I deny it. It is not natural' (*Works*, v, 97). As for the idea that if they have good health, women should hide the fact, Wollstonecraft is incredulous: 'In the name of truth and common sense, why should not one woman acknowledge that she can take more exercise than another? or, in other words, that she has a sound constitution' (*Works*, v, 97). Sentiments such as Gregory's have actually altered the shape of women's bodies: 'enervated by confinement and false notions of modesty, the body is prevented from attaining that grace and beauty which half-formed limbs never exhibit' (*Works*, v, 92). Wollstonecraft blames women's 'sedentary employments' and lack of physical exercise for making them 'sickly' (*Works*, v, 145). While critics generally agree that Wollstonecraft admits men are, at base, physically superior to and stronger than women, in fact she questions this with a direct challenge: 'Let us then, by being allowed to take the same exercise as boys, not only during infancy, but youth, arrive at perfection of body, that we may know how far the natural superiority extends' (*Works*, v, 155).[20] Women would not be so childish if they were allowed physical exercise and were not imprisoned and stifled: 'I am persuaded we should hear none of these infantine airs, if girls were allowed to take sufficient exercise, and not confined in close rooms till their muscles are relaxed, and their powers of digestion destroyed' (*Works*, v, 131). In other words it is the advice of such writers as Gregory that has encouraged women to live in ways that exacerbate any pre-existing natural difference.

Perhaps because she approved of some of Rousseau's ideas and sentiments, Wollstonecraft is particularly disappointed by his theories on the education of girls. Rousseau had also employed the tactic of turning to natural history to bolster his ideological position. Immediately upon beginning Book Five of *Emile*, on the education of Sophie, Emile's future wife, Rousseau determines to examine 'the similarities and the differences between her sex and ours' – thus alerting us to the sex of his intended reader – and, accordingly turns to 'comparative anatomy' (Rousseau 1979, 357). After acknowledging that 'the machine' of both men and women 'is constructed in the same way', he admits how difficult it is to determine 'what in their constitution is due to sex and what is not' (Rousseau 1979, 357). In other words, which parts of our bodies are common to all humans and which are distinctive to each sex?

The differences that he discovers in men and women, he writes, 'must have a moral influence' (Rousseau 1979, 359). His research leads him to conclude that 'woman is made specially to please man' (Rousseau 1979, 359). Not only this, woman is 'made to please and be subjugated to man' (Rousseau 1979, 359). The key to women's character then is found in their bodies: they are made to behave in a certain manner. Wollstonecraft notes that Rousseau 'pretends to draw [his arguments] from the indications of nature' (*Works*, v, 94). When the evidence from comparative anatomy does not support his ideology, Rousseau finds a way around this: 'If females among the animals do not have the same shame, what follows from that' (Rousseau 1979, 359). For her part, Wollstonecraft finds Sophie, Rousseau's ideal woman, 'grossly unnatural' and she endeavours to prove that obedience and subjection are not natural to her sex by herself using the knowledge gained by natural history (*Works*, v, 93). This reveals that she is aware of Rousseau's tactical use of natural history for political purpose – and rejects it. Such moments also indicate her own knowledge and opinion of what natural history tells us. The next section gives a single but persuasive instance of this in her review of Smellie, which again reveals Wollstonecraft's engagement with natural history.

1.3 Animal instinct and human reason

The period in which Wollstonecraft was reading and reviewing books of natural history by Smellie, Bewick and Beilby, and Buffon, is precisely that same period in which she was thinking about and writing *Vindication of the Rights of Men* and *Vindication of the Rights of Woman*. There are certainly textual echoes between these reviews and *Vindication*; specifically, ideas picked out for discussion in reviews re-emerge in *Vindication*. Unsurprisingly, when writing these reviews Wollstonecraft is mulling over the arguments she intends to make in *Vindication* and thinking about the uses to which natural knowledge has been and can be put.[21] In this section I focus on Wollstonecraft's review of Smellie's *Philosophy of Natural History*, examining in detail an aspect of his work with which she vehemently disagrees. She refuses to believe, as Smellie does, that reason is an extension of instinct, instead arguing that they are 'essentially different' (*Works*, vii, 297). This debate is crucial for Wollstonecraft because she has to defend women against the idea that they do not have reason enough to be given rights or to be capable of improvement by means of virtue. She has a strict sense of the difference between humans and animals based, in part, on her religious views. Smellie is too radical for Wollstonecraft because he sees more similarities than differences in his comparisons between humans and animals.

S.W. Brown praises William Smellie (1740–95) for having 'made natural history accessible to women' (*DNB*). Smellie's work as an editor, author, and publisher reveals his 'commitment to the popular dissemination of knowledge', a commitment that may have originated with his attendance at John Gregory's medical lectures in Edinburgh (*DNB*; see also Kerr 1811).[22] He was a radical Whig in his politics and throughout his life challenged various forms of authority; his politics can be seen in his natural history. Daniel O'Neill argues that, for Wollstonecraft, improvement in society came from 'bringing reason to bear on a given field of human endeavour and benefiting from its incremental accretion over vast stretches of time'; this differs from Scottish Enlightenment figures, such as Smellie, who saw progression occurring by means of the 'refinement of instinctive impulses' (O'Neill 2007, 121). For my purposes, Wollstonecraft's review of Smellie demonstrates her serious engagement with scientific debate, and we can see the arguments she formulates through this disagreement emerge again in *Vindication*.

In her review of an abridged translation of Buffon's works in January 1792 Wollstonecraft praises another 'voluminous translation of Buffon' and it is likely that the translation she refers to was Smellie's (*Works*, VII, 411).[23] Smellie had taught himself French in order to undertake this translation, which was published in eight volumes in 1780 and nine volumes in 1785 (*DNB*). It is clear that Wollstonecraft was familiar with Buffon's *Natural History*, and not just the abridged version: in *Vindication*, Wollstonecraft refers to 'some naturalists' who assert 'that men do not attain their full growth and strength till thirty; but that women arrive at maturity by twenty' (*Works*, V, 138). This refers directly to Buffon's comment that 'A woman at twenty years is as perfectly formed as a man at thirty', as translated by Smellie (Buffon 1780, II, 436). This passage does not appear in the two volume abridged version that Wollstonecraft reviewed, but Smellie does refer to it in his *Philosophy of Natural History*.[24] Crucially, Wollstonecraft rejects the naturalists' assertion in *Vindication*: 'I apprehend that they reason on false ground, led astray by the male prejudice, which deems beauty the perfection of woman – mere beauty of features and complexion' (*Works*, V, 138). In other words, she interprets these statements not as purely scientific but as prejudiced by cultural opinion. Buffon (and Smellie) assume that woman is 'perfect' when she is at her most beautiful; instead Wollstonecraft urges them to consider perfection as a matter of bodily maturity and strength. In her 'Hints', intended for the second part of *Vindication*, Wollstonecraft again used material gained from Buffon via Smellie: 'It has been observed that the most adventurous horses, when tamed or domesticated, are the most mild and tractable' (*Works*, v, 272; Buffon 1780, III, 309).[25] Wollstonecraft's interest in natural history often focuses on the changes that occur when animals are domesticated and in *Vindication* these offer her a way of understanding what has happened to women in her society, now far removed from their 'natural state'.

At first glance Wollstonecraft's authorship of these reviews may seem surprising, but it is less so when she identifies Smellie's remit as primarily educational. Smellie writes that:

> Upon the whole, the general design of this publication is, to convey to the minds of youth, and of such as may have paid little attention to the study of Nature, a species of knowledge which it is not difficult to acquire.
>
> (*Philosophy*, p. viii)

This was, therefore, exactly the kind of book that Wollstonecraft was likely to review.

As she wrote in *Thoughts on the Education of Daughters*: 'A taste for the beauties of nature should be early cultivated: many things, with respect to the vegetable and animal world, may be explained in an amusing way; and this is an innocent source of pleasure within every one's reach' (*Works*, IV, 11). As we have seen, natural history books were not necessarily 'an innocent source of pleasure': they presented opinion concerning human characteristics as if it were scientific truth and even posited that physiological differences justified notions of proper behaviour. Wollstonecraft notes in her review Smellie's particular aim to see '*How far peculiarities of structure are connected with peculiarities of manner and dispositions*' by comparing the 'human structure' with that of 'quadrupeds, birds, fishes, and insects' (*Works*, VII, 295; *Philosophy*, 44). In other words, how far are our characters determined by our bodies?

Wollstonecraft does not comment on all such instances in Smellie's natural history. For example, immediately after the passage that Wollstonecraft does comment upon – that women reach their physical maturity at twenty while for men this comes at thirty – Smellie asserts:

> A similar observation is applicable to the minds of the two sexes. Man is, comparatively, a bold, generous, and enterprising animal.

> Women, on the contrary, are timid, jealous, and disposed to actions which require less agility and strength. Hence they are entitled to claim, and, by their amiable weakness, they actually receive our protection.
>
> (*Philosophy*, 236–7)

The language of address is clearly gendered: 'their' refers to women and 'our' to Smellie and his male readers. In opposition to Smellie's ideas here Wollstonecraft would state in *Vindication* that it is wrong to give 'a sex to mind' (*Works*, v, 111). Smellie, however, goes further and draws a link between female anatomy and character: 'The laxity and softness of [their 'muscular fibres'] may, in some measure, account for the timidity and listlessness of their disposition' (*Philosophy*, 237). He considers the texture of women's 'muscular fibres' 'more feeble and lax than those of men'; this is the reason for their reaching maturity earlier than men but may also partly account for their comparative 'timidity and listlessness' (*Philosophy*, 236, 237). Assuming that she reads these sections (and their proximity to sections we know her to have read should give some confidence in this), it seems likely that Wollstonecraft is ignoring or rejecting Smellie's ideas out of hand. This is a further example of an attempt to regulate and control social behaviour by reference to a physical explanation.

Revealing her natural history reading in *Vindication*, Wollstonecraft admits that 'In the government of the physical world it is observable that the female in point of strength is, in general, inferior to the male' and that this is the 'law of nature', but she does not agree that this means that women's characters are correspondingly weaker (*Works*, v, 74). In this, she engages directly with natural history but disputes what she reads. Instead she argues that weak women in the upper classes of her society are not naturally so but have been formed this way through the advice of men. Thus she selects as a matter of particular interest Smellie's view that anatomy and physiology determine human behaviour and character.

Smellie begins his *Philosophy* by establishing at great length that it is extremely difficult to distinguish between the animal and plant world; he argues 'that plants make a very near approach to animals' and that there is great difficulty in 'fixing the precise boundaries' between the 'two great kingdoms of nature' (*Philosophy*, 11). Wollstonecraft seems not to be persuaded of this and sarcastically notes that while the 'distinguishing characters [...] baffle all philosophical definition, and slip from the accurate investigator', they are 'clearly discriminated by common sense and unassisted organs'. So much so 'that they seem for all the purposes of life, to be distinguished with the most scrupulous exactness' (*Works*, VII, 294). From the outset, then, she is not persuaded that there are likenesses between different categories of living beings. Smellie's view fits Arthur Lovejoy's account of the shift in thinking about the 'Chain of Being' that took place in the eighteenth century, where the chain began to be seen as having almost imperceptible gradations within it, and particular interest was paid to species that might provide what we would now call the 'missing link' between the human, animal, plant, and mineral worlds.[26] Given that women were thought by some to be 'the link which unites man with brutes', Wollstonecraft had political reasons to reject the idea that there were blurred boundaries between the animal and human worlds (*Works*, V, 104). More than this, though, Wollstonecraft is determined that the gap between humans and animals be recognized and not reduced. According to her, animals are not capable of improvement; they do not have reason and therefore cannot achieve virtue. It is important to her that humans are seen as superior to animals.

In her review Wollstonecraft objects to Smellie's notion that animals have 'minds' (*Works*, VII, 295). It is when he discusses the 'distinction between reason and instinct', however, that she describes how in reading his book:

> we were obliged to stop, and taking a cursory view of the human mind, we could not coincide in opinion with him, though it was not always easy to confute some artful inferences which appeared naturally to flow from a highly coloured view of the sagacity so apparent in the animal kingdom.
>
> (*Works*, VII, 295)

Smellie attempts to prove in *Philosophy* that 'no such distinction exists' between rational and instinctive motives, 'and that the reasoning faculty itself is a necessary result of instinct' (*Philosophy*, 145). Wollstonecraft, however, 'cannot agree with Mr S. that instinct is only a lesser degree of reason' (*Works*, VII, 295). She quotes Smellie at length on this; her reference to the examples he gives of the 'sagacity' of animals includes an anecdote about his own cat, which had learned to lift the latch on the window so that she could get out (*Philosophy*, 152). When Smellie posits that there is 'perhaps, a greater difference between the mental powers of some animals than between those of man and the most sagacious brutes', Wollstonecraft responds with 'Here we differ – Again; – Again; – ' (*Philosophy*, 156; *Works*, VII, 295). In *Maria, or the Wrongs of Woman*, Maria is mortified by the idea that 'an ape had claimed kindred with me' (*Works*, I, 157).

Instincts, Smellie argues (and Wollstonecraft quotes him on this), 'may be considered as so many internal senses [...] these senses in different species, are likewise more or less ductile' (*Philosophy*, 156; *Works*, VII, 296). This statement elicits another passionate response from his reviewer:

> We acknowledge that we do not clearly comprehend what the author means to infer from *by more or less ductile* – unless in his ardour to prove that animals have minds similar to the human intellect, he meant to deprive us of souls. If the beaver, the bee, or the termites, are directed by reason; the faculty of thinking, of comparing ideas and profiting by experience, they are superior to men; yet we do not find that their *ductile* senses ever enables them to transmit any portion of their acquired knowledge to their posterity.
>
> (*Works*, VII, 296)

In this passage, Wollstonecraft uses a phrase that will reappear in *Vindication*. There, Milton is the author railed against with his efforts to prove with the character of Eve that women were 'formed' to be frail, soft, and sweet. Wollstonecraft writes: 'I cannot comprehend his meaning, unless, in the true Mahometan strain, he meant to deprive us of souls' (*Works*, V, 88). In *Vindication* it is women who are to be denied a soul if they do not demonstrate the possession of reason. In the 'Introduction' to *Vindication*, Wollstonecraft refers to 'the true style of Mahometanism', which treats women 'as a kind of subordinate beings' and 'not as part of the human species' (*Works*, V, 73). The importance of the soul is clear: 'if woman be allowed to have an immortal soul, she must have [...] an understanding to improve' (*Works*, V, 132). The reference to what can be transmitted to posterity through future generations as evidence of a species' improvement or degeneration is another phrase that reappears in *Vindication*. There it is 'servitude' that 'not only debases the individual, but its effects seem to be transmitted to posterity' (*Works*, V, 152). We see Wollstonecraft pick her way carefully through Smellie's arguments, disagreeing with those points that contradict her political and religious views. She is confident in her opinion and in arguing that if it were the case that animals had reason we would see evidence of it in future generations, she disputes with him on the grounds of natural history. The religious argument is partly pragmatic for Wollstonecraft, who, like abolitionists, presented religious, natural rights, economic, scientific, and literary arguments in an effort to make the strongest case.[27]

According to Wollstonecraft only humans possess reason. In *Vindication*, she defines it as the 'power of improvement' and cites Lord Monboddo approvingly when he declares that 'The brutes [...] remain in the state in which nature has placed them, except in so far as their natural instinct is improved by the culture *we* bestow upon them' (*Works*, v, 122n.). She uses the word 'instinct' often in her writing elsewhere and the way it is often used, such as in the phrases 'animal spirits and instinctive feelings' in *Vindication*, clearly refers to the part of us that is perhaps more animal than intellectual or spiritual (*Works*, v, 176).[28] Instinct means, therefore, a mechanical, natural, or an unthinking response to the world. Also in *Vindication*, Wollstonecraft writes that: 'The feelings of a parent mingling with an instinct merely animal, give it dignity' (*Works*, v, 208). Thus instincts, which are 'merely animal', can be added to by civilized affection. Wollstonecraft describes 'sensibility' as, similarly, 'the most exquisitely polished instinct' (*Works*, v, 132). She is adamant in *Vindication* that 'sensibility is not reason' (*Works*, v, 133). In *Vindication*, she puts forward, momentarily, the alternative view:

> And if the dignity of the female soul be as disputable as that of animals – if their reason does not afford sufficient light to direct their conduct whilst unerring instinct is denied – they are surely of all creatures the most miserable! and, bent beneath the iron hand of destiny, must submit to be a *fair defect* in creation.
>
> (*Works*, v, 114)

If women are denied both reason and instinct they must be considered a defect of nature because they have neither the characteristic that distinguishes men nor that which distinguishes animals. Wollstonecraft is playing devil's advocate here of course. She does believe women capable of reason, of virtue, and of improvement.

Wollstonecraft denies the 'sagacity' of animals that Smellie regards as signs of their ability to reason. Rather than interpreting the many instances of an ability to imitate as evidence of reason, she sees an animal wanting to please its master, having learned (the hard way) the result of a failure to do so. In *Vindication*, Wollstonecraft uses this idea to compare women to tamed animals: women are 'Smiling under the lash at which [gentleness] dare not snarl' (*Works*, v, 102). Domesticated animals are discussed again in *Vindication* and women in their present, debilitated state in her society are explicitly compared to such animals. Their behaviour is artificial rather than natural. What Wollstonecraft finds in the women around her is not the reason of which she knows they are capable, but a desire to please men, using foibles and frivolous tricks that they have learned to achieve this. Wollstonecraft refers to Smellie as an authority for the view that 'the principle of imitation' is greater where the 'rational faculties' have been less cultivated. Imitation is perceived in the behaviour of domestic animals and Wollstonecraft cites Smellie's argument that women are more prone to imitation than men in 'Hints': '"Most women, of course, are more influenced by the behaviour, the fashions, and the opinions of those with whom they associate, than men." (Smellie.)' (*Works*, v, 276). Again here she disputes Smellie's natural history on its own terms:

> The human species, considered collectively, appear to have an infancy, youth, etc. – Has any thing similar ever been observed in the brute creation? On the contrary, it is evident that the horse, dog, and sheep, and many others which it would be tedious to enumerate, transmit to their posterity *only* physical improvement.
>
> (*Works*, VII, 297–8)

The issue of what can be transmitted to future generations is key to Wollstonecraft's objection to Smellie's notion of animal mind, or reason: if such a faculty existed it would be revealed in future generations. In *Vindication*, the spaniel is offered as an example of the transmission of physical change through time. Wollstonecraft writes that 'a naturalist' (identified as Buffon by Butler and Todd) has observed that the spaniel's ears used to be erect but now 'custom has superseded nature, and a token of fear is become a beauty' (*Works*, v, 152). The spaniel is likened directly to women of Wollstonecraft's society, who similarly, after years of servitude, 'hug their chains, and fawn like the spaniel' (*Works*, v, 152).[29] Wollstonecraft uses the image of the spaniel elsewhere in *Vindication*, referring twice to women's 'spaniel-like affection' for man (*Works*, v, 102, 212). In the case of the spaniel the species has not improved but degenerated from its natural state – it has become 'artificial' – and this is what Wollstonecraft believes has happened to women in her society.

After examining natural history books and Wollstonecraft's reviews of them, it is possible to see *Vindication* as borrowing from their genre and ambition: 'I shall first consider women in the grand light of human creatures, who, in common with men, are placed on this earth to unfold their faculties' (*Works*, v, 74). Women are human, primarily, asserting her firm conviction that gendered behaviour was learned through education and experience. Seen in this light, *Vindication* is a kind of natural history of woman. The middle classes offer Wollstonecraft woman in her most 'natural state' because she has not been affected by the damaging effects of hardship and physical suffering that accompany poverty, nor by the enervating effects of extravagant opulence and luxury common to the upper classes. The latter are discussed particularly in *Vindication*. Mental as well as physical exertion are required to achieve this 'natural state', coupled with that 'natural soundness of constitution' of which women are capable (*Works*, v, 107). The 'bodily labour' of the lower classes may result in the 'robust tone of nerves and vigour of muscles' but the 'mind is quiescent' (*Works*, v, 107). Instead the ideal is for strength of both body and mind. Wollstonecraft states in *Vindication* 'I wish to persuade women to endeavour to acquire strength, both of mind and body' (*Works*, v, 75).[30]

As is clear from these passages, for Wollstonecraft the mind and the body are closely linked.[31] She urges women to acquire so-called 'manly virtues',

> or, more properly speaking, the attainment of those talents and virtues, the exercise of which ennobles the human character, and which raise females in the scale of animal being, when they are comprehensively termed mankind.
>
> (*Works*, v, 74)

This reference to the 'scale of animal being' suggests that when women are considered within the inclusive term 'mankind' they are higher up this scale than when they are considered as merely 'females'. In *Vindication*, Wollstonecraft admits that men are physically stronger than women but rejects the idea that women should deliberately weaken their constitutions to make them more attractive:

> Nature has given woman a weaker frame than man; but, to ensure a husband's affections, must a wife, who by the exercise of her mind and body whilst she was discharging the duties of a daughter, wife, and mother, has allowed her constitution to retain its natural strength, and her nerves a healthy tone, is she, I say, to condescend to use art and feign a sickly delicacy in order to secure her husband's affection?
>
> (*Works*, v, 98)

If a woman is contented with such a 'paltry crown' as obtaining a husband, she is 'scarcely raised by her employments above the animal kingdom' (*Works*, v, 101). The desire of women to 'establish' themselves in this manner makes 'mere animals' of them (*Works*, v, 76). Milton's portrayal of Eve, who is held to embody many of the characteristics considered ideal for her sex, is angrily rejected: 'How grossly do they insult us who thus advise us only to render ourselves gentle, domestic brutes!' (*Works*, v, 88–9). Reading and reviewing Smellie's book, Wollstonecraft engaged with the natural history of the relationship between humans and animals, specifically whether animals were capable of reason. The debate offers her support for her political objective and allows her to understand and describe what has happened to women now so far removed from their 'natural state'. Smellie's examples of domesticated animals' 'sagacity' she views as merely imitation, aping humans in order to please. In this she finds a model for women's condition in contemporary society, which she uses to great effect. Wollstonecraft proves that she is alive to the political purposes to which natural knowledge is put and that she is as adept as others in using natural knowledge to assert her own political agenda.

1.4 Botany

Wollstonecraft also objects to Smellie's *Philosophy* on the grounds that it refuses to follow Linnaeus's system of the sexes of plants. In this her scientific viewpoint is more radical than his. Linnaeus's system draws further analogies between the animal and plant kingdoms, where plants are regarded as either male, female, or hermaphrodite, and as engaging in various forms of intercourse in order to generate. In *Philosophy*, Smellie joins other writers in objecting to the smuttiness of these new botanical terms (George 2005, 2–3; George 2007). He is dismayed by what he regards as the 'truly ridiculous' level to which analogy has been pushed, noting that it has gone 'far beyond all decent levels' (*Philosophy*, 248). In his 'Botany' entry for the *Encyclopaedia Britannica* the issue is described at greater length. Smellie writes there that 'obscenity is the very basis of the Linnaean system' and that 'there is such a degree of indelicacy in the expression as cannot be exceeded by the most obscene romance-writer' ([Smellie] 1771, I, 653). It is no accident that, as Ann B. Shteir has pointed out, 'The Linnaean system of plant sexuality was promulgated during the period when sexual difference became a reiterated theme in medicine and other areas of natural knowledge' (Shteir 1996, 17). Shteir writes that 'Linnaeus's sexual system reads as a conservative gender construction. It embodies clear and naturalized sexual differences and distinct gender boundaries' (Shteir 1996, 17). These are precisely the distinctions that Wollstonecraft recognized as having been made to seem natural in human society, but which, she argued, had little real basis in nature itself. While this section may be treading well-worn critical ground I am primarily interested in the way that botany offered Wollstonecraft another example of how plants (like animals), though they cannot improve, can degenerate.

Sam George makes the point that it seems odd that Rousseau should be one of those who encouraged women to study botany, as his *Lettres Élémentaires sur la Botanique* (1771–73) clearly did, despite the fact that in *Emile* he seems very much against women studying science (George 2005, 14). George accounts for this by linking Rousseau's interest in this to other of his philosophical ideas: 'To Rousseau, the "true" study of botany was "understanding plants in their natural state, before they had been cultivated and denatured by the hands of men"', and unlearned women, similarly 'closer to a state of nature, had a special affinity for this kind of exploration, which even Linnaeus lacked' (George 2005, 14). As Bewell puts it: 'What has often been said about Rousseau's "state of nature" can equally be said about his botanical musings: for him, plants are as noble as savages' (Bewell 1989a, 134). Using Wollstonecraft's phrase, Rousseau places women lower down the 'scale of animal being' and this position, closer to the plant kingdom, permits their study of botany (*Works*, v, 74). Wollstonecraft, in her response to the issue of an analogy between flowers and women, was able to use Rousseau's idea of the natural state of flowers as a metaphor for the 'natural state' of women. Like him too, though, she was able to point to the corrupting influence of cultivation, which had produced sickly, barren, disease-prone, but beautiful flowers, known as luxuriants, a clear symbol in the plant world of the upper-class, overly-sensitive women that Wollstonecraft saw in contemporary society (Bewell 1989a, 137–8; *Works*, v, 75). Analogies can be drawn between the degenerate condition of wealthy women in Wollstonecraft's society and both hot-house plants and domesticated animals: all have degenerated from their natural state to artificial beings. These analogies are present in Wollstonecraft's writings despite a general refusal to consider woman as closer to the animal and plant kingdoms than man.

In the opening paragraph of the introduction to *Vindication*, Wollstonecraft uses botanical metaphors to compare society's women to flowers that have been 'planted in too rich a soil', where their 'strength and usefulness are sacrificed to beauty' (*Works*, v, 73). Later, she writes that modesty needs to be 'cultivated', or it becomes a sickly 'hot-house plant' (*Works*, v, 196). Quoting David Williams in a review of his *Lectures on Education*, Wollstonecraft notes ideas that we find again in *Vindication*:

> The business of fashionable education, conducted with ostentation and expence [*sic*] in private families, is on the principles of artificial gardening; and the pupils are hot-house plants. Their progress and beauties dazzle or surprize [*sic*] superficial observers; but they sicken at the first breath of common air; they have latent insipidities discernible to a natural or accurate taste, and they fade or perish with the direct execution of my plan.
>
> (*Works*, VII, 147; see also Calè 2000)

Wollstonecraft sees the forcing of hot-house plants as analogous to women's subjection and 'cultivation' by civilized society. This very brief look at the uses of botany in *Vindication*, confirms both that botanical knowledge was used to political ends and that Wollstonecraft used it in this way herself. For my purposes, her interest in botany lies particularly in the idea that species can degenerate, like the spaniels in the natural history of animals, and should be placed within the context of a general focus upon change and development through time. Changes from the natural state enabled by the cultivation of plants, like that of the domestication of animals, created unnatural and artificial beings.

1.5 Race theory

As is clear from her selections from the animal world (the spaniel) and the plant world (the hot-house plants), Wollstonecraft is interested in the capacity for degeneration. She believes that humans are capable of improvement and that this allows for women's potential to improve beyond, for example, 'the present race of weak mothers' that Wollstonecraft sees around her (*Works*, v, 249). Wollstonecraft may have developed these ideas not only from natural history books but also from reading and reviewing travel writing and writing about race.[32] In this section I focus on Wollstonecraft's review of Samuel Stanhope Smith's *An Essay on the Causes of the Variety of Complexion and Figure in the Human Species* and of the translation of Le Vaillant's *New Travels into the Interior Parts of Africa*. In texts such as these, as well as in the natural history works considered earlier, Wollstonecraft finds much to support her belief in human equality, and uses evidence found in these books to further her own feminist agenda.

The role of science in communicating racist ideology has come under scrutiny recently, as has the intersection between travel and science in the colonial world (see Kitson 2007 and Fulford et al. 2004). On the *Beagle* voyages, for example, Charles Darwin not only catalogued plant and animal life but also mused on the differences between races. When he met the inhabitants of Tierra del Fuego on 18 December 1832 he wrote: 'I could not have believed how wide was the difference between savage and civilized man: it is greater than between a wild and domesticated animal, inasmuch as in man there is a greater power of improvement' (Darwin 1846, I, 263). Darwin's comparison between Fuegian men and animals is distinctly uncomfortable for the modern reader but to many at the time it would have seemed uncontroversial. Stories of encounters with the peoples of other continents were greedily consumed by British readers. Travel narratives were often salacious, filled with accounts of the depravity of native peoples, described as being in a more primitive or barbaric stage of civilization than the white European. Even when represented as a kind of Rousseauian 'noble savage', a concept to which Wollstonecraft clearly subscribes, stereotyping remains racist and patronizing. Wollstonecraft herself had to counter similar ideas in responding to those who claimed that women were merely animals, or that they constituted the link between men and animals, and she finds much to support her feminist and abolitionist cause in writings on race.

Wollstonecraft is specifically interested in evidence that humans can change in response to environmental conditions, making parallels possible with her interest in the effect of domestication on animals. These analogies occur elsewhere in the period, for example, S.T. Coleridge's 'To a Young Ass' has long been recognized as an abolitionist poem in the guise of a poem about subjugated animals (Kenyon-Jones 2001, p. 68). In *Vindication*, women are compared to oxen or other animals by means of the image of a yoke: 'to shew that she ought to have her neck bent under the yoke' (*Works*, V, 95). Wollstonecraft's agenda, of course, primarily concerns female equality, and it is possible to see domestic animals and slaves as, for her, primarily symbols of female oppression. Moira Ferguson notes that *Vindication* contains 'more than eighty references' to slavery, and that 'the constituency Wollstonecraft champions – white, middle-class women – is constantly characterized as slaves' (Ferguson 1993, 9).

In a review in May 1797 of a translation of Le Vaillant's *New Travels into the Interior Parts of Africa*, Wollstonecraft finds evidence that undermines the so-called civilizing efforts of whites on the Khoikhoi people of the Cape of Good Hope. She writes:

> The hottentots have been considered as the most disgusting and brutal of 'the various tribes of the many peopled earth;' a real lover of mankind must then be highly gratified by the lively and artless pictures that occur in this narrative of the domestic virtues, and moral sensibility, of the untutored wanderers in those vast rocky deserts.
>
> The hottentots, in the vicinity of the Cape, as has ever been observable in the case of a hasty adoption of very contrary manners, have degenerated from the simple virtues common to their state of civilization; but accompanying our traveller to those hordes, never visited by the rapacious whites, from whose bosoms commerce has eradicated every human feeling, we find them just and affectionate, with the distinctive characteristics of man. The dirty customs attributed to them are evidently proved to be false, as well as the charge of tyrannizing over the weaker sex.
>
> (*Works*, VII, 480)

Here she is delighted to find in the description of these people evidence of 'distinctive characteristics of man', or, in other words, the characteristics that distinguish humans from animals and that are shared by all human races. The 'rapacious whites' she associates with trade and commerce, regarding these as having 'eradicated every human feeling' from their hearts: in fact it is they who have changed and degenerated from their original natural state. The Khoikhoi are, she points out, 'untutored' – they have not learned their behaviour – it is natural to them. While such sentiment can be regarded as shot-through with Rousseau-inflected racism, it nonetheless posits a natural goodness in mankind regardless of race. Where colonization has occurred, described here as the 'hasty adoption of very contrary manners', the manners (of the white people) are seen as responsible for the 'degeneration' from otherwise natural 'simple manners'. If there were any question remaining over Wollstonecraft's authorship of this review, the language of this passage is recognizably hers, particularly in the values she upholds in human society: 'domestic virtues', 'moral sensibility', and the humane treatment of women.

Ferguson has written on Wollstonecraft's use of a comparison between the position of women in patriarchal society and the African slave (another comparison with which the modern reader may feel distinctly uncomfortable) (Ferguson 1993, 8–33). She does at one point in *Vindication* specifically write that when she calls women slaves she means this 'in a political and civil sense' (*Works*, v, 239). In the passage where she notes the natural history of the spaniel, Wollstonecraft makes a specific reference to slavery: women, like the spaniel, have learned to 'hug their chains' (*Works*, v, 152). Immediately before this passage, Wollstonecraft quotes Rousseau's *Emile* in which he states that for women, 'a state of dependence being natural to the sex, they perceive themselves formed for obedience' (cited in *Works*, v, 152). To counter this, Wollstonecraft puts forward the idea that submission to slavery can be learned, and that it seems possible that this lesson can be transmitted to future generations: 'for servitude not only debases the individual [...] its effects seem to be transmitted to posterity' (*Works*, v, 152). In Stanhope Smith's *Essay*, which Wollstonecraft reviewed in December 1788, he intends to establish 'the unity of the human species' and Wollstonecraft was clearly much impressed by his work.[33] In her review the issue of physical or moral characteristics being transmitted to future generations is again raised.

Scott Juengel has written on this review, arguing that it informs Wollstonecraft's *Letters Written During a Short Residence in Sweden, Norway and Demark* (1796), which he describes as 'a journey into the heart of whiteness through which Wollstonecraft can meditate on the (failed) promise of historical progress and the limits of human adaptability' (Juengel 2001, 900; see also Ferguson 1993, 24). Quoting Nicholas Hudson, Juengel notes that the definition of 'race' had changed around this time, from its 'original sense of a people or single nation, linked by origin, to its later sense of a biological subdivision of the human species' (Juengel 2001, 900). This subdivision increasingly became understood as 'an innate and fixed disparity in the physical and intellectual makeup of different peoples' (Hudson, cited in Juengel 2001, 900). Unlike polygenetic racial theory, which posited that the '"darker races" are inherently, irredeemably inferior', Stanhope Smith believed that there was a connection between 'geography and complexion' (Juengel 2001, 902, 904). For Stanhope Smith, race is not fixed but plastic and mutable, influenced by social, moral, and environmental causes (see Kitson 2007). This accords broadly with Enlightenment thinking on both race and gender as Russett also has argued: while convinced of European racial superiority to the 'lesser rank of dark-skinned, non-European peoples', ethnologists 'usually understood their inferiority to be the result of environment rather than biology' (Russett 1991, 25). This opinion allows, in principle, for optimism for the future: different races were 'not the cause but the result of cultural and environmental diversity, and their inferior status could in principle be remedied' (Russett 1991, 25). It is possible to draw certain analogies between the ways in which both race and gender were understood at the time, and these analogies could be used positively as well as negatively. For my purposes, the race theory Wollstonecraft puts forward here accords with decided views expressed elsewhere on the topic of animals and plants in natural history. For Wollstonecraft, if women could be seen to have learned certain behaviour and to have degenerated from their 'natural state' – physically as well as mentally and morally – this meant at least that they were capable of change. If gender as well as race was mutable according to cultural and environmental conditions, a 'revolution in female manners' was truly possible; and of course, for Wollstonecraft, the remedy by which this could be effected for women was education (*Works*, v, 114).

Wollstonecraft, in her review of Stanhope Smith's book, couches this enquiry into human diversity as an exploration of what it means to be human. She writes:

> An acquaintance with the human heart has ever been thought important and interesting; those who feel lively emotions wish to know if the same string vibrates in another bosom – if they are indeed tied to their species by the strongest of all relations, fellow-feeling – in short, if the world without resembles that within.
>
> (*Works*, VII, 50)

Such sentiments are often at the heart of Wollstonecraft's writings, from *Maria, or the Wrongs of Woman* to *Letters Written [...] in Sweden, Norway and Denmark*. She writes in this passage that individuals want to find others who feel as they do, and that in this they desire to know whether what they feel is shared by all of mankind. Her use of the word 'vibrate' alludes to David Hartley's idea of sensations as vibration, a theory that similarly imagines a link between the inner and the outer worlds of the mind and body.

While there are, she admits, 'innumerable modifications' among the many varieties of 'man':

> yet there is a degree of uniformity in their variety which silently affirms that they proceed from the same source. The untutored savage and the cultivated sage are found to be men of like passions with ourselves: different external circumstances, such as the situation of the country, forms of government, religious opinions, etc. have been

> traced by the ablest politicians as the main causes of distinct national characters.
>
> (*Works*, VII, 50)

Here we find her strong belief, shared by William Godwin, in the shaping force of institutions, such as government, in creating people's identities, the way, for example, as Wollstonecraft writes in *Vindication* that 'females [...] are made women of when they are mere children' (*Works*, V, 186).

Using language that is very like that used in *Vindication*, Wollstonecraft in her review of Stanhope Smith speaks of the 'secondary causes' that also produce changes in human form and complexion and quotes him at some length:

> Various secondary causes are assigned, which the naturalist will allow to have great force, and they produce the pertinent reflections which follow.
>
> 'Colour and figure may be styled habits of the body. Like other habits, they are created, not by great and sudden impressions, but by continual and almost imperceptible touches. Of habits both of mind and body, nations are susceptible as well as individuals. They are transmitted to offspring, and augmented by inheritance. Long in growing to maturity, national features, like national manners, become fixed, only after a succession of ages. They become, however, fixed at last'.
>
> (*Works*, VII, 51)

It is tempting to consider this passage a prefiguring of Judith Butler's idea in *Gender Trouble*. Where Butler talked about the '*stylized repetition of acts*', Wollstonecraft here speaks of 'habits of the body', and just as Butler could imagine that the body was not a neutral, innocent blank slate on which gender was written, Wollstonecraft can also imagine the body's malleability, its openness to reinvention, though Butler is thinking of quite different means through which this reinvention might take place (Butler 1990, 140). Ultimately though, Wollstonecraft firmly believes that such habits can be transmitted to future generations and eventually become fixed. Pessimistically, this means that women and slaves (she uses these ideas in writings on both) may never be able to break their chains, but, optimistically, a few pages later, she quotes Stanhope Smith's observation that education produces the 'greatest difference between men in society' (cited in *Works*, VII, 54). Education is key to positive change and improvement. While Wollstonecraft is at times despairing – 'and, who can tell, how many generations may be necessary to give vigour to the virtue and talents of the freed posterity of abject slaves' – she also sees in this the way forward (*Works*, v, 145). At the end of *Vindication*, she tells us that she has only tried to prove that the faults she perceives in women are the 'natural consequence of their education and station in society' (*Works*, v, 266). Following this argument, it is reasonable to assume that once conditions have changed so will character. Put in the context of the natural rights debate, such sentiments reveal that natural knowledge was at the heart of one of the most important concepts for the later Romantics.

This chapter has shown how Wollstonecraft appropriated for her own purposes the natural history and medical knowledge she encountered in her reading and reviewing. She rejects Smellie's idea that reason is an extension of instinct because she cannot see evidence that animals are capable of improvement. Conversely though, she takes up the idea of domesticated animals being socialized out of their natural behaviour to understand and describe metaphorically what has happened to women in her society. In this she reveals her awareness of the way that scientific knowledge can be used as authority, claiming to reveal the laws of our nature, and she is alive to the uses to which such knowledge can be put. In particular, the potential of natural history, at the intersection of nature and culture, is understood as a tool used by others to bolster gender stereotypes and as a weapon in her own political armoury.

Perhaps the key idea that Wollstonecraft is interested in is the capacity for 'improvement'. While it is clear that many of her ideas on this subject come from the eighteenth-century traditions of dissenting religion, and from educationalists such as John Locke, this chapter reveals another source. What Wollstonecraft learns from her natural history, botanical, and race theory reading is that humans are capable of physical 'improvement'. She learns that the human body itself is capable of change and development and that these changes can be handed down to future generations. This is not yet an acceptance of evolution but it is the grounds upon which she can build her sense of optimism for a future of greater equality between men and women through reason and education. Recognizing this interest in and use of natural history and medicine in Wollstonecraft's writings deepens our reading of her work. Wollstonecraft takes a confident and assured position within contemporary debates of this nature and presents her answer to these issues in *Vindication*. Scientific and medical knowledge is not merely ancillary to her political argument, at times it offers her the evidence that she needs to prove her point. It is also not the case that Wollstonecraft is merely influenced by what she reads; instead she challenges and disputes it.

In the next chapter I consider another instance where Wollstonecraft expresses distrust of the assumed authority of scientific thought, and her understanding of the political purposes to which it is put, beginning with her anger at the women who are duped by those quack doctors, the mesmerists. The chapter deals in the main with William Godwin whose knowledge of mesmerism, the efficacy of which was much debated in the 1790s and beyond, informs his understanding of the way that the vulnerable and ignorant are duped into thinking that class is a natural rather than an artificial distinction. Godwin also imagines a physical dimension to his Enlightenment sense of 'perfectibility'. His opinion that environment, particularly government, determines character, enables him to see his current society as corrupt but also, like Wollstonecraft, to think positively for the future.

2
William Godwin and the Imagination

Towards the end of *Vindication of the Rights of Woman*, Mary Wollstonecraft expresses her annoyance at the women who are taken in by the 'fashionable deceptions' of the animal magnetists (*Works*, v, 253).[1] This instance of gullibility is dwelt upon because it particularly reveals the 'folly which the ignorance of women generates' (*Works*, v, 251). Her husband, William Godwin, had particular knowledge of these 'priests of quackery' as she called them (*Works*, v, 254). In 1785, he had translated from the French an important report that aimed once and for all to dispel the myth of animal magnetism.[2] This chapter looks at the scientific knowledge that Godwin gained through undertaking this translation, through the medical lectures he attended, and from conversations with some of his close scientific and medical friends. This knowledge extended and added to his political ideas – ideas that are instrumental for later Romantic writers. For example, the idea that environment shapes individuals and that circumstances determine action can be seen as a feature of both scientific and political theory of this time. More specifically, Wollstonecraft and Godwin both concern themselves with the ways in which obedience to authority can be obtained through deceptive means. In addition, Godwin is particularly interested in ideas of sympathy between parts of the body as well as between individuals, in longevity, and in the possibility of immortality. The optimism that Godwin shared with Wollstonecraft was based upon a conviction that people can change and improve; Godwin was convinced that there was a physical as well as a moral aspect to human perfectibility.

Where Wollstonecraft used natural history to prove that women's inferiority was not natural but learned, Godwin uses his knowledge of animal magnetism to prove that authority can be assumed by a show of power and that the victims of tyranny are, in part, complicit in their deception. The role of the imagination in this was key: it was the imagination that mesmerists played upon in their theatrics, and which deceived patients into believing they had been treated and cured. Indeed, the example of animal magnetism revealed the power of the imagination. The imagination is also key to Godwin's role as a transitional figure between the Enlightenment and Romanticism. Gary Handwerk and Arnold Markley regard Godwin's personal development from 'the reputed apostle of pure rationalism' as dependent upon a 'revaluation' of the imagination and emotion (Godwin 2001, 9). *Fleetwood*, for example, a novel written later in Godwin's career, offers a medical case study of the 'diseased imagination' of the main character, recognizing it as a motivating force (*Novels and Memoirs*, v, 237). An important recent essay by Richard Sha warns that critics have not paid enough attention to the 'physiological imagination' (2009).[3]

Lorraine Daston traces what she perceives as the systematic opposition drawn between the imagination and science in the period 1780 to 1820, when 'fact hardened, the imagination ran riot, and art and science diverged in their aims and their collective personae' (Daston 2001, 81). She cites the original animal magnetism *Rapport* as a key text in this split. The French commissioners' experiments, made with the express aim of proving animal magnetism to be an imposture, thoroughly convinced them that all effects witnessed were produced by the imagination alone. Conversely the effects they witnessed also convinced them of the very real power of the imagination. Daston writes:

> They concluded that the cures wrought by animal magnetism were often genuine, and the convulsions mostly sincere, but that all were the work of the imagination [...] Despite their palpable disapproval of such excesses of the imagination, the savants of the Royal Commission paid tribute to its extraordinary power over mind and body. No romantic poet was ever more firmly convinced of the force of the unfettered imagination than the Parisian savants.
>
> (Daston 2001, 80)

This is seen as a turning point, a shift from Enlightenment science to Romantic psychology: while the French commissioners' report detailed the many subtle ways in which patients were duped into believing that they had been affected and changed by the treatment, it still acknowledged the physical effects that magnetism appeared to have.[4] It is this that attracted Coleridge (and other Romantic writers) to animal magnetism: it showed the power that the imagination could hold over the mind and the body.

Godwin is not known for his interest in science and few people have commented upon this aspect of his work.[5] As discussed in the introduction, my categorization of ideas into 'scientific' and 'medical' is in many respects an anachronism. Identifying Godwin's participation in specific scientific debates, such as that which surrounds animal magnetism, reveals the degree to which writers of the period simply used the intellectual tools that were available to them. The knowledge Godwin gained aided his philosophical and political thinking, contributing to ideas that survived beyond the Romantic period and to the position he is now seen to hold as the founder of philosophical anarchism. He supported the private judgement and reason of the individual rather than the force of institutions such as governments: the animal magnetism case is exemplary in showing how power works in society and the ways in which the people are coerced into thinking that they are changed for the better by the experience.

In their discussions of animal magnetism Godwin and Wollstonecraft seem to be aware of science as a discourse, and both question and interrogate its claim to truth. Jan Golinski points out that to regard science either now or in the past as 'entirely open, egalitarian, and consensual is naively unrealistic' (Golinski 1992, 2). Instead science should be recognized as 'a system of authority, the tool of powerful interests in society' (Golinski 1992, 2). Writing of physicians in *The Enquirer* (1797), Godwin comments: 'The regular and the quack have each their several schemes of imposition, and they differ in nothing so much as in the name.'[6] In *Romantic Liars* Debbie Lee discusses our complicity in the act of deception; often, she writes, we are 'willing victims', wanting to believe that impostors are telling us the truth (Lee 2006, 11). Godwin could see this too. Echoes of the specific imposture of animal magnetists on their vulnerable patients can be found in *Caleb Williams*. Godwin's argument in this novel and elsewhere, in Marilyn Butler's words, is that 'Obedience to authority is thus not a virtue, even in children; it is only by making us believe in obedience, through exhortation, fiction and other devices of imposture, that our governors maintain their position.'[7] In other words, a multitude of devices are employed to deceive us into obedience to authority. Revealing these 'devices of imposture' in *Caleb Williams*, Godwin hopes that people will finally recognize the ways in which they are being deceived. In his work on the translation of the animal magnetism report, Godwin found evidence to support this more general political point. For example, in the 'Historical Introduction' written to accompany the *Report*, Godwin writes: 'it can no longer be concealed that the system of the animal magnetism is to be regarded as an imposture' (*Report*, xv). The 'devices' used by both mesmerists and Falkland in *Caleb Williams* are theatrical and spectacular. This chapter explores the links between mesmerism and politics, and the theatrical tricks used to dupe ordinary people into obedience.

The first section of the chapter examines in close detail Godwin's translation of the animal magnetism report, placing its findings within the context of Godwin's philosophical and political ideas, both those that he expressed at the time and those that emerged later in his career. In the second section I examine some of Godwin's specific links with medical and scientific worlds. His diary shows how many physicians, anatomists, natural historians, and chemists he knew and saw regularly. I consider the lectures that Godwin went to and pay attention to men he knew particularly well: Anthony Carlisle, William Nicholson, and Humphry Davy. Godwin was writing important political, philosophical, and literary works at the same time as he socialized with these men and I find evidence in the works of the knowledge that he gained from their society. The chapter proceeds broadly chronologically, examining Godwin's writing in the first half of the 1780s before looking closely at friendships first formed in 1786, and then moving on to consider his novel of 1794.

Primarily using William Godwin's novel, *Caleb Williams*, in the third section of this chapter, I examine the model of authority witnessed in the character of Mr Falkland, and link his pretence to the supernatural and the sublime with the equally fictitious though equally effective claims of the animal magnetists. Godwin's comments on magnetists, medical practitioners, politicians, and the aristocracy, suggest that he considered all of these figures to be, in some respects, encouraging people to think they had authority simply by giving the appearance of it. In *Caleb Williams* Godwin expressly wished to delineate 'the modes of domestic and unrecorded despotism, by which man becomes the destroyer of man'.[8] In this, the novel followed the purpose of *Enquiry into Political Justice*, which in the words of Gary Handwerk and A.A. Markley, was intended to reveal 'the psychological basis for and consequences of political oppression':

> Godwin's goal in [*Caleb Williams*] was to show how the 'mind-forg'd manacles' described in a poem like Blake's 'London' came to be created and, even more importantly, how it was that they had managed to persist for so long.
>
> (Godwin 2000, 11)

The animal magnetists offer an insight, then, into the way that people can be manipulated and persuaded by the mere force of suggestion, just as Godwin believed they were imposed upon politically. In translating the report, Godwin learned about the 'science' of animal magnetism as well as the experiments of Benjamin Franklin and the other commissioners that disproved its legitimacy. He added to the report his own 'Historical Introduction', which gave particular attention to the influence of the imagination upon the body, a theme to which he would return in *Caleb Williams*, *Political Justice*, and future texts. Caleb can be seen as the victim of an imagined gothic horror similar to that of the patients described in the *Report*. Like the medical imposture of animal magnetism, Godwin believed in what he called the 'political imposture' of such men as Falkland. He devoted an entire chapter to 'Political Imposture' in *Political Justice*, the system by which, as Marilyn Butler has put it, 'the population must be duped into obedience' (Butler 1995, 349). *Political Justice* states, for example that 'monarchy is founded in imposture' and discusses the 'means by which the imposture is maintained' (*Political Writings*, III, 230). In the animal magnetism report Godwin found scientific evidence of how this imposture worked on the imaginations of its victims.

2.1 Godwin's scientific and medical writings

By his own account, the early years of the 1780s were financially difficult for Godwin. He describes how, in 1783, despite prolific literary output in a variety of genres, 'for the most part I did not eat my dinner, without previously carrying my watch or my books to the pawnbrokers to enable me to eat' (*Novels and Memoirs*, I, 45). His writing was prolific during these years in his efforts to advance himself and to make money enough to live, objectives that were sometimes at odds with each other. William St Clair records how between 1782 and 1785 Godwin:

> had produced a life of Chatham, a volume of sermons, a translation of Lord Lovat's memoirs, a pamphlet on education, three novels, a book of literary parody, digests of two years of British and foreign history for the *New Annual Register* each equivalent to a substantial volume in itself, and [a] quantity of reviews for the *English Review*.
>
> (St Clair 1989, 32)

Godwin's translation from the French of the commissioners' report on animal magnetism was yet another labour of these busy years.

Translation was the work of the 'less prosperous members of the profession' to which Godwin belonged at this point in his life (St Clair 1989, 19), and the translation to which St Clair refers, the *Memoirs of the Life of Simon, Lord Lovat,* also from the French, was commissioned by John Murray and completed in 1785 but not published until 1797 by George Nicol.[9] Suggestively for my purposes, Godwin declares in the 'Preface' that these *Memoirs* have been 'faithfully translated; without any further liberty being taken with the original work, than dividing it into sections and adding the marginal notes, by the Translator' (Lovat 1797, 2). The *Report* is similarly translated, with notable adherence to the original *Rapport* and the addition of a 'Historical Introduction'.[10]

A letter written on 12 October 1784 from Benjamin Vaughan to William Temple Franklin, Benjamin Franklin's grandson and his aide in Paris from 1776 to 1785, introduces Godwin with: 'My dear sir, Pray oblige me by giving the bearer Mr Godwin such information as may occur to you respecting Animal Magnetism, as he is translating the Commissioners Report.'[11] Denis I. Duveen and Herbert S. Klickstein first discovered Godwin's authorship of the translation in 1955 (Duveen and Klickstein 1955, 300). The main text of the *Report* comprises two texts translated from the French, which were bound together with pages numbered separately: the report of a Committee of the Royal Society of Medicine on Michel Augustin Thouret's *Recherches et Doutes sur le Magnétisme Animal* (1784) and the *Rapport des Commissaires charges par le Roi, de l'Examen du Magnetisme Animal* (Anon. 1784d). In addition to the evidence provided by the letter to W.T. Franklin in which Godwin is named as author of the *Report* the 'Historical Introduction' and the *Report* itself bear marked characteristics of Godwin's other writings and ideas.[12]

From 1783 Godwin recalls 'writing for the English Review, published by Murray in Fleet Street, at two guineas a sheet, in which employment it was my utmost hope to gain twenty four guineas per annum' (*Novels and Memoirs,* I, 44). Pamela Clemit writes that Godwin was employed specifically 'to write the literary sections' of this periodical and that this employment ended in November 1786 'when he was dismissed on account of his political views' (Godwin 2011, I, 28, n. 5). It is unclear how much of the content of these 1783–86 issues of the *English Review* Godwin wrote, but there are indications that he was certainly close to the inner circle of authors writing for the journal. For example in August 1784 there was a very positive review of Godwin's *Imogen, a Pastoral Romance,* and in October of the same year a good, though brief, review of his *Italian Letters* (Anon. 1784a; Anon. 1784b). In April 1785 the *English Review* also reviews the translated *Report* beginning with

> Having already laid before our readers a copious account of the subject of this pamphlet*, we can only at present lay before our readers a brief extract from the introduction, as a specimen of the abilities of the person to whom it is indebted for its English dress.
>
> (Anon. 1785, 304)

After quoting a few passages from the 'Historical Introduction', which is acknowledged as the translator's own, the review ends with 'Upon the whole the publication is executed, in a style somewhat superior to the common run of translations' (Anon. 1785, 305). Thus, reviewers at the *English Review* were favourable to Godwin's novels and to the *Report*, indeed both could have been written by the same person sympathetic to him and his ideas; the latter could even have been written by Godwin himself.

The allusion in the review of the *Report* to the 'copious amount of the subject of this pamphlet' already published (with the asterisked note) is to a review in November 1784 of two key works discussed and translated from the French in the *Report*: Thouret's text and the *Rapport*. There are striking similarities in the language and style of this review (signed 'A') and the translated *Report*, which may suggest that Godwin was the author of both. The review begins with:

> The subject of these publications demands a place in a literary review, not so much on account of the performances that have been written respecting it, as from the extraordinary attention it has excited in our neighbour kingdom, and the singular incident it furnishes in the history of the human mind. It has excited the enquiries of the lively and intelligent inhabitants of Paris, with the well-known discovery of the aerostation, and it has been in a greater or less degree a subject of disquisition for a much longer time. Their journals and newspapers have been filled with it for years; and, as M. Thouret informs us, it has finished with becoming a mode, a matter warmly taken up, and an interest dear to the hearts of the fashionable world.
>
> (Anon. 1784c, 381–2)

In the translator's 'Historical Introduction' to the *Report* we initially hear of the 'extremist attention' that the subject has been given in France, and which has 'for years filled [the] Journals and Mercures' of our 'neighbour kingdom' (*Report*, iii). Later the translator speaks of the 'universal attention' animal magnetism has 'excited at Paris, where it seems to have divided the public speculations with the celebrated and incomparable discovery of the aerostatic globe' (*Report*, xvi). The aerostation or aerostatic globe refers to the experiments of the Montgolfier brothers who had in 1783 successfully lifted a silk balloon over 6000 feet into the air, and by 1784 had created a balloon that carried seven passengers over Lyon. The 'Historical Introduction' also notes the importance of these findings to 'the history of the human mind' (*Report*, xvii). When both texts translate the same passage from Thouret, the *Report* has: 'as M. Thouret observes, the animal magnetism became a mode, an affair of bon ton, an interest, extremely precious and warmly espoused by the fashionable world' (*Report*, xiv). Compared to the equivalent passage in the *English Review*, the *Report* is more faithful to the original: for example, in retaining the French phrase 'bon ton', which does not translate as 'a matter warmly taken up' but means sophisticated manners or breeding. We could speculate that the review, published in November 1784, could have been written at the same time as Godwin is trying to find out more information about animal magnetism (according to the letter written to Franklin's grandson in October), and might be a first draft or work in progress of the translation that would become the *Report*.

Both the reviewer in the *English Review* and the translator of the *Report* take in the 'remarkable coincidence between the magnetism asserted by Paracelus, and the animal magnetism of Mesmer' (Anon. 1784c, 386; see also *Report*, xix). The protagonist of Godwin's *St Leon* is an alchemist and one of Godwin's final works, the *Lives of the Necromancers*, was written for a reason not unlike the one for which the *Report* on animal magnetism was undertaken: 'The main purpose of this book is to exhibit a fair delineation of the credulity of the human mind' (Godwin 1834, v). In the 'Preface' to the *Lives*, Godwin lists among man's delusions the attempt 'of producing miraculous cures upon the bodies of our fellowmen' (Godwin 1834, ix).[13]

Both Mark Philp and St Clair note that many of the ideas that would be made famous in *Political Justice* had formed or were being formed in Godwin's mind around this time (*Political Writings*, I, 13). It is possible to track Godwin's political views at this point and find ideas echoed in the animal magnetism *Report* and, later, in *Political Justice*. His contributions to the *Political Herald and Review* offer an opportunity to see his opinions in 1785, the year the *Report* was published. For example, he decries man's inability to see through the 'supple courtier' of the politician and realize he is instead 'the cat's-paw of despotism' (*Political Writings*, I, 195). Already, at this early stage in his career, Godwin shows a firm commitment to private judgement:

> No doubt can be made that, upon a system of pure morality, every man ought to be left to the simple dictates of his own judgment and conscience, and that every kind of influence, except that of superior virtue, is illegitimate and improper.
>
> (*Political Writings*, I, 212)

He laments, though, the difficulty that the 'vulgar among every class of mankind' have in 'thinking and deciding for themselves' (*Political Writings*, I, 222). We can already see here the beginnings of his antagonism to obedience, which in *Political Justice* would become a prominent concern: in 1785, he writes of men becoming 'voluntary slaves', 'paltry puppets', and notes that 'To comply' is to 'degrade' oneself (*Political Writings*, I, 222, 223). He compares William Pitt specifically to a quack doctor: 'the mountebank who cures the most rooted distempers by the bare inspection of an urinal. In this quack we have the image of our adventurer' (*Political Writings*, I, 234). He also draws attention to style and manner because they can be used to delude others (*Political Writings*, I, 234). These issues are precisely those raised by animal magnetism and which feature in the *Report*.

In 1785 animal magnetism was such a concern to medical practitioners in France that Franklin and others were 'charged' by King Louis XVI to investigate and discredit it. Animal magnetists, or mesmerists as they were also known after the German Franz Anton Mesmer who performed these treatments most famously in Paris, argued that there was a magnetic fluid that flowed through the body until illness caused a blockage or obstacle to this flow.[14] The magnetist believed that this obstacle could be removed by causing the patient to have convulsions or a 'crisis', which would restore the natural equilibrium. The practitioner could effect this crisis in a number of ways, using the magnets in his body to attract those in the patients' bodies: by pressing a finger into the chest of the patient; by running their hands across the patient's body; by the patient touching something that had been magnetized; even by being pointed at from afar by the magnetist. The effects were hugely spectacular and the treatment an elaborate performance. Robert Darnton notes that 'Everything in Mesmer's indoor clinic was designed to produce a crisis in the patient' from the carpets, to the wall decorations, drawn curtains, the lighting and music (Darnton 1968, 8). If other treatments failed, 'Mesmer himself would approach, dressed in a lilac taffeta robe, and drill fluid into the patient from his hands, his imperial eye, and his mesmerized wand' (Darnton 1968, 8). The French commissioners' report argues, in part, that patients believed themselves cured by the treatment of animal magnetism because of the outward show of power that the medical profession (as with other professions) used to convey a sense of their authority.

Speaking of the state of the medical profession in 1823 in the 'Preface' to the first volume of *The Lancet*, the editor Thomas Wakley writes:

> We hope the age of '*Mental Delusion*' has passed, and that mystery and concealment will no longer be encouraged. Indeed, we trust that mystery and ignorance will shortly be considered synonymous. Ceremonies and signs, have now lost their charms; hieroglyphics, and gilded serpents, their power to deceive.[15]

Wakley expressly hopes that by reading *The Lancet*, 'Man' will be furnished 'with a test by which he could detect and expose the impositions of ignorant practitioners' (Wakley 1823, 2). That the medical profession felt threatened by impostors or 'quacks' was real enough, and *The Lancet* set out to dispel the mystery with professional knowledge. Doctors, lawyers, and the clergy were not above the 'mystery', 'ceremonies and signs' that Wakley speaks of in the *Lancet*. The use of spectacle as a force to impose authority and compel obedience is something that Godwin also objected to on the London stage. David O'Shaughnessy writes: 'Spectacle is conceived of by Godwin as a morally corrosive force that debilitates its antithesis: free and frank conversation which promotes the spread of political justice' (O'Shaughnessy 2010, 15). O'Shaughnessy argues that Godwin's play *Antonio* and his novel *St Leon* were both 'anti-spectacle', demonstrating Godwin's belief that 'external show and spectacle has deliberate ideological force, exploited by the powerful throughout history' (O'Shaughnessy 2010, 15, 109). This conviction would have been bolstered by his work on the animal magnetism translation, which emphasizes Mesmer's use of spectacle.

Penelope Corfield has examined the kinds of mechanisms (such as regulations and institutional recognition) that helped to legitimate the medical, legal, and clerical professions as they rose in status between 1700 and 1850. The late eighteenth and early nineteenth centuries particularly, she argues, 'belonged to the doctor' (Corfield 1995, 137). Trust in the professional knowledge of physicians and surgeons needed to be gained and fostered, and the numerous caricatures of medical practitioners of this time attests both to 'the cultural power' of these figures and to the reiterated complaints concerning them (Corfield 1995, 63). They were accused in these cartoons of being 'mercenary, often brutal, and prone to hide their ignorance behind grand-sounding diagnoses' (Corfield 1995, 43). Events such as the alleged verification of Joanna Southcott's pregnancy in 1814 by 'nine medical gentlemen' did not do much to aid public faith in the profession.[16] Doctors were often accused of quackery, and high-profile cases, such as that of James Graham with his 'Earth baths' and 'Celestial Bed', were equally damaging.[17] As Corfield argues, the professions relied upon a degree of 'mystery', enabled by the clothes they wore, the way they travelled, their technical language, in order to 'enforce obedience' among the public (Corfield 1995, 21). This mystery enabled medical practitioners to exercise their power over the public. For Godwin, the use of spectacle in aiding the imposture that would ensure obedience was not limited to the professions; in *Political Justice* he includes politics, religion, and the monarchy as institutions that also resort to such tactics. For example, Godwin writes on the subject of kings: 'To conduct this imposture with success it is necessary to bring over to its party our eyes and our ears. Accordingly kings are always exhibited with all the splendour of ornament, attendance and equipage' (*Political Writings*, III, 230). In other words, monarchies impose upon us through their sumptuous shows of authority.

It is in this context that the report, attributed to Jean Sylvain Bailly (one of the commissioners) and published in 1784, on the trial of animal magnetism should be considered. Darnton reveals that animal magnetism, far more than a passing fad in France at this critical political moment appeared 'as a challenge to authority', not only to the authority of the church but also to the authority of 'established scientific bodies and even to the government' (Darnton 1968, 61–2). The government was particularly worried after the Paris police presented a secret report revealing that 'some mesmerists were mixing radical political ideas in their pseudoscientific discourses' (Darnton 1968, 62). As a result a royal commission was set up to investigate the truth of mesmerism, comprising some of the most prestigious doctors from the faculty of medicine in Paris, and members of the Academy of Sciences. These men listened to the lectures of Mesmer's chief convert, Charles Deslon, who had been expelled from the faculty of medicine in the University of Paris for his association with Mesmer, but had since parted company with him. The commissioners witnessed the convulsions and crises of patients Deslon had magnetized, and those he had not magnetized (but who believed he had), and concluded that 'Mesmer's fluid did not exist; the convulsions and other effects of mesmerizing could be attributed to the overheated imaginations of the mesmerists' – and of their patients (Darnton 1968, 64).

In the 'Historical Introduction', Godwin asks rhetorically why it is worth translating the *Rapport* when animal magnetism has been so effectively exploded. He believes that the treatment touches on one of the most important of questions in both metaphysics and medicine 'respecting the influence of the imagination upon the animal frame', and that the *Rapport* 'seems to throw new light' upon this question, 'and to have a tendency to add precision and accuracy to our notions in regard to it' (*Report*, xvi–xvii). Godwin was one among many who believed that the imagination could have very real effects on the body. An entire section of Godwin's 1793 *Political Justice* was devoted to examining the way that 'Impressions upon our senses may act either as physical [or] moral causes' (*Political Writings*, III, 33). Later in the same text he expresses his firm belief in the powerful connection between the mind and the body, a connection that contemporary surgeons called 'sympathy'. This is another medical concept that seems to have distinct parallels in the literature of the time: Godwin may well have learned of John Hunter's notion of 'universal sympathy' from one of the surgeons he knew and whom I discuss in the next section.[18] Godwin points out how:

> Emotion excited by some unexpected word, by a letter that is delivered to us, occasions the most extraordinary revolutions in our frame, accelerates the circulation, causes the heart to palpitate, the tongue to refuse its office, and has been known to occasion death by extreme anguish or extreme joy.
>
> (*Political Writings*, III, 460–1)

Similarly the *Report* notes: 'there most certainly exists a sympathy, communication or correspondence between all parts of the body' (*Report*, 88). To 'account for the physical disorders produced by the imagination', the *Report* asserts that 'Surprise occasions the colic, terror causes a diarrhœa, melancholy is the origin of icterical distempers' (*Report*, 88–9). Drastic physical change can accompany situations such as 'terror occasioned by fire', which might remind us of the decisive scene during the fire in *Caleb Williams* where the confusion is described as being transmitted by 'contagion' (*Report*, 89; *Novels and Memoirs*, III, 121). The imagination, then, or more properly the mind, can have very real effect on the body and both the *Report* and Godwin's later work confirm this.

Godwin's translation contains not only the commissioners' report on animal magnetism but also translates in its first seventeen pages the report of a commission of members of the Royal Society of Medicine, 'which condemned mesmerism in a report of its own separate investigation' (Darnton 1968, 62). The Royal Society of Medicine was specifically charged with the examination of Thouret's *Enquiries and Doubts Respecting the Animal Magnetism*, the author himself a member of this society, and Godwin supplements his translation of this report with notes, 'chiefly extracted' from Thouret's work (*Report*, 1). The society's report begins by looking into the history of animal magnetism, finding its roots in a time 'when suppositions were admitted to hold the place of facts' and vanishing 'when experimental philosophy began to dissipate the impostures of the imagination' (*Report*, 2). The report describes how seventeenth-century physicians thought such treatments worked but they note that: 'in order to call [the magnetism] into action, they did not, like M. Mesmer, desire to touch, or so much as to approach the patient' (*Report*, 4, n. 1). The sexual aspect of mesmeric treatment posed the greatest concern among mainstream medical practitioners, particularly because the patient was often female and the practitioner male.

The *Report* lists ten of Thouret's 'doubts' concerning animal magnetism, one of which is the idea that the theatrical nature of the treatment predisposed patients to thinking that they would feel an effect from the magnetism:

> 3. That in subduing the imagination by solemn preparations, by extraordinary proceedings, by the confidence and enthusiasm inspired by magnificent promises, it is possible to exalt the tone of sensible and nervous fibres, and afterwards to direct, by the application of the hands, their impulse towards certain organs, and to excite in them evacuations or excretions, without there resulting any addition to the sciences, either of philosophy or medicine.
>
> (*Report*, 10)

Once the scene has been prepared and the 'solemn preparations', 'extraordinary proceedings', and 'magnificent promises' have the patient believing that the treatment will work, the *Report* notes that the animal magnetists only produce crises, or convulsions in those subjects who are predisposed to be 'extremely irritable, extremely nervous, and above all, in women, whose sensibility has been already excited by the means we have described' (*Report*, 11). The 'power of nervous influences over diseases' is also proven by the fact that 'history has also transmitted to us a great number of cures operated by fear, by joy, or the commotion of any violent passion' (*Report*, 11). The *Report* notes the spectacle of the magnetists' performance in delivering treatment, who 'in many instances' 'seem to bestow a greater attention to excite surprise in the spectators, than salutary effects in their patients' (*Report*, 13–15). In other words, the practitioners are more concerned with their performance and its effects upon their audience than with the efficacy of their remedies.

The translation of the commissioners' report comprises the remainder of the *Report* (*Report*, 19–108). It describes the experiments of a group of highly influential physicians and natural philosophers, including Franklin, Lavoisier, and Guillotine. Initially, the commissioners witnessed a treatment session in which a number of patients are arranged around the magnetic 'bucket' (a 'baquet'), either touching this directly or connected to it and each other by means of ropes, and by placing a thumb between the forefinger and thumb of the person next to them (*Report*, 23). Music was played because, as Deslon informed the commissioners, music can also transmit magnetism to the patients (*Report*, 24). The results witnessed by the commissioners are described as spectacular – 'Nothing can be more astonishing than the sight of these convulsions' – particularly given that the commissioners, having tested the bucket with an 'electrometer' and an iron needle, discovered that it 'contained no substance either electric or magnetical' (*Report*, 27, 24). The commissioners note, however, that as soon as one person has a convulsion, others follow, that more women than men have these crises, and that the music is used to encourage these fits, accelerating to further 'agitate' the patients (*Report*, 26–8). The commissioners then determined to be magnetized themselves but individually and in private as opposed to the public displays they had witnessed. They conclude that it is the 'public' nature of these treatments (in the manner of a theatrical performance) that cause such effects and, consequently, 'Not one of the commissioners felt any sensation' (*Report*, 42). The links between the treatment and the theatre are often explicit and reveal the commissioners' views of the theatre as a potential site of mass hysteria.

The next set of experiments set out explicitly to take account of the class of persons magnetized: the commissioners resolve to experiment 'upon persons really diseased' who were chosen from the 'lower class' (*Report*, 44). Of these patients, 'four felt no sensation at all' while 'three experienced some effects from the operation' (*Report*, 46). After these experiments, the commissioners:

> resolved to make the experiment upon patients, placed in other circumstances, and selected from the polite world; such as could

> not be suspected of sinister views, and whose understanding made them capable of enquiring into and giving a full account of their sensations.
>
> (*Report*, 46)

The class of the patient was seemingly of the highest importance, since this was understood to determine not only the honesty of their response (if from the upper classes, they could not, it seems, 'be suspected of sinister views') but also their ability clearly to communicate their sensations during the treatment. In the commissioners' opinion, lower-class patients' accounts of themselves were not to be trusted. What Godwin thought while translating this report can perhaps be seen in his later writings, particularly *Political Justice* and *Caleb Williams*, to be discussed later in this chapter.

The commissioners also treat female patients with noticeable suspicion. Where some effect of magnetism is felt, the commissioners account for this by ascribing the sensation to the fact that the patient is encouraged to dwell upon her illness. The experience recounted by '[M]adame de V—', for example, is explained away with the following:

> It is easy to judge what ought to be expected from a woman, whose nerves are extremely irritable, and who, being magnetized for an hour and nineteen minutes, had during that time no other subject of reflection than that of the disorders which are habitual to her. She might have had a nervous crisis more considerable than that we have described, without our having a right to be surprised at it.
>
> (*Report*, 51)

It seems that little 'ought to be expected' of such a woman as is described here. On the subject of women's bodies, the *Report* adds, alluding to the still common idea of female hysteria: 'The empire and extensive influence of the uterus over the animal œconomy is well known' (*Report*, 87). A letter from one magnetist, 'M. Sigault', attempting to show that 'magnetism is merely an imaginary power', very clearly makes the point that it is the magnetist's performance in treating a patient that makes them feel they are being magnetized (*Report*, 63, n.). He writes of his female patient that 'The magisterial tone and the serious air I affected, together with certain gestures, made a very great impression on her' (*Report*, 63, n.). These theatrical scenes are held responsible for the quite extraordinary effects he witnesses. He then tries the 'same trick' on other people 'and succeeded more or less, according to their different degrees of sensibility and credulity' (*Report*, 63, n.). The patients become convinced of the doctor's abilities; he writes of one: 'He doubted no longer of the power I possessed over him' (*Report*, 64, n.). Alison Winters writes that 'Mesmeric performances [...] explored the very nature of theatricality' (Winters 1998, 31). More than this, for Godwin they make explicit the links between political shows of authority and theatricality. Key for Godwin would be the 'power' that a mesmerist (or an aristocrat, such as Falkland in *Caleb Williams*) 'possessed over' another man. The links between politics, mesmerism, and the theatre, where all are considered as using devices of imposture by which the vulnerable are duped, are there to be made.

The *Report* asks us to consider the experience of being part of this experiment, for a lower-class, 'and of consequence ignorant', patient, who is perhaps rather overwhelmed at their situation, being 'introduced with some degree of ceremony, to a large company, partly composed of physicians' (*Report*, 52). It seems, then, that commissioners were aware of the authority their profession carries and the feelings this produces. The 'ceremony' with which the treatment is offered is held to be partly responsible for the fact that the patient is convinced even before receiving the treatment 'that he is about to experience prodigious effects' (*Report*, 52). The commissioners remind us also that the patient is paid for his involvement and that he wishes to please the commissioners by, 'professing to experience sensations of some kind' (*Report*, 52–3). These conclusions lead the commissioners into new area of research: 'to determine to what degree the power of the imagination can influence our sensations, and to demonstrate whether it can be the cause, in whole or in part, of the effects attributed to the magnetism' (*Report*, 54). This is a shift in the *Report* but it is the point considered most important by Godwin in his 'Historical Introduction'.

Mesmer's 'imperial eye' was one of the chief methods of magnetizing patients (Darnton 1968, 8). The commissioners' report also notes particularly the 'power, which the sense of sight exercises over the imagination' (*Report*, 76). Signs and gestures are of no effect where the patient has not already been 'mastered by the employment of the eyes', and the *Report* notes that: 'The eyes possess in an eminent degree the power of magnetizing' (*Report*, 77, 76). The commissioners account for this peculiar power with the following:

> it is the eyes that convey the most energetic expressions of passion, it is in them that is developed all that the human character has of the commanding or the attractive. It is natural therefore

> that the eyes should be the source of a very high degree of power; but this power consists merely in the aptitude they possess of moving the imagination, and that in a degree more or less strong in proportion to the activity of the imagination. It is for this reason, that the whole process of the magnetism commences from the eyes of the operator; and their influence is so powerful and leaves traces so strong and lively, that a woman, newly arrived at the house of M. Deslon, having encountered a look of one of his pupils, who had performed the operation upon her, just as she was recovering from a crisis, had her eyes set in her head for three quarters of an hour. For a long time she was haunted with the remembrance of this look; she always saw before her this very eye fixed to regard her; and she bore it uninterruptedly in her imagination sleeping as well as waking for three days.
>
> (*Report*, 77)

This case reveals to the commissioners 'what an imagination is capable of doing' (*Report*, 77–8). The eyes are used particularly to command and attract others, and the peculiar power of the eyes is that they can 'move' the imagination of the person looked upon. The power that the eyes have in this regard depends upon the degree of 'activity' of the imagination of the patient. In other words, if they are more susceptible – because more prone to the power of the imagination – the eyes of the magnetist can have an even greater effect. This is why the magnetist uses his eyes at the beginning of the treatment and it is this gaze that can remain with the patient long after the treatment has finished. In the final section of this chapter I look particularly at references to Falkland's eyes in *Caleb Williams* and to the power they hold over Caleb's imagination.

In its conclusion the *Report* again makes the point that it is the public nature of much of the treatment that produces the effects witnessed. It also notes, speaking of female patients, that usually crises do not take place until around two hours after the treatment begins, and here makes the specific comparison with the theatrical:

> By little and little the impressions are communicated from one to the another, and reinforced, in the same manner as the impressions which are made by theatrical representation, where the impressions are greater in proportion to the number of the spectators, and the liberty they enjoy of expressing their sensations.
>
> (*Report*, 91)

A comparison is made with the way in which enjoyment of a theatrical performance can be affected by the size and reaction of the audience: where impressions are spread like a contagion from one person to the next and the noise and enthusiasm of an audience encourages general emotion. Later, this 'public process' is described as having the character of a 'spectacle' (*Report*, 97). It is partly, therefore, the communal and public nature of the activity that encourages the spread of certain behaviour, such as the example of the applause of individuals encouraging others to clap their hands at the theatre (*Report*, 91). Likewise, using the example of the day before battle, 'the enthusiasm of courage, as well as the impressions of terror, are propagated with so amazing rapidity' (*Report*, 91). This is accounted for by the impression made by sounds (the shouts, drums, and 'general disorder'), which 'exalt the imagination in the same degree' (*Report*, 91). In a striking (though not uncommon) comparison, given the political situation unfolding in France, rebellions, similarly, are considered to result from this form of 'contagion' (*Report*, 93). Riots and mobs were commonly seen as the result of a contagious hysteria that gripped the populace. Godwin makes the connection himself in a passage written much later in *Thoughts on Man* (1831): 'We [humans] touch each other, as the members of a gay party are accustomed to do, when they wait the stroke of an electrical machine, and the spark spreads along from man to man. It is thus that we have our feelings in common at a theatrical representation' (*Political Writings*, VI, 42). The *Report* notes: 'The magnetism then, or rather then operations of the imagination, are equally discoverable at the theatre, in the camp, and in all numerous assemblies, as at the bucket' (*Report*, 95). The real cause in all of these instances is the imagination, the power of which can be seen at the theatre, on the battlefield, and in the animal magnetists' treatment.

It is intriguing to think that it was Godwin who translated this *Report*, which was hugely important at the time and has now come to hold a significant position in critical accounts of animal magnetism and the role of the imagination in science and medicine. Godwin's addition to the original events – his 'Historical Introduction' – identifies animal magnetism as an 'imposture' a word that has significant connotations for him. There are clear links to be made between his understanding of the 'imposture' of this treatment and other forms of imposture that he encountered or of which he was aware. The *Report* details the theatrical means by which the mesmerist achieves this imposture and is explicit in its claims that lower-class men and women generally were more susceptible than others to the mesmerist's spectacle. Later in this chapter

I consider how the ideas found in this early translation re-emerge in *Caleb Williams*, with Falkland figured as the mesmerist. First, though, I look at further evidence of Godwin's interest in science and medicine, beginning with the evidence to be found in his diary.

2.2 The evidence of Godwin's diary

Between 1788 and 1836 William Godwin kept a diary, eventually comprising over thirty-two notebooks, carefully recording, almost every day, the people he met or dined with, the plays he went to, the reading he did, the exhibitions and lectures he attended, and the deaths of contemporaries (*Godwin Diary*). From 1827 onwards Godwin also regularly noted the temperature inside his house according to his thermometer.[19] Godwin's diary confirms that literary and scientific interests were not considered mutually exclusive in the period they cover. Godwin himself attended medical and scientific lectures and socialized with physicians, anatomists, natural historians, and chemists. He was also a patient, and his diary constitutes a major resource for the diagnosis and treatment of illnesses in this period. There are 660 entries relating to his personal health, including the names of doctors that he consulted and medical treatments undergone. The number of people in Godwin's diary who are categorized as scientific or medical by editors is striking. In this section I will pick out just a few who are particularly important to Godwin: William Nicholson, Humphry Davy, and Anthony Carlisle.

It seems likely that Godwin first met William Nicholson in 1786, perhaps at the same time as he met Thomas Holcroft, whom Nicholson already knew.[20] The diary mentions Nicholson 516 times – though he was not at home 33 times, and his house was a venue for meetings 351 times – between 1788 and Nicholson's death in 1815 (*Godwin Diary*, entry for Nicholson).[21] Nicholson is best known now as the editor of *A Journal of Natural Philosophy, Chemistry, and the Arts*, which ran from 1787 to 1813 and, with Anthony Carlisle, for the first use of an electric current to decompose water into its constituent parts. This was the first example of electrolysis, which Davy would exploit to the full, using apparatus to isolate many elements, including potassium, calcium, and magnesium. Nicholson's politics are difficult to ascertain but he is believed to be the author of *The Doubts of the Infidels* (1781), which aligns him with religious dissenters.[22]

Nicholson was heavily involved in the composition of *Enquiry into Political Justice*. Godwin had intended to dedicate this book to both Nicholson and Holcroft, but finally decided not to name them in what might be considered a dangerously inflammatory text (*Political Writings*, I, 9). Nicholson's influence on the book can be seen in the many discussions recorded in Godwin's diary during the period of composition (Godwin began work on *Political Justice* in September 1791 and it was published on 14 February 1793). The following discussions all took place either while dining with, at tea with, or in the presence of Nicholson, often only with Nicholson present and sometimes also with Holcroft: 'criticize the Introduction; talk of économistes, taxation & commerce' (*Godwin Diary*, 30 September 1791); 'talk of property, marriage & immortality' (12 March 1792); 'talk of language, alphabet & necessity' (4 April 1792); 'talk of animals, innate, infinite, space & causation' (19 April 1792); 'talk of literary societies, taxation, promises & coercion' (6 May 1792); 'talk of immortality, abstraction, causation, majorities & promises' (13 May 1792); 'talk of government, contract, associations & instinct' (30 May 1792); 'talk of obedience, delegation, secrecy & abstraction' (12 June 1792); 'talk of causation' (12 July 1792); 'talk of France, matter & Hartley' (27 July 1792); 'talk of obedience, war & property' (25 September 1792); 'talk of punishment, education, cooperation & cohabitation' (5 October 1792); 'talk of constitutions' (21 October 1792); 'talk of government, property, punishment' (8 November 1792).

The process of writing *Political Justice* can be traced through these discussions. Each of the topics covered appear in *Political Justice* and Godwin's progress with the book can be measured by the dates given. It is fascinating to think that Nicholson was present at all of these conversations even if we do not know what part – if any – he took in them. It is tempting to imagine that he had an important role in formulating the ideas of the book, but it is difficult to verify this without further knowledge of Nicholson's politics and views. The combination of topics is often intriguing and may perhaps indicate the influence of Nicholson. While most topics seem purely political and to pertain to the current political situation, others suggest a branching out into other fields, such as 'talk of animals' and 'matter & Hartley'. The words 'innate' and 'instinct' might refer to the debate concerning whether animals had instinct or reason that had interested Wollstonecraft in her review of William Smellie.[23] The phrase 'talk of obedience' reminds us that this was an important topic in *Political Justice*, one which had been also been discussed in the animal magnetism report. Immortality is a subject I shall come to later in this chapter.

Nicholson also helped with the preparation of the manuscript: for example, 'Carry the ms to Nicholson' (14 April 1792); 'Sup at

Nicholson's, revise Book VIII avec lui' (25 December 1792). Nicholson also helped with the second edition of *Political Justice* (see Godwin 2011, I, 119). Conversation was key to Godwin's sense of how ideas were generated and developed. From the diary entries it is clear that Nicholson was an important collaborator on the book – though in what capacity remains unclear – that made Godwin famous and which was highly influential on such Romantic writers as Coleridge, Hazlitt, the Shelleys, and Wordsworth.

St Clair tells us that 'It was to Nicholson that Godwin turned for information on the latest theories in chemistry, physics, optics, biology, and the other natural sciences' as well as on scientific method (St Clair 1989, 61). Using the principles set out in Nicholson's 1782 *Introduction to Natural Philosophy*, St Clair argues that Godwin was attempting to apply these principles to 'human psychology, to history, to politics, and to other "social sciences"' (St Clair 1989, 61). There is evidence of scientific learning in *Political Justice*, such as in the chapter 'Of the Mechanism of the Human Mind' where in a discussion of the theory of the mind as 'a system of mechanism' we also have a detailed account of 'the essential properties of matter' and the laws of motion (*Political Writings*, III, 175, 185). Godwin's interest in science can be seen in the fact that on 19 November 1799 he records his attendance at 'Nicholson's lecture' (*Godwin Diary*). Little is known about the content of this lecture but it was part of a series giving a grounding in the topics that Nicholson had covered in *An Introduction to Natural Philosophy*.[24]

These were not the first or last scientific lectures that Godwin attended. In 1796 he attended an entire series of lectures given by Anthony Carlisle, a surgeon at Westminster Hospital. From 1795 the diary reveals an acquaintance between Godwin and Carlisle, continuing until 1814. Carlisle eventually became surgeon-extraordinary to the Prince Regent, and was knighted for his services after the prince's coronation.[25] Godwin was Carlisle's patient and Carlisle saw other members of the Godwin household; he was called to Wollstonecraft's bedside in her final illness. Carlisle clearly considered himself Godwin's friend; see, for example, a letter written to Godwin on 7 July 1804 after attending to his children: 'It gives me much satisfaction to afford the little extent of my professional aid to all my Friends, and to none more than yourself' (Oxford, Bodleian Library, MS. Abinger c. 8, fol. 72). It is difficult to tell what his politics were but he did oppose man-midwives on the conservative 'grounds of modesty and incompetence' (*ODNB*).

The diary shows intense periods of meetings between Godwin and Carlisle, particularly in the last few years of the 1790s. Godwin attended a series of Carlisle's lectures, 'On the Elements of Anatomy', every two days from October to December 1796. The lecture series was designed to be accessible to 'Gentlemen of general information who may be desirous of gaining a knowledge of the Structure and Phenomena of Animal Bodies' as well as to medical students (*Oracle and Public Adviser*, cited in *Godwin Diary*). William Bewick also writes about attending some of Carlisle's lectures with William Hazlitt, though no date is given for this (Bewick 1871, I, 140–2).[26] From Bewick's account it seems that Carlisle's lectures could be spectacular; he remembers Hazlitt apparently fainting at the sight of a human brain and heart being passed around the room on dinner plates (Bewick 1871, I, 141–2). Godwin shows an interest in the body, particularly in its relation to the mind, in texts such as *Political Justice*, where he discusses the ways that 'Indisposition of the body operates on the mind' (*Political Writings*, III, 33). In a section already alluded to, Godwin acknowledges that his 'theory of the human mind' is drawn from Hartley; thus, he considers the 'human body to be so constituted as to be susceptible of vibrations, in the same manner as the strings of a musical instrument' (*Political Writings*, III, 176n, 175). He goes on to describe in some detail the way that 'a system of association' is 'carried on by traces to be made of the medullary substance of the brain' (*Political Writings*, III, 176). Godwin's interest in the body extended to reading John Thelwall's medical lecture on vitalism given at Guy's Hospital on 26 January 1793 (Thelwall 1793). The diary records that Godwin read 'Thelwal on Vitality, 40 pages' (23 August 1793) and 'Thelwal on Vitality, pp. 40' (25 January 1794) (*Godwin Diary*). The whole of this text comprises only 41 pages, so presumably Godwin read it twice.

According to the diary, on most days that Godwin attends Carlisle's lectures he also writes a few pages of *The Enquirer* and we can speculate on connections between the two (published on 27 February 1797). Godwin tends, in *Political Justice* and elsewhere, to advocate a healthy mind and body and, as already discussed, to emphasize the dependence that exists between the physical and the mental. In an essay in *The Enquirer* he discusses those religious groups who believe in 'the superiority of the mind to the body' to the extent that they promote 'self-denial' (*Political Writings*, V, 184). This leads him to reveal a knowledge of contemporary medical theory that he might well have gleaned from Carlisle's lectures:

> A wise man would wish to have a sound body, as well as a sound mind. [...] For this purpose he would exercise and strengthen the

> muscles of every part of his frame. He would prepare his body to endure hardship and vicissitude. He would exercise his digestic powers. [...] There is a harmony and a sympathy through every part of the human machine. A vigorous and animated tone contributes to the advantage of the intellect, and an improved state of intellect heightens and refines our sensible pleasures. A modern physician of great character*, has maintained life to be an unnatural state, and death the genuine condition of man. If this thesis is to be admitted, it seems to follow, that true wisdom would direct us to that proceeding, which tended most to inform with life, and to maintain in activity, every portion of our frame and every branch of our nature. It is thus that we shall most effectually counterwork an enemy who is ever in wait for us.
>
> (*Political Writings*, v, 185)

By this time Godwin has read Wollstonecraft's *Vindication of the Rights of Woman* and his idea that a strong body is crucial for a strong mind echoes her own advice to women. Given that *The Enquirer* is being written on the same day as he attends Carlisle's lectures perhaps we can also see the influence of the surgeon's view of the body's relationship to the mind. Certainly Godwin puts forward a particular regimen, advocating physical exercise and development of strength. In this essay Godwin coins the word, 'digestic' (the *OED* gives this instance as the first time it was used).[27] His emphasis on the stomach and the powers of digestion perhaps specifically refer to Hunter's ideas. The asterisk leads to a note at the bottom of the page identifying the physician as '*Brown'. Godwin here demonstrates his knowledge of one of the theories of life most prevalent in this period: John Brown's theory that we had an allotted portion of what he termed 'excitability', which was at one time influential on Wordsworth and Coleridge.[28] Godwin alludes here to the idea that death is the natural state to which all matter tends and life is the constant struggle against this 'enemy' lying 'in wait for us'.

Godwin argues that a strong body aids the intellect and, conversely, an 'improved' intellect 'heightens and refines' the pleasures of the body. His notion of the 'harmony and sympathy' that exists throughout the 'human machine' will have been confirmed by many of his medical acquaintances. The importance of diet would also have been impressed upon Godwin from a number of quarters. He was the good friend of Joseph Ritson, the antiquarian ballad collector who famously kept to a vegetarian diet. Godwin's diary notes that they first met in 1793 and their friendship continued until Ritson's death in 1803 when

Godwin wrote an obituary of him, noting his unusual diet (*Godwin Diary*; Godwin 1805, 293). One diary entry notes, on the occasion of a visit from Ritson, 'talk of animal food' (15 December 1793). Godwin also knew well John Frank Newton, another vegetarian, who wrote *The Return to Nature* (1811) (*Godwin Diary*). Godwin himself after a period of bad health in 1803 cut down on both wine and meat (St Clair 1989, 261). At the end of the essay on self-denial in *The Enquirer* Godwin argues that looking after the body helps us to be independent rather than enslaved to the senses and to luxuries. He makes the comparison with animals that are bribed with the prospect of food to learn tricks: 'He is like those brute animals, that are allured to the learning innumerable postures and ridiculous tricks, by the attraction of a morsel of meat' (*Political Writings*, v, 187). The tone of contempt might remind us of Wollstonecraft's similar statements in *Vindication*.

One topic of discussion that is raised repeatedly in the diaries during the time he was writing *Political Justice* and that features in this text, is that of immortality. Godwin's notion of human perfectibility had a physical dimension.[29] In the first edition of *Political Justice*, Godwin imagines an ideal society in which the rational mind would gain control 'over the matter of our own bodies', asking 'In a word, why may not man be one day immortal?' (*Political Writings*, III, 460). Godwin offers evidence for the likelihood of this future condition in instances where 'thought modifies the external universe', from the more usual operations of the body, such as the stretching out of one's hand at will, to involuntary modifications (*Political Writings*, III, 460). Godwin also points to the 'power of the mind in assisting or retarding convalescence' (*Political Writings*, III, 461). His argument for future immortality proceeds from these grounds; if involuntary thoughts can have these real effects what might be the result if we were able to govern and direct such thoughts? His idea of immortality fits his notion of human perfectibility, that the mind's power will continue to improve, and he discusses the possibility of this at some length. In some far distant future, Godwin imagines that men 'will cease to propagate', there will be no disease, and 'In addition to this they will perhaps be immortal' (*Political Writings*, III, 465). The protagonist of Godwin's 1799 novel *St Leon* has conquered disease and death: 'I am invulnerable to disease. Every sun that rises, finds the circulations of my frame in the most perfect order. Decrepitude can never approach me' (*Novels and Memoirs*, IV, 13). Longevity was a subject Carlisle was also interested in; in 1818 he published *An Essay in the Disorders of Old Age, and on the Means of Prolonging Human Life*. While Godwin tempered his statements on immortality in later editions of *Political Justice*, it is clear that in 1793 he believed it was possible, and that the idea emerges from his interest in the relationship between the body and the mind.

Another scientific figure who greatly impressed Godwin was Humphry Davy, who became the foremost chemist of the day. Davy had met William Godwin before moving to London, but they saw each other a great deal after Davy was appointed to lecture at the Royal Institution in 1801. The first date we can be certain of a meeting between Davy and Godwin is 4 December 1799 and already on 1 January 1800, Coleridge tells Davy: 'Godwin talks evermore of you with lively affection' (*Coleridge Letters*, I, 557). On 23 March 1802 Godwin went to one of Davy's lectures, part of the course that Davy's *Syllabus* (1802) describes, and he also dined with Davy that night (*Godwin Diary*). Coleridge had introduced Davy to Godwin and Davy's sympathetic youthful radicalism can be seen in the early manuscript versions of Davy's *Discourse*, which are far more politically radical than the final lecture. Unsurprisingly, lines such as: 'The most powerful & most respected part of the human species have squandered away much of their thought in luxury & the vanity of pleasure' are omitted from the final lecture given to the landed gentry at the Royal Institution (RI MS HD 13c, 56–7). The influence of Godwin might be seen in an intriguing revision of one of the most famous passages of Davy's *Discourse*. The original manuscript version reads: 'In this hope we do not amuse ourselves with visionary theories; with thoughts concerning the infinite perfectibility of the human species, the annihilation of disease, labour & even death' (RI MS HD 13c, 58). In the final published version this becomes: 'In this view we do not look to distant ages, or amuse ourselves with brilliant, though delusive dreams, concerning the infinite improveability of man, the annihilation of labour, disease, and even death' (Davy 1802, 22). As noted above, Godwin believed that human perfectibility would be realized as physical strength, resistance to disease, and even, eventually, immortality. In the notebook version, besides the use of the Godwinian word 'perfectibility' (replaced with 'improveability' in the published version), these ideas are still seen as 'visionary' but not yet 'delusive'.

The majority of contact between Davy and Godwin recorded in the diary occurs in the early years of Davy's London career, particularly in 1801 and 1802. It seems that Davy's radicalism was replaced by conservatism as his career progressed and by May 1802 the mere mention of a visit from Godwin was enough to alarm him. Southey writes: 'I have terrified Davy with the news of his coming. He actually perspires at the thought' (Southey 1965, I, 277, 10 May 1802).[30] It is the case though that an unpublished letter from Davy to Godwin, asking him to dine on 28 September 1802 gives a different picture; Davy writes: 'It is one of my unfeigned regrets that the hurry of a busy life has prevented me from seeking after the enjoyment of your society as much as I have wished' (*Davy Letters,* 26 September 1802).[31] In any case mentions of Davy in the diary thin out considerably after 1802, though, as with many other friends and also famous figures, Godwin notes Davy's death in 1829.

To conclude this section, from the evidence of the diary, Godwin's interest in science and medicine takes in contemporary ideas of sympathy between parts of the body (particularly the stomach and the rest of the body); reveals some knowledge of contemporary medical theory, particularly as it concerns vitalism and the importance of diet to the body's health; he also shows an interest in the role of the imagination in diseases and in the relationship between the mind and the body. Others have noted Godwin's interest in phrenology: on 24 February 1831 Godwin attended a lecture given by Johann Gaspar Spurzheim on the subject, which he also writes about in *Thoughts on Man* though he expresses much scepticism at the individual's lack of agency within this system of thought (*Political Writings,* VI, 231–40).[32] In this late text, published in 1831, Godwin returns to ideas he had expressed earlier. He begins with a first essay 'Of Mind and Body' in which he discusses such matters as the physical effect caused by the mind in the act of blushing (*Political Writings,* VI, 42). He also refers to a remark made 'many years ago by an eminent physiologer and anatomist', whom editor Mark Philp thinks might be Anthony Carlisle, that: 'when I find my attention called to any particular part or member of my body, I may be morally sure that there is something amiss in the processes of that part or member' (*Political Writings,* VI, 43). He continues, therefore, to emphasize the dependency that exists between the mind and the body. Godwin's engagement in a network of medical and scientific figures can clearly be seen. During the writing of some of his most famous works he was involved in worlds we would now call scientific or medical and the ideas he gained from conversations with friends, lectures, and texts that he read emerge again in his own work. The next section considers the way that these surface in his novel *Caleb Williams.*

2.3 Imagination and theatrical performances of authority

Godwin's 1805 novel *Fleetwood* has been read as revealing Godwin's philosophical transition from pure rationalism to his recognition of the importance and centrality of the imagination and emotion 'in the development of the human mind' (Godwin 2001, 9). In this novel, the protagonist, believing himself subjected to the will of his wife describes himself as being like a patient of an animal magnetist:

> I felt like the persons I have somewhere read of, acted upon by a magnetic influence, who wore no chains or fetters, and yet were prisoners, struggling, perhaps, to advance in an opposite direction, but always compelled to follow the steps of him who exerted this ascendancy over them.
>
> (*Novels and Memoirs*, V, 218)

The language of this passage echoes some of the ideas that would remain consistent throughout Godwin's writings: the idea of obedience to authority, which was not informed by personal judgement but was the result of political 'imposture', can be found in his early and later writings. Godwin is also interested in the tacit complicity that enables unfair hierarchies to continue to operate: in the extract, these prisoners wear 'no chains or fetters' but are nonetheless in thrall to the magnetist. In this section, I look at the ways in which the example of animal magnetism may have contributed to Godwin's ideas, particularly as they are revealed in *Caleb Williams*, a text that also shows the power of the imagination when it is worked upon.

There are a number of links to be made between Godwin's novel *Caleb Williams* and the findings of the commissioners' report. The novel itself has been read as a 'theatrical novel', in that 'it contains a noticeable amount of theatrical language, allusion, and even plot borrowing (mainly from Shakespeare) and it is structured in such a way that it reflects contemporary dramatic technique' (O'Shaughnessy 2007, 55). Gothic novels also often use what Max Fincher has described as the 'penetrating gaze' of the gothic villain and *Caleb Williams* is no exception (Fincher 2007, 24). Falkland's authority over Caleb is often exerted by shows of power, particularly using the language of the sublime to achieve a hold over Caleb's imagination in the same way that magnetists persuaded patients of their skill. In one particular scene, Falkland, acting in the manner of a gothic villain, tells Caleb to beware an unspecified 'power' that he exercises over him. His finger (which, with the eyes, was one of the most effective of the magnetist's tools) is alluded to particularly and we might imagine this being accompanied by a gesture of the hand:

> Why do you trifle with me? You little suspect the extent of my power. At this moment you are [surrounded with the engines of my

> vengeance, and before you are aware] they will close upon you. You might as well think of escaping from the [reach] of the omnipresent God, as from mine! If you could touch so much as my finger, you should expiate it in hours and months and years of a torment, of which as yet you have not the remotest idea.
>
> (*Novels and Memoirs*, III, 130)[33]

Butler was the first to notice that the 'rhetoric of terror' in this passage owes its influence particularly to Burke's *A Philosophical Enquiry into the Origin of our Ideas of the Sublime and Beautiful* (1757), which Godwin had re-read in the 1790s (Butler 1995, 352; *Godwin Diary*; see, for example 11 July 1792 and 16–17 June 1974). Caleb, in this scene, experiences the sublime – 'the strongest feeling of which the human mind is capable, [...] evoked, characteristically, by contemplating power' (Butler 1995, 352). Indeed the *Report* describes the imagination as 'that terrible and active power' (*Report*, 98). Without wishing to deny the fact that Falkland's power over Caleb, simply by virtue of his being one of the landed gentry, has very real effects, particularly in the fact that the law favours the interests of his class, Falkland's words here are full of bombast, highly theatrical and succeed in their purpose by appealing to the imagination rather than to reason.

Caleb's peculiar degree of sensibility has been remarked upon by many critics, and has been seen as evidence that his role is that usually played by the female gothic victim (see Bour 2005). Godwin himself, in his 1832 account of the writing of the novel, refers to Caleb as 'the wife' to Falkland's Bluebeard (Godwin 2000, 449). Caleb frequently describes a physical reaction to emotional or psychological events, and in many instances he evinces the same symptoms as the susceptible magnetic female patients, or those drawn from the lower classes, as described in the French commissioners' report. Peter Melville Logan believes it is 'the particular social conditions that literally make Caleb into the nervous character who narrates the story of his nervous incarnation' (Logan 1996, 206). Caleb often assumes the role of a patient, describing the symptoms he is experiencing, and Logan points out that a characteristic of patients with nervous illnesses was believed to be their tendency to talk about their illnesses; but Caleb's physical sufferings are usually the result of imagined horrors, which have been put into his mind by the terror Falkland's gothic rage produces (Logan 1996, 206).

Magnetism is itself mentioned in the novel. In a conversation about Alexander the Great, Caleb alludes by accident to Mr Falkland's crime of murder. He describes the effect of his words as producing a kind of 'magnetical sympathy' between them:

> The [instant] I had uttered these words, I felt what it was that I had done. There was a magnetical sympathy between me and my [master], so that their effect was not sooner produced upon him, than my own mind reproached me with the inhumanity of the allusion. Our confusion was mutual. The blood forsook at once the transparent complexion of Mr. Falkland, and then rushed back again with rapidity and fierceness.
>
> (*Novels and Memoirs*, III, 100)[34]

He draws attention to Falkland's eyes again, but in this 'mutual confusion', it is Falkland who suffers convulsions: 'He gave me a penetrating look as if he would see my very soul. His eyes were then in an instant withdrawn. I could perceive him seized with a convulsive shuddering' (*Novels and Memoirs*, III, 101). In another similar incident, where Falkland commands Caleb to 'cease to contend with insurmountable power!' Caleb tells the reader: 'The speech I had heard was the dictate of frenzy, and it created in me a similar frenzy' (*Novels and Memoirs*, III, 138). The contagion of this 'frenzy' might remind us of episodes described in the *Report*. This scene demonstrates what Fincher has also described as the 'sublime effect' that Falkland has upon Caleb, in whose presence he is 'irresolute, overawed and abashed' (Fincher 2007, 117; *Novels and Memoirs*, III, 138). Describing the incomprehension and ineffability of the sublime experience, Caleb asks, 'Why was it, that I was once more totally overcome by the imperious carriage of Mr Falkland, and unable to utter a word?' (*Novels and Memoirs*, III, 138).

The 'penetrating' gaze which passes between Falkland and Caleb shows that Caleb can also take the role of the magnetist, and Eric Daffron has pointed out that these '"magnetical" techniques [...] have the potential to subvert Falkland's political authority' (Daffron 1995, 220). Daffron has also connected their constantly changing roles, persecutor becoming persecuted, with the looks they exchange. The gaze can also have a 'sublime effect', as Fincher argues: 'The novel suggests that men feel afraid at the spectacle of the ambiguously gendered subject who gazes back and threatens their identity' (Fincher 2007, 110). On many occasions described in the commissioners' report it seemed that the magnetist had to be in view of the patient for them to feel any effect, and in a remarkably similar episode to that described in a quotation given earlier, Falkland is described as suffering particularly from eye contact with others. Caleb writes that 'He was scarcely able to look at [Mr Forester] without shuddering', for example (*Novels and Memoirs*, III, 129).

At other times, the superiority and integrity of Falkland seems unquestionable to the people in the novel because of his social position, which might remind us of the social position of medical practitioners; indeed, Butler describes Falkland as exercising 'a powerful spell over everyone in the world' (Butler 1995, 351). In these instances the eyes are particularly mentioned as a source of Falkland's power: they 'emitted sparks of rage' (*Novels and Memoirs*, III, 120). At a particularly low moment, when Caleb comments 'I now took it for granted that I was once more in the power of Mr Falkland', the submission is described as 'inexpressibly mortifying and afflictive to my imagination'. He questions whether Falkland is indeed supernatural: 'Did his power reach through all space, and his eye penetrate every concealment?' (*Novels and Memoirs*, III, 214). The 'power' that Falkland exerts over Caleb, reminds us of the magnetist's claim to exert power over the mind and body of a patient. In the words of one magnetist already quoted: 'He doubted no longer of the power I possessed over him' (*Report*, 64, n.). Even after Falkland's death his image continues to haunt Caleb: 'Waking or sleeping I still behold him' (*Novels and Memoirs*, III, 276). This last statement echoes closely the example given of a peculiarly susceptible patient who bore the look of the magnetist's eye 'uninterruptedly in her imagination sleeping as well as waking for three days' (*Report*, 77).

Magnetism is not only a source of power; it also offers Caleb an analogy for the sympathy he desires to experience between himself and others. In the third, fourth, and fifth editions of the novel, after Laura's rejection, Caleb concludes: 'To me the whole world was as unhearing as the tempest, and as cold as the torpedo. Sympathy, the magnetic virtue, the hidden essence of our life, was extinct' (*Novels and Memoirs*, III, 334, n. 320). Sympathy here is used to describe the connections between all humans, in a larger extension of its contemporary medical definition as the connection between all parts of the body, but particularly the mind and body, and the stomach and other parts of the body. It is interesting that Caleb alludes to the torpedo fish here, which John Hunter had famously dissected to reveal the anatomical structure that produced electric shocks (see Moore 2005, 352–3). In a letter to Mary Jane Clairmont Godwin wrote 'of the animal magnetism which drew them together' in another rare example of his positive metaphorical use of the term (St Clair, 1989, 243).

Godwin's translation of the French commissioners' report may have offered him a model for the highly-strung and peculiarly sensitive Caleb.

The commissioners repeatedly pointed out that it was the appearance of authority in the magnetist that encouraged patients to believe that they would experience an effect; and one could argue that in the same way, Caleb's refusal to betray his master's confidences, his complicity in a system that believes someone is truthful or honest simply because they are in a position of authority, contributes to the treatment he experiences. Godwin himself pointed out, in *Political Justice*, that 'Implicit faith, blind submission to authority, timid fear' are among 'the chief obstacles to human improvement.'[35] It seems that many of the lower-class characters in the book, including Thomas and Collins, are unable to see the truth of the question of who murdered Tyrrel. They simply find it impossible that it could be Falkland, unable to see past his status as master, or to acknowledge that a gentleman may be a murderer. When Caleb overhears the group of labourers talking about the 'notorious housebreaker, Kit Williams', one says that he could have forgiven Caleb any robbery but that of robbing his master (*Novels and Memoirs*, III, 210). On another occasion, the old man set to watch over Caleb, who has all the appearance of good-nature, benevolence and sensibility, regards him as a 'monster', primarily, it seems, because of Caleb's recriminations 'against so generous a master' (*Novels and Memoirs*, III, 222). Caleb's early and naive evaluation of Hawkins's rebellion against Tyrrel is indicative of a similarly misplaced loyalty. He considers that Hawkins is 'guilty' of a 'double imprudence', both in talking to Tyrrel in 'a more peremptory manner than the constitution and practices of this country allow a dependent to assume' and in not thinking about the consequences of his actions, which Caleb considers are obvious to all (*Novels and Memoirs*, III, 39). As Butler argues, one of Godwin's purposes in this novel is to reveal that the 'naturalness of obedience' of which Burke is so keen to persuade his readers is not natural at all (Butler 1995, 347). As was clear to the French commissioners, class (and gender) played a role in patients' reactions to the authority of the medical profession. The animal magnetist trials showed in relief the way authority worked more generally.

Caleb Williams, then, is an effort to show that some things – though they appear to be true – may be false; one of these false perceptions is the apparent naturalness of the class system. Caleb and Hawkins are almost the only characters in the book who feel some degree of equality with their class superiors, though the society of robbers is also set apart in this regard:

> They did not impose upon themselves the task, as is too often the case in human society, of seeming tacitly to approve that from which

> they suffered most; or, which is worse, of persuading themselves that all the wrongs they suffered were right; but were at open war with their oppressors.
>
> (*Novels and Memoirs*, III, 194)

This 'tacit approval', Blake's 'mind-forg'd manacles', is witnessed repeatedly in *Caleb Williams*. At the end of the novel, one could argue that Caleb seems still to remain within its traps, considering himself to be in the wrong, and to be Falkland's 'murderer' (*Novels and Memoirs*, III, 276). Others, such as Grimes, experience a kind of superstitious awe at the prospect of nobility: 'he reverenced the inborn divinity that attends upon rank, as Indians worship the devil' (*Novels and Memoirs*, III, 70). Godwin equates religion with superstition and associates wrong-headed religious belief with the idea that birth and rank are naturally deserving of honour. Both *Caleb Williams* and the *Report* explore circumstances in which authority is assumed and then enforced through the use of spectacular displays that appeal to the imagination rather than to reason. Their effectiveness reveals complicity in the act of imposture – and the need to fully appreciate the power of the imagination in the perpetuation of 'things as they are'.

The influence of the French commissioners' report extends beyond the circles and texts explored here.[36] Animal magnetism was of particular interest to many Romantic writers, particularly Coleridge, and had specific links to radical French politics (see Levere 1980; Rzepka 1986, 106–15; and Fulford 2004). Jennifer Ford argues that it was the *Rapport*, specifically, that encouraged Coleridge's interest in magnetism: 'He was ready to give magnetism a fair hearing in the light of the French Royal Commission's 1784 conclusion that its effects and cures were the results of the imagination' (Ford 1998, 104). Indeed in Coleridge's marginal comments on Carl Alexander Ferdinand Kluge's 1815 book on animal magnetism, he writes: 'I am persuaded, that it is the Imagination at once producing and beholding' (Coleridge 1969–2002 XII. III, 376). Editors H.J. Jackson and George Whalley note that while the 'commissioners may have intended thus to discredit animal magnetism; refining their speculations. C[oleridge] can take their findings as evidence of the power of the imagination' (Coleridge 1969–2002 III, 376–7, n.). Coleridge finds correspondence between the description of the effects of magnetism and his trials of nitrous oxide in the 1790s, commenting: 'This sensation is the first noticeable effect of the nitrous Oxyd of Davy, when inhaled' (Coleridge 1969–2002, III, 375). Coleridge's interest in magnetism 'periodically reignited' throughout his lifetime and he even drafted 'the beginnings of an essay on the subject' (Ford 1998, 101). He was particularly interested in the idea of a magnetic torpor or sleep (see also Wilson 2006). Robert Rix has discovered William Blake's sympathies with Swedenborgian magnetizers (Rix 2002). Robert Southey also begins his 1807 'Account of Animal Magnetism' (one of his *Letters from England*) with recognition of the importance of the *Rapport*. He writes that animal magnetism 'was put a stop to in France' as a result of 'an unfavourable report on Mesmer's performances made in 1784 by a Committee that included Lavoisier and Benjamin Franklin' (Southey 1951, 304 and n.). Thomas de Quincey, surveying the subject in *Tait's Edinburgh Magazine* in 1834, explicitly declares his antipathy to the report's conclusions, perhaps signalling a shift between Enlightenment and Romantic sentiments concerning the power of the imagination:

> The famous Report, which these gentlemen drew up as their definitive verdict on the question submitted to them, is the most memorable instance on record of violent prejudice, and the extent to which it paralyses the judgment. [...] In fact, if any phenomena occurred of a nature to startle the mind, and to call for further investigation, they set them down to the force of *imagination*: and by the one cabalistical word they evaded all investigation.
>
> ([de Quincey] 1834, 459)

De Quincey's use of italics perhaps demonstrates his opinion that the commissioners viewed the imagination as below their consideration, and because of this the 'force' of the imagination was not properly investigated. In the 1820s Percy Shelley was fascinated by magnetism and, in the thoroughly Romantic manner of self-experimentation, was magnetized himself in Pisa in 1820. He writes about magnetism in 'The Magnetic Lady to her Patient' (see Leask 1991 and Dawson 1986). It is fascinating that Godwin translated the 'famous report', as de Quincey puts it, which was read by and influenced so many others.

Godwin's knowledge of, and intervention in, this specific medical debate had ramifications for his own writing and ideas as well as extending beyond this to advance a key concept of the Romantic period: the power of the imagination. Animal magnetists had attempted to establish their practice as a 'science', with all that this suggests of rigour and method. In turn, the commissioners, led by some of the most prominent Enlightenment thinkers, had exploded belief in animal magnetism with their own scientific experiment and observation. The commissioners' report confirms that, even before the word 'scientist' was coined there were ongoing conflicts regarding the position of authority and the voice of truth. What Godwin does is to exploit the emergent or incipient Romantic aspects of the animal magnetism debate. In the 'Historical Introduction' to the *Report* he notes that, most importantly, the commissioners' report 'seems to throw new light' upon the question 'respecting the influence of the imagination upon the animal frame' and it is this particular aspect of animal magnetism that fascinates other Romantic writers (*Report*, xvi–xvii). The next chapter opens with Godwin's writings on the physical condition that best accompanies literary composition and his advice for the bodies of geniuses. Godwin's interest in the connections between the mind and body, and in psychology, extend naturally into these subjects, which preoccupied medical as well as other literary writers.

3
Romantic Creation

This chapter considers a selection of texts, many written in the 1790s, which describe literary creation using metaphors of organic and biological creation. Some of these texts have been considered as themselves involved in the creation of what we now call Romanticism, and in some cases this claim has been challenged. The chapter concerns the act or process of literary creation and the product of this process, the text that is created. Its general argument is that the metaphors used by writers about writing are determined by contemporary understandings of how the world was thought to have been created, how living beings were created, and the role of the creator within this process.

There are questions that continue to revolve throughout the texts considered here that bear relation to larger issues: can something be created from nothing (*ex nihilo*), or can nothing be created from nothing? Is a genius born or made? What is the relation between God's and man's creation? In what sense are literary texts to be thought of as reproduction, the offspring of the author's imagination? If the latter is the case, how did critics think about those texts of which they did not approve, texts that are considered 'monstrous' or in some way malformed?[1] This chapter takes in questions of the changing taste of the period, as it is represented in metaphors of literary creation, whether poetry is compared to a natural forest, a landscaped park, a wilderness, or a pleasure garden. These metaphors reveal the shifting taste for the man-made, the ordered lawns and the picturesque landscapes of the eighteenth century.[2] Other texts selected here use the metaphors of biological growth to imagine literary creation as parenthood, and the text as a living being with the same function as the human body.

I begin with William Godwin, writing in 1831, because his *Thoughts on Man* covers many of the issues involved: the question of whether genius is innate and a predisposition of the body as well as the question of whether literary creation has to be the creation of something entirely new rather than a new combination of existing materials. Godwin also uses the language of reproduction and of the failures of reproduction (abortion and deformity). His desire to exempt monstrosity from the normal scheme of things is in stark contrast to the work of William Lawrence, John Hunter, and Étienne Geoffroy Saint-Hilaire who sought to categorize and taxonomize the 'monstrous' and bring it within the parameters of the 'normal' healthy body. Godwin's views changed on many of these issues: in 1797 he was adamant that genius is not born but made, in accordance with his ideas that environment and education are of vital importance. In 1831 he is equally sure that creativity is a 'gift of nature' (*Political Writings*, VI, 56).

I then look at a number of texts that have been seen as formative in various ways in the creation of 'Romanticism'. I start with Edward Young's 1759 *Conjectures on Original Composition* and move through the Joseph Weston and Anna Seward debate of 1789–91 to Joanna Baillie's 'Introductory Discourse' to *A Series of Plays* in 1798, before looking finally at S.T. Coleridge's *Biographia Literaria* (1817). I end the chapter with a look at Mary Shelley's 1831 introduction to *Frankenstein*. Young's attempt to distinguish between an original and an imitation is set out in the terms of organic and biological reproduction. An original is something born, that grows, and has life. An imitation is something that is manufactured with labour and skill. For Young, true literary creation is the creation of an entirely new thing, which has never existed before. When we get to Shelley's account of literary creation, she uses the opposite terms: it is impossible to create *ex nihilo*; nothing can come from nothing. For her, creation should be renamed invention, with all its attendant meanings and implications (Shelley 1993, 195).

The context for this discussion of literary creation, though, is contemporary scientific accounts of generation and reproduction. The chapter looks at the theory of maternal impressions influencing the sex and health of the embryo and examines the work of Lawrence, Hunter, and Geoffroy on so-called 'monsters'. Shelley's *Frankenstein* is read in the light of these developments and I compare the author's creation to Victor's creation to see how 'monstrous' the Creature really is. Ideas of literary creation evidently respond to (and interrogate) these scientific debates and discussions.

The word 'creativity' was coined in 1659 according to the *OED*, but as Rob Pope notes, it was not widely current until the 1940s (Pope 2005, 19).[3] He also notes that '"creativity" has *not* been a favoured term in literary and cultural theory of the past twenty or thirty years' (Pope 2005, 6). For Romanticists, the term is very much associated with the anachronistic views of mid-twentieth-century critics such as Abrams, most famously, who represented the writing of the period as a kind of lamp (as opposed to eighteenth-century literature, which was like a mirror), where the source of light and heat comes from within the individual author (Abrams 1953). We might see Abrams's view of Romanticism as predicated upon the idea that a poet is born and not made; it ignores the sociability, networks, and collaboration that we now know to have taken place among these writers. Creativity, then, is a term with particularly negative associations for the Romantic scholar; it seems old fashioned, outmoded, and a throwback from a critical past which we have moved beyond. It is true that the word 'creativity' does not seem to be used in titles and texts of the Romantic period.[4] Yet, it is the case that many Romantic-era writers do write about the act of literary creation, and use associated terms, such as originality, genius, and inspiration.[5] Rob Pope also looks at the historical uses of the word and considers the influence of scientific and medical ideas; he looks at how science offers metaphors for creativity and how we understand the idea of creation partly through scientific knowledge. His examples are from later periods though, concerning knowledge relating to fields such as evolution, genetics, and neuroscience.

There are many aspects of creativity that might be covered here but which the scope of the chapter will not accommodate: for example, the ability to 'half-create' the external world rather than simply passively receive impressions from it, as expressed by Wordsworth working within a clear philosophical tradition (Wordsworth 1992, 119, l. 107). The period's fascination with originality has also been persuasively linked to parallel developments in intellectual property and copyright (see Rose 1993). The term is associated uncomfortably now with ideas of divine creation; for Terry Eagleton the less mysterious and more accessible Marxist notion of literary production is preferred, which I do touch on at the end of the chapter (Eagleton 1987, 45; also cited in Pope 2005, 7). Much work has been done to historicize these concepts, and to emphasize their historical contingency, such as David Higgins's consideration of the way that the idea of genius shifted in the early nineteenth century to pay more attention to the characters and lifestyles of 'men of genius' (Higgins 2005, 3). Thus, while 'creativity' is an anachronistic term, efforts are made in this period to define literary creation. Writers discussed here try to proscribe the limits of taste (defining what is, and is not, genuine creation as opposed to imitation), to account for creativity in the body and mind of the literary genius, and to describe it using physical models of creation. The texts that I examine here do not form a comprehensive list but they do contribute to the emergence of a Romantic-era discourse.

The chapter starts with William Godwin because he discusses in a single text many of the issues to be considered later, and there is evidence that his thought on some of these matters has shifted considerably since the 1790s. Godwin quotes Robert Burton's *The Anatomy of Melancholy* (1632) in the first essay of *Thoughts on Man*, 'Of Body and Mind', perhaps wishing to suggest that his book too will range from the physical to the metaphysical. Godwin quotes the opening of *Anatomy*, where man is praised as the best creation of God, and moves, in the next paragraphs to consider man's 'corporeal structure' in detail as the means by which great achievements can be accomplished (*Political Writings*, VI, 39).[6] The body of man – the joints, muscles, veins, hands, face – is particularly praised, but despite this admiration of the physical 'Man is a godlike being' because he is not limited to the prison of the body and his mind can range through time and space (*Political Writings*, VI, 43). The body can be an encumbrance and a potential distraction from, specifically, 'That sublimity of conception which renders the poet, and the man of great literary and original endowments "in apprehension like a God"' (*Political Writings*, VI, 46). In other words, while the human body is a thing of wonder, it can distract men of great literary talent with its failings and inconveniences. After quoting *Hamlet*, Godwin tells us that he has even looked upon his own body as a poor host for 'so divine a guest' as his mind when it is in its 'loftiest' moods (*Political Writings*, VI, 46).[7]

In the next essay, 'Of the Distribution of Talents', Godwin considers it likely that Horace's idea that 'The poet is born a poet, and cannot be made so by the ingenuity of art' is true because the poet perceives and experiences the world differently to his fellow man (*Political Writings*, VI, 55). This debate is found in other texts discussed in this chapter; whether literary genius is thought of as born or made determines the kinds of metaphors used to describe it. At this point in *Thoughts on Man* Godwin quotes from *A Midsummer's Night's Dream*: the poet's 'imagination bodies forth / The forms of things unknown' (Shakespeare 1994b, V.1.14–15). In this allusion, it is the poet's ability to create new entities, things that have never before existed, which is specifically 'godlike', rather than his understanding or perception. The poet can create something from nothing. Percy Shelley quotes Tasso in *The Defence of Poetry*, 'Nom merita nome di creatore se non Iddio ed il Poeta' ('None merits the name of creator except God and the Poet').[8] This chapter explores the period's interest in the idea of literature as the creation of new worlds as opposed to, say, what Mary Shelley calls 'invention' in her 1831 introduction to *Frankenstein*.

The ability to create is probably a 'gift of nature', Godwin writes in *Thoughts of Man*, and, despite his earlier statement that the body can be an encumbrance to the mind, he gives this gift a physiological basis:

> it may reasonably be presumed, that there are varieties in the senses, the organs, and the internal structure of the human species, however delicate, and to the touch of the bystander evanescent, which may give to each individual a predisposition to rise to a supreme degree of excellence in some certain art or attainment, over a million of competitors.
>
> (*Political Writings*, VI, 56)

Ultimately, therefore, the origin of such mental abilities is physical and so cannot be worked upon or consciously improved. We do not have 'innate ideas' at birth but we do have 'predispositions' to certain professions or type of work (*Political Writings*, VI, 56). According to Godwin, it is man's 'structure' that makes him 'best fitted to excel' in this particular kind of pursuit (*Political Writings*, VI, 56).

In *Thoughts of Man*, he contradicts the earlier conclusions he reached in *The Enquirer* (1797) on the subject of whether 'genius be born with a man, or may be subsequently infused' (*Political Writings*, V, 87). In the earlier text, while acknowledging that the only 'essential' difference between children at birth could be in the 'structure of their bodies' not in their minds, he denies that genius is 'connected with any particular structure of the organs of sense' and is dubious of the idea that genius is 'connected with a certain state of nervous sensibility originally existing in the frame' (*Political Writings*, V, 87). If one were to dissect a man of genius, he writes, it would be impossible to 'point out those differences in his structure which constitute him such' (*Political Writings*, V, 88).[9] In 1797, Godwin is unequivocal: 'Genius [...] is not born with us, but generated subsequent to birth' (*Political Writings*, V, 89). Clearly Godwin changed his mind on this subject between 1797 and 1831; this change strikes at the heart of his most fundamental ideas, and the concerns of my previous two chapters. His earlier statements accord with his and Wollstonecraft's belief that education and environment are the primary influences on character and ability. Alan Richardson also notes the change in Godwin's thinking on this issue, influenced, he argues, by the 'new brain-based theories of mind, particularly Gall's "organology"' (2001, 95). The shift in his ideas is fascinating and, when linked to the body, as it is in Godwin's thinking, invests the physiology of the genius with far more importance than before. Such discussions come to the fore with the publication of *Frankenstein*, where creation, monstrous or otherwise, is the subject of the text. The novel seems to explore further Godwin's 1790s sense that genius or its creations can be 'made' in its discussion of what we would now call the nature versus nurture debate. In *Frankenstein* we see a creature very deliberately assembled from body parts, and in a similar shift, in 1831, Mary Shelley herself alludes to the creative process as 'invention'. The idea that a genius is born, conversely, is crucial to the phenomena of the 'natural genius' of the labouring-class poet in this period.

Throughout the *Thoughts on Man*, Godwin is at pains to make clear that he is speaking only of normative bodies: when he writes of man he does not 'regard any aberrations of form' as part of his subject (*Political Writings*, VI, 39). He writes that 'All men, the monster and the *lusus naturae* excepted', share the same form; once 'deformities of body and abortions of intellect' are disregarded, men are more alike and equal to each other than some will admit (*Political Writings*, VI, 53). He repeatedly puts 'idiots and extraordinary cases out of the question' in his *Thoughts on Man* (*Political Writings*, VI, 53, 59). Other writers (both medical and literary) of this period were particularly interested in the 'monstrous' and extraordinary. Later in this chapter I examine the work of contemporary surgeon Lawrence and naturalist Geoffroy on teratology, which argues that monstrosity should not be regarded as an exception but as on a continuum with the 'normal', healthy body. I also look at Erasmus Darwin's view of why monstrosity occurs – he describes his literary creations in *The Botanic Garden* as 'monsters' – and I compare the creation of Mary Shelley's 'hideous progeny', *Frankenstein*, to Victor Frankenstein's 'monster' in the novel itself (Darwin 1791, 58; Shelley 1993, 197).

Godwin uses the language of reproduction when he describes what happens when men are placed in situations for which their physiological 'organisation' makes them unfit, in his third chapter of *Thoughts on Man*, called 'Of Intellectual Abortion' (*Political Writings*, VI, 68). On some occasions, the men themselves choose an unsuitable activity, 'in which all of their efforts must necessarily terminate in miscarriage' and he gives the example here of a would-be playwright (*Political Writings*, VI, 68). Godwin urges that men need to wait to fulfil their ambitions until their body demonstrates its readiness to embark upon the proper career, until the mind swells, 'his blood flows fitfully and with full pulses through his veins till his eyes sparkle with the intenseness of his conceptions, and his "bosom labours with the God"' (*Political Writings*, VI, 69–70). The use of a language of pregnancy and its failures is not uncommon in writing about literary endeavour. Neither is the use of a language of organic growth; Godwin laments the many causes that can result in even the 'richest soil, impregnated with the choicest seeds of learning and observation' failing to produce a good 'crop' (*Political Writings*, VI, 72). In 1591, Philip Sidney in *Astrophil and Stella* found he was 'great with Childe to speake' but had to look to his own heart in order to invent something original.[10] This chapter looks closely at specific Romantic-era uses of such metaphors, including ideas of monstrous births as well as the key medical writing on these topics. Of course, Mary Shelley's *Frankenstein* exploits to the full any discomfort the reader might feel at the idea of a male pregnancy.

In this chapter I look at specific instances where writers describe and define the act of literary creation and the product of this act, the creation itself, using organic and biological metaphors. The texts chosen have been considered as particularly important in the act of themselves creating 'Romanticism'; they have been credited with developing the sentiments associated with the era's sense of itself and its writing.

3.1 Literary composition and organic creation

In this section I examine in detail a key eighteenth-century theory of composition that privileges the idea of poet as creator: Edward Young's 1759 *Conjectures on Original Composition*, which is often represented as a 'showcase for emerging ideas, a mileage-marker on the road from Neoclassicism to Romanticism'.[11] Young uses the word 'composition' to refer to the writing of poetry but does not mean it in the sense of putting something together, where the existing elements are combined into new arrangements. Young belongs within a tradition of writing opposed to the neoclassical idea that imitation is the highest form of art, and which instead privileges originality in literature. Ironically, it is now accepted that Young's 'particular reflections on original composition [...] by 1759 were no longer original' in themselves (Wickman 1998, 900). In 1711 Joseph Addison had likewise argued that 'An Imitation of the best Authors, is not to compare with a good Original' (Addison 1711, [320]). Young, though, was perhaps responding specifically to Joseph Warton's criticism of Pope, published in 1756, in which he wrote that Pope lacks the 'creative and glowing IMAGINATION' that alone makes a poet.[12] Richard Hurd's *A Dissertation on the Idea of*

Universal Poetry published ten years later also notes that poetry 'peoples all creation with new and living forms'.[13] These kinds of sentiments can be contrasted with a critic such as Samuel Johnson writing in 1765 about Shakespeare:

> his drama is the mirrour of life; [...] he who has mazed his imagination, in following the phantoms which other writers raise up before him, may here be cured of his delirious extasies [*sic*] by reading human sentiments in human language.
>
> ('Preface', Johnson 1765, I, n.p.)

While here the creations of other writers are considered 'phantoms' rather than fully living forms, Johnson praises Shakespeare because he reflects or imitates real life. Reading Shakespeare can cure the reader, whose imagination is amazed and full of wonder at the supernatural creations of others. The positions taken by these critics introduce a number of topics to be explored further: there is a kind of writing that is regarded as truly original and this is considered superior to writing that simply imitates. Originals are defined thus by their bringing into being something that has never existed previously. In the mid-eighteenth century, this discussion often revolves around Shakespeare and Pope, the former's work being compared to a natural-grown forest, and that of the latter to a man-made, landscaped garden.[14] The idea of a kind of unnatural, phantom-like life achieved by lesser writers emerges again, as does the idea that writing is a therapy that can cure the reader diseased by these dangerous literary productions. M.H. Abrams drew attention to Young's 'vegetable concept of genius' or his 'metaphors of vegetable growth' in 1953 – though my approach is different to his (Abrams 1953, 198, 199). These metaphors are common in literary criticism of the eighteenth century, with a number of key critics using organic, agricultural, or gardening metaphors to express their sense of what constitutes genuine literary creation. For Addison at the beginning of the century there are two types of genius, typified by Shakespeare and Milton: both begin with 'rich Soil' but the first 'produces a whole Wilderness of noble Plants [...] without any certain Order or Regularity' while the second 'has been laid out in Walks and Parterres, and cut into Shape and Beauty by the Skill of the Gardener' (Addison 1711, [320]). Johnson uses the same metaphors many years later though not to the same ends: 'The work of a correct and regular writer is a garden accurately formed and diligently planted [...] the composition of *Shakespeare* is a forest' (Johnson 1765, I, n.p.). We find these metaphors continuing into the last decade of the eighteenth century, further influenced by theories such as those of William Gilpin on the picturesque, and anxieties concerning the pleasure garden.

Young's essay has been influential more generally in studies of the development of theories of the imagination. James Engell finds in Young's image of the imagination as a kind of seed or germ the origins of later Romantic ideas similarly expressed by Goethe, Percy Shelley, and Coleridge (Engell 1981, 4). Young was well known as the author of *Night Thoughts* and his *Conjectures* was published as part of his *Works* in a posthumous edition of 1777. Wordsworth acknowledged that his phrase 'half create' in 'Tintern Abbey' was owed to Young's *Night Thoughts* and Bjorn Tydahl also finds evidence of Wordsworth's engagement with *Conjectures* in his 'Intimations Ode.'[15] David Higgins refers to Young's essay in tracing the development of the concept of genius (Higgins 2005, 2). It is possible therefore to argue for this text as one that, in its ideas of creation, also helped to create 'Romanticism'.

One of Young's central conceits is his comparison of genius to organic life. It is not merely the flower – which adorns the plant – but the root of the plant itself:

> An *Original* may be said to be of a *vegetable* nature; it rises spontaneously from the vital root of genius; it *grows*, it is not *made*: *Imitations* are often a sort of *manufacture* wrought up by those *mechanics, art,* and *labour,* out of pre-existent materials not their own.
>
> ([Young] 1759, 12)

He claims that original compositions are new in every sense of the word; they have not existed in any form before. The question of whether genius can be learned or is innate is one that continues into the late eighteenth century and a conviction such as Young's – that an original '*grows*' – aligns it with organic life, specifically, the life of plants and vegetables. This also gives us an idea of how he thought plant life began; his idea that vegetable life 'rises spontaneously from the vital root' perhaps suggests Aristotelian ideas that plants can be 'spontaneously generated'.[16] An original composition for Young must appear and grow from nothing rather than being made or compiled from pre-existing components. He particularly contrasts with originality those imitations that are produced by physical labour, manufacture, and machinery. In her 1831 introduction to *Frankenstein*, Shelley writes exactly the opposite; for her nothing can come from nothing and she characterizes literary composition as 'invention'.

A few pages earlier, Young uses another metaphor that involves the organic world, though here, perhaps contradictorily, he compares the writer to a magician:

> The pen of an *original* Writer, like *Armida*'s wand, out of barren waste calls a blooming spring: Out of that blooming spring an *Imitator* is a transplanter of laurels, which sometimes die on removal, always languish in a foreign soil.
>
> ([Young] 1759, 10)

The writer of original compositions can transform and revitalize; he (it is always a 'he') can breathe life into an otherwise dead landscape, though this is likened to a magical rather than a natural act. Armida, a female magician in Tasso's *Jerusalem*, lures a knight to a garden where he is bewitched.[17] This comparison is somewhat suspect therefore; while the act does describe creating something from nothing, in Armida's case at least this is for the purposes of deception. In Young's text, an imitator of others' writing simply moves the fruits of genius from one place to another and this removal is not beneficial to the life of the plant. There is play in the word 'transplanter' here, which contains the word 'plant' and describes the act of moving it. An imitator merely moves ideas from one place to another; he does not create new ones.

Young is optimistic that there will be more 'Originals', assuring the reader that it is not the case that the 'human mind's teeming time is past', and nor is it 'incapable of putting forth unprecedented births'; both of these phrases use a language of reproduction, which Godwin also uses and which we see again in Romantic-era accounts of literary creation ([Young] 1759, 17). For Coleridge, Darwin, and Mary Shelley the 'unprecedented birth' could specifically be a monstrous one. Young warns, though, that there is a kind of imitation life, a non-life, which the author-magician conjures up: 'That is, where art has taken great pains to labour undramatic matter into dramatic life; which is impossible' ([Young] 1759, 93). Using a metaphor of pregnancy here – which is interesting given the gendering of the poet – he describes a kind of stillbirth. On the other hand, original writers such as Shakespeare and Otway in Young's opinion 'would have outdone *Prometheus*, and, with their heavenly fire, have given [...] not only life, but immortality' ([Young] 1759, 93). Referring to the version of the Prometheus myth, where the Titan is credited with the creation of man, as well as having stolen fire for man's benefit, Young finds that the literary creation of these authors will continue to exist beyond their lifetime. Male authors use a language of pregnancy (labour, pain, conception) to describe their literary creation just as Frankenstein uses this language to describe his task in creating the Creature (see Huet 1993, 132).

Young reminds us that we have not yet 'fathomed the mind of man' and makes the comparison with measuring the infinite universe: 'Its bounds are as unknown, as those of the creation' ([Young] 1759, 48). This reveals Young's understanding of the size of the universe and his sense of the limitless capacities of man. Such comparisons between God's and man's creations were not unusual though they did potentially court danger. Indeed Young argues that scientific progress and discoveries will provide an ever-evolving source of inspiration:

> Yet, consider, my Friend! knowlege [*sic*] physical, mathematical, moral, and divine, increases; all arts and sciences are making considerable advance; with them, all the accommodations, ornaments, delights, and glories of human life; and these are new food to the Genius of a polite writer; these are as the root, and composition, as the flower; and as the root spreads, and thrives, shall the flower fail? As well may a flower flourish, when the root is dead.
>
> ([Young] 1759, 74–5)

Initially he describes the advances of the arts and sciences as 'food' to the genius, imagining the objects and ideas that inspire writers to be their sustenance and the means by which they thrive. Then he imagines this growing body of knowledge as the root upon which the 'flower' of literary composition appears. The flower depends upon the root; advances in knowledge inspire literary composition; and where the root is healthy the flower will be too. Young clearly felt that scientific knowledge had a place in literary writings, and considered Bacon and Newton to be 'great *Originals*' just as Shakespeare and Milton were ([Young] 1759, 76).

Young describes genius as being like 'the Body's natural strength', locating it as Godwin would in 1831 in the physical make-up of the man; whereas in contrast, learning is compared to the 'superinduced Accoutrements of Arms' ([Young] 1759, 30). Throughout the essay he considers genius to be natural and innate. For him, a genius seems not to work at his art and this ability is what makes us believe that genius 'partake[s] of something Divine' ([Young] 1759, 27). Rather than be rule-bound like '*Learning*', genius often owes 'its supreme Glory' to 'Liberty' or freedom ([Young] 1759, 27). Due to this particular nature of genius, Young thinks it might be found working at the plough: 'Many a Genius, probably, there has been, which could neither write, nor read' ([Young] 1759, 35). This leads him to conclude that genius may be more common than has been thought previously. These ideas continue in the label of 'natural genius' given to labouring-class poets of the Romantic period, a label sometimes cultivated by the poets themselves and at other times exploited by the poet's publishers. Robert Burns promoted himself in this way, thus masking his intensely radical agenda and was famously described as a 'heaven-taught plowman' by Henry Mackenzie, while Wordsworth also imagined him 'Following his plough, along the mountain-side' in 'Resolution and Independence'.[18] The debate about whether genius is born or made thus continues into the Romantic era with significant ramifications for a poet's marketability and success.

Young alludes to a number of scientific or medical ideas when formulating his theory of composition. For example, he imagines that literature has a medicinal effect on its readership: for him, where Addison 'prescribed a wholesome and pleasant regimen, which was universally relished, and did much good', Pope's writing was more in the nature of 'a purgative [...] which, tho' wholesome, was too painful in its operation' ([Young] 1759, 97–8). Swift's writing was 'a large dose of ipecacuanha, which, tho' readily swallowed from the fame of the physician, yet, if the patient had any delicacy of taste, he threw up the remedy, instead of the disease' ([Young] 1759, 98). Ipecacuanha is 'a South American small shrubby plant, which possesses emetic, diaphoretic, and purgative properties', which around this time was also used specifically to induce vomiting (*OED*). Swift's is the least successful of the remedies if the patient tends to throw up the remedy but not the disease. While Addison and Pope are both good for you, Pope offers a more violent and painful treatment. This shows Young using contemporary medical ideas concerning how to maintain good digestive health. Reading can be good for you – indeed, it can cure you – but how it does so depends upon the violence of the treatment. Conversely, later in the century Wordsworth imagines certain kinds of writing to be physically bad for the reader, 'frantic novels, sickly and stupid German Tragedies' (*Prose Works*, I, 128).[19] Novels, according to Hurd, appeal to a 'vitiated, palled, and sickly imagination — that last disease of learned minds' (Hurd 1766, 22). Later in this chapter I look at the prevalence of the theory of maternal impressions to which Hurd seems to refer – the diseased imagination of the author produces a defect in the literary creation. Indeed Hurd, using the language of reproduction, describes such creations as either not fully formed or monstrous. In his 1766 *Dissertation*, Hurd describes novels as 'hasty, imperfect abortive poems' that may have been 'spawned' from either the 'dramatic or narrative species' (Hurd 1766, 5).[20] Hurd quotes – as illustration – from Pope's *Essay on Criticism*: 'Unfinish'd Things, one knows not what to call, / Their Generation's so equivocal' (Hurd, 1766, 21; Pope 1711, 5). Novels have a kind of life, but one that is not properly or fully formed, and this suits the diseased imaginations of their readers.

The metaphors used by Young and the other critics discussed so far continue into the later decades of the eighteenth century. The question of whether critics favour Dryden or Pope is often key to their theories about how literary creation is defined. John Williams argues that the public disagreement between Joseph Weston and Anna Seward on this and related matters bolsters Marilyn Butler's thesis that Wordsworth's 'Preface' to the *Lyrical Ballads* 'represented strands of thinking and of taste typical of the last half century', rather than being the originary moment of Romanticism (Williams 2001, 146). The Weston-Seward debate (1788–91) therefore, has been held to be representative of a kind of thinking associated with the Romantic period and might be considered as having had a part in creating 'Romanticism'. On the question of literary taste, Weston prefers Dryden (Weston 1788). Again comparing literary creation to creation itself, here, specifically, the earth, Weston asks: 'Would the Face of Creation appear more lovely, were it—instead of "rising into Inequalities, diversified by the varied Exuberance of abundant Vegetation"—to exhibit one immensurable "Velvet Lawn, shaven by the Scythe, and levelled by the Roller?"' (Weston 1788, xi; Johnson 1781, 172). Weston, like Johnson, complains of the 'tiresome Uniformity of [Pope's] Versification', but then goes on to concede that 'so material a Change in the Constitution of Poetry could not be expected to take Place, without some literary Convulsions' (Weston 1788, xiii).

It is unlikely that Weston refers here to geological theories of catastrophism.[21] Instead, he probably refers to convulsions of the body, which is certainly the way in which Johnson uses the word most often in his works (see, for example, Johnson 1752, I, 90). This would also accord with his use of the word 'Constitution', which is often used to refer to the health of the physical body. In other words, some crisis needs to take place before poetry can move forward.[22] The interest in landscape continues in Weston's literary criticism though, perhaps with specific contemporary reference to William Gilpin on '*picturesque* Versification' (Weston 1788, xix, xxii) (Gilpin 1768; see also Barrell 1983). Weston criticizes the idea that art can be taught, exclaiming: 'as if Poets, like Peers, not happening to be born such, could be made!'

(Weston 1788, xiv). There were no life peers at this point in the House of Lords, and the idea is ridiculous to Weston. It is equally ridiculous to imagine that poets could be made rather than born.

Anna Seward's public response to Weston's 'Preface' to the *Woodmen of Arden* (Weston 1788), in the pages of the *Gentleman's Magazine* from 1789 to 1791, boldly ranked 'SEVEN celebrated Female Poets' among her list of modern poets worth reading (Seward 1789a, 292; see also Hawkins 2011). She also mentions in her list the 'unschooled sons of genius', including Burns, Yearsley, and Chatterton (Seward 1789a, 292). Seward was the correspondent of Humphry Repton (Seward 1811; see also Barnard 2009). Using gardening metaphors to talk of both the product and the process of Dryden's poetry, which she thinks more like a wilderness than an ordered landscaped park, Seward writes in another article that:

> He trusted to the majestic trees of this wilderness, 'laden with blooming gold,' for the preservation of his fame; and they *will* preserve it. But he little dreamt that their fruits should so far intoxicate the brain of a brother poet, in future time, as that he should assert the superior beauty of this wilderness on *account* of its weeds, and abuse the majestic parks and lawns of succeeding bards, from which the nettles and switch-grass have been rooted up.
>
> (Seward 1789b, 510)

There are weeds, or imperfections, but in the wilderness of Dryden's literary creation also 'majestic trees'. The produce of these trees, their fruit – here she quotes Milton's *Comus* – has intoxicated the 'brain of a brother poet' Weston himself, who is criticized for asserting the superiority of Dryden's verse because of, rather than in spite of, its weeds (Milton 2009, I. 394, 100). Again, taste is imagined as bodily – the product of Dryden's creation intoxicates Weston into madness. This has led Weston to abuse the 'parks and lawns', which probably refers to Pope's poetry, where under much stricter self-regulation there is no evidence of such weeds. As I shall discuss, Coleridge uses these metaphors when describing Wordsworth's poetry but there the metaphors are further invested with a belief that poetry is itself organic.

Joanna Baillie's 'Introductory Discourse' to *A Series of Plays* on the passions (1798) is another work of literary criticism that has been seen as an important precursor to Wordsworth's 'Preface' (see Yudin 1994; Brewer 1991). As such it can be regarded as another text that helps create 'Romanticism'. Published before the 'Preface' to the *Lyrical Ballads*,

Baillie's text argues for a new naturalness in language and emphasizes feeling, passion, and emotion above reason. Baillie's text also features metaphors that we see in earlier texts. Here speaking of how fiction about the middling sort and lower-class people will interest us more than that on the upper classes, Baillie writes:

> The one is a dressed and beautiful pleasure-ground, in which we are enchanted for a while, amongst the delicate and unknown plants of artful cultivation; the other is a rough forest of our native land; the oak, the elm, the hazle [*sic*], and the bramble are there; and amidst the endless varieties of its paths we can wander for ever.
>
> ([Baillie] 1798 20)

Writing about the upper classes is likened not to a landscaped park here but to a pleasure garden. Baillie criticizes the 'higher sentimental novels' that have attempted to interest readers in 'the delicacies, embarrassments, and artificial distresses of the more refined part of society', figuring them here as an artificial garden with which we are temporarily enchanted. The plants here are Wollstonecraft's 'hot-house' flowers, exotic and highly cultivated (*Works*, v, 196). Instead, Baillie urges us to read texts that are like 'rough forests'. Rather than visit a garden filled with exotic plants, she argues that it is better to walk in a forest full of British trees. Such metaphors alert us to changing literary tastes as well as to changing contemporary cultural signs, from the landscaped garden to the wilderness and now the pleasure garden.

Baillie's links to medicine are well known. Her brother, Matthew, was a physician; he and Joanna were the niece and nephew of surgeons William and John Hunter; and the Hunter-Baillie family has been described as 'the most famous medical family of the period' (McMillan 1998, 70). Matthew Baillie was best known for his 1793 publication *Morbid Anatomy*, which begins: 'The object of this work is to explain more minutely than has hitherto been done, the changes of structure arising from morbid actions in some of the most important parts of the human body' (Baillie 1793, i). His object of study, then, was not the healthy body but the diseased body, and his book described the anatomy of diseased body parts. This accords with the shift, described later in this chapter, toward studying 'monstrous' deformities in humans and animals. Matthew Baillie acknowledged that 'The subject in itself is extremely difficult, because morbid actions are going on in the minute parts of an animal body excluded from observation' (Baillie 1793, ii). There are comparisons to be made with Joanna Baillie's plays, such as *De Monfort*, which focuses in minute detail on a mind distorted by the disease of intense hatred.[23] Joanna began her literary career while living in Great Windmill Street, the famous school for dissection that was set up by her uncle William; she dedicated the second volume of her *Plays* to her brother – she even rescued a cat that had been experimented on nearly to death by the surgeon Benjamin Brodie (Edgeworth 1971, 316–17). Tellingly, Matthew Baillie was thought to be the author of his sister's *Series of Plays* when it was first published anonymously (Baillie 2000, 17).

There seems to be a kind of scientific methodology at work in the title page of Joanna Baillie's first collection of poems, published in 1790, which had the subtitle '*Wherein it is Attempted to Describe Certain Views of Nature and of Rustic Manners; and also, to Point Out, in Some Instances, the Different Influence which the Same Circumstances Produce on Different Characters*' (Baillie 1790). The 1798 *Series of Plays* had the subtitle 'in which it is attempted to delineate the stronger passions of the mind'. This categorizing tendency, and the experimental manner – she will observe and 'point out' the way that the same circumstances can have different influences on different characters – may be likened to her brother's efforts in his *Morbid Anatomy*, a work that also intends to observe and note the different effects of the same diseases within different bodies. Fredrick Burwick also notes the way that Baillie chooses to 'represent dramatic character [...] in relation to the accounts of mental pathology in contemporary medical science' (Burwick 2004, 48).

Baillie makes an explicit connection with science when she writes that if we did not have a 'sympathetick [*sic*] curiosity' for our fellow men, our interest in them would quickly wane; it would be as 'insipid, as examining the varieties of plants and minerals, is to one who understands not natural history' (Baillie 1798, 4). Perhaps in reference to her own natural history knowledge, she uses the word 'varieties' and 'species' often in the 'Introductory Discourse'; most often the former is used to refer to the varieties of the human mind, its passions and character. There are linguistic echoes in Wordsworth's later 'Preface', both authors describe their activities as 'tracing': Wordsworth is 'tracing [...] the primary laws of our nature' through 'common life', while Baillie will 'trace passion through all its varieties, and in every stage' many of which would for various reasons be otherwise 'overlooked' (*Prose Works*, I, 122–3; Baillie, 1798, 59).[24] As with her brother's study, Baillie admits that observation of the closest kind is necessary: 'even the smallest indications of an unquiet mind, the restless eye, the muttering lip, [...] will set our attention [...] anxiously upon the watch' (Baillie 1798, 10). She determines to pay attention to these minute details since herein lie the clues to the case. Her observation is that of a physiologist, if not what we would now know as a psychologist. In deciding to make the diseased body (or mind) the object of her study, she follows her uncle, John Hunter, who similarly studied monstrosity. Burwick notes, too, that Baillie 'enters into the very same province of aberrational psychology that Matthew Baillie had begun to explore in his 1794 lectures on the nervous system' (Burwick 2004, p. 51). Richardson also finds 'a number of correspondences between Baillie's guiding "ideas concerning human nature" in the "Introductory Discourse" and the emergent biological psychologies of the time' (Richardson 2004, 132). Not only this, he asserts that the 'moments of original psychological insight' found in such writers as Baillie 'not only adapted but significantly extended the embodied approach to mind being worked out in Romantic brain science' (Richardson 2004, 140).

Though the metaphors used to describe literary creation hitherto have all been organic, often comparing literature to plant or other life forms, they are employed for a variety of purposes. Young was adamant that an original was something created from nothing (*ex nihilo*), corresponding to his conviction that a genius was born and not made. Critical opinion diverges according to the taste of the time: critics find comparison (and grounds for superiority) in the images of the forest, landscaped garden, wilderness, and picturesque scene. This enables a discussion of the best conditions for literature; imagined as the soil in which plants best grow or the degree of cultivation that is rendered necessary. Pregnancy metaphors are commonplace, with the author imagined as labouring at his work and producing something that has a life independent of his own. Both the author and the reader are capable of diseased minds and imaginations too though, which then produce something that has only an imitation, phantom life, or is regarded as an abortion, only half-formed. Literature can be seen as the cure for the reader's mind or the disease, though the method of cure varies in extremity. Conversely, Baillie's works are conceived as scientifically studying the diseased mind, recording in minute detail the problem and its effects.

The final critic I want to look at briefly in this section is the one who is best known for using metaphors of organic growth in his description of literary creation, S.T. Coleridge. In the *Biographia Literaria*, though published in 1817, Coleridge reflects upon his work in the 1790s – particularly the collaboration with Wordsworth – and this text might also be regarded as having created what we anachronistically call 'Romanticism'.[25] Coleridge's use of organicism in his theory of literary creation has been written about a great deal, from the New Critics to the historical work of Trevor Levere and Ian Wylie (Levere 1981; Wylie 1989). Here I look at the way that metaphors seen already in this chapter continue and develop in his work before examining the idea that poetry for Coleridge is conceived as a living organism.

Coleridge is explicit about the link between poetic creation and God's creation of the universe. In his most famous statement he contrasts objects, which are 'essentially fixed and dead' with the imagination. The latter is divided into the primary imagination ('a repetition in the finite mind of the eternal act of creation in the indefinite I AM') and the secondary imagination, which is 'essentially *vital*' and which 'dissolves, diffuses, dissipates, in order to re-create' or if this is impossible 'struggles to idealize and unify' (*Biographia*, I, 304). In 1804, he had applied these ideas to Wordsworth, whom Coleridge regarded as 'a most original Poet' whose poetry synthesizes thought and feeling and combines these with poetic forms, with 'pleasurable passion', and imagination (*Coleridge Letters*, II, 1034). The imagination is described here, as in the *Biographia*, as 'the *modifying* Power' and is opposed to fancy, the '*aggregating* power' (*Coleridge Letters*, II, 1034). Where the latter simply collects images, the former transforms them. This division is used repeatedly in *Biographia*: the imagination is a 'shaping and modifying power' whereas the fancy is an 'aggregative and associative power' (*Biographia*, I, 293). In other words, the imagination is a living power and imparts some of this life to the poetic creation itself.

There is some evidence of the conventional metaphors used earlier in the eighteenth century in the *Biographia*. When comparing his and Wordsworth's projects in their literary criticism, Coleridge describes how Wordsworth 'has drawn a masterly sketch of the branches with their *poetic* fruitage', while Coleridge wishes with the *Biographia* 'to add the trunk, and even the roots as far as they lift themselves above ground' (*Biographia*, I, 88). Indeed Coleridge's objective is philosophical and goes beyond the scope of Wordsworth's 1815 'Preface' to the *Lyrical Ballads*. Again applying these metaphors when recalling Wordsworth's *Descriptive Sketches* of 1793, Coleridge finds in the 'form, style, and manner' of the poem a 'harshness and acerbity', 'which might recall those products of the vegetable world, where gorgeous blossoms rise out of the hard and thorny rind and shell, within which the rich fruit was elaborating' (*Biographia*, I, 77). To elaborate is 'to fashion or develop (an animal or vegetable tissue, etc.)' from raw materials (*OED*). Coleridge's point is that something lovely emerges from an unlikely source. At a later point in *Biographia*, Coleridge finds that a description of a specific Georgian soil given in William Bartram's *Travels* through America provides the most apt metaphor to describe Wordsworth's poetry (*Biographia*, II, 155; Bartram 1792, 36).

Coleridge claims that it is 'the prerogative of poetic genius to distinguish by parental instinct its proper offspring from the changelings', thus using the metaphor of parenthood to describe the author's relation to his work, but also suggesting that there are false children, 'which the gnomes of vanity or the fairies of fashion may have laid in its cradle or called by its names' (*Biographia*, II, 83; see also Toor 2007). Indeed, the poet gives life to his creation: 'a human and intellectual life is transferred to [poetic images] from the poet's own spirit' (*Biographia*, II, 23). These metaphors are commonplace by the time that Coleridge employs them but he invests them with a particular significance, making the idea of the imagination as the vital principle of the living, organic poem his central theory. The imagination is 'the living Power' (*Biographia*, I, 304). He states that 'The *rules* of the IMAGINATION are themselves the very powers of growth and production' (*Biographia*, II, 84). In other words the way that the imagination operates, the system within which it works, its rules, its laws and principles, are the same principles as those that govern organic growth. One of these principles is 'that *all* the parts of an organized whole must be assimilated to the more *important* and *essential* parts' (*Biographia*, II, 72). Here he uses language informed by the contemporary physiological debate on the nature of life, to which I will shortly return.

According to Coleridge, poetic genius is 'a very rare plant' (*Biographia*, II, 132). It 'may be cultivated and improved, but can never be learnt'; for this reason, '"Poeta nascitur non fit"', or, the poet is born and not made (*Biographia*, II, 20). Coleridge makes explicit links between the act of literary creation and natural (and therefore God's) creation. For example, he quotes Perdita from *The Winter's Tale*: there is an art that 'shares / With great creating nature' (*Biographia*, II, 66). Not only this, Polixenes then makes the point that this art, which can 'change' nature, also 'is nature'; it is created by nature too (*Biographia*, II, 66; Shakespeare 2007, IV.4.86–7, 95–7). Coleridge draws a distinction between a copy and a true imitation and in using these terms distinguishes his theory from Edward Young's. As James Engell and W. Jackson Bate further elucidate, an imitation 'is more of a "living" thing [...] a true "imitation" duplicates the process of nature itself, by presenting, in itself, the organizing spirit (*natura naturans*)' (*Biographia*, II, 72–3, n. 4). The genuine literary creation, then – as opposed to something fashioned by a 'mechanical art' – is itself alive, possessed of a vital principle and able to do all that the living body can do (*Biographia*, II, 83). It assimilates, blends, fuses, synthesizes, unifies, and idealizes. These are functions of the imagination, paralleling the functions of the living body as they were currently understood.

Coleridge's knowledge of various branches of science is revealed throughout *Biographia*. He uses the term 'mordaunt', a 'well-known phrase' he tells us, which is borrowed from 'technical chemistry' to describe the affinity that must exist between other aspects of poetry and the metre that is 'superadded' to it (*Biographia*, II, 71).[26] He also demonstrates his chemical knowledge earlier in the *Biographia* when he illustrates his point that a pedant might ask his wife to '*make the tea*' using technical language: he should 'bid her add to the quant. suff. of thea sinensis the oxyd of hydrogen saturated with caloric' (*Biographia*, I, 170). In his use of caloric, it is clear Coleridge no longer uses the by now old-fashioned ideas of phlogiston, but caloric was still regarded as a subtle fluid, or a substance that explained the presence of heat in matter. The way such substances operate have an affinity with the 'vital principle', which was thought by many, including Coleridge, to explain life.

Coleridge demonstrates his knowledge of vitalist ideas when he describes – three times – metre as 'superadded' to poetry in *Biographia* (*Biographia*, II, 11, 69, 71). This is a word that has particular resonance, since it was an important notion in the very public debate on the nature of vitality that was taking place in the Royal College of Surgeons between 1814 and 1819 (see Ruston 2005). The idea that the vital principle was 'superadded' to an otherwise inert body was a central tenet of the surgeon John Abernethy's theory of life, which Coleridge knew.[27] Indeed, Coleridge claimed in *The Friend* that Abernethy's 1817 *Physiological Lectures* were 'dictated solely by the writer's [Coleridge's] wishes' (Coleridge 1818, 180, n.). Abernethy attended Coleridge's lectures in 1818–19 and Coleridge attended Abernethy's *Hunterian Oration* on 15 February 1819 where he was quoted (see Levere 1981, 46). Coleridge also wrote his own *Theory of Life*, a serious intervention into the debate between Abernethy and another surgeon, William Lawrence (Coleridge 1848). In this text, Coleridge attacked Lawrence, whose position had become associated with French materialism and atheism, but he also had problems with Abernethy's views: Coleridge's religious and moral beliefs did not allow him to regard the vital principle as some kind of imponderable fluid analogous (if not identical) to electricity. In *Biographia* then, Coleridge uses the terms of the debate: for example he writes: 'For aught I know, the thinking Spirit within me may be *substantially* one with the principle of life' (*Biographia*, II, 139). In other words, thought might be identical with the vital principle.

Other terms are used in the *Biographia* that have particular resonance with the debate on the nature of life: for example, the body's ability to assimilate food and other substances and to convert them to its own nature was seen as a particular function of the living body. Abernethy writes that the 'principle functions' of life are 'assimilation, formation, and multiplication' (Abernethy 1817, 204). Similarly, Coleridge speaks of the 'blending, *fusing* power of Imagination and Passion' (*Biographia*, II, 150). The word 'powers' is also at issue in the debate between Abernethy and Lawrence; this word occurs fifty-four times in Abernethy's *Physiological Lectures*, often in phrases such as 'vital powers' or 'powers of life' or cognates (Abernethy 1817, pp. 28, 31, 33, 34, 170, 182, 219, 245, 246, 302, 311). On one occasion the ovum is described as having 'plastic powers' (Abernethy 1817, 303).[28] The power referred to in this debate is one that enables the transformation of matter; as, for example, the kidneys, which have 'powers of converting various kinds of animal matter into a peculiar and very soluble substance, lately recognized and denominated urea' (Abernethy 1817, 255). Levere also reminds us that the *Naturphilosophen* influenced Coleridge, and that J.F. Blumenbach's idea of a 'formative power provided a suggestive metaphor that was almost a model for imagination' (Levere 1981, 37). The imagination, described as '*essentially* vital' in *Biographia* can be seen as the vital principle that animates poetry. With Coleridge we see biological metaphors being used that are informed by an understanding of contemporary debates on the nature of life. While Young's *Conjectures* is important to Coleridge's theory of poetry, particularly his sense of a genuine original, there has been an important shift in Coleridge's thinking about the living nature of a true imitation.

3.2 Monstrous births and literary invention

Plant and animal reproduction and generation, as well as speculation on the beginning of the universe, earth, and life on earth, were among the favourite topics of the poet-physician Erasmus Darwin. Much has been written about Darwin and his discussion of such subjects; he is such an important figure in the 1790s that it would be odd not to discuss his work in this chapter however briefly. His influence on the writers of the Romantic period has been well documented and Mary Shelley mentions 'Dr Darwin' as an influence on *Frankenstein*, the novel most concerned with the idea of creation (Shelley 1993, 195; see also King-Hele 1986). Martin Priestman has summed up Darwin's connection to Romantic writers thus: 'If not quite part of the Romantic literary revolution, then,

Darwin gave its formative stages something to kick against, after first supplying some of its key ideas and images' (Priestman 2006). In this sense, and with all of the usual disclaimers, Darwin should take his place among the many who 'created' Romanticism. Darwin's interest in issues of generation and reproduction shows again how much discussed these subjects were at the time and his ideas can be placed within the historical context sketched out above (see also Wilson 2005). As Maureen McNeil has written, Darwin's theories often elude 'the neat categories of "materialist", "mechanist", or "vitalist"' (McNeil 1987, 167).

When *The Botanic Garden* was published in 1791, Darwin told readers that his general design was 'to inlist Imagination under the banner of Science' (Darwin 1791, v). He wished to lead readers from the 'looser analogies' often made in poetry to the 'stricter' analogies made possible with knowledge of science (Darwin 1791, v). The topics of the first part of the poem, *The Economy of Vegetation*, as described in the '*Argument of the First Canto*', include the origin of the universe, 'Animal Incubation', 'Phosphoric Acid and Vital Heat produced in the Blood', and 'Buds and Flowers Expanded by Warmth, Electricity, and Light' (Darwin 1791, xi–xii). The Second Canto of the poem, *The Loves of the Plants*, presents the sexual system of Linnaeus as a series of relationships between personified plants and flowers. Taken as a whole, *The Botanic Garden* shows how important reproduction was to Darwin's mind, and also emphasized analogies between the human and animal worlds on this topic.

With *Zoonomia* (1794–96), Darwin entirely concentrated on '*the laws of organic life*', extending this beyond plant life to include all living beings, and included a section dedicated to generation near the end of the first volume (Darwin 1794–96). Darwin states that he does not believe in preformation, and it becomes clear that instead his view is epigenesist (1794–96, I, 490). He objects to Buffon's 'organic particles', which are 'supposed to be partly alive, and partly mechanic springs', on a number of grounds and instead claims that matter has 'appetencies' that encourage it to 'embrace or absorb' other matter and so develop and grow (1794–96, I, 491–2). Darwin imagines this process as being akin to 'chemical affinities' but he also awards the advanced foetus power of 'volition' (1794–96, I, 499, 500). For Darwin, 'new animal appetenc[ies] are produced' with every change and development of the embryo and so it grows and acquires new powers and appetencies (1794–96, I, 500). Such notions of self-sufficient active matter could easily be identified as materialist to thinkers like William Paley, who reacted with outrage in his 1802 *Natural Theology* (Paley 1881, 279–80).

Radically, Darwin concluded that 'all animals have a similar origin, viz. from a single living filament'; statements such as these have been seen as proto-evolutionary, leading the way for his grandson's work (Darwin 1794–96, I, 498).[29] In the posthumously published *The Temple of Nature* (1803), Darwin moves from discussing the origin of the universe – according to his editor, Priestman, offering a theory akin to the modern 'big bang' – to positing his theory that all life on earth originally came from the sea (Darwin 2006, I, 227, 234). Each 'successive generation' of living being acquires 'New powers' and so species grow and develop in a movement like that of the embryo in microcosm (Darwin 2006, I, 299–300). Darwin's Lucretian-influenced idea is of a 'vital chain' that links old and young in a never-ending 'long line of Being' (Darwin 2006, II, 19–20). He is convinced that living beings are progressing while they develop and that they are in 'a perpetual state of improvement' (Darwin 2006, Additional Note 1).

Darwin makes important changes to his view of one aspect of human reproduction between the first and the third editions of *Zoonomia*. In 1794, 'the embryon is produced by the male, and the proper food and nidus by the female' (Darwin 1794–96, I, 484). Also in this edition, it is the imagination of the man that determines both the gender and the characteristics of the child being conceived: 'the imagination of the male at the time of copulation' will cause 'the production of similarity of form and of features, with the distinction of sex' (Darwin 1794–96, I, 519). In the third edition (1801), however, Darwin gives women a more equal role in these matters (Wilson 2005, 125). Darwin's theory of the growth of the organism also helps him to account for the existence of 'monstrous births' (Darwin 1794–96, I, 496). Preformation theories could not explain deformities, according to Darwin, whereas epigenesis does: it particularly explains the 'duplicature of limbs' where there is a 'superfluity of the first nutritive particles' (Darwin 1794–96, I, 496). As Gigante writes, 'once life came to be seen as power, monstrosity came to represent life's relentless fecundity and "the monstrous" a mode of uncontainable vitality' (Gigante 2009, 6). Darwin refuses to blame the imagination of the woman during pregnancy for deformities in the child, though this was the usual explanation given (Darwin 1794–96, I, 515). For Darwin, 'monstrous conformations become less difficult to comprehend, when they are considered as an effect of the imagination' but he is speaking about the male imagination (Darwin 1794–96, I, 521). The existence of monstrous births was difficult to square with religious beliefs that God had created man perfect and in his image: preformation theory would mean that God had deliberately created human deformity.

In ascribing monstrosity to the male imagination, Darwin was of a different opinion to many in the medical profession of his day who believed that the maternal imagination shaped the foetus and deformities were often explained with reference to something that the mother had seen, dreamed, or imagined (see Huet 1993). The famous hoax of Mary Toft, who in 1726 persuaded a number of eminent physicians that, after being startled by a rabbit during pregnancy, she had given birth to seventeen rabbits was simply the best-known example of a commonly held belief, that the mother's imagination was paramount in the formation of the child in her womb (see Todd 1995). Links have been made between these ideas and the act of composition: Marie Hélène Huet argues that for those who believe in maternal imprinting the 'imagination functions *like* writing, particularly in its capacity to imprint the image of absent objects on the fibers of the brain' (Huet 1993, 53). As Kiran Toor puts it, the 'body of the child becomes a literal *text*' (Toor 2007, 259). The imagination becomes a powerful force, the most important force in the generation of living beings.[30]

Early in the eighteenth century, surgeons Daniel Turner and James Blondel had been involved in a very public debate on the issue of maternal impressions; Turner's epigenesist view of the embyro, as a malleable entity that was impressed upon by the mother's imagination, accounted for monstrosity by 'suggesting a mass of infinite potentiality residing within it, and out of which new parts and organs appear' (Toor 2007, 259). Blondel's theory of preformation, on the other hand, did not permit the woman any power to influence the foetus (Toor 2007, 260; see Todd 1995, chapter 4). Either the mother was held responsible for any sign of deformity in her child or was denied any power to influence it at all. These ideas persisted well into the nineteenth century, particularly in the popular imagination, and can also be found in the literature of the period. Huet finds a shift in the Romantic period though, when she writes: 'Romanticism reassigned the *vis imaginativa* to the father alone' (Huet 1993, 8). She links this to the changing perception of imagination more generally, which was no longer thought to reproduce images but now was thought to have 'the power to create them' (Huet 1993, 8). Coleridge, for example, was particularly fascinated by the idea of maternal impressions and more generally uses theories of embryonic development to describe the imagination (Toor 2007).

By 1819, theories of what caused monstrosity had changed. In Abraham Rees's *Cyclopædia*, William Lawrence defined what was meant by the term 'monster' as 'a creature in whom the body in general, or some large and conspicuous part of it, deviates remarkably from the accustomed formation' ([Lawrence] 1819b, n.p.). He lists a number of examples, ranging from the union of body parts, extra digits, 'hare-lip', to 'the want of the brain', 'club feet', spina bifida, and the resemblance of humans to animals, though in the last instance he is sceptical and leaves identification of these 'to the imagination of the observers' ([Lawrence] 1819b, n.p.). Lawrence's *Cyclopædia* entry is significant for a number of reasons and reveals that a shift has taken place in the way in which monsters are thought. Whereas previously monsters were considered as marvels, or aberrations of nature, Lawrence places them within the parameters of the natural.[31] In Lawrence's view they exist on a continuum with the natural, healthy body.[32] Lawrence even pointed out that monstrosity was difficult to define because it was difficult to 'draw very accurately the line of distinction between varieties and monstrous formations, which differ rather in degree than in kind' ([Lawrence] 1819b, n.p.). As Stephen T. Asma notes, this could suggest that in some way 'all of us deviate from the norm' (Asma 2009, 160). In the *Cyclopædia* entry Lawrence is clear that neither maternal impressions nor physical knocks during pregnancy can cause deformities in the child; instead monstrosity was the result of the irregular operations of the 'powers of generation' ([Lawrence] 1819b, n.p.).

Lawrence's very different view of monstrous births was in consequence of the work that had been done by men such as John Hunter and Étienne Geoffroy Saint-Hilaire. Hunter's interest in monsters is immortalized at the Royal College of Surgeons in London, where his specimens – such as the comb of a cockerel with a human tooth implanted into it – can still be seen (Moore 2005, 217–18). Hunter applied serious thought to the question of monsters and his extensive collections 'sought to display the underlying laws of abnormal growth' (Asma 2009, 155). He had already posited in 1779 that every animal had the potential for monstrosity, and in 1780 argued that this propensity was present in the embryonic beginnings of all life (Moore 2005, 407). In *Monstrosities: Bodies and British Romanticism*, Paul Youngquist argues that Hunter's work (among others) 'produces and enforces a cultural norm of human embodiment' at this time (Youngquist 2003, xi). He shows how the abnormality of bodies acquired by Hunter, such as the Sicilian dwarf, Caroline Crachami, or the Irish Giant, Charles Byrne, helped medical authorities to manage and control monstrosity. During this period, Youngquist argues, there was an attempt to install a 'norm of embodiment', which he calls the 'proper body', and monstrous bodies played a large role in the development of this category because norms need exceptions to prove the rule (Youngquist 2003, xiv). Efforts were made to reduce the terror caused by monstrosity, to master it and bring it under the institutional control of medicine (Youngquist 2003, 9).

In France, Geoffroy was developing his own ideas about what caused monstrosity – and courting controversy with his answers. He is widely credited with the creation of teratology, the study of monstrosity. He argued against Cuvier who believed that the physical form of the parts of living beings had been divinely created to perfectly suit the functions those parts had to fulfil (see Appel 1987). Instead Geoffroy claimed to have found similarities in the bodies of many different kinds of animals despite their existing in radically different environments and thus having quite different needs (see Asma 1996). Such similarities proved to him what he called 'unity in composition': that living bodies – whether monstrous or not – developed in the same ways (see Desmond 1992). As Huet puts it, when writing of the work of Geoffroy and his son, Isidore: 'Nothing could illustrate more explicitly the normalization of the monster by the scientific gaze: its submission to rules, norms, and variations' (Huet 1993, 109). Geoffroy attempted with some success to reproduce monsters (using chick embryos) in the laboratory, and with such activities, Huet writes, the 'scientist now takes the place of the mother' and 'male intervention has been substituted for female imagination' (Huet 1993, 111, 119). Of course such a shift is highly suggestive for such texts as *Frankenstein*.

For Geoffroy and Hunter then, while monsters deviated from normality, they still helped to reveal how normal human and animal generation worked and proved that the monstrous and the normal developed along the same lines. In other words, the monster was not that different after all. Lawrence's debt to Geoffroy and Hunter is clear in his *Cyclopædia* entry. It is important to study monsters, he writes, because they can help us to understand normal, healthy development since both proceed along the same lines:

> Monsters, in which considerable parts are wanting, seem particularly likely to assist in the prosecution of physiological researches. If we never saw animals, except in a perfect state, we would not form ideas of the comparative importance of the different organs.
>
> ([Lawrence] 1819b, n.p.)

Having examined children born without a heart or brain, Lawrence concludes that contrary to what was previously thought an otherwise organized body may be born and live for a few days without one or either. This makes him realize that the 'whole growth and formation of the foetal body depends upon the actions of the vascular system' ([Lawrence] 1819b, n.p.). In turn, this leads him to deny that the embryo is perfectly formed from conception, as preformation theory would have it, or, 'that the young animal is originally perfect, and degenerates into a monster through the action of external forces'; in fact, we should think that 'man, considered at the epocha of his first formation, and with respect to his corporeal frame, is a secretion' ([Lawrence] 1819b, n.p.). He admitted this might offend the pride of his readers but this was 'the simple truth' ([Lawrence] 1819b, n.p.).

By the time that Mary Shelley came to write her novel about a monster, then, much work had been done to categorize and understand monstrosity and to re-evaluate it as a condition not so far removed from the normal body.[33] In *Frankenstein*, a novel that concerns the non-natural creation of a living being, knowledge of contemporary thought on issues of generation and reproduction is particularly important. There are two acts of creation here, Mary Shelley's in writing the novel, and Victor Frankenstein's in creating the Creature: Shelley suggests a connection between these two herself when she describes the novel in 1831 as her 'hideous progeny' and her 'offspring' (Shelley 1993, 197).[34] Thus it seems appropriate to examine the novel in the light of contemporary and past understandings of generation and reproduction. The question of maternal impressions, for example, offers an interesting metaphor for the relationship between an author and her literary creation: as Shelley recalls in 1831, she was very frequently asked '"How I, then a young girl, came to think of and to dilate upon so very hideous an idea?"' (Shelley 1993, 192). Much critical attention has been paid to attempts to answer this question, which, crudely put, asks what was in Shelley's mind that made her come up with this idea.[35] The failings of Frankenstein's imagination might also be seen as the reason why the Creature is created a monster: he 'selected' the Creature's 'features as beautiful' but did not consider what they would look like when the Creature was alive and his face was mobile (Shelley 1993, 39). Alternatively, the condition of Frankenstein's mind – his removal from society, friends, and family and his nervous illness – could be seen as having had an adverse influence on his creation and even of creating the Creature's monstrosity. These questions of how a biological creation is conceived, how far characteristics are passed on from the parent to offspring, and whether the female merely provides the vehicle for child's development but does not shape or influence it, can be asked metaphorically of Shelley's creation in the novel. The application of metaphors of generation is particularly warranted in this instance because the novel concerns the act of generation and its consequences.

Shelley mentions 'Dr. Darwin' in the 1831 introduction to the novel but he was also present in Percy Shelley's original 1818 'Preface': 'The event on which this fiction is founded has been supposed, by Dr. Darwin, and some of the physiological writers of Germany, as not of impossible occurrence' (Shelley 1993, 3). Marilyn Butler notes that Blumenbach might have been in Percy Shelley's mind here, given that Lawrence, the friend and doctor to the Shelleys, had translated his *Comparative Anatomy* into English in 1807 (Shelley 1993, 252). In any case, it has long been established that the novel taps into contemporary debates concerning the nature of life, particularly those between Abernethy and Lawrence, which were represented in an overly simplistic manner by contemporaries as debates between vitalist and materialist views of life (see Marilyn Butler's comments in Shelley 1993 and Ruston 2005). Shelley's 1831 introduction – which always needs to be read cautiously given the many years that had passed since the novel's first publication and the many changes that had occurred in Shelley's life since that date – seems to confirm the possibility that 'galvanism' might be the means by which Frankenstein achieves the creation of a living being without the help of a woman or God.

The idea that the vital principle was electricity was a sticking point in the debate between Abernethy and Lawrence. Abernethy presented a number of ways in which electricity and vitality corresponded and even suggested that they might be one and the same thing. Lawrence poked fun at this idea and portrayed it as ridiculous (Ruston 2005, 43–50). In the 1818 edition of the novel, there is much evidence to support the idea that the 'spark of being' with which Frankenstein 'infuse[d]' the Creature was electricity (Shelley 1993, 38). During the creation scene itself Frankenstein describes how he 'collected the instruments of life around me, that I might infuse a spark of being into the lifeless thing that lay at my feet' (Shelley 1993, 38). In addition to this language, there is the formative memory of the tree destroyed by lightning; Professor Waldman's praise of man's power to 'command the thunders of heaven', which has been read as referring to Benjamin Franklin's electric kite; and the clear influence in the words of Waldman of Humphry Davy, who was best known by this time for his use of electro-chemical apparatus to isolate elements (Shelley 1993, 24, 30; see Crouch 1978).

Even Frankenstein's language when describing his Eureka moment – the moment when he realizes what the principle of life actually is – perhaps metaphorically suggests electricity:

> from the midst of this darkness a sudden light broke in upon me—a light so brilliant and wondrous, yet so simple, that while I became dizzy with the immensity of the prospect which it illustrated, I was surprised that among so many men of genius, who had directed their inquiries towards the same science, that I alone should be reserved to discover so astonishing a secret.
>
> (Shelley 1993, 34)

The surprise that Frankenstein voices here – that he should be the first to discover the principle of life when so many 'men of genius' have searched for it – fits one reading of him as an inept natural philosopher: according to Butler, 'Frankenstein the blundering experimenter, still working with superseded notions, shadows the intellectual position of Abernethy, who proposes that the superadded life-element is analogous to electricity' (Shelley 1993, xx–xxi). Naomi Hetherington likewise sees *Frankenstein* as 'a short satire of Abernethy's position, exposing it as nonsense. The being animated by the infusion of a "spark", apparently of electricity, is not human but a grotesque distortion of our form, which the humans in the story cannot acknowledge' (Hetherington 1997, 4). Such views can be heard in Ebenezer Cobham Brewer's 1870 edition of *Brewer's Phrase and Fable*, who also sees Frankenstein's creation, as, ultimately, a failure: 'It was only animal life, a parody on the creature man, powerful for evil, and the instrument of dreadful retribution on the student who usurped the prerogative of the creator' (quoted in Baldick 1987, 3). In these readings, Frankenstein's act of creation only achieves a non-life, with the Creature represented as a kind of automaton or imitation of human life. This belies the true achievement of Frankenstein though; no matter what the Creature looks like, he is a living, breathing, thinking, self-aware, and highly sensitive being.

The verbs that Frankenstein uses to describe his new found ability to create life betray his vitalism: he describes how he can 'bestow', 'endue', 'infuse', and 'give' life (Shelley 1993, 36, 37, 39, 40). In turn, the monster 'receives' life from his creator (Shelley 1993, 55). Once he has discovered the principle of life, Frankenstein is left with the problem of housing it. We are told that he was unable to use a corpse for this purpose, and accordingly he sets about making a body: 'to prepare a frame for the reception of it, with all its intricacies of fibres, muscles, and veins' (Shelley 1993, 35). Despite Frankenstein's mindfulness of its intricacies, the body is merely the receptacle of life, which is superadded to the frame that contains it. This confirms the identification of Frankenstein's science with Abernethy's vitalist notions. Butler argues that 'Lawrence's sceptical commentary on that position finds its echo in Mary Shelley's equally detached, serio-comic representation' (Shelley 1993, xxi). In other words, Victor represents a view that Shelley does not herself subscribe to. In a complex argument, according to Butler, we hear Lawrence in Shelley's silence.[36] The question remains over whether Frankenstein's creation is to be regarded as a successful achievement or a failure. His creation might be no more than an imitation life, not the true creation of an original composition, as Edward Young would have it.

The Creature is clearly categorized as a monster in the novel; indeed he identifies himself as such (Shelley 1993, 90, 96, 120). He has been created from human and animal body parts; he is 'gigantic'; and his limbs may not be in proportion (Shelley 1993, 37, 35, 186). He calls himself an 'abortion' and describes himself as 'hideously deformed' (Shelley 1993, 189, 96). He is physically repulsive to humans who cannot bear to look at him; his appearance instils fear, terror, and disgust in everyone who sees him. Despite this, it is still possible to see Frankenstein's creation as a successful achievement rather than as a defective imitation life created by an inept and ill-informed natural philosopher. For one thing, the Creature of the novel – not his counterpart in later multimedia spin-offs – is a complex, emotionally sophisticated, and verbally expressive being, far more complex than any animal known apart from man. Frankenstein had determined when planning his creation to 'give life to an animal as complex and wonderful as man' and it seems that he achieves this (Shelley 1993, 35). The Creature is capable of sympathy, love, hatred, moral reflection, and revenge. I have argued elsewhere that it is interesting to think of the Creature as a 'new species' of the *homo* genus rather than as a deformed man (Ruston 2012). He could be considered an advance on natural man, built to be stronger, faster, more capable of endurance – and a vegetarian. It is also possible to see no small degree of humanity in his expressed feelings and reflections. After Lawrence's and Geoffroy's work, the Creature could be thought of as existing on a continuum with the 'proper body', as Youngquist calls it; not so different from the 'norm' as might once have been thought and instead causing us to reflect upon our own potential degree of monstrosity in human society's treatment of him (Youngquist 2003, xiv; see also Cooper 2008).

There can surely be little disagreement on the question of whether the author's creation is successful given the life that the novel has continued to have in the popular consciousness, even while these appropriations are liberal with the source text. Chris Baldick's book, *In Frankenstein's Shadow*, uses the language of generation when it describes *Frankenstein* as an original myth rather than the reworking of an existing myth. Since its publication, *Frankenstein* has given birth to a multitude of reworkings and reinterpretations of itself. Baldick's language in describing this process is alive to the metaphorical potential:

> The vitality of myths lies precisely in their capacity for change, their adaptability and openness to new combinations of meaning. That series of adaptations, allusions, accretions, analogues, parodies, and plain misreadings which follows upon Mary Shelley's novel is not just a supplementary component of the myth; it *is* the myth.
>
> (Baldick 1987, 4)

Myths are here imagined as having lives of their own, and this life is typified by an ability to change, transform, adapt, and form new myths by combining with others. Baldick describes his book as 'a study of that process of adaptation, allusion, and revision by which a modern myth is born and sustains its life' (Baldick 1987, 9). He makes the point that the revisions and adaptations that the Frankenstein myth goes through (before the 'closure' of the myth in the form of Boris Karloff's definitive interpretation in 1931) typify the 'openness of literary revisions and allusions' to which any literary text is prone (Baldick 1987, 4, 5). The peculiar characteristic of the *Frankenstein* myth, though, is that the novel's narrative concerns the process of creation and generation and because of this particularly calls attention to it. Baldick sees the advent of the story as a result of the historical moment in which it is written: Shelley writes a myth of creation, he argues, because she lived in 'an age in which humanity seizes responsibility for re-creating the world, for violently reshaping its natural environment and its inherited social and political forms, for remaking itself' (Baldick 1987, 5). Similarly, Shelley lived at a time when the processes of creation were under scrutiny in the scientific world.

Finally, I want to examine further Shelley's language when she describes her creation all those years later in the introduction to the 1831 edition: she speaks of the idea that a creature might be 'manufactured', for example, and of her art as 'invention' (Shelley 1993, 196, 195). Many years have passed since Young's 1759 *Conjectures*, where he imagines genuine original literary composition as creating something from nothing. It is true that he is there describing poetry (and many of the authors I have used in this chapter have been writing specifically of poetry) whereas Shelley is writing about the creation of a novel, though I am not sure that Shelley is necessarily speaking specifically of the novel genre here. Shelley is also writing at a time of far more advanced industrialization. Her novel has been read in these terms as alive to a Marxist understanding of the nature of capital and property (Moretti 2005). It is also possible to read her description of literary creation as informed by science:

> Everything must have a beginning, to speak in Sanchean phrase; and that beginning must be linked to something that went before. The Hindoos give the world an elephant to support it, but they make the elephant stand upon a tortoise. Invention, it must be humbly admitted, does not consist in creating out of void, but out of chaos; the materials must, in the first place, be afforded: it can give form to dark, shapeless substances, but cannot bring into being the substance itself. In all matters of discovery and invention, even those that appertain to the imagination, we are continually reminded of the story of Columbus and his egg. Invention consists in the capacity of seizing on the capabilities of a subject: and in the power of moulding and fashioning ideas suggested to it.
>
> (Shelley 1993, 195)

Shelley confronts the eternal problem of imagining the origin of all things, and is clear that even at the beginning of one thing, there must be another that went before and that helped to create it. In fact, the new composition is created from materials already present. She alludes to the Hindu myth of the World Turtle – a myth used to explain the creation of the world – as an analogy for her description of her creation in the novel, and of literary creation in general. Editing Darwin, Priestman notes a similar predicament in Darwin's theory about the beginnings of the universe: '"Ere Time began" suggests the paradox — which still bedevils attempts to explain the "big bang" — of an initiating temporal event in a previously timeless context' (Darwin 2006, I, 227–50, n.). In other words, how can time begin in a world where time has not existed previously? Rob Pope begins his book *Creativity* with the words: 'Practically speaking, there is no "creation from nothing" (*ex nihilo*). There is always something "before the beginning", just as there is always something "after the end"' (Pope 2005, xv; see also 137). In this respect, Shelley's point is a very modern one. She notes that every moment of conception, such as the beginning of an idea for a novel, is not only a beginning but also a summation of what had gone before.

In his 1794–96 *Zoonomia*, Darwin uses very similar language to Shelley's 1831 introduction:

> Invention is an operation of the sensorium, by which we voluntarily continue to excite one train of ideas, suppose the design of raising water by a machine; and at the same time attend to all other ideas, which are connected with this by every kind of catenation; and combine or separate them voluntarily for the purpose of obtaining some end.
>
> For we can create nothing new, we can only combine or separate the ideas, which we have already received by our perceptions: thus if I wish to represent a monster, I call to mind the ideas of every thing disagreeable and horrible, and combine the nastiness and gluttony of a hog, the stupidity and obstinacy of an ass, with the fur and awkwardness of a bear, and call the new combination Caliban. Yet such a monster may exist in nature, as all his attributes are parts of nature.
> (Darwin 1794–96, I, 132)

The example that Darwin gives for 'invention' is a scientific one, the use of technology to raise water. This may allude to a particular definition of invention as a specifically scientific device or contrivance where claim to having invented it is important because of patent issues. He defines invention as a particular process of the brain whereby we concentrate on one project but at the same time consider other ideas, which are connected in a kind of chain with our main project, and 'combine or separate' these in order to achieve our aim. His language here is reminiscent of chemistry with its interest in combining and separating elements, and it is perhaps unsurprising that the term 'catenation' is taken up by chemistry to describe the chains of carbon atoms to form elements such as Benzene. Rob Pope reflects on the differences George Steiner perceives between creation and invention as 'between competing, but also potentially complementary world-views: with science dedicated to "discovery" and technology to "invention", while religion, mythology and the arts are concerned with "creation"' (Pope 2005, 30). While this is a modern view, there is also clearly some sense of these differentiations of meaning in history too.

Denying that anything can be created which is new and has had no existence in any form before, Darwin writes that all invention occurs through this process of combining and separating already known elements into new arrangements. The next example he gives is of the representation of a monster, which, if he wishes to invent such a creature, will consist of many parts of his former recollections of and associations with monsters. It will itself be a monstrous combination formed of the characteristics of different kinds of animals with the addition of a literary reference to Shakespeare's Caliban. Darwin then claims that this monster is not new in the sense that it has never existed before because all of its parts have come from nature itself.

Shelley could be using the term 'invention' to apply specifically to literary invention. Definition 3b in the *OED* refers specifically to 'art and literary composition: The devising of a subject, idea, or method of treatment, by exercise of the intellect or imagination.' In other words, invention is the moment when the writer has thought of a subject for their composition: accordingly, in 1667 Dryden writes that 'The first happiness of the Poet's imagination is properly Invention, or finding of the thought' (*OED*). This certainly works with Shelley's use of the term because in the paragraph previous to this she has been recalling the difficulty she had in coming up with a ghost story for the competition: 'I felt that blank incapability of invention which is the greatest misery of authorship' (Shelley 1993, 195). Invention also of course means to make something up, or to fabricate, which is particularly apt when speaking of literary fiction though even in these terms there is a sense of technology at work.

The reference seems also to allude to an older sense of invention as, in Rob Pope's words: '"finding or discovering what already exists" rather than, as now, "making or bringing into being what never before existed" (cf. *OED* "invention" senses 1 and 3)' (Pope 2005, 63). This is reminiscent of Percy Shelley's comment in the 'Preface' to *Prometheus Unbound*: 'The mass of capabilities remains at every period materially the same; the circumstances which awaken it to action perpetually change' (Shelley 2003, 231). In other words, the capacity is always there to produce great art but for Percy Shelley, the stimulus comes with specific historical and political events. Mary Shelley seems also to be alluding to this idea in her reference to the story of Columbus and his egg. The point of the story is that the Americas were always there to be discovered, and discovery of them seemed easy after the fact, but this was only because Columbus had shown people where they were. Using this analogy, Shelley does not deny herself genius but redefines it. She writes that the key is recognizing opportunities to be exploited: 'Invention consists in the capacity of seizing on the capabilities of a subject: and in the power of moulding and fashioning ideas suggested to it' (Shelley 1993, 195). In this formulation, literary genius is made not born (invented not created); it does not give birth to the idea but moulds, fashions, or gives form to the substance, which is always already present. Given the significance of criticism that reads Shelley's novel in the light of her personal issues as a mother, it is striking to read her remark that the author 'cannot bring into being the substance itself' (see Moers 1976). The metaphors used to describe the process of literary composition are radically different to those examined in this chapter from the eighteenth century. While this difference may be partly due to the individual circumstances of the particular author writing, there has also been a substantial change in the way biological creation has been thought to take place.

In Young's *Conjectures*, he speaks of an original composition as something that '*grows*, it is not *made*' and in *Frankenstein* we have a Creature who is made rather than naturally born and who suffers as a consequence ([Young] 1759, 12). Young writes that '*Imitations* are often a sort of *manufacture* wrought up by those *mechanics, art,* and *labour*, out of pre-existent materials not their own' ([Young] 1759, 12). In her 1831 introduction to the novel, Shelley confronts this position and argues that all literary creation is the result of labour, and all is 'wrought' from materials already in existence. She does not deny the work involved in the task nor the originality of the conception that results. It is easy to see how an egg might be made to stand on its tip once you have seen someone do it but the brilliance of the idea is none the less for that. The shift that can be perceived in the way that things are thought to come into being – from creation to invention – can be witnessed when comparing Young's and Shelley's statements. In the next chapter I examine Humphry Davy's use of the idea of the sublime, which he borrows from aesthetics and philosophy to apply to chemistry, to describe the discipline just emerging at this time but which promised great things. The study of the transformation of matter between states while it retained its chemical properties, was nothing short of sublime to Davy, the chemist and poet.

4
Humphry Davy and the Sublime

This chapter explores the poetry and the science of the chemist Humphry Davy and his fascination with the sublime. In the work of Davy during and beyond the 1790s there is a special relationship between poetry and chemistry. When Coleridge asks 'What is poetry?' and 'what is a poet?' in his *Biographia Literaria* he uses a number of terms in his answer to this question that are to be found in contemporary chemistry and which may well be the result of his earlier connection with Davy (*Biographia*, VII; II, 15). Specifically, Coleridge uses the word 'sublime' as a verb in *Biographia* to describe the poetic imagination, making reference to the chemical process of sublimation. Chemical metaphors help Coleridge to define his understanding of poetry. His friend Humphry Davy, poet and chemist, similarly sees a connection, using the aesthetic category of the 'sublime' as an adjective to describe the discipline of chemistry itself. Davy appropriates the sublime for science in this period because of its association with grandeur, awe, power, and for the role played by the imagination, fear, and pleasure.

This chapter argues that the Romantic-era concept of the sublime was a product of medical and scientific thought as well as literary and aesthetic thought, and that it was appropriated by natural philosophers for their own purposes. The sublime had worrying implications: it might imply a world with or without God, a world that may or may not have been designed intentionally. The possible, alternative interpretations of the sublime experience – whether it was an experience that was contained within the body or an experience that went beyond the self and transcended the body – connected with the very current debate about the relationship of the mind and the self to the body and their possible interdependence (see Richardson 2001). This debate in turn was linked to materialist and atheistic views. Davy's early notebooks show that the young Davy flirted with materialism but by 1802, when he had been appointed to the Royal Institution, and even though his sublime experiments suggested that the mind could be controlled by substances such as nitrous oxide, he stated his political allegiance categorically, declaring that he 'will uniformly appear as the friend of tranquillity and order' in unsettled political times (*Collected Works*, II, 326). It has long been understood that the sublime is a cultural category, historically contingent and intimately connected to contemporary political events and issues of gender; Davy's use of the sublime confirms the idea that science is not immune to the cultural weight of meaning when it uses and appropriates such a term for its own ends.

Coleridge's answers to his own questions, 'What is poetry?' and 'what is a poet?', are to be found, he writes, in 'poetic genius itself, which sustains and modifies the images, thoughts, and emotions of the poet's own mind' (*Biographia*, VII; II, 15). In other words, poetic genius acts upon the products of the poet's mind and it both 'sustains' (as in keeps them alive, perhaps) and 'modifies' (alters, adapts, or transforms) them. Coleridge continues with his description of the poet thus: 'He diffuses a tone, and spirit of unity, that blends, and (as it were) *fuses*, each into each, by that synthetic and magical power, to which we have exclusively appropriated the name of imagination' (*Biographia*, II, 15, 16). Coleridge is using words that have specific resonance with chemistry: the imagination is here described as a power that has the ability to transform 'a tone, a spirit of unity' through the medium of poetry into something different.[1] This is perhaps an example of Coleridge having increased his 'stock of metaphors' by attending Davy's 1802 chemistry lectures (Paris 1831, 92). More than this though, I want to argue here that literature and chemistry have particular potential for symbiosis during the Romantic period because of contemporaries' claims for their respective power to transform. For Coleridge, poetry has the power to transform and for Davy, chemistry has this power.

Below, I look at Coleridge's use of sublimation to describe the poetic imagination, considering it as a modifying principle that changes one thing into another, especially, the images in the poet's mind into poetry. This is followed, in Section 4.1, with an exploration of the role that scientific and medical thought had on the development of the aesthetic of the sublime in this period. I examine Edmund Burke's use of medical knowledge and scientific methodology in his efforts to produce an exact theory of the laws and fixed principles that govern our passions. His particular attention to the role of the body in the experience of the sublime is explored, as is his idea that the mind is affected through the means of the body. Joseph Priestley's concept of the 'sublime of science' is of particular relevance to Davy, and I look at the way in which Priestley uses what he calls 'corporeal' metaphors to describe non-material things as sublime. For Priestley the power of the sublime lies not in the natural object itself but in the words used to describe it; for Kant, the sublime resides in the perceiving object. Davy's own sense of the sublime does not subscribe to the annihilation of the self in the sublime experience that we find in Burke but to the transcendent, exalted, and superior self that we find in Kant. The emphasis on reason and the superiority of man over nature can also be seen in Davy's use of the term. It is helpful to use the theories of Burke, Priestley, and Kant to explore how Davy understood the term himself. Ultimately, Davy's sublime is his own concept, and I have found perhaps surprising consistency in the way he uses the idea in his poetry. Though I concentrate on poetry written in the 1790s, I supplement this with relevant later poetry, which confirms his lifelong fascination with the sublime. Davy's sublime is distinct from the beautiful and expressed in the same gendered language that we find in Burke; it is also figured as a violent jolt to the system, which enables the higher thinking needed by both poets and natural philosophers. The sublime is experienced in the body but it transports its subject beyond the body, though not necessarily beyond the self. Davy's masculine sublime is superior to nature, an experience that exalts and enlarges him: he becomes himself sublime.

From his earliest publication in 1799, Davy reveals that he thinks the 'motions of matter', the way that matter changes into other states and other forms, the most 'sublime' idea of all (*Collected Works*, II, 29, n.). In 1807, he repeats an idea he has voiced many times before, that it is these 'continual transmutations and changes of external objects' that occupy the attention of chemistry: 'The variety of the forms of things, their unceasing modifications, but, for chemistry, would be unintelligible enigmas.'[2] Again in *Elements of Chemical Philosophy* (1812) he reiterates the point that 'Most of the substances belonging to our globe are constantly undergoing alterations in sensible qualities, and one variety of matter becomes as it were transmuted into another.' He adds that 'The object of Chemical Philosophy is to ascertain the causes of all phenomena of this kind, and to discover the laws by which they are governed' (*Collected Works*, IV, 1). Such sentiments can be found throughout Davy's career. It seems clear through his writings and his poetry that Davy thinks there is a modifying principle in living matter, which might also be called a principle of life, and that is the most sublime idea that he can imagine. There is evidence, particularly early in his career, that Davy is in fact searching for this modifying principle and that light, heat, and electricity – which were commonly thought of as modifications of a single principle at this time – are strong contenders. For Coleridge, the imagination is another such modifying principle and the process of sublimation is used to describe its power to transform. Modifying principles, whether electricity or the imagination, have the power to transform one thing into another. Chemistry, then, is the study of this sublime process but is also itself sublime; chemistry has the power to modify elements and forms, to make solids into gases or to reveal new elements through a chemical process (such as galvanism) and it is for this reason that for Davy it is a sublime science. This chapter, overall, considers Davy's developing Romantic sentiment and the importance of the sublime to this as witnessed in his letters, notebooks, and publications of the period 1796–1802.[3] The final section looks at Davy's use of the sublime in his earliest scientific writings, in his nitrous oxide experiments, and in his bombastic *Discourse, Introductory to a Course of Lectures*, published by Johnson in 1802.[4] I find that during these years he is consistent in his search for the 'laws of life', the 'active powers' inherent in all matter, which are themselves sublime.

Before moving on to Davy, then, I briefly explore Coleridge's unusual and suggestive use of chemical terms, particularly the idea of sublimation in his *Biographia Literaria*. Though the *Biographia* was not published until 1817 it reflects upon earlier times and influences, and Coleridge's most sustained period of interest in chemistry must surely have been the years of his friendship with Davy, including particularly his participation in the Bristol circle in 1799 and his attendance at Davy's 1802 lectures in London. The many pages of notes that Coleridge took at these lectures are thorough and detailed (Coleridge 1957–2002, I, 1098, 1099). He often notes how to do experiments, with the suggestion that he may have had thoughts of doing these himself: 'N.B. Be sure to hold your face close to the glass' (Coleridge 1957–2002, I, 1099*f*31^{v}). He records who discovered the gases oxygen (Priestley), hydrogen (Cavendish), and nitrogen (Rutherford) and notes some of the practical uses of the information he is given, such as a substance that can be used for 'whitening Prints & old Books' and another for 'fumigating putrid rooms' (Coleridge 1957–2002, I, 1098*f*30, 1098*f*30^{v}). Some of his notes have specific connections to Davy's research at this time, such as that 'Silver and Platina', though they will not burn, 'are however combustible if a power sufficiently strong be applied; & this power exists in Galvanic Electricity' (Coleridge 1957–2002, I, 1098*f*14). Coleridge devotes a good deal of space to writing about the various combinations of and ways to procure nitrous gases, such as nitrous acid gas and 'Nitrous Oxyd' (Coleridge 1957–2002, I, 1098*f*25ᵛ).

There are a few lovely descriptions, such as how ether burns, 'but o! how brightly whitely vividly beautiful in Oxygen gas' (Coleridge 1957–2002, I, 1098*f*5), which clearly demonstrate Coleridge's interest and excitement in the lecture; for example, on the detonation of hydrogen he writes: 'Hold the Cannon over the Bottle containing Hydrogen Gas—applied a Leyden Phial to it—*bang!*' (Coleridge 1957–2002, I, 1098*f*8ᵛ). Coleridge also makes a sly political reference that reminds us of his political affiliations at this point in time: 'If all aristocrats here, how easily Davy might poison them all' (Coleridge 1957–2002, I, 1098*f*31). It is possible roughly to follow Coleridge's attendance at the course of lectures by means of Davy's *A Syllabus of a Course of Lectures on Chemistry* (1802), though the *Syllabus* does not clearly divide its text into individual lectures (Davy 1802).[5] Coleridge's notes do give a real sense of the lectures though, and show particular interest in the colours and qualities of elements when they burn, how to procure different gases, and, often at the beginning of the notes offer a description accompanied by an '*Exper.*' that will detail the experiment to use to achieve the effect Davy is describing. The first lecture of this course Davy published as *Discourse, Introductory to a Course of Lectures*, which I will return to at the end of this chapter and which was also discussed in the Introduction.

It is likely then, perhaps, that Coleridge's knowledge of chemistry came from his early friendship with Davy. In the quotation given from the *Biographia Literaria* above, Coleridge mentions the action of fusing, which is found in a number of contemporary manuals of chemistry, and is often specifically used to describe the action of fusing metals. Davy uses the word himself on many occasions in his published works on chemistry; indeed he uses this term in his account of one of his most famous experiments – the isolation of potassium. In the course of this experiment, Davy describes how 'a vivid action was soon observed to take place. The potash began to fuse at both its points of electrization' (*Collected Works*, V, 60). According to his brother and biographer, John Davy, the resulting globules of potassium that were produced made Davy bound 'about the room in extatic [*sic*] delight' (*Collected Works*, I, 109). While the word 'fuse', it may be argued, is pretty common – perhaps Coleridge was not necessarily using it with specific reference to chemistry – the word 'synthetic' is more obviously a word used with specific scientific connotations. Again, Davy uses this word repeatedly in his published works and explains in his *Elements of Chemical Philosophy* that when elements are fused together this is a 'synthetical experiment', meaning that bodies are brought together and unified (*Collected Works*, IV, 133). Coleridge had used these terms previously; in a fragmentary note dated May–June 1812, he states 'Imagination is the synthetic Power', which modifies and fuses (Coleridge 1995, I, 289; see Duff 2009, 177 and Levere 1981, 29). On 4 May 1801, Coleridge wrote to Davy that he felt relatively confident using some chemical terms: 'As far as *words* go, I have become a formidable chemist—having got by heart a prodigious quantity of terms &c to which I attach *some* ideas' (*Coleridge Letters*, II, 727).

In Coleridge's account of poetry, the elements that are blended and harmonized in the poetical process are opposites, such as 'the general, with the concrete; the idea, with the image' and so on (*Biographia*, II, 17). Coleridge then quotes, or, rather, misquotes, a poem written by Sir John Davies published in 1599, which is addressed to the soul. In *Biographia* Coleridge applies the poem instead to the 'poetic IMAGINATION' (*Biographia*, II, 17). Coleridge uses it to describe the transformative power of the poetic imagination, which is enabled by means of a process akin to a chemical process. Davies's poem uses chemical, or perhaps given its historical context, alchemical terms:

> Doubtless this could not be, but that she turns
> Bodies to spirit by sublimation strange,
> As fire converts to fire the things it burns,
> As we our food into our nature change.
>
> From their gross matter she abstracts their forms,
> And draws a kind of quintessence from things;
> Which to her proper nature she transforms
> To bear them light, on her celestial wings.
>
> Thus does she, when from individual states
> She doth abstract the universal kinds;
> Which then re-clothed in divers names and fates
> Steal access through our senses to our minds.
>
> (*Biographia*, II, 17)

Coleridge almost entirely rewrites the third stanza of this quotation when he, 'with slight alteration', applies them to the poetic imagination (*Biographia*, II, 17; Davies 1599, 24). The word sublimation means here: 'The chemical action or process of subliming or converting a solid substance by means of heat into vapour, which resolidifies on cooling'

(*OED*). William Nicholson, in his *First Principles of Chemistry*, describes the process of sublimation thus: 'In the distillation of such bodies as are solid, in the usual temperature of the atmosphere, the vapours are scarcely condensed before they become solid' (Nicholson 1790, 34). Sublimation is a noun formed from the verb 'to sublime', which is itself transitive, meaning that it needs a direct object. Even this rule enacts the process being described, elements must be 'sublimed' to or from or with something else. The action is one of transmutation, a chemical change from one thing to another. This, then, according to Coleridge is what the poetic imagination does. This capacity appears elsewhere in Coleridge's description of the secondary, poetic imagination, such as when he describes the 'activity of the assimilative and of the modifying faculties' of Shakespeare's imagination (*Biographia*, II, 26).

In another passage in *Biographia*, this time taken from Milton's *Paradise Lost*, we see these chemical metaphors being used again. For Coleridge, sublimation is a useful concept to describe what the poetic imagination does. Coleridge quotes Milton as an epigraph at the beginning of chapter thirteen of *Biographia*. This chapter is concerned with 'the imagination, or esemplastic power' and presumably Coleridge feels that the quotation illustrates this:

> O Adam, One Almighty is, from whom
> All things proceed, and up to him return,
> If not deprav'd from good, created all
> Such to perfection, one first matter all,
> Endued with various forms, various degrees
> Of substance, and, in things that live, of life;
> But more refin'd, more spiritous and pure,
> As nearer to him plac'd, or nearer tending,
> Each in their several active spheres assign'd,
> Till body up to spirit work, in bounds
> Proportion'd to each kind. So from the root
> Springs lighter the green stalk, from thence the leaves
> More aery: last the bright consummate flower
> Spirits odorous breathes: flowers and their fruit,
> Man's nourishment, by gradual scale sublim'd,
> To vital spirits aspire: to animal:
> To intellectual![6]

In this passage, the archangel Raphael explains to Adam that all matter ('all things') come from and return to God. God is, therefore, the unity of all things although there is a variety in the forms of things created from this single unity. Some of these forms have life and some have more 'substance' than others, which seems to mean that they have more or less heavy bodies. The next line further explicates this, the closer that beings are to God, the more 'refined' they are, the 'more spirituous and pure'. This might remind us of chemical or industrial processes by which elements are purified; I think Milton refers to both senses, the moral and the physical.

Milton speaks of differently assigned spheres with heavier, material bodies on earth giving way to spiritual, immaterial bodies the closer one gets to heaven. He likens this to the physical appearance of the flower, with the heavy root planted in the earth, giving way to the lighter stalk, which in turn gives way to the leaves, the flower, and finally the scent of the flower, which is entirely immaterial. In the 'Chain of Being', he tells us that animals, and then intellectual beings, in the same kind of trajectory, succeed flowers and fruit. Flowers and their fruit are 'by gradual scale sublim'd' to these other more complex beings. Here the verb 'to sublime' does not simply mean a transmutation but also the 'Elevation to a higher state or plane of existence; transmutation into something higher, purer, or more sublime' (*OED*). Coleridge's application of this term to the poetic imagination may incorporate this: the poet does not simply change his ideas into another form, he raises and elevates them in the process. It is surely significant that Coleridge chooses sublimation rather than other possible chemical processes; the movement from solid to gas is a movement from gross, inert matter to ethereal spirit. The poetic imagination, then, also purifies and reifies in this process.

Stuart Sperry writes that Keats imagines poetic process as a sublimation or distillation in the same manner. Using, for the main part, Davy's chemical publications to show that words such as 'sublime' had 'more or less exact meanings in the chemistry of his day', Sperry argues that for Keats, poetry can 'distill higher or ideal elements that transcend the limited aspects of any particular stage of human experience' (Sperry 1973, 37, 46). Sperry argues that Keats uses this chemical metaphor to describe what happens in the poetic process: 'poetry can be said to operate through the laws by which the mind, and more especially the imagination, assimilates and transmutes the impressions it derives from nature' (Sperry 1973, 41). He expressly likens this to Davy's sense of the natural world as 'constantly' transmuting one variety of matter into another (Sperry 1973, 41). Jennifer Wunder expands this to consider alchemical processes and she also finds that 'the natural wonders that

Keats describes and the nightingale who sings of golden histories and mysteries are located in Elysian realms where nature has been refined to a sublime state' (Wunder 2008, 74). For Coleridge too, sublimation offered a useful metaphor for the way that the poet modified the external natural world and transformed it into something else. The process of sublimation is only one of the many ways in which matter can be transformed from one form into another; often such processes involve heat and one of Davy's greatest contributions to science was in realizing the potential of electricity to do the same. As I will explore later in this chapter, the mutability of matter through such processes as sublimation was a truly sublime idea for Davy.

In the next section of this chapter I look at ideas of the sublime in the writing of Burke, Priestley, and Kant, particularly in relation to the influence of science and medicine upon their formulations. I then turn to Davy himself, to see what he means by the term 'sublime' in his poetry and letters, before examining his application of this term to science itself. As one would expect, Davy refers often to the chemical process of sublimation in his letters and scientific writings, but he does not use the word metaphorically in the way that Coleridge does.[7] He does, though, apply the language of the sublime to his chemical pursuits, in particular his nitrous oxide experiments. Breathing nitrous oxide was described in a multitude of ways as a sublime experience: as an experience that was beyond language, as something that transported him beyond his self, as an encounter with power, and as a form of spectacle. The sublime is one of Davy's favourite tropes in his poetry but its appearance in his scientific writings and his appropriation of this idea, taken from literature and aesthetics and applied to chemistry, shows the imagination at work in scientific endeavour.

4.1 Science and the sublime

In this section I argue that Romantic-era concepts of the sublime might be thought of as a product of philosophy, aesthetics, literature, medicine, and science, or as a nexus where these perspectives come together. I begin with Burke in his *Philosophical Enquiry* (1757), the most important text for the British Romantic sublime.[8] Burke attempts a kind of scientific theory of the sublime and the beautiful, and identifies and is wary of the methodological pressures and challenges experienced by Newton in his scientific writings (Burke 1998, 64). Burke sets out to discover whether another law like those laws discovered by Newton regulated the passions.[9] This aspect of Burke was recognized by Coleridge, who calls him a '*scientific* statesman': one who 'sees all things, actions, and events, in relation to the *laws* that determine their existence and circumscribe their possibility. He referred habitually to *principles*' (*Biographia*, I, 191). The *Philosophical Enquiry* discusses the bodily experience of the sublime, and details the physical effects that terror has upon the body. While he is not to be drawn into the contemporary physiological debate about whether these effects are the result of the nerves contracting or tensing, Burke is clear that the sublime demonstrates that the mind and body are intimately connected (Burke 1998, 120–1). Davy's sublime seems indebted to Burke for a number of reasons. Davy accepts Burke's distinction between the sublime and the beautiful and uses Burke's gendered language to describe these. More interesting for the purposes of this book, Davy, like Burke, also imagines the sublime as a bodily experience.

Burke tells the reader in his original 'Preface' to the *Philosophical Enquiry* that he felt the need to write this work because despite having thought for some time on this subject he still had nothing like 'an exact theory of our passions' (Burke 1998, 1). He wished to be able to 'reduce his notions to [...] fixed or consistent principles' but hitherto had been unable to do so (Burke 1998, 1). The implication then is that this treatise will present his particular 'exact theory', based on 'fixed and consistent principles'. He expresses his determination to untangle the sublime and the beautiful through a 'diligent examination' of our passions, a 'careful survey' of the properties of those things that excite our passions, 'from a sober and attentive investigation of the laws of nature' by which these properties are able to affect the body and thus excite our passions (Burke 1998, 1). From the outset, then, his language suggests a methodical approach that might be considered 'scientific' and makes it clear that he thinks that regular and universal laws inform the reason why our bodies are affected in this way. From the outset, the body's experience of the sublime is given importance. In addition, he hopes by his enquiry to deduce 'rules' that can then be applied to the 'imitative arts' or any other field to explain how the sublime works.

Burke's *Enquiry* claims to use scientific methodologies. In the 'Preface' to the second edition, he tells the reader that his is a 'theory founded on experiment and not assumed' (Burke 1998, 5). Critics have commented upon Burke's specifically empirical mode of approach: Philip Shaw points out that one reason for Burke's particular interest in the body and in the 'observable effects' of the sublime is his 'instinctive empiricism' (Shaw 2006, 53). Burke discusses his choice of method a number of times in the *Philosophical Enquiry*. For example, when presenting his observations on the physical effects of love, Burke reveals that he is using inductive reasoning although he does not call it this. He refers instead to Newton's 'judicious rule laid down [...] in the third book of his Optics' (Burke 1998, 136). Clearly following Newton's inductive method, Burke allows that 'some odd and particular instance' might be found that contradicts his observation, but notes that even if this should occur his more general conclusion may still be found to stand with the recognition of this exception. Earlier Burke had expressed his disappointment with Newton because in later life the natural philosopher had attempted to trace the cause of gravity rather than be content with describing its effects. When Newton 'quitted his usual cautious manner of philosophising' and speculated that gravity was the result of a 'subtle elastic æther', he went beyond what Burke considered the proper realm of investigation (Burke 1998, 117). We should not, in Burke's words, go 'beyond the immediately sensible qualities of things', or, in other words, we should not venture beyond what we can see and experience empirically (Burke 1998, 117). These methodologies are those most commonly associated with Bacon and Newton.

Continuing to justify his choice of method, Burke informs the reader that he thinks his 'method of investigation' is best because rather than presenting 'a few barren and lifeless truths' it leads the reader to investigate for themselves the 'stock' upon which these truths were grown (Burke 1998, 12). This method encourages the reader to pursue his or her own 'track of invention' and to follow the paths by which 'the author has made his own discoveries' (Burke 1998, 12, 13). His language is one we might now consider to be scientific, particularly since his express aim is to discover the 'principles' upon which taste works. He makes the argument that taste, like truth and falsehood, is fixed and universal; the reason he gives for this is because 'the conformation of their organs are nearly, or altogether the same in all men' (Burke 1998, 11, 13). In other words, since our organs of sense are pretty much the same, we will experience the world in the same way. For Burke, taste is instinctive though it can vary in degree according to how much 'natural sensibility' a person possesses (Burke 1998, 21). Taste can be vitiated though, for example by alcohol or drugs (Burke 1998, 14–16). It is also possible to cultivate taste beyond its natural and instinctive capacity (Burke 1998, 25). So, taste is something we are born with which is affected by the way that we treat our bodies, though we can also learn to improve it. Burke believes that in the same way as taste has 'fixed principles' so the imagination is affected 'according to some invariable and certain laws', and if this were not the case there would be no point to his *Philosophical Enquiry* (Burke 1998, 12). He is convinced that passions such as 'Love, grief, fear, anger, joy [...] do not affect [the mind] in an arbitrary or casual manner, but upon certain, natural and uniform principles' (Burke 1998, 22). His undertaking in this text is to discover these principles or laws, not to enquire into the causes of them, but to describe them and examine their effects. This is obviously an Enlightenment endeavour: the search for laws and truth in human nature that we have seen in Wollstonecraft, Godwin, and Wordsworth, and here in Burke, is paralleled by Davy's scientific efforts to find the same in the natural world.

Perhaps surprisingly for a book on aesthetics, Burke's *Enquiry* devotes much space to the body, sometimes considering it in extreme physical conditions. These sections clearly demonstrate Burke's medical knowledge.[10] Having already established the close resemblance between terror and pain in Part Two, Burke decides to 'explain the nature' of pain in Part Four and he does so by describing the physical symptoms of a 'man in great pain' (Burke 1998, 53, 119). The man who 'suffers under violent bodily pain':

> has his teeth set, his eye-brows are violently contracted, his forehead is wrinkled, his eyes are dragged inwards, and rolled with great vehemence, his hair stands on end, the voice is forced out in short shrieks and groans, and the whole fabric totters.
>
> (Burke 1998, 119)

Burke seems to suggest here that these are the universal expressions of pain, and he writes of them as effects rather than as symptoms of pain. Burke goes on to claim that 'Fear or terror' (clearly counting these as a single item by the grammar of his sentence) 'exhibits exactly the same effects' as pain (Burke 1998, 119). In his language, then, fear is one and the same thing as terror; and both fear and terror are simply the 'apprehension of pain or death' rather than the experience of pain itself. For these reasons, fear of pain evinces 'exactly the same effects' as does pain. In Burke's theory, then, mental states evoke physical effects that are the same as those evoked by bodily states. Vanessa Ryan has commented on what she calls Burke's 'physiologism' noting that his text is 'remarkable for its emphasis on the physiological aspects of experience' (Ryan 2001, 269). For her, it is Burke's move 'to derive the mental reaction from the physical rather than the reverse', which reduces 'the role of conscious and reflective mental activity', that makes his theory different from both contemporary associationist views and Kant's idea of the sublime

(Ryan 2001, 269, 270). Alan Richardson also discovers that 'at least one Romantic version of the sublime can best be understood not in relation to Kantian notions of transcendence but to a materialist, brain-based conception of mind' (Richardson 2010, 12). This he calls the 'neural sublime', finding examples in Burke, Shelley, Wordsworth, and Keats. Theirs is 'a nontranscendent or even anti-transcendent sublime', which rather than offering us a glimpse into the Kantian supersensible realm shows us what our ordinary brains can do (Richardson 2010, 13, 34). Both critics, while they emphasize different characteristics of Burke's sublime – physiological and neural – are alive to its particularly material nature.

Burke's universalizing drive to discover a law of nature that explains the sublime experience leads him to claim that it is not only the case that the whole 'human race' exhibits the same symptoms when experiencing fear or terror, he even witnesses similar effects in dogs (Burke 1998, 119). This leads him to conclude generally that pain and fear 'act upon the same parts of the body, and in the same manner, though somewhat differing in degree' in all living creatures (Burke 1998, 119). Specifically, pain and fear act upon the nerves; they 'consist in an unnatural tension of the nerves' and this is the cause of the effects witnessed (Burke 1998, 119). While he acknowledges that there is a difference in degree between the effects of pain and fear or terror, he also notes that they operate in slightly different ways. The 'things which cause pain operate on the mind, by the intervention of the body', whereas, the 'things that cause terror' affect the 'bodily organs by the operation of the mind suggesting the danger' (Burke 1998, 120). In other words, pain works on the body and affects the mind through means of the body, whereas terror works on the mind and affects the body through means of the mind or the imagination. The symptoms described above are immediate for the victim of pain, whereas a person in terror has these bodily symptoms because the mind has suggested that he or she may be in imminent danger. Davy's nitrous oxide experiments seem to validate Burke's idea.

The larger point being made by Burke, which is also something that Davy sets out to explore in his nitrous oxide experiments, is that our minds and bodies are 'closely and intimately connected' (Burke 1998, 121). Though Burke concedes in a footnote that he does not intend to enter into contemporary physiological debates concerning whether pain is the effect of a tensing or a contraction of the nerve, finding these ideas equally fit for his purpose, he usually prefers the term and action of tension in the nerves in the *Enquiry*.[11] He describes, for example, how terror produces 'an unnatural tension' in the nerves but argues that in general a certain degree of this tension is necessary for good health (Burke 1998, 121). Rest and indolence, conversely, are bad for one's health. Labour is essential, Burke argues, to keep our bodies in good order. States of relaxation bring on such moods as 'Melancholy, dejection, despair' and even thoughts of 'self-murder' (Burke 1998, 122). Later in *Philosophical Enquiry* the physical effects of love are described in a similar manner; one's posture, carriage and bearing is characterized by a relaxed languor (Burke 1998, 135–6). Beauty, which gives us pleasure, also acts in this way upon our bodies, 'by relaxing the solids of the whole system' (Burke 1998, 136). Again, these symptoms of love are universal, 'common in all times and in all countries', and consist in 'being softened, relaxed, enervated, dissolved, melted away' (Burke 1998, 136). It seems, then, that being in love is bad for one's health. Shaw has noted how in passages such as this, 'Burke's masculinity is thus shown to be constantly at the mercy of feminine stupefaction' (Shaw 2006, 61). Burke's characterization of these states is a thinly veiled censuring of women's behaviour. Again, I am particularly interested in the distinctly physiological description of these emotional states; Burke's masculine sublime has a violent, bracing effect upon the body, whereas the experience of feminine beauty is of a lethargic, unhealthy condition. Davy genders these categories in the same way and also represents the masculine sublime as a kind of physiological awakening from a pleasurable but relaxed state.

Burke imagines the sublime as a kind of therapy and describes it in medical terms. The sublime is like physical labour and does the work that labour does for the body's general health. The body needs labour, Burke claims, because when it falls into a state of relaxation the nerves are not able to perform their usual office; nerves no longer have 'the vigorous tone of fibre which is requisite for carrying on the natural and necessary secretions' (Burke 1998, 122). Burke here is repeating the advice of George Cheyne in his *Essay on Health and Long Life* (1724): exercise is 'absolutely necessary' to keep the Fibres in 'due *Tension*'.[12] 'Labour' is one of the key elements of good health according to Cheyne (Cheyne 1724, 20). Also according to Cheyne, 'a *Relaxation, Weakness,* and *want of Spring* in the *Fibres,* is the *Origin* of all *nervous* Distempers' (Cheyne 1724, 117). It may even be the case that the closeness Burke finds between fear and terror comes from Cheyne who describes the physical effects of anxiety, concern, and fear, in much the same way: for example, 'the Hair stands on end in a *Fright,* and the whole *System* of the Nerves becomes so *rigid* and *stiff,* as to lose their *Elasticity*' (Cheyne

1724, 155).[13] In Burke, the nerves need to be 'sufficiently braced and strengthened', which is not the case while the person is in a 'languid inactive state' (Burke 1998, 122). The best means to do this is through 'exercise or *labour*' (Burke 1998, 122). Labour is characterized as 'an exertion of the contracting power of the muscles' and therefore it 'resembles pain, which consists in tension and contraction'; in other words, labour and pain operate in the same manner but differ in the degree to which they act (Burke 1998, 122). Burke tells the reader that labour is important not only for 'the coarser organs' but also for the 'finer and more delicate organs' which are needed for the imagination (Burke 1998, 122). He proves this by describing how mental exertion 'induces a remarkable lassitude of the whole body' and how, on the other hand, 'great bodily labour, or pain, weakens, and sometimes actually destroys the mental faculties' (Burke 1998, 123).

Burke believes that these 'finer parts' of the body, so crucial for the imagination and other mental faculties, need to be exercised in exactly the same way as the body: 'to have them in proper order, they must be shaken and worked to a proper degree' (Burke 1998, 123). While Burke represents the sublime as a kind of paralysis of the mind, producing astonishment and suspending the faculty of reason, it is simultaneously a violent attack on the body (Burke 1998, 53). It might be compared to a kind of purgative, or some other violent intervention, shocking the lethargic body and re-regulating it. Terror is the means by which to achieve this much needed shock, and Burke tells the reader that terror offers equivalent exercise for 'the finer parts of the system' as 'common labour' does for the 'grosser' parts of the body (Burke 1998, 123). Befitting the idea of the sublime as a kind of laxative, Burke writes that terror can 'clear the parts, whether fine, or gross, of a dangerous and troublesome incumbrance' (Burke 1998, 123). Burke's sublime is a short, sharp shock to the system, bringing it back into working order. Tom Furniss also connects Burke's idea that labour and exercise are needed with Cheyne's concept of the 'English Malady', his better-known guide to health published in 1733 (Furniss 1993, 44–5). For Furniss, the sublime is 'the resort of the "civilized" classes whose lives no longer involve the appropriate kinds of mental and physical exertion or variety to prevent their degeneration into corruption' (Furniss 1993, 44). In this respect, 'Burke's sublime functions as an antidote against, but also as a symptom of, a disease thought to be already internal to eighteenth-century bourgeois England' (Furniss 1993, 44). Despite the different emphasis here in Furniss's work, the medical language is still explicit. Ryan also writes of Burke's sublime as a kind of 'physiological hygiene';

the analogy drawn with physical exercise and the power of the sublime as an antidote to melancholy make explicit for Ryan its particular 'social utility' and 'moral power' (Ryan 2001, 276). It is clear then that Burke's theory of the sublime is very much engaged with contemporary medical knowledge and ideas.

As I will show later in this chapter, Davy's nitrous oxide experiments share some aspects of Burke's 'physiological sublime'. Davy's poetry in general and his scientific writings on the sublime experience of inhaling nitrous oxide in particular concentrate on bodily effects. In other important ways though Davy's use of the sublime does not seem to follow Burke's account. Burke's sublime is an overpowering force that robs the mind of its independence; it denies to the self mastery, expansion, transcendence, and control. It is likely that the writings of both Burke and Kant were available to Davy, as was the work of an early scientific influence, Priestley, on the sublime.[14] Priestley's 'Of the Sublime' was published as one of *A Course of Lectures on Oratory and Criticism* (1777).[15] These lectures were expressly written to illustrate 'the doctrine of the *association of ideas*' (Priestley 1777, i). In his description of the encounter with the sublime Priestley allows for greater autonomy of the self than Burke does: in his account, the mind must 'enlarge' itself to 'conceive a great object' and this experience is pleasing since it demonstrates our abilities – 'the strength and extent of our own powers' – even if we are not necessarily explicitly aware of the exercise of these powers (Priestley 1777, 151). Richardson argues that the metaphors Priestley uses imagine 'the mind as an organ or a muscle'; there is an effort involved in the sublime act, 'a labor of conception' (Richardson 2010, 26). Given Davy's knowledge and praise of Priestley's work, particularly during his early career, it would not be implausible to think that he had read this text. It may also have recommended itself to Davy when he was thinking about his own oratorical lecturing skills. For the purposes of this book, Priestley's most important addition to the development of the concept of the sublime was the consideration of it as a term that was particularly appropriate to describing scientific pursuits. This would also have appealed to Davy who continues to use it in this way in his own writings.

Priestley's lecture proposes a number of rhetorical devices that can be used to invoke the sublime. Shaw notes that for Priestley 'sublime qualities such as grandeur and awfulness are derived not from objects but rather from the ideas we "annex" to objects', and that 'what the sublime embodies is nothing less than the transformational power of language, its ability to link disparate entities (both physical and mental objects) by analogy' (Shaw 2006, 45, 47). This is, after all, part of a lecture series on oratory, and Priestley's point is not that material objects themselves convey the sublime but that the language used to describe them does. Priestley makes the point in his lecture that 'there are a variety of things, not material, which raise sensations similar to those which are excited by objects which have corporeal magnitude and elevation' (Priestley 1777, 156). Among these he includes '*sentiments* and *passions*' such as 'patriotism, and universal benevolence' (Priestley 1777, 154). He proves his point by noting the number of spatial metaphors, or what he calls 'terms borrowed from corporeal magnitude, extension and elevation' used to describe non-material things, such as the epithets '*proud, haughty*, and *lofty*' (Priestley 1777, 156). His point is that such sentiments – for example, universal benevolence – are 'attended with a consciousness of a feeling' that we also experience with the sublime (Priestley 1777, 156). After showing this to be the case for sentiments and passions, Priestley moves to another example where corporeal terms are applied to non-corporeal matters, which he calls the 'sublime of science', a category that is seen again in Davy's writings (Priestley 1777, 157).

Priestley thinks that there are many instances of the 'genuine sublime' in geometry and algebra, while natural philosophy and astronomy 'exhibit the noblest fields of the sublime that the mind of man was ever introduced to' (Priestley 1777, 157). All of these sciences, according to Priestley, 'present the idea of *vastness* to the mind' (Priestley 1777, 157). When such activities are considered on their own, they are not sublime, but when we 'join' ideas of the '*causes*, the *adjuncts*, or the *effects*' of such things, then they become sublime, and when contemplated 'they fill and charm the soul' (Priestley 1777, 157). Priestley had already identified one of the most sublime sciences in his *History and Present State of Electricity* (1767). He describes the history of electricity as a 'field full of pleasing objects, according to all the genuine and universal principles of taste', in which there is 'a gradual rise and progress' (Priestley 1767, i). This perception of improvement and progress is pleasurable to us: the 'association of ideas has annexed crouds [*sic*] of pleasing sensations to the contemplation of every object, in which this property is apparent' (Priestley 1767, i–ii). It is for this reason that science is particularly an object of the sublime. Using what he would call a corporeal metaphor, Priestley describes how an object in which we see 'a perpetual progress and improvement is, as it were, continually rising in its magnitude' (Priestley 1767, ii).

An examination of the history of electricity gives a clear sense of the progress and improvement that has taken place, and contemplating this makes him think about its future potential for progress and improvement, 'which is a prospect really boundless, and sublime' (Priestley 1767, ii). In other words, the progress that has been achieved so far in the science of electricity and which looks certain to continue offers the kind of sublime prospect that is dizzying and magnificent. This way of representing science's former and potential achievements would have appealed to Davy who similarly thought of chemistry – including galvanism – in these terms.

There are also aspects of Davy's sublime that might suggest the influence of Immanuel Kant's *Critique of Judgement*, particularly his view that ultimately the sublime experience offers the perceiving subject a sense of superiority over nature (Kant 1987, 120). While it is the case that Kant was not widely read in Britain, during his time at Bristol Davy was in a good position to have encountered Kant's ideas.[16] Thomas Beddoes may well have introduced Coleridge to Kant's writing, but certainly they both knew of him by 1796 and Davy would have had access to Kant's work in Beddoes's library.[17] Beddoes wrote a review of Kant's *Critique of Judgement* in the May 1796 issue of *The Monthly Magazine* (Beddoes 1796). The main difference between Burke and Kant for my purposes, and which seems to suggest that ultimately Davy's sublime was more Kantian than Burkean, is that after an initial feeling of being overpowered in an encounter with the sublime, Kant feels a sense of empowerment: 'we found in our mind a superiority over nature itself in its immensity' (Kant 1987, 120). This superiority in the face of natural objects arises through the power of reason: though we experience a 'momentary inhibition of the vital forces', this is 'followed immediately by an outpouring of them that is all the stronger' (Kant 1987, 98). In the case of what Kant calls the 'mathematical sublime', we are initially overwhelmed by the magnitude of the natural object in question, which seems infinite, but then we reflect that the mind exceeds the senses simply because we can understand the concept of infinity: 'to be able even to think the infinite *as a whole* indicates a mental power that surpasses any standard of sense' (Kant 1987, 111). In other words, just being able to think of and imagine the idea of infinity means that, in Shaw's words, 'the mind discovers within itself a faculty that transcends the realm of sensible intuition' (Shaw 2006, 82).

For Kant, the sublime exists within the perceiving subject rather than the natural object: 'true sublimity must be sought only in the mind of the judging person, not in the natural object' (Kant 1987, 113). This emphasis on the self also chimes with Davy's sense of the sublime though he also seems to find sublimity in the natural world. Opposed to Burkean paralysis, where the mind is robbed of reason, and the self is annihilated, experience of the Kantian sublime is an uplifting and expansive experience: 'we like to call these objects sublime because they raise the soul's fortitude above its usual middle range' (Kant 1987, 120). Kant's sublime offers a form of transcendence. Not only this, the Kantian sublime reinforces confidence in one's self and in human capability; it also pitches man against nature and finds man superior. Vast natural objects, according to Kant, 'allow us to discover in ourselves an ability to resist which is of a quite different kind, and which gives us the courage [to believe] that we could be a match for nature's seeming omnipotence' (Kant 1987, 120). The language here (admittedly in translation) suggests a contest between man and nature that is at times reminiscent of Davy's words. These kinds of sentiments can be found in Davy's 1802 *Discourse,* which I will turn to at the end of this chapter and which find their way into the mouth of Professor Waldman, Victor Frankenstein's tutor at Ingolstadt University. In both texts the contest is of a decidedly sexual nature, figured as the penetration and conquest of a feminized nature by the masculine natural philosopher (Crouch 1978; see also Mellor 1988).

A crucial difference between Kant and Burke helps to explicate Davy's own sense of the sublime. The Kantian sublime 'elevates [*erhebt*] our imagination' (Kant, 1987, 121). The perceiving mind is not lost or annihilated before it, as Burke imagined, but is raised, transported, and exalted. Kant also thought that it was possible to perceive in an encounter with the sublime an underlying, *a priori,* transcendental knowledge; these kinds of 'fundamental principles' might be likened to natural laws (Shaw 2006, 74). For these reasons, and the emphasis placed on man's ability to know, comprehend, and thus conquer nature, it is possible to see the Kantian sublime as more attractive for Davy than Burke's sublime, which downplayed reason in favour of the body in the sublime encounter. Priestley's model of the 'sublime of science' was also available for Davy to use.

Jan Golinski has noted the importance of the sublime for natural philosophers of the Romantic period: scientific lecturers and writers deliberately invoked the sublime with different motivations (Golinski 2009). While some (and Davy would be among these) invoked the sublime 'to inspire further efforts to conquer nature', others wished to show how nature continued to 'elude human curiosity' (Golinski 2009, 532). Golinski also makes the point that the sublime 'evoked the theological dimension of natural philosophy', in some ways fulfilling 'functions previously fulfilled by the deity in scientific discourse' (Golinski 2009,

532–3). While acknowledging that Kant's work was 'not widely read in Britain', Golinski recognizes that 'his manoeuvre of inserting mental reflection into the aesthetics of the sublime was matched by British commentators'; locating the sublime in the perceiving subject's mind rather than in the object itself allowed natural philosophers to assert their 'apprehension of the powers of natural phenomena' above an 'irrational – even superstitious – fear of them' (Golinski 2009, 534). In Golinski's discussion, the use of the sublime offers another example of the ways in which science was invested with different theological and political views: it was held by such as Davy to be a 'sign of the deity' but by religious sceptics to point 'to the absence of God' (Golinski 2009, 534). For these reasons among others, Golinski writes, the sublime was a theme that 'featured centrally in scientific discourse of the period' (Golinski 2009, 528).[18] It reaffirms Golinski's point that in this period science was no monolith but was invested with cultural and political meaning. Priestley even characterized the natural philosopher as himself sublime: he should be 'something greater, and better than another man'. Contemplating God's works should give 'a sublimity to his virtue' and such philosophers have the capacity to be 'great and exalted beings' (Priestley 1767, xx). In the next section we see Davy's sense of himself as a sublime being.

Burke, Priestley, and Kant engage with contemporary medicine and science in their development of the concept of the sublime; whether, as in the case of Burke, this is the clear influence of medical knowledge and his desire to produce a scientific theory that identifies a law of nature, or as with Priestley, the term is applied to the sciences themselves. Kant's emphasis on reason and the primacy of the self allows for arrogant, masculinist assertions of the natural philosopher over nature. The concept of the sublime is a nexus where scientific, medical, literary, philosophical, and aesthetic perspectives – themselves clearly shaped by the politics of the period – interact.

4.2 'I seemed to be a sublime being, newly created and superior to other mortals'[19]

This section will offer an introduction to Davy's poetry written in the 1790s, and consider it as what we would now call 'Romantic' in subject matter and form. Davy's lifetime (1778–1829) spans the years usually ascribed to the Romantic era in Britain and his time in Bristol placed him at the heart of a community that included Coleridge and Robert Southey and which can be seen as key to the creation of British Romanticism. In many ways, Davy was thoroughly immersed in this context, and thinking about Davy's part within this community should help us to reach a fuller, more culturally-rounded understanding of the term 'Romantic'. After briefly surveying Davy's poetic oeuvre, I look at his use of the word 'sublime' in his letters and poems: examining how his own version of the sublime borrowed from and rejected the various possibilities put forward by Burke, Priestley, and Kant and discussed in the previous section. The word 'sublime' is a favourite for Davy; he uses it often in his poetry with some degree of consistency throughout his lifetime. It is a word he can invest with particular religious, philosophical, and aesthetic properties, which reveal the work of the imagination in scientific endeavour and which acknowledge the dynamic forces or powers of nature.

While some excellent biographies of Davy have considered his poetry, there is not yet any full-length study of Davy as a poet despite the fact that he wrote poetry throughout his life.[20] Although the vast majority of his poetry was never published in his lifetime, in *Middlemarch*, which was published in 1874, George Eliot makes reference to Davy as a poet. In response to hearing that Sir James Chettam is reading Davy's *Agricultural Chemistry*, Mr Brooke tells of how he once dined with both Wordsworth and Davy: 'Davy was there: he was a poet too. Or, as I may say, Wordsworth was poet one, and Davy was poet two. That was true in every sense, you know' (Eliot 2003, 16). John Ayrton Paris presented some of his poetry in the first biography of Davy (Paris 1831); Davy's brother, John, published selections of his poetry posthumously in his 1836 *Memoirs* (some deliberately mistranscribed to protect his brother's reputation), and this poetry was the subject of a *Gentleman's Magazine* article in 1837.[21] There is also evidence that Davy circulated some of his poetry in manuscript and even authorized publication, albeit anonymously: for example, in 1823, Davy sent Joanna Baillie a poem for a collection she was putting together to raise money for a friend and this was published without his name.[22] While it is difficult to be sure of how Davy thought about his poetry, this does suggest that, at this late date at least, he was happy to publish his work, albeit anonymously; the poem itself is a reworked version of one first mentioned in 1800, the many different versions of which show his commitment to the pursuit.[23] Even though he decides upon a scientific career rather than choosing to become a poet, I think that Davy considered his interest in poetry as something that gave him a particular and unusual perspective on the world. It is during the 1790s, arguably, that Davy becomes a 'Romantic'. The aesthetic of the sublime is key to his thinking about the role of the imagination in scientific pursuit.

Davy's earliest poetry is perhaps most reminiscent of Thompson's *The Seasons* and the poetry written in the late 1790s and early 1800s conveys an appreciation of the sublime as marker of genius.[24] These poems trace Davy's sense of his own awakening in the arresting Cornish landscape in which he grew up. Davy contributed five poems to the first volume of Robert Southey's *Annual Anthology* (1799) and one to the second volume (1800). In this chapter I concentrate on poems written in the 1790s but supplement the discussion with later, connected poems. In Bristol Davy fell in love with Anna Beddoes, his mentor's wife, to whom he dedicated much sentimental verse.[25] In Davy's poetic oeuvre there are conversation poems in the style of Coleridge, odes, the occasional satirical poem, and a variety of verse forms.[26] Davy wrote a parody of Wordsworth's lyrical ballad form, 'As I was walking up the street'.[27] He also proposed an orientalist epic ('Moses'), of which extracts are extant, to be written with a poet friend.[28] His early poetry has been compared in content and style to Wordsworth's 'Tintern Abbey'.[29] As well as seeing the second edition of the *Lyrical Ballads* through the press, Davy also helped Southey with the publication of *Thalaba*.[30] It is alleged that Davy also wrote the blank verse 'Prologue' for John Tobin's successful play, *The Honey Moon*, performed on 31 January 1805 at Drury Lane.[31]

For the main part, Davy's poetry has survived in notebooks and letters, on scraps of loose sheets, often accompanied by drawings and in among accounts of his scientific experiments and discoveries. His later poetry was often inspired by his travels abroad and within Britain, including poems on Alpine scenes and poems written at friends' country houses. Long after leaving Bristol and in much later poems, the influence of the younger generation of Romantic poets on Davy is perhaps more evident: there are two poems written about Byron, for example.[32] As he approaches death, his poems become more philosophical. As this brief survey makes clear, there are many ways in which Davy's poetry can be regarded as Romantic, not least in his fascination with the sublime. There is the sense of an early Pantheism in his 1790s poetry, to be replaced by more orthodox religious sentiment, with the occasional hint of Platonism in his late poems. His poetry can be related to his scientific endeavours, and in this chapter his lifelong preoccupation with light – whether moonlight, the sun's rays, the light of fire-flies or glow worms – is linked to his scientific researches into light and heat.[33] Modern critics have called Davy a 'Romantic scientist' with the epithet usually taken to refer to his search for underlying, dynamic forces in the natural world (see Knight 1990). Equally, and related to this understanding, we could use this epithet to refer to his lifelong interest in a distinctively Romantic sublime.

Coleridge certainly seemed to have regarded Davy as a kind of bridge between poetry and science, describing him in 1823 as 'the Man who *born* a Poet first converted Poetry into Science and *realized* what few men possessed Genius enough to *fancy*'.[34] The sublime is an idea that brings together poetry and science for Davy; in his poetry he describes it as something to which natural philosophers are particularly alive. Davy's use of the sublime is often unconventional; clearly well versed in Burke's theory of the sublime and the beautiful, Davy also rejects parts of this and adds to it a Kantian confidence in reason. Repeatedly for Davy, discovery of the 'laws of nature' is a sublime activity and this is one reason why science is capable of being considered itself sublime. In the next section of this chapter I discuss Davy's interest in what he considered the most sublime idea of all – that there was a modifying principle at work behind the constant transmutation of living forms.

It is clear from the evidence of 'The Sons of Genius' and other poems that Davy has read Burke.[35] He is careful to distinguish between the sublime and the beautiful and to gender these accordingly: the beautiful is 'soft and fair', while the 'grander scenes of nature' are described as 'great, sublime, and terrible' (ll. 53–6). The 'sons of genius' are delighted and moved by both kinds of scenes. A letter to John King written a few years later refers to the 'vallies of Derbyshire' as being 'in the highest degree beautiful' and notes that 'they confine the imagination' when compared to the 'fine & grand features' of the Wye (1 September [1802]); *Davy Letters*).[36] In a poem published in the same volume of the *Annual Anthology*, 'Ode to St Michael's Mount, in Cornwall', Davy makes a similar rhetorical move, which makes a clear distinction between the sublime and the beautiful. Davy remembers his youth as a time when he was pleased and content with beauty but makes a sharp division between this state and his experience of the sublime:

> Then BEAUTY bade my pleasures flow,
> Then BEAUTY bade my bosom glow
> With mild and gentle fire!
> Then mirth, and cheerfulness, and love,
> Around my soul were wont to move,
> And thrill'd upon my lyre.
>
> But when the Dæmon of the deep
> Howl'd around thy rocky steep,
> And bade the tempests rise,

Bade the white foaming billows roar,
And murmuring dash the rocky shore,
    And mingle with the skies;

Ah, then my soul was rais'd on high,
And felt the glow of ecstasy,
    With *great* emotions fill'd;
Thus joy and terror reign'd by turns,
And now with LOVE the bosom burns,
    And now by FEAR is chilled.

(Davy 1799c, ll. 37–54)

This poem is written in six-line stanzas with a pattern of two rhyming lines of iambic tetrameter and a single line of iambic trimeter producing a rhyme scheme of AABCCB (using some half and eye-rhymes). It is dated 1796 in the anthology, which would mean that it was written when Davy was eighteen years old. Despite his youth, he writes that he has gone through a formative experience, having passed from being moved by pleasurable thoughts inspired by beauty to the '*great* emotions' inspired by the sublime. He describes how this change has affected the kind of poetry that he writes: the pleasurable emotions he experienced 'thrill'd upon [his] lyre'. The change comes with the word 'But' at the start of the stanza; all is altered after he witnesses a storm around St Michael's Mount. This encounter with the sublime raises his soul and he experiences ecstasy.

As the repeated word 'bade' implies, Davy is largely passive in both experiences; after being 'fill'd' with '*great* emotions' as opposed to merely pleasurable ones, he is subject to alternating positive and negative feelings, which reign over him 'by turns'. The rhyming pattern works well to imitate this. Joy and terror, love and fear, are among the emotions described by Burke and similarly Davy's sublime encounter is felt in the body; it alternately burns and chills his heart. This extreme is far different from the 'mild and gentle fire' urged by beauty, which reminds us that Burke considered the experience of beauty as one that relaxed the nerves. Interestingly, Coleridge in his 1802 poem 'Dejection: An Ode' also uses the 'And now [...] / And now' device that we see in this poem, similarly to describe two different sounds of the wind that inspire his own 'lyre' (Coleridge 1985, 113–17, ll. 124–5).

The word 'awful' appears a great deal in Davy's poetry and it is often used to describe natural objects. His love of the sublime was clearly fostered in his native Cornwall but he writes a good deal on mountains later in his life, when he travels abroad. There are poems on 'Mont Blanc', 'The Canigou' (in Southern France), as well as a poem on 'Carrara' (a city in Tuscany), which describes Carrara's quarries as 'sublime' (*Collected Works*, I, 170–1, 173–5, 177–8). There is a poem on 'The Tempest' also dated 1796 in the first volume of the *Annual Anthology*, which imagines a sublime scene (Davy 1799a). The poem 'Vaucluse' describes the river Sorgue in France that Petrarch loved as 'sublime'; as the streams descend with 'more of power [...] Amidst their basins awful cliffs impend' (*Collected Works*, I, 175–7, ll. 52, 21–2). Davy can see why Petrarch was so enamoured of this particular scene:

> I wonder not the poet loved thy wave,—
> Thy cavern'd rocks,—thy giant precipice;
> For such a scene was suited well to break
> The tyrant-spell of love, and to controul
> A passion that was often hopeless love
> Call'd for impressions strong and vigorous,
> Such as this scene sublime might well bestow
> Upon a mind alive to sympathy
> With all created forms that bear the stamp
> Of loveliness, or majesty, or grace.
>
> (ll. 46–55)

The reason that Davy gives for why Petrarch so loved the place again suggests a Burkean understanding of the sublime, which can 'break / The tyrant-spell of love'. Love is imagined here as a kind of spell that imprisons the poet and from which he must be jolted; this unrequited passion needs 'impressions strong and vigorous', such as those offered by this 'scene sublime' to provide the bracing, violent, action needed to break the spell of love. The switching of the usual pattern of stress in this otherwise blank verse poem at the beginning of line fifty-one enacts the 'strong and vigorous' awakening needed.

The kinds of natural objects Davy considers sublime are the same as those identified by Burke, Priestley, and Kant, including: 'vast cataracts, raging storms, thunder' (Burke 1998, 75); 'large rivers, high mountains, and extensive plains; the ocean, the clouds, the heavens, and infinite space; also storms, thunder, lightning, volcanos [*sic*], and earthquakes, in nature; and palaces, temples, pyramids, cities, &c. in the works of men' (Priestley 1777, 154); 'bold, overhanging and, as it were, threatening rocks, thunderclouds piling up in the sky and moving about accompanied by lightning and thunderclaps, volcanoes with all their destructive power, hurricanes with all the devastation they leave behind, the boundless ocean heaved up, the high waterfall of a mighty river, and so on' (Kant 1987, 120). In 'The Sons of Genius', for example, Davy identifies the sublime with 'rough precipices', the 'stormy night', the 'thunders of the threatening deep', and with atmospheric lightning and thunder (Davy 1799b, ll. 58, 59, 60).

In a late poem written at Ullswater in 1825, reference is made to certain of Burke's 'qualities' of these sublime objects though here it is applied to an abstract concept rather than natural object:

> The great is ever
> Obscure, indefinite; and knowledge still,
> The highest, the most distant, most sublime,
> Is like the stars composed of luminous points,
> But without visible image, or known distance.
>
> (*Collected Works*, I, 321, ll. 15–19)

There is a section on 'Obscurity' in Part Two of Burke's *Philosophical Enquiry*, as well as a further section 'Of the difference between CLEARNESS and OBSCURITY with regard to the passions' where he writes that a 'very obscure and imperfect *idea*' can do far more to engage the emotions than a clear idea (Burke 1998, 55). The indefinite is mentioned twice in Burke's treatise as a characteristic of the sublime (Burke 1998, 67, 90). Burke also considers the stars to be sublime because of our being unable to count them; their 'apparent disorder' and 'confusion' makes them seem infinite (Burke 1998, 71). For Davy, the stars are sublime but for different reasons, though these accord well with other points made in Burke's treatise: for Davy, the stars are so far away as to give us no real sense of what they look like or their exact distance, and the most important knowledge, likewise, is sublime for the same reasons.

In his letters describing travel in Britain and abroad Davy often uses the language of the sublime. In 1802 in the Peak District in England he finds 'Dove-dale' to be 'inferior, in point of sublime scenery' to Chee Tor (15 August 1802; *Davy Letters*; Paris 1831, 101). From North Wales a few months later, he writes to John King: 'North Wales has given me conceptions that I never had before of the great & sublime in Nature' (1 September [1802]; *Davy Letters*).[37] In a letter written in 1811 describing Snowdon rising from the clouds, Davy writes: 'Nothing could exceed the sublimity of this scene' (14 October 1811; *Davy Letters*).[38] Connemara in Ireland he describes as 'savage, wild, & sublime'

(1 November 1811; *Davy Letters*).[39] When he travels further afield we hear of the Simplon in the Alps having 'sublimity' ([?] July 1814; *Davy Letters*).[40] In 1824, he writes that 'all the southern coast of Norway abounds in peculiar & extraordinary fine & even sublime features', while the 'scenery in Sweden is of a wilder & I think inferior [kind?]' (20 July 1824; *Davy Letters*).[41] Only the next day in a letter to Jons Jakob Berzelius he contradicts this – perhaps in an attempt to flatter the Swedish chemist's national pride: 'I should have been happy to have seen more of your interesting peninsula which abounds in grand & sublime features' (21 July 1824; *Davy Letters*).[42] The mountains of 'Appenzel' [*sic*] in Switzerland are also 'sublime' (13 July 1827; *Davy Letters*).[43] While visiting what we would now call Austria and Slovenia, he writes: 'It is scarcely possible to imagine a country of more sublimity & beauty' (1 June 1828; *Davy Letters*).[44]

He also uses the term to describe a number of other kinds of things. Coleridge's description in 1803 of the projects he intends to pursue, but which Davy suspects he will not, is described as sublime. Davy is disappointed in him and writes to their mutual friend, Thomas Poole: 'What talent does he not waste in forming visions, sublime, but unconnected with the real world!' (1 May 1803; *Davy Letters*; Paris 1831, 115). In this use, the sublime is characterized by greatness and ambition, but has nothing of reality about it. In a letter written to his soon-to-be wife, then Jane Apreece, Davy describes the experience of the sublime as one that transports the viewer, but he also makes the point that there is a 'moral sublime' more readily to be found in Milton and Shakespeare than in alpine scenery:

> You write with great eloquence & truth on the effects of mountain Scenery on the Mind — Whatever exalts the imagination, purifies the affections — but even our noblest & best thoughts have their archetypes in sensation; the eye is the most perfect of all the senses & the one that most feeds the intellect. When surrounded by the grand forms of nature —. — We give to the earth something of the indefinite character of heaven — Great objects excite great thoughts the standard of our being rises; — all our low & grovelling associations disappear & our sympathies are more strongly awakened with regard to the moral sublime the excellent — the decorous & the great in philosophy. We are more fitted to enjoy the blaze of light of Milton, to pass into the proteus forms of humanity with Shakespeare or to move through the heavens with Newton.
>
> (26 August 1811; *Davy Letters*)[45]

Here describing the relationship between the sensation of sight and its effect upon the mind, Davy concedes that there are 'archetypes' of thoughts in our sensations, particularly in what we see. In other words, changes in our body affect our mind and the eye has the most direct access to our thoughts. The 'great objects' such as mountains 'excite' within us corresponding 'great thoughts' and so we become better people. He imagines our metaphorical rising to a higher standard of being because of this process.

Once this has happened we are even more sympathetic to the 'moral sublime' of philosophy, used here to refer to Milton, Shakespeare, and Newton. If we are receptive to the natural sublime, we will be even 'more fitted' to appreciate these thinkers, and again the process by which we appreciate their sublimity is imagined as a kind of transportation in two of the examples; we become Shakespeare's many characters — and 'pass into the proteus forms of humanity' he has created — or 'move through the heavens with Newton'. This sense of movement, of being raised and transported, is not in keeping with Burke and yet it is to be found often in Davy's poetry on the sublime. In 'Ode to St Michael's Mount', for example, Davy writes that his 'soul was rais'd on high' (Davy 1799c, ll. 49). In a later poem to Athens, he ascribes the power of expanding the soul to the beautiful as well as the sublime; Athens is said to have 'loved whatever could expand / The soul, — the beautiful, the grand' (*Collected Works*, I, 139–40, ll 50–1).

In only one later poem, 'The Sybil's Temple', does Davy characterize the sublime – as Burke does – as a force that potentially annihilates the self:

> In the sympathy sublime,
> With natural forms and sounds, the mind forgets
> Its present being'
>
> (*Collected Works*, I, 185–6, ll. 21–3)

However, this is not necessarily a limiting or restricting emotion; Davy imagines the emptying of the mind as a precursor to the inspiration of prophecy. In Davy's poetry we see far more often what Keats described as the Wordsworthian or egotistical sublime than the chameleon poet.[46] In his poetry Davy is often a participant rather than a spectator – the sublime becomes internalized, and enlarges rather than diminishes his consciousness. In the poem written about his nitrous oxide experiment – a sublime experience that is literally ingested – Davy describes how his limbs 'with inward transport fill[']d' are 'clad with new-born mightiness around' (RI MS HD 13c, p. 6, ll. 7, 8). In the sublime encounter he himself becomes sublime; he is raised and exalted to a new, more powerful state.

In this poem and others 'rapture' and 'ecstasy' are often used to describe his emotions during the sublime experience and these states are usually taken to refer to what we might call out-of-body experiences. For example, in the 'The Sons of Genius', Davy writes that 'raptures fill the soul' when he reads of 'Attic' war, presumably referring to the *Iliad* or other works on the Trojan wars (Davy 1799b, ll. 81, 82). In 'The Sons of Genius', he feels 'the glow of ecstasy' when filled with '*great* emotion' (Davy 1799b, ll. 50, 51). Richardson notes how the word 'ecstasy' means 'the state of being taken beyond or above one's ordinary state' and that, correspondingly, in Burke, 'the terms *rapture* and *transport* drop away altogether':

> Locating the sublime in the body rather than in an out of the body phenomenon, Burke makes the sublime a corporeal experience that, in the last analysis, depends on changes in the central nervous system, a stretching and subsequent relaxation of the nerves.
>
> (Richardson 2010, 26)

Davy does feel the effects of the sublime 'in the body', particularly in his account of the nitrous oxide experiments where the purpose of the reports written were to detail physical effects, the 'thrill' through the body that is also found in his poetry on the subject (RI MS HD 13c, p. 6). This 'thrill' is of course understood as the vibration caused by the movement of the nerves. However, it is also the case, as Golinski has pointed out, that the gas seemed to offer 'a means of transcending normal body conditions' (Golinski 2009, 542). I shall return to this later in this chapter.

Though the influence of Burke is clear, then, so are the points on which Davy deviated from Burke's theory. It is also possible to see the influence of Kant on Davy's sublime, because he allowed for the idea that the soul would expand, rise, and be transported in the sublime experience. In many of the poems already discussed the sublime is trumped by reason, a calmer and more sovereign force on the self, and this might remind us of Kant's insistence on the superiority of man's reason over nature. In 'The Sons of Genius' Davy pictures a 'poor shepherd' who 'Surveys the darkening scene with fearful eye', imagining that he sees 'haggard sprites' in the 'moon-beams' (Davy 1799b, ll. 13–16). Superstition, in this poem, 'rules the vulgar soul' and does not allow 'the energies of man to rise' (Davy 1799b, ll. 17–18). In contrast, 'Aspiring genius' loves the moonlit night because then 'Reason extends her animating sway, / O'er the calm empire of the peaceful mind' (Davy 1799b, ll. 20, 27–8). The power of reason is described as governing the mind and – gendered female – her reign is described, in a commonplace metaphor, as an 'all-enlightening ray' that drives all the 'gloomy terrors' of superstition away (Davy 1799b, ll. 29, 31). The effect of 'Reason' upon the sons of genius may be superficially like that of the sublime: 'Inspired by her', they 'rise', and are 'Enraptur'd' (Davy 1799b, ll. 33, 36). Scientific work can bring greater calm though: 'To scan the laws of Nature, to explore / The tranquil reign of mild Philosophy' (Davy 1799b, ll. 77–8). The 'sons of genius' are 'By science calm'd' and peace 'drives the fury passions away' (Davy 1799b, ll. 91, 94). In other words, science brings calm while reason excites.

Moonlight is one of Davy's favourite settings and is often a source of the sublime. On 5 May 1800, in Bristol, Davy deliberately went for a moonlight walk by the Avon with his green bag of nitrous oxide gas in an attempt to enhance by artificial means the experience of the sublime (*Collected Works*, III, 291–2). Later in 1800, he, John King and Charles Danvers travelled to the Wye specifically 'to see Tintern Abbey by moonlight' (20 October [1800]; *Davy Letters*). In the *Collected Works*, John Davy excerpts from what he calls 'a sketch of a reverie', which clearly comes from the experience of the moonlight at Wye, quite possibly from the same time in the autumn of 1800 (*Collected Works*, I, 64). Davy wakes, seemingly from a nightmare, and the moonlight is transformed from a beautiful to a sublime experience. This occurs by means of the 'restless and uneasy feeling which superstition, almost conquered by reason, is capable of awakening in the mind'; this feeling disappears before or is combined with the beautiful to produce the sublime encounter (*Collected Works*, I, 65). He continues, addressing an unknown person, 'You know a moonlight scene is peculiarly delightful to me; I always considered it as beautiful' but so much has occurred to him while 'beneath the moonbeams', since 'Nature first spoke' to him in Cornwall, that he now has changed his mind: moonlight 'is now become sublime' (*Collected Works*, I, 65). References to the sublimity of moonlight continue through Davy's life until his final text *Consolations in Travel*, where the narrator, Philalethes (often regarded as Davy himself), admits that 'the full moon has always a peculiar effect on these moods of feeling in my mind' (Davy 1830, 15).

For Kant, while we may experience the laws of nature empirically, they are ultimately transcendent truths, which are necessary and universal (see Kant 1987, 18–20 and Shaw 2006, 73–5). Our contingent, sensory experience of these laws alerts us to the *a priori* unities of nature, which may not be visible to us. It may not be necessary to invoke Kant for this since, during his galvanism experiments in particular, Davy was explicitly trying to discover a new law of nature to explain the phenomena found: namely, that chemical affinity was at base electrical in nature. Kant's idea of the sublime would have had some appeal for Davy, though; man is superior to nature because he can understand the concept of unity that binds together natural phenomena to make an underlying law of nature. In the blank verse 'Extract from an Unfinished Poem on Mount's Bay', also published in the *Annual Anthology*, Davy imagines an intrepid follower of nature who stands 'unawed' in the face of the sublime:

> Thy awful height Bolerium is not loved
> By busy Man, and no one wanders there
> Save He who follows Nature: He who seeks
> Amidst thy craigs [*sic*] and storm-beat rocks to find
> The marks of changes teaching the great laws
> That raised the globe from Chaos. Or He whose soul
> Is warm with fire poetic, He who feels
> When Nature smiles in beauty, or sublime
> Rises in majesty. He who can stand
> Unaw'd upon the summit clad in tempests
> And view with raptured mind the roaring deep
> Rise o'er thy foam-clad base, while the black cloud
> Bursts with the fire of heaven.
>
> (Davy 1799d, ll. 40–52)

Bolerium is another name for Land's End, as Davy explains in an earlier footnote. This poem shares some characteristics with 'The Sons of Genius' in imagining an elite group of people (presumably men) who are more in sympathy with the sublime in nature. Here, in a technique used elsewhere in his poems, he imagines a single man, 'He', held to be representative of a type, though not of man more generally. In contrast, worldly man, 'busy' with material cares, is not interested in this ragged and bare rock, but the natural philosopher seeks and can find 'marks' in this rock that tell him of the earth's past. Land's End can teach him of the 'great laws' that first created the earth. Poets would also be interested in 'Bolerium'; they are equally men who have the ability to appreciate Nature at her most beautiful or sublime. Davy plays with the metre to help produce his desired effect: the sublime 'Rises' with inverted stress in a trochee; likewise, the black cloud 'Burst[s]' into the line and the scene. This representative man, and we have to assume that Davy considers himself among those 'He' represents, is able to stand 'Unaw'd' upon the most sublime natural landscapes, himself 'clad in tempests', viewing the sublime scene. To borrow Kant's ideas, this man is assured of his superiority over nature because he sees in this scene evidence of the *a priori*, transcendent laws underlying matter. He also, in some respects, becomes himself sublime. In the next section, I look at Davy's claims that chemistry – and in particular the work that he was doing – was sublime.

4.3 'Thus would chemistry, in its connections with the laws of life, become the most sublime and important of all sciences' (*Collected Works*, II, 86)

As is clear from the comment above, made at the end of his first scientific work, 'Essay on Heat, Light, and the Combinations of Light', published in Beddoes and Watt's 1799 *Contributions*, Davy was convinced of the idea, to which Priestley also subscribed, that the sciences could be and were sublime. While he refers to astronomy and geology a few times as 'sublime' sciences, he is also at pains to prove that chemistry is too.[47] In this section, I consider the reasons why Davy thinks of chemistry as a sublime science and the ways in which he thinks of his own chemical projects as potentially sublime. While working on seemingly different projects – heat and light, nitrous oxide, and galvanism – Davy's object was strikingly similar. These pursuits might, he believed, reveal the 'laws of life', a phrase that recurs during these years in his scientific writings and letters. Davy's confidence in this period can be seen in his bombastic 1802 *Discourse, Introductory to a Course of Lectures*, which invokes the sublime in order to imply the potential importance of what chemistry can achieve.

In a letter to Davies Giddy, dated 10 April 1799, Davy discusses a topic that he would return to repeatedly in his early scientific writings and in the poetry he writes throughout his life:

> The supposition of active powers common to all matter, from the different modifications of which all the phenomena of its changes result, appears to me more reasonable than the assumption of certain imaginary fluids alone endowed with active powers, and bearing the

> same relation to common matter, as the vulgar philosophy supposes spirit to bear to matter.
>
> (*Davy Letters*; Paris 1831, 54)

The 'imaginary fluids' here are, presumably, phlogiston and caloric; it was the existence of the latter that Davy expressly set out to disprove in his 'Essay on Heat, Light, and the Combinations of Light'. In this letter, he makes it clear that he believes all matter has 'active powers' within it, rather than these powers being attached – as people believe the soul is attached to the body – to certain 'imaginary fluids'. Instead, these 'active powers' are inherent within matter. In his 1802 *Discourse*, Davy describes the chemist as also having 'active powers', which is very like Wordsworth's description of the poet's special ability in his 'Preface' to the *Lyrical Ballads*, which likewise 'enabled him to modify and change the beings surrounding him' (*Collected Works*, II, 319). For Davy, and contemporaries, these 'active powers' are responsible for modifying matter and producing all the changes that we see in the world. In the 1790s, Davy set out to find out more about these active powers, which he considered to be sublime. As Burke wrote, 'I know of nothing sublime, which is not some modification of power' (Burke 1998, 59). Likewise, Davy conceives of the transmutation of matter, of the changing states of living forms, as the result of an inherent power within matter.

Levere, in his study of Coleridge's interest in and use of contemporary scientific thought, notes that the poet considered nature to be determined by processes 'not mechanical, but dynamic, governed by powers' and believed that the powers of mind and of nature 'correspond[ed] to one another' (Levere 1981, 3). Levere finds that the lengthy, controversial 'Essay on Heat, Light, and the Combinations of Light', which Davy contributed to Beddoes's and Watt's *Contributions*, and which he would later repudiate, accords with Coleridge's own views at this time (Levere 1981, 23).[48] In this essay, Davy wanted to prove that light 'is not a modification, or an effect of heat' (*Collected Works*, II, 7). He proposes instead that light combines with oxygen to form what he calls 'phosoxygen', and in this combination light is essential to the 'perceptive existence' of all organic bodies (*Collected Works*, II, 49, 84). Life, for Davy, is the constant motion and the transmutation of matter from one form into another and this is the most 'sublime idea' of all.[49] Davy argues that 'all matter is governed by the same laws' and finds that all matter has 'active properties' (*Collected Works*, II, 73). Light may well be the principle of life in Davy's essays; by entering into the human body, it is responsible for 'perception, thought, and happiness' (*Collected Works*, II, 74). These terms are used again in his researches into nitrous oxide.

Davy's 'Essay' was begun in Penzance, and in a letter to his mother dated 11 October 1798 Davy alludes to 'my Theory', to which he tells her Beddoes has 'become a convert' (*Davy Letters*).[50] In a letter to Henry Pennick, Davy tells him: 'I intend in the course of this year if I can compleat my exp^ts to publish a much larger work in the Laws of Corpuscular Motion & the connexion of chemistry with the Laws of life' (26 January 1799; *Davy Letters*).[51] While he will profess himself in print later the same year 'a sceptic with regard to my own particular theory of the combinations of light, and theories of light in general', it is clear from his letter to Davies Giddy that he is still convinced on 3 July 1799 that chemistry will reveal the 'laws of life', though by this time it is galvanism that he credits with this potential (*Collected Works*, II, 126).[52] There is evidence therefore, that Davy was hoping to discover these laws of life and animation in these early researches.

At this stage, Davy sounds as though he agrees with David Hartley's theory that ideas are the product of sensations conveyed by means of the nerves; certainly, there is a link between the mind and body in Davy's 'Essay':

> Life, then, may be considered as a perpetual series of peculiar corpuscular changes; and the living body as the being in which these changes take place. Perceptions, ideas, pleasures, and pains, are the effects of these changes. They are consequently found to be continually varying. The laws of mind then, probably, are not different from the laws of corpuscular motion. Every change in our sensations must be accompanied with some correspondent change in the organic matter of the body.
>
> (*Collected Works*, II, 84)

Where Davy differs from Hartley in his 'Essay' is in the importance he gives to light in these processes. He imagines 'the sun and the fixed stars' to be 'immense reservoirs of light destined by the great ORGANISER to diffuse over the universe organization and animation' (*Collected Works*, II, 85). It is not impossible, he argues, that only 'one law alone may govern and act upon matter: an energy of mutation, impressed by the will of the Deity, a law which might be called the law of animation' (*Collected Works*, II, 85). For Davy, life is typified by change at a corpuscular level: our emotions and ideas are the result of these bodily changes and this is the reason why they themselves are so variable. The body accounts for the mind in this theory. Light is the active principle in effecting these changes at all levels (within the individual and within the entire universe). These are the kinds of 'sublime investigation' that chemistry can pursue (*Collected Works*, II, 85). This investigation is sublime partly because to understand and comprehend the laws of life is sublime. To use Kant again, the perceiving mind is superior to nature because it can understand the concept behind the phenomenon. We also perhaps see the influence of Priestley, even in the wording that Davy uses to describe this science: 'An extensive field for sublime investigation is open to us. The laws of perceptive life as yet are but partially known' (*Collected Works*, II, 85). I think that Davy went on with similar purpose to investigate these laws in his nitrous oxide experiments. His experiments of the 1790s show him applying the aesthetic term 'sublime', used confidently and consistently in his poetry, to scientific matters.

When Davy began to explore the effects of nitrous oxide, his letters (but not his later published *Researches*) show that he interpreted his results as confirming his 'theory' regarding 'phosoxygen'. Taking nitrous oxide is repeatedly referred to as a 'sublime' experience in his *Researches Chemical and Philosophical*. On 9 April 1799, Davy breathed sixteen quarts of nitrous oxide for seventeen minutes, proving to himself and others 'how necessary it is to repeat experiments' since the American chemist Samuel Mitchill had claimed it would be fatal.[53] Davy finds that breathing nitrous oxide has far more effect than breathing pure oxygen:

> Pure oxygen gas produced no alteration in my pulse, nor any other material effect; whereas this gas raised my pulse upwards of twenty strokes, made me dance about the laboratory as a madman, and has kept my spirits in a glow ever since. Is not this a proof of the truth of my theory of respiration? for this gas contains more light in proportion to its oxygen than any other, and I hope will prove a most valuable medicine.
>
> (10 April 1799; *Davy Letters*; Paris 1831, 56)

The nitrous oxide experiment proves his theory about phosoxygen because 'this gas' contains more light than pure oxygen, which is why it has this effect. Indeed, Davy calls the compound 'nitrous phosoxyde' in his letters, including two letters written to William Nicholson and published in his *Journal* (11 April [1799], 17 April [1799]).[54] Davy argued in his 'Essay' that sensations, including perceptions, ideas, pleasures, and pains, were caused by a corresponding change in the body; the nitrous oxide experiments seemed to show him that this was the case. This letter makes it clear that he thinks the reason is because of the proportion of light that there is in nitrous oxide. Borrowing the terms of his 'Essay', nitrous oxide seemed to bring him closer to the discovery of 'the laws of our existence' and may well enable 'in a great measure to destroy our pains and to increase our pleasures' (*Collected Works*, II, 85–6). Thus, the theory of heat and light is applied to the practical experiment with nitrous oxide and seems to be confirmed. Breathing nitrous oxide was a sublime experience for a number of reasons, which I will now explore: it mixed fear and pleasure, was a means to reach the mind through the body, and seemed to transport the subject beyond the body and the self.

The nitrous oxide experiments in Bristol excited Davy because he thought they indicated that pleasure could be administered and controlled. Davy referred to the gas in a letter as the 'pleasure-producing air' (12 January 1801; *Davy Letters*; *Collected Works*, I, 81). The language in which Beddoes publicly announced the discovery of a 'new pleasure' was replete with overtones of mastery and power reminiscent of the masculine sublime: 'Man may, some time, come to rule over the causes of pain and pleasure, with a dominion as absolute as that which at present he exercises over domestic animals and the other instruments of his convenience' (Beddoes 1799, 16, 27). At the outset of Davy's trials nitrous oxide seemed to promise the ability to give and control pleasure according to how many quarts were inhaled.[55] The experiments proceeded upon strict Brunonian principles and effects were interpreted within these parameters. Nitrous oxide was described as a stimulant – unlike alcohol – with no subsequent 'fatigue or sadness' (Beddoes, 1799, 8). Beddoes's early optimism for gas treatment claimed to put at '*our disposal an infinite series of powers*' (Beddoes 1799, 26). Beddoes speculated, for example, that it might be capable of 'renovating excitability' in the body and even that it might be the means of 'converting torpid into vivacious, cold-blooded into warm animals' (Beddoes 1799, 27).

There are parallels to be drawn between these nitrous oxide experiments and the animal magnetists' experiments discussed in my second chapter. Again, the majority of patients were drawn from the lower classes; Beddoes describes how 'paupers' came in numbers to be treated for free at the institute (Beddoes 1799, 6). There is also a particular concern with the propriety of treating 'hysterical' women (Beddoes 1799, 17). Beddoes claimed in the early days of the trials that the treatment promised new insight into certain 'nervous affections', pointing to the similar effects experienced by 'females of similar temperament, and by two or three males' (Beddoes 1799, 17). The effects of inhalation were as spectacular as anything witnessed by the French commissioners in their trials of animal magnetism and, likewise, the danger was that they were similarly the result of the imagination rather than of the treatment.[56] When Beddoes describes the first time he saw Davy take the gas, he writes 'the scene exhibited was the most extraordinary I had ever witnessed' (Beddoes 1799, 7). There are similar overtones of power and authority in Davy's dealings with poor patients. One story that John Ayrton Paris claims was 'lately communicated to me by Mr. Coleridge' involved a paralytic patient falsely being given the impression that he felt the effects of the treatment after Davy merely put a thermometer in his mouth. Davy played along with this delusion repeating this action every fortnight until the patient 'was dismissed as cured, no other application having been used but that of the thermometer' (Paris 1831, 51).[57] While this episode was not undertaken with the intention to delude, it was continued in Davy's full knowledge that no treatment was being undergone. It was also the case that the ridiculousness of the spectacle of those experiencing nitrous oxide made some people reluctant to try the gas.

Southey exclaimed to his brother 'Davy has actually invented a new pleasure for which language has no name.'[58] The inadequacy of language to represent this 'new pleasure' is a common theme among accounts of those who tried it.[59] Beddoes apologized for the failings of his early report on the trials with: 'it is impossible for the combined endeavours of the spectator and the subject of experiment adequately to represent what was sometimes seen and felt' (Beddoes 1799, 8). In this respect, inhaling nitrous oxide fits another characteristic of the sublime experience, one that the twentieth-century theorist Jean-François Lyotard considered an extension of the Kantian sublime, the idea that the sublime was 'unrepresentable' (Shaw 2006, 116). At the end of a letter which was supposed to detail the effects of taking nitrous oxide, James Thomson writes: 'we must either invent new terms to express these new and particular sensations, or attach new ideas to old ones, before we can communicate intelligibly with each other on the operation of this extraordinary gas' (*Collected Works*, III, 306). Thomson complained that our vocabulary was 'very defective' in the expression of sensation (*Collected Works*, III, 305).

This need for a new language might also be linked to Wordsworth's complaints in his 'Preface' to the *Lyrical Ballads* that poetry needed a language that more faithfully expressed emotion, and that this language was to be found among the lower classes (*Prose Works*, I, 124). Davy's own recollections lamented the 'imperfections' of the 'language of feeling': 'I have endeavoured to give as accurate an account as possible of the strange effects of nitrous oxide, by making use of terms standing for the most similar common feelings' (*Collected Works*, III, 293).[60] He had to use the terms that we have for the 'most similar' feelings when in fact the effects of nitrous oxide were very much stranger than our common feelings. James Webbe Tobin wrote of his experiences breathing the gas:

> It is giving but a faint idea of the feelings to say, that they resembled those produced by a representation of an heroic on the stage, or by reading a sublime passage in poetry when circumstances contribute to awaken the finest sympathies of the soul.
>
> (*Collected Works*, III, 297)

Here, breathing nitrous oxide is compared directly to the effect felt upon reading a 'sublime passage in poetry' and Tobin explains the feeling further with: 'my mind was elevated to a most sublime height' (*Collected Works*, III, 297). Davy uses this word to describe his own experiences a number of times: he feels 'sublime emotions connected with highly vivid ideas'; his 'emotions were enthusiastic and sublime'; later, his 'emotions are generally much less intense and sublime than in former experiments'; in general, nitrous oxide is capable of giving 'sublime pleasure' (*Collected Works*, III, 275, 290, 291, 327). Although the word clearly means a number of things for Davy, in the conclusion of his *Researches* he defines it in a footnote: 'Sublime emotion with regard to natural objects, is generally produced by the connection of the pleasure of beauty with the passion of fear' (*Collected Works*, III, 327, n.). Pleasure and fear are combined while breathing nitrous oxide: pleasure is often the effect but the subject may reasonably experience fear at the idea of breathing a gas thought until recently to be fatal and which caused people to behave in ridiculous ways.

Mike Jay argues that Coleridge and Kant influence Davy's representation of breathing nitrous oxide (Jay 2009, 193–4). Jay identifies a 'new subjectivity' in Davy's 'conception of the material world' around this time, which encouraged him to 'postulate a science of life that was animated by vital and mysterious forces' as was his earlier phosoxygen (Jay 2009, 194). This accords with Golinski's view that Davy was engaged throughout his life in a 'profound enquiry into—and molding of—his own subjectivity' (Golinski 2011, 25). Stephanie Snow has written that the fact that a chemical such as nitrous oxide 'had the power to intensify engagement with the natural world harmonized with Enlightenment philosophies' (Snow 2008, 13). The chemical's operation on the interface between self and nature can also be likened to the Romantic poet's objective to become more intimately connected with nature. Davy's experiments on 26 December 1799, reported in his *Researches* and involving an 'air-tight breathing box' designed by James Watt, affect his body first (*Collected Works*, III, 288). He describes a thrilling through his limbs, magnified sensations of sight and sound, a lightness and 'power of exertion' in his muscles (*Collected Works*, III, 289). The bodily sensations eventually give way to a changed perception of the world:

> By degrees, and as the pleasurable sensations increased, I lost all connection with external things; trains of vivid visible images rapidly passed through my mind, and were connected with words in such a manner, as to produce perceptions perfectly novel. I existed in a world of newly connected and newly modified ideas.
>
> (*Collected Works*, III, 289)

In this experience, Davy encounters entirely new perceptions. Language plays a role in this as images are connecting words in new ways as to produce new ways of seeing. While downplaying his active role in producing these images and words, it is clear that this is a world of his own making. When he is recalled to himself by others and tries to remember the ideas he had, 'they were feeble and indistinct', but he is left with the following words: '*Nothing exists but thoughts!—the universe is composed of impressions, ideas, pleasures and pains!*' (*Collected Works*, III, 290). Golinski has questioned whether this outburst is evidence of a belief in materialism or Berkleyan idealism (Golinski 2011, 20). On the one hand, it suggests that the mind depends upon the body; on the other, it suggests a move beyond the body into the realms of thought alone.

Davy's use of the sublime demonstrates that science is not immune to or innocent of the cultural and political implications of such terms. Davy had flirted with materialism; a few years earlier (dated 1797 in a notebook), he had made the materialist case that 'The Thinking Powers depend on Organisation' though these notes are angrily crossed through at some later date (RI MS HD 13f, 12).[61] In another notebook, Davy writes that it is probable 'that the phænomena of life are capable of chemical solution' and his nitrous oxide experiments must have seemed to prove this (RI MS HD 13h, 17). His first published work, 'Essay on Heat, Light, and the Combinations of Light', claimed that phosoxygen is the '*pabulum vitæ* of organic beings' (*Collected Works*, II, 50). When he begins his work on galvanism, he tells Davies Giddy that

'Some of the new facts on this subject promise to become instruments capable of destroying the mysterious veil which Nature has thrown over the operations & properties of etherial fluids' (20 October 1800).[62] In November 1800, he told Coleridge that he had made 'some important galvanic discoveries which seem to lead to the door of the temple of the mysterious god of Life'.[63] To John Tonkin, he writes that galvanism 'promises to unfold to us some of the laws of our nature' (12 January 1801; *Davy Letters*). It seems then that even after he has turned from nitrous oxide to galvanism, Davy is searching for the laws of life, and feels increasingly close to discovering something of them. Given that some contemporaries believed light, heat, and electricity were modifications of the same principle, it seems that Davy considered these early projects as being connected.[64] Certainly he believed the idea that we might comprehend the laws of animation was a sublime one.

While Davy might privately have expressed materialism, his publications – even his earliest ones – are in no manner atheist. All that he reveals in his 'Essay' Davy finds to be proof of the 'simplicity and unity of design' of the 'great ORGANISER' (*Collected Works*, II, 85). His letters are full of references to God, and after his second lecture at the Royal Institution he writes to his mother of his gratitude to 'the Supreme Being' (23 January 1802; *Davy Letters*). There is some suggestion of Pantheism though in his early poems and of Platonism in his later poems, such as in 'Thought' written in 1827 in Ravenna when, 'the human intellect' is but a feeble after-image of the '*One*' imagined as the 'glorious and eternal source' of individual life (*Collected Works*, I, 335, ll. 8, 12). The Platonism of these poems becomes even clearer when Davy calls the 'human intellect' 'but a type' of the eternal '*One*' (*Collected Works*, I, 335, ll. 8, 9). Since his first poem, 'My eye is wet with tears', Davy had worried about whether there was a future existence after death. He consistently expresses a strong conviction that our material bodies return to atoms and renew themselves in other life forms. We see this in poems such as 'The Spinosist', written sometime before 1800, the ending of which Coleridge objected to in a letter of 9 October 1800 on the grounds of its materialism (*Coleridge Letters*, I, 630).

Davy believed that there were powers at work – underlying natural forces – that were responsible for the mutability of matter. The Lucretian idea that atoms never die but are constantly changing is suggested by his sense of the laws of life. In 'Extract from an Unfinished Poem on Mount's Bay', Theora 'scann'd the laws / That move the ruling atoms, changing still, / Still rising into life' (Davy 1799d, ll. 83–5). In 'Many days have pass'd', Davy describes how he learned to 'trace': 'The mystic laws from whose high energy / The moving atoms, in eternal change, / Still rise to animation' (*Collected Works*, I, 59, ll. 24–6).[65] Perhaps the clearest expression of this sentiment comes in his 1815 poem 'On the Immortality of the Mind', where he writes when the inert rocks and stones, though they are 'to Nature lifeless bones' are reduced again to dust, this dust becomes atoms in other living forms such as rain or dew because 'Nothing is lost' (*Collected Works*, I, 234–5, ll. 4, 13). Where he has worried before that there seems to be no such afterlife for the mind and self, in this poem he confidently asserts: 'If *matter* cannot be destroy'd, / The *living mind* can *never* die' (*Collected Works*, I, 235, ll. 21–2). To use the language of Davy's first published 'Essay', this is the most sublime idea of all: 'No more sublime idea can be formed of the motions of matter, than to conceive that the different species are continually changing into each other' (*Collected Works*, II, 29, n.). This idea, intimately connected with the laws of life, takes on further significance when it comes to convince Davy that there is life after death.

Finally, I want to look at Davy's 1802 *Discourse, Introductory to a Course of Lectures*, which he began writing in Bristol but delivered in the Royal Institution in London. This short text uses the word 'sublime' seven times, and testifies to Golinski's point that popular scientific lecturers, and Davy in particular, '[gave] way to transports of rhetorical intensity' (Golinski 2009, 547). Davy uses the language of the sublime in these lectures to impress his audience, to excite and awe them. From the outset, Davy writes that the subject of these lectures – chemistry – is sublime (*Collected Works*, II, 310). He writes that chemistry and natural history are intimately related, for while the latter concerns itself with the bodies of the external world 'in their permanent and unchanging forms', chemistry instead looks at 'the laws of their alterations' and the 'active powers' within them (*Collected Works*, II, 312).

There are slight, possible references to his previous work, which suggest a desire to qualify his earlier claims: admitting that man knows 'little of the laws of his own existence', he has still 'derived some useful information concerning the nature of respiration' (*Collected Works*, II, 314). In the next sentence though he comments that the connection of chemistry and physiology has 'given rise to some visionary and seductive theories', which coming so close to a reference to respiration might suggest that he is referring to the nitrous oxide experiments (*Collected Works*, II, 314). The lecture concerns the many ways in which chemistry is a useful science, detailing all of the sciences it aids. The invention of glass is held to be a particularly important achievement of chemistry, without which 'the sublime researches of the moderns concerning heat and light would have been wholly lost to us' (*Collected Works*, II, 317–18). He goes on to compare 'primitive' man with civilized man who has all the benefits and enjoyments provided by scientific knowledge. 'Science' has given to man 'creative' powers that enable him to:

> modify and change the beings surrounding him, and by his experiments to interrogate nature with power, not simply as a scholar, passive and seeking only to understand her operations, but rather as a master, active with his own instruments.
>
> (*Collected Works*, II, 319)

The chemist, then, does not simply study the active powers of nature, he is himself in possession of active powers, able to 'modify and change' other beings. The chemist can change matter into other forms, such as solids into gases through sublimation, reveal the existence of previously unknown elements through the use of processes such as galvanism, and control other transformative activities and processes. In the style of the Kantian sublime, Davy's chemist is not the subject of nature but superior to it.

Though chemistry is a branch of 'sublime philosophy' it has much still to achieve. It can:

> produce, by means of our instruments of experiment, an almost infinite variety of minute phænomena, yet we are incapable of determining the general laws by which they are governed; and in attempting to define them, we are lost in obscure, though sublime imaginations concerning unknown agencies.
>
> (*Collected Works*, II, 320)

Here again, Davy may be referring privately to his own speculations on the laws that govern existence. Such thoughts are 'sublime' though and they are also to be encouraged. He continues by saying that he is confident that these general laws 'may be discovered' (*Collected Works*, II, 320). Later in the *Discourse*, he writes that 'The study of nature, therefore, in her various operations must be always more or less connected with the love of the beautiful and sublime' (*Collected Works*, II, 325). This means, specifically, that chemistry is connected with the beautiful and the sublime, and 'in consequence of the extent and indefiniteness of the views it presents to us, it is eminently calculated to gratify and keep alive the more powerful passions and ambitions of the soul' (*Collected Works*, II, 325). The views gained by chemical study are themselves sublime (characterized as large and indefinite), and they have a sublime effect upon us.

Given that Davy's scientific work was so important to the Romantics – not just Wordsworth and Coleridge, but also Anna Letitia Barbauld, Baillie, the Shelleys, Byron, and quite probably Keats – his concept of the sublime should be taken seriously. This chapter shows how the usual tradition invoked in a history of the sublime – Burke, Priestley, Kant – was itself informed by scientific and medical ideas. Not only this, Davy proceeded to form his own idea of the sublime, taking and appropriating ideas from each of these writers. His poetry demonstrates the formulation of the idea but his scientific writing sees the application of this idea to chemistry itself. These investigations lead to a re-evaluation of the 'sublime', one of the key concepts of Romantic-era discourse.

Conclusion

Romantic writers' engagement with science and medicine is complex, sophisticated, and at times critical and challenging. Scientific and medical ideas are accepted and appropriated for political purposes, a process which reveals that poets, novelists, and essay writers were fully alive to the cultural weight of these ideas. Conversely, explicitly scientific and medical texts can be seen to borrow the language, images, metaphors, and aesthetic practices we would usually associate with more literary kinds of writing. Even where chapters in this book consider what appears to be one-way influence from science to literature or vice versa, this is rarely straightforward. These writers of all genres were astute political thinkers who identified and utilized what they needed from the work of others. Just as science is not a cultural monolith, despite the singular noun used to describe it, Romanticism should more properly be recognized as Romanticisms, and the plurality and variety of genre, politics, and style can be seen in the many texts discussed in this book. It is difficult to conclude that there was a particular method, practice or approach in the Romantics' use of science and medicine, although we can say that clearly they were very interested in it, whether defining themselves against it or adopting it for their own ends.

With all of this taken into account, it is possible to be more confident about a number of things which might help towards understanding how our perception of the period changes once we include science and medicine in the picture. The 1790s, the decade with which this book is mostly concerned, was a crucible for what we now call 'Romanticism'. We see some of the key concepts that we now associate with the period's literature and politics being formed in this decade, such as natural rights, the creative imagination, and the sublime. This was a decade in which poets struggled to define what poetry was and what they thought it should be, at the same time as natural philosophers and 'men of science' struggled to become 'scientists'. These efforts are connected: Wordsworth's attempt to demarcate what he does from 'Matter of Fact' develops as he gains greater understanding of what 'science' means from the work of Davy (*Prose Works*, I, 135). Reading natural history helps Wollstonecraft to formulate the ideas that we find in *Vindication of the Rights of Woman*; translating the French commissioner's report offers Godwin a model for both Falkland and Caleb in *Caleb Williams*. In turn, Davy's sense of the importance of his scientific work is illuminated by the concept of the sublime. This book covers much more than these examples and in doing so confirms the idea that science, medicine, and literature were not separate cultures.

This book also argues for the centrality of Davy – who features in the introduction and final chapter of the book but whose presence is felt throughout – to Romantic-period culture. His links to many poets, novelists, and political writers often situate him in particularly interesting moments of history: the circle at Bristol that he is part of at the end of the 1790s is an exciting one for poetry as well as for science and medicine. His first attempts at scientific experiment are characterized by an ambition of purpose matched by those being made for other subjects by Wordsworth and Coleridge. Later in his life, and beyond the scope of this book, Davy becomes friends with other poets, Joanna Baillie, Thomas Moore, and Lord Byron among them. His own poetry is characteristically Romantic: intensely personal lyrics that find solace and inspiration in nature. It is fascinating to consider how Davy was important to texts that helped create the aesthetic and sentiment of the time, such as the 'Preface' to the *Lyrical Ballads* and *Biographia Literaria*, and that in his own poetry he continued this project. This book rejects the idea, now hopefully laid to rest, that the Romantics were solitary, introverted geniuses, and instead shows the many communities, networks, and circles to which they belonged. It extends this to take in the scientific and medical communities, represented by the new scientific periodicals and by audiences at public lectures as well as through friendships and through relationships between patients and their doctors. Returning to concepts such as Coleridge's organicism or creativity with a historicist approach reveals the work that is still to be done on ideas often now considered old-fashioned and outmoded. The Romantic period, and the 1790s in particular, experienced an exciting explosion of the public sphere, with ideas jostling with each other for recognition and significance. While many critics in the discipline of English Literature have given up using the term 'Romanticism' because of its anachronism, critical history, and past associations, I think it should be usefully re-considered as a more culturally-inclusive term that incorporates science and medicine with literature.

Notes

Introduction

1. Major works cited in abbreviated form within the text and manuscript sources are detailed in the preliminary pages.
2. I use the word 'science' in its modern meaning for ease of reference throughout this book, though I do not mean to imply by this that it was in any way a monolithic entity. However, I avoid the word 'scientist', which was not coined until 1833.
3. His use of the word 'enthusiasm' here confirms Jon Mee's thesis that enthusiasm had to be regulated and controlled since it had become associated at the end of the eighteenth century with the riotous mob (Mee 2003).
4. Throughout the book, I regard medicine as a scientific discipline, though it is such an important one in this period that it is often referred to independently.
5. See, in particular, work in the bibliography by the following: Allard, Budge, de Almeida, Duffy, Earl, Fulford, George, Gigante, Heringman, Holmes, Jackson, Kitson, Lawlor, Lussier, O'Connor, Richardson, N. Roe, Sha, Shuttleton, Underwood, Vickers, Wallen, E. Wilson, and Youngquist. I have deliberately excluded eco-criticism from the scope of this book, though there has been some excellent work done in this area.
6. Beer (1993). Stefan Collini describes the development of 'a whole sub-field or "interdiscipline" of "science and literature"' in his Introduction to C.P. Snow's *The Two Cultures* (Collini 1993, liii). G.S. Rousseau was one of the first to attempt to configure the fields of both literature and science and literature and medicine (Rousseau 1991, 2–25, 202–12; see also Ruston 2008a).
7. See Golinski (1992). See also Fulford et al. (2004). This period saw the creation of the Linnean Society (1788), the Royal Institution (1799), the Geological Society (1807), and the British Association for the Advancement of Science (1831). This picture has been complicated more recently by work that emphasizes the multitude and variety of forms and locations in which science was found (see Fyfe and Lightman 2007). Essays written by John Money and Trevor Levere in Wood (2004) both also emphasize the links between provincial and metropolitan science at this time.
8. According to a 2006 survey, most of these concepts are among those themes and ideas most often taught by UK academics. Full details of the survey results are available on the British Association for Romantic Studies website: 'Survey Results: Teaching Romanticism Questionnaire' (2006), *BARS Website* <http://www.bars.ac.uk/teaching/survey/surveyresults.php> (accessed 24 January 2013).
9. See, for example, Whale (2000), Barrell (2000), Clark (1997), and Pope (2005).
10. The books particularly relevant here are *Madness and Civilisation*, *The Birth of the Clinic*, and *Discipline and Punish*.
11. '[W]hatever the actual achievements of the [Victorian] poets, the name "Poetry" too often became a vague short-hand term for a lost lyrical

directness of first-person feeling, an ideal of Romantic transcendentalism that was seemingly no more, alongside other religious and spiritual losses' (Davis 2002, 225).

12. Klancher's point is noted by O'Connor (2007, 14) and Heringman (2004, 7).
13. John Christie and Sally Shuttleworth also locate the differentiation made between science and literature in the 1600s 'on the terrain of expression, of language and discourse', arguing that with the establishment of the Royal Society 'science would now forgo the whole realm of rhetorical persuasion and of figuration', whereas, simultaneously, literature developed as 'a kind of expressive practice termed rhetorical and figural'. They remind us too that 'What we take as "creative imagination", "rationality", "method", "objectivity" [...] are historical artefacts produced by institutionally located practices and their communicative forms' (Christie and Shuttleworth 1989, 2–3).
14. In support they quote Thomas de Quincey (Daston and Galison 2007, 31).
15. I am aware of the problems associated with using the *OED* as an authority but find it a useful tool when distinguishing between meanings current at particular times (see Williams 1983, 18).
16. Letter to Benjamin Bailey, 22 November 1817 (Keats 2002, 36).
17. The SciPer Project examined, among other subjects, the interactions of scientific and literary articles in periodicals from 1800 to 1900, *Science in the Nineteenth-Century Periodical* <http://www.sciper.org/> (accessed 19 February 2013).
18. The understanding of this word as referring specifically to a scientific context is given in the *OED* as: '3. An action or operation undertaken in order to discover something unknown, to test a hypothesis, or establish or illustrate some known truth. a. in science'. This meaning of the word was not only current in 1798 but is offered as the earliest appearance of the word 'experiment' more generally.
19. Olivia Smith brings to the fore the ways in which 'The experimentation of Wordsworth and Coleridge proves to be one of many and diverse experiments concerning the relation of language to class' (Smith 1984, vii).
20. See Chapter 3 for the use of similar metaphors to describe literary creation.
21. Wordsworth also thinks that children are closer to nature because they are more in touch with their 'animal sensations' (*Prose Works*, I, 142). See also 'Tintern Abbey':

    For nature then
    (The coarser pleasures of my boyish days,
    And their glad animal movements all gone by,)
    To me was all in all

    (Wordsworth 1992, 118, ll. 73–6)

22. In Chapter 4, for example, I examine Davy's determination to discover the laws of life.
23. According to Wordsworth a poet is, of course, 'a man speaking to men' and so I shall follow his gendered terms (*Prose Works*, I, 138).
24. Unless otherwise stated, italics are in the original text.

25. The first time that the word 'scientific' is used in this way, to mean systematic or methodical is in 1794 according to the *OED*. In any case it is not a word that Wordsworth uses himself in the 'Preface' although he does use other words that might be considered to be related to this meaning.
26. See also Teresa Kelley: 'Wordsworth's most radically antithetical claim about poetic language emerges when he defends (and appropriates) the materiality of poetic figures, whether the figure of this materiality is the durability of the language really spoken by men or the epitaphic monument' (Kelley 1988, 193).
27. See Budge (2007a). Budge's article is particularly persuasive as to the currency of the Brunonian metaphors and contemporary readings of Wordsworth's poetics in this light.
28. Wallen writes that 'though Coleridge did not read Brown's *Elementa Medicinae*, he was receptive to Beddoes's ideas which were informed partly by Brunonianism' (Wallen 2004, 7; see also Vickers 1997).
29. See Bynum and Porter (1988). For Coleridge's preference of Schelling's modification of Brown's theory over the original, see Levere (1981, 202–3).
30. Beddoes reports that during lectures, when Brown 'found himself languid, he sometimes placed a bottle of whisky in one hand, and a phial of laudanum on the other'. Such treatment produced correspondingly extreme material: 'Between the effects of these stimulants and voluntary exertion, he soon waxed warm, and by degrees his imagination was exalted into phrenzy' (Brown 1795, I, lxxxvii).
31. See Vickers, too, on the significance of Brown's theory: 'The exciting powers which enable us to live, in the end, cause us to die. Insofar as the causes of health are identical to the causes of illness, health and disease are different manifestations of a single principle' (Vickers 1997, 65). Beddoes stated this with 'IV. *Life is a forced state;* if the exciting powers are withdrawn, death ensues as certainly as when the excitability is gone' (Brown 1795, I, cxxvii).
32. According to an unpublished letter written by Davy on 26 January [1799] Beddoes soon gave up on Brown's theory of excitability: 'Both Browns and Darwins Theories seem to be daily loosing [*sic*] ground. I have had a number of conversations with Dr Beddoes on this subject. Dr Beddoes himself seems to give up altogether Browns Theory' (*Davy Letters*; the original is in the American Philosophical Society).
33. Coleridge to Davy: 'In Wordsworth's case, which I have sent to Beddoes, you will see a curious instance of ideas, linked with feeling habitually, at length forming blind associations with a particular pain, probably in the right hypochondrium—so as immediately to excite that pain' (*Coleridge Letters*, I, 606 (15 [16] July 1800)). Coleridge also asked James Webbe Tobin not to forget to bring 'a bottle of Davy's Acid for Wordsworth' on 17 September 1800 (*Coleridge Letters*, I, 623). This 'perfectly new Acid' discovered by Davy is described in a letter from Coleridge to Godwin because it might help Mary Robinson: 'For Davy has discovered a perfectly new Acid, by which he has restored the use of limbs to persons who had lost them for many years, (one woman 9 years) in cases of supposed Rheumatism. At all events, Davy says, it *can* do no harm, in Mrs Robinson's case—& if she will try it, he will make up a little parcel & write her a letter of *instructions* &c.' (*Coleridge Letters*, I, 589).

34. See also Vickers for Coleridge's 'final estimate of Brunonian medicine' (Vickers 1997, 81–3).
35. In the *OED* 'vitiated' is defined as: 'To reduce the value or impair the quality of. To corrupt morally; debase. To make ineffective; invalidate.' Wollstonecraft's *Vindication of the Rights of Woman* is offered by way of illustration: 'These pretty [superlatives], dropping glibly from the tongue, vitiate the taste, and create a kind of sickly delicacy that turns away from simple unadorned truth' (*Works*, v, 76).
36. Mill uses the terms of Wordsworth's revised 'Preface': 'What made Wordsworth's poems a medicine for my state of mind, was that they expressed, not mere outward beauty, but states of feeling, and of thought coloured by feeling, under the excitement of beauty' (Mill 1981, 153).
37. Coleridge also visited Currie in person in July 1800 by which time Currie had published a new edition of his 'Life' (see Roberts 2003). Roberts's article finds other persuasive points of comparison between the 1798 'Advertisement' to the *Lyrical Ballads* and Currie's 'Life of Burns'.
38. Kirstie Blair (2007) has written about the links between poetic rhythm and the heart's pulse.
39. Blair describes this as 'a curious phrase which seems to substitute "along" for the more common and easily imagined "within", links heart and circulation by implying that these sensations run throughout the body, moving in each vein' (Blair 2007, 7).
40. Darwin presumably alludes here to Christopher Anstey's anonymously published 1766 *The New Bath Guide; or, Memoirs of the B-r-d Family.*
41. Coleridge first mentions Davy in a letter to Southey dated [19 December 1799] (*Coleridge Letters*, I, 547–50). Earl Leslie Griggs thinks they first met just before Coleridge went from Bristol to Sockburn in October 1799 (*Coleridge Letters*, 548, n.1).
42. The same letter announces 'As soon as I have disembrangled my affairs by a couple of months' Industry, I shall attack chemistry, like a Shark —' (I, 605).
43. Wordsworth to Davy (28 [29] July 1800) (Wordsworth 1967, I, 289). The *Lyrical Ballads* was extended to two volumes for the second edition.
44. 'Longman deems it best for you to publish *a Volume*, & be determined by the Nature of the Sale at what interval you will publish a second—the Volume of what size you find convenient. And you may of course begin printing when you like' (*Coleridge Letters*, I, 556 (1 January 1800)). In the event it was published by Joseph Johnson.
45. Sharrock (1962, 64); *Coleridge Letters* (I, 592–3); See also Moorman (1957, I, 488–92). Wordsworth told Josiah Wedgwood in July 'ill health has for some time rendered literary labour inadvisable for me' (Moorman, I, 489). Duncan Wu confirms that the 1800 *Lyrical Ballads* was 'formally published *c.* 26 Jan.' (Wu 1995, 250).
46. Wordsworth was disappointed with the printing: 'After much, perhaps most of the edition was sold, Longman provided new pages of *Michael* and a page of "Errata and Corrections," comprising both corrections of printer's errors and revisions by Wordsworth' (Wordsworth 1992, esp. Introduction).
47. 'I shall emphasize interchange rather than origins and transformation rather than translation' (Beer 1996, 173).

48. Sharrock notes that 'Davy echoes Wordsworth's thought and phraseology' in this passage (Sharrock 1962, 68).
49. Davy's 1802 *Discourse* formed the first session of the course described in the *Syllabus*.
50. Owen and Smyser accept that these echoes occur; they tell us that Wordsworth 'probably revised the Preface and wrote the Appendix between June 1801 and April 1802' but note that these echoes suggest at 'least some of the revision was probably undertaken between late January and April 1802' (*Prose Works*, I, 112).
51. Compare 'those particular parts of nature which are the objects of his study' ('Preface', *Prose Works*, I, 140).

1 Mary Wollstonecraft and Nature

1. See *Works*. Hereafter I shall refer to *Vindication of the Rights of Woman* as *Vindication*.
2. *Vindication* is one of the texts R.S. White considers a product of 'the crucible [in the 1790s] in which ideas were established and fought for, and what came after was a conflict that built upon certain intellectual positions established then' (White 2005, 7).
3. I am following Janet Todd and Marilyn Butler here in assigning these reviews to Wollstonecraft (see *Works*, VII).
4. Wollstonecraft quotes Smellie's use of this word and uses it herself, and different forms of it, in her *Analytical Review* writings; see for example *Works* (VII, 295, 298). Wollstonecraft's and Smellie's ideas are not proto-evolutionary, having more in common with a more general Enlightenment sense of development and progress. See Peter J. Bowler on pre-Darwinian evolutionary thought (Bowler 1989, 51). Erasmus Darwin, of course, was one of only two figures (the other is Lamarck) 'whose ideas seem to come much closer to the modern concept of organic development' (Bowler 1989, 81). Sapiro notes that for Wollstonecraft 'Human imperfection and its attendant potential for improvement are part of the perfect system of nature', which is God's system (Sapiro 1992, 48). Both Godwin and Percy Shelley similarly thought that moral progress would be accompanied by physical improvement.
5. Mary Wollstonecraft to Everina Wollstonecraft, 7 November 1787 (Wollstonecraft 2004, 139).
6. See Schiebinger (1989, 208) and McGrath (2002, 107).
7. Wollstonecraft quotes this passage in her review of this book (*Works*, VII, 312).
8. Paul Youngquist also makes the point that for Wollstonecraft 'An independent woman is physically fit' and that 'To this end, Wollstonecraft includes body in the process of cultivating mind' (Youngquist 2003, 152).
9. For Johnson's publications and specific connections, see Braithwaite (2003). For the literary dissenting circles of the period, see White (2006). For Wollstonecraft's indebtedness to dissenting traditions, see Taylor (2003).
10. *Thoughts on the Education of Daughters* (1787), *Original Stories from Real Life* (1788), *The Female Reader* (1789), some of her translations, *Young Grandison* and *Elements of Morality* (1790), and unfinished work (such as 'On the

Management of Infants' and 'Lessons') can be thought of as related to these genres.

11. Vivien Jones argues that 'Her first publication, *Thoughts on the Education of Daughters* (1787), was a kind of conduct book, and *Rights of Woman* itself still bears more than a passing resemblance to the genre' (Jones 2002, 140).
12. The Royal College of Physicians published a number of editions of *Pharmacopoeia Collegii Regalis Medicorum* in 1788 with Joseph Johnson. Johnson published many of the books reviewed and it seems as though the *Analytical Review* was intended partly to act as a vehicle for advertising these books.
13. On animals in Romantic literature see Kenyon-Jones (2001) and Perkins (2007).
14. Sha also notes passages in *Vindication* where, in his words, 'biology slides into culture' (Sha 2009, 91).
15. George Fordyce is mentioned a number of times in Wollstonecraft's *Letters*. Despite her misgivings about James Fordyce's *Sermons*, which she would 'instantly dismiss' from her pupil's library Wollstonecraft describes dining at the house of 'Dr [George] Fordyce' with: 'I have seldom been in company with more intelligent pleasing women than his two daughters. There [*sic*] education has been attend[ed] to, I may say with emphasis; and there [*sic*] father is now rewarded for his care' (*Works*, v, 162; Wollstonecraft 2004, 213, December 1792).
16. See also Jones's essay on the 'sometimes surprisingly close' connections between Wollstonecraft's writings and those of figures such as Gregory, which also plots 'her discriminating, and shifting, relationship with them' (Jones 2002, 120).
17. I agree with Mary Catherine Moran 'that the *Legacy*'s assumptions about female nature are best understood when placed alongside the account of human nature that Gregory offered in his earlier *Comparative View*' (Moran 2007, 9).
18. Lawrence (1819b, n.p.).
19. Wollstonecraft explains women's interest in clothes with the following: 'Men order their clothes to be made, and have done with the subject; women make their own clothes [...] and are continually talking about them' (*Works*, v, 144).
20. Claudia Johnson writes that Wollstonecraft 'is arguing that man's physical superiority will guarantee their deserved preeminence no matter how strong or "masculine" women should ever become' (Johnson 1995, 41).
21. Marilyn Butler and Janet Todd also claim Wollstonecraft's possible authorship of reviews of other scientific and medical works in *Analytical Review*, such as: *Observations on the General and Improper Treatment of Insanity* (April 1790), George Adams's *An Essay on Vision* (July 1790), and Samuel Shaw's translation of *Physiognomy* (August 1792) (*Works*, vii, 18).
22. His friendship and respect for Gregory is clear from his posthumously published *Literary and Characteristical Lives of John Gregory, M.D. Henry Home, Lord Kames. David Hume, Esq. and Adam Smith, L.L.D.* Smellie also printed, with J. Balfour, Gregory's 1772 Edinburgh edition of *Elements of Physic*.

23. The book Wollstonecraft reviewed was Buffon (1792). There was another multi-volume translation of this text published before Wollstonecraft's review (Buffon 1775–76) but it was not as 'voluminous' as Smellie's.
24. Wollstonecraft's paraphrase in *Vindication* seems nearer to Smellie's translation of Buffon than the version in his *Philosophy*: 'He does not acquire his full growth, and best form, till he arrives at the age of thirty years. But, in women, the parts are rounder, and their muscular fibres more feeble and lax than those of men, and their growth and form are perfect at the age of twenty' (*Philosophy*, 236).
25. See also *Philosophy* (454). Wollstonecraft's version is again close to Smellie's translation: 'it has been remarked, that those which are the most adventurous and expert in these natural exercises, are the most generous, mild, and tractable, when reduced to a domestic state' (Buffon 1780, III, 309).
26. 'Thus the general habit of thinking in terms of species, as well as the sense of the separation of man from the rest of the animal creation, was beginning to break down in the eighteenth century' (Lovejoy 1936, 231).
27. I am grateful to Brycchan Carey for help with this point.
28. There is a brief discussion of 'animal sensations' in the introduction to this book.
29. The spaniel is commonly used as a symbol of female servitude. See for example, *A Midsummer Night's Dream*, where Helena declares 'I am your spaniel' to Demetrius, while under the influence of the love potion (II.1.211). See also, Kelley (2003, 233).
30. Adriana Craciun has also noted the importance of bodily strength to Wollstonecraft's argument in *Vindication* (Craciun 1997).
31. Dependence of the mind upon the body and vice versa was promoted by both radical and conservative women. See William Stafford: 'no woman writer, when she consciously confronts this issue, thinks that weakness of the body is at all desirable, and there are calls for women to become more robust' (Stafford 2002, 175).
32. Wollstonecraft is credited with the review of a number of such books in the *Analytical Review*, including Samuel Stanhope Smith's *An Essay on the Causes of the Variety of Complexion and Figure in the Human Species* (December 1788); Olaudah Equiano's autobiography (May 1789); William Hamilton's *Letters Concerning the Northern Coast of Antrim* (August 1790); Joseph Lavall Bois-Robert's novel, *The Negro Equalled by Few Europeans* (August 1790); and a translation of Le Vaillant's *New Travels into the Interior Parts of Africa* (May 1797).
33. Stanhope Smith (1788, 165). See also Sapiro (1992, 46) on this review.

2 William Godwin and the Imagination

1. Wollstonecraft is prepared to consider the existence of 'subtle electric fluid' within our bodies, allowing that according to 'materialists', 'the most powerful effects in nature are apparently produced by fluids, the magnetic, etc.' She asks why, in this case, 'the passions might not be fine volatile fluids' also (*Works*, V, 185, n.).

2. Godwin's translation was published anonymously ([Godwin] 1785). It will be referred to as *Report* for the remainder of this chapter. Where I am referring to the French original ([Bailly] 1784) I shall use the title *Rapport*.
3. Sha discusses the French commissioners' report but unfortunately did not know that this was translated by Godwin.
4. The nature of the French commissioners' report might be likened to the shift Terry Castle perceives with regard to the Enlightenment's view of apparitions and ghosts. She describes this as an 'act of internalization' or a realization that ghosts are figments of the mind rather than external bodies; this act 'was actually a momentous event in the history of Western consciousness, with paradoxical consequences for the modern theory of imagination' (Castle 1995, 171).
5. One exception is an essay by Angela Monsam in which she argues that '*Memoirs* was influenced by, if not modelled after, contemporary medical writings, particularly dissection reports. Specifically, Godwin's apparently insensitive, factual detailing of Wollstonecraft's life may have been influenced by his interest in contemporary science, including anatomy' (Monsam 2008, 110).
6. *Political Writings* (v, 178). Corfield also cites this passage (1995, 59).
7. Butler (1995, 348). Wollstonecraft writes something very similar in an October 1789 review where she criticizes the educational books of Madame de Genlis: 'With respect to filial and religious duties, she inculcates blind faith instead of a submission to reason; this error, must ever give the mind an indolent, servile turn' (*Works*, vii, 175).
8. 'Preface' to second and later editions of *Caleb Williams* (*Novels and Memoirs*, iii, 279).
9. Mark Philp did not include the *Memoirs*, which he calls Godwin's 'one work of translation' in the *Political Writings* (i, 43). St Clair describes it as 'a book of quite exceptional dullness' (St Clair 1989, 23). The National Library of Scotland has an edition of this text published by J. Murray and dated 1785. Thanks to David McClay for confirming this.
10. Roger McLure, a French language specialist, has examined the *Report* comparing it to the original, attributed to Jean Sylvain Bailly: he notes that the translation is 'remarkably good throughout, in places inspired in its syntactic recastings and inventions. It reveals an excellent knowledge of French and is faithful in the sense that [Godwin] translates *all and only all* of the substance of the French text: neither by unwarranted additions of meaning (as distinct from just words) nor by omissions, nor by any other device, does he give rise to the suspicion of promoting a personal agenda' (unpublished report prepared by Roger McLure). I acknowledge the financial support of the Research Institute for the Humanities at Keele University in funding this work.
11. William Temple Franklin Papers, American Philosophical Society, CVI, 94. I am grateful to the curator of the American Philosophical Society archive for sending me a copy of this letter and to the society for permission to quote from it.
12. In terms of style, the *Report* features the removal of the second 'l' in names such as Marshall, which St Clair considers (not speaking about this text) as 'a surer proof of Godwinian authorship than stylistic analysis alone can

usually expect' (St Clair 1989, 22). In the 'Historical Introduction' the name 'Maxwel' is spelled in Godwinian fashion (*Report*, xix) but it is also spelled this way in Thouret's original text, which is being discussed and on occasion, quoted, in the *Report*. See, for example, Thouret (1784, xxiv).

13. Simon Schaffer notes that Godwin's translation refers to this context as further evidence of the way that 'the history of astro-meteorology was of necessity produced as part of the debate about mesmerism's roots and rights' (Schaffer 2010, 162).
14. Mesmer used the name 'animal magnetism' to suggest it was 'an application of Newtonian philosophy to bodily health; skeptics gave his therapy the (initially pejorative) name of "mesmerism" to deny that physical forces were involved' (Winters 1998, 2).
15. Wakley (1823, 2). Corfield also quotes this passage (1995, 165).
16. Southcott was sixty-one years old at this time and convinced that she was carrying the second Messiah (see Lee 2006, 72–7). For the purported medical evidence, see Southcott ([1814]).
17. On Graham and other quacks, see Porter (1989) and Syson (2008). Tim Fulford has also written on Graham and his associations with Mary Robinson, see Fulford (2002).
18. Godwin may have learned of these ideas from John Abernethy who publicized Hunter's ideas. Abernethy described Hunter's ideas as 'that sympathy which the whole system seems to have with its several parts' (Abernethy 1814, 99–100). For more on Godwin's connections with these surgeons and on Romantic sympathy, see Ruston (2005, chapter 2).
19. There are 3135 entries giving thermometer readings. See Jan Golinski (2007) on the Enlightenment project of daily recordings of weather and temperature. In *Thoughts on Man* Godwin considers that a 'fitting temperature, neither too hot nor cold' is needed for good health (*Political Writings*, VI, 43).
20. Nicholson lived with Holcroft from 1778 for three years until Nicholson's marriage. Iain Watts, 'Natural Philosophy and Chemistry in Monthly Numbers: Editorship, Authorship, and Anonymity in *Nicholson's Journal*, 1797–1813' (unpublished article). I am very grateful to Iain Watts for sharing this unpublished article with me.
21. There are two William Nicholsons in Godwin's Diary. I refer to the one who was born in December 1753 and is described by the editors as 'chemist; inventor'.
22. *The Doubts of the Infidels; or, Queries relative to Scriptural inconsistencies and contradictions ... By a Weak Christian* (see [Nicholson] 1781).
23. See Chapter 1 for a discussion of Wollstonecraft's review.
24. Iain Watts has discovered from newspaper advertisements that the 'lectures were on Tuesday and Friday evenings at 7 o'clock, starting from the 29 October, and consisted of two courses (12 lectures each) on "Mechanics, Hydraulics, Electricity, Optics, Astronomy &c", and one course on "Philosophical and Technical Chemistry". The venue was Nicholson's house at 10 Soho Square, there were experimental demonstrations, and the lectures were marketed at a "mixed audience".' I am grateful to Iain Watts for sharing this with me. See Nicholson (1782).
25. Anthony Carlisle has been proposed as the author of a number of gothic novels, writing under the pseudonym 'Mrs Carver', such as *The Horrors of Oakendale Abbey* (1797) (see Shelton 2009).

26. I am grateful to Sarah M. Zimmerman for this source.
27. There is not much evidence that this word was used commonly after Godwin's coinage and the *OED* describes it as both obsolete and rare. It only offers one other instance in 1799 of the use of the same phrase, 'digestic powers'. There are other instances of the phrase, such as in Ewell (1816, 84). William Hone also speaks of John Abernethy's book on the 'Digestic Organs' in his almanac, first published in 1825 (Hone 1839, I, 304).
28. See the introduction for a discussion of Brown's theory.
29. Ni Chonaill tells us that 'While previous writers such as La Mettrie had discussed the connection between the mind and physical health, Godwin was the first philosopher to take the doctrine of perfectibility a step further by establishing a link between human progress and physical immortality' (2007, 36).
30. Southey does not allude to Godwin by name but draws a profile of a man with a very large aquiline nose presumed to be Godwin.
31. This letter is held in the Bodleian Library, Oxford. Godwin did dine as invited (*Godwin Diary*).
32. St Clair writes about the phrenology studies that used Godwin's own head as illustration of argument, as well as Godwin's personal interest in the subject (St Clair 1989, 262). On 28 August 1830 Godwin records 'Cast at Spurzheim's', which has led diary editors to suggest that he had his skull cast for a phrenology reading (*Godwin Diary*).
33. In later editions of the novel Godwin writes 'power' instead of 'reach', a word used repeatedly in the *Report* and which has particular associations with the sublime (*Novels and Memoirs*, III, 303, n. 115).
34. See also Daffron (1995, 220).
35. *Political Writings* (III, 268); cited in Butler (1995, 348).
36. Mesmerism influences literature beyond the Romantic period to a significant degree. See, for instance, Willis (2006) and Willis and Wynne (2006).

3 Romantic Creation

1. I use the words 'monster' and 'monstrous' in this chapter because these were the terms used at the time, but the scare quotes should be understood hereafter.
2. In chapter 4 I also briefly examine Edmund Burke's view of taste.
3. Rob Pope's book *Creativity* has been very helpful in the writing of this chapter, particularly in setting parameters around a potentially huge topic (Pope 2005). See also Williams (1976, 83–4).
4. See Clifford Siskin (2011, p. 281 and n. 1). The project of rehabilitating 'creativity' has already begun with the publication of this special journal issue, which was based on the conference 'Contesting Creativity, 1740–1830' at the University of Leeds in September 2008.
5. Clark's project is similar to Rob Pope's, to give serious consideration to what is now thought of as 'trite, mystifying, and even embarrassing', the 'spurious and exploded theory' of inspiration (Clark 1997, 1).
6. Godwin uses the word 'man' throughout. Burton's *Anatomy* was published in 1800 after a period of being out of print.

7. Godwin slightly misquotes *Hamlet* (Shakespeare 1994a, II. 2. 303–4).
8. Translated by the editors (Shelley 2003, 698, n. 835).
9. He gives the example of Gibbon and finds instead in the circumstances of his early life a clue to the source of his genius (*Political Writings*, V, 93).
10. Sidney (1989, 153, Sonnet 1, l. 12). Sidney uses the term 'invention' three times in this opening sonnet, thus demonstrating the different possible meanings for the word and the way the word's meaning has changed over time. See also Toor (2007, 261).
11. Chibka (1986, 541). Pope (2005, 57) discusses Young's text as one that 'marks the turning point' in the meaning of the word 'original'.
12. Warton (1756, v). This was dedicated to Young.
13. Hurd (1766, 10). Hurd also wrote a *Discourse on Poetical Imitation* (1751).
14. For more on these kinds of metaphors, see Dixon Hunt (1976). Thanks to Stephen Bending for this reference.
15. Wordsworth acknowledged the debt of this phrase to *Night Thoughts* in a note (Wordsworth 1992, 119, l. 107n; see Tydahl 1962, 128, n. 3).
16. Aristotle writes: 'of these spontaneously-generated plants some derive their nourishment from the earth, while some come into being in other plants'. He thought that animals could do the same (Aristotle 1970, V. 1, 99).
17. Tasso (1987, 341). My thanks to Clare McManus for identifying this reference.
18. MacKenzie (1808, VI, 389; Wordsworth 1990, 156). For an extensive list of labouring-class poets, see Goodridge (2006).
19. This passage is discussed in the Introduction.
20. Duff also quotes this passage (2009, 175).
21. Hutton's theory of the earth was first given as a paper to the Royal Society of Edinburgh in 1785, then published in the society's *Transactions* in 1785, and published as a book in 1795. Cuvier's work was also not published until the end of the century.
22. This was the idea informing the convulsions brought on by animal magnetism discussed in Chapter 2.
23. Other critics have pointed out the parallels that exist between Joanna and Matthew Baillie's work. See, for example Burwick (2004) and Richardson (2004).
24. 'Trace' can also have a specific scientific meaning as discussed in the introduction. Davy uses the verb 'to trace' in both his poetry and scientific writing, see Chapter 4.
25. For the importance of this text, see the 'Editor's Introduction' (*Biographia*).
26. The term ('mordant') comes from the process of dyeing and refers to a 'substance which combines with a dye that has low affinity for a particular textile fibre, enabling it to become firmly fixed in the fibre' (*OED*). It was a word that Coleridge used elsewhere in a figurative sense. See Duff on the biological and chemical metaphors used by Coleridge and in the period more generally (Duff 2009, 160–200).
27. See Abernethy (1814, 39, 94; and 1817, 26, 44, 46, 269, 277) for his uses of this word.
28. Coleridge coined the term 'esemplastic' to describe the imagination (*Biographia*, I, 168–70; *OED*). See Wylie (1989) on Coleridge's sources for this term.

29. See Porter (2004) and also the discussion of proto-evolutionary ideas in Chapter 1.
30. The *Rapport* on animal magnetism by J.S. Bailly, discussed in Chapter 2, was used as 'a striking example of the general credit given to the power of the imagination' by the French King's physician, Benjamin Bablot, writing in favour of the theory of maternal impressions in 1788 (Huet 1993, 71).
31. Katherine Park and Lorraine J. Daston show that the representation of monsters had already evolved some way during the sixteenth and seventeenth centuries: 'As the period progressed, they appeared more and more as natural wonders – signs of nature's fertility rather than God's wrath' (Park and Daston 1981, 23).
32. Though she does not discuss Lawrence, Huet writes that by this time 'within the framework of rational thought on natural deviations, the monster became nothing more than a variation, a definable category of living species' (Huet 1993, 101).
33. Lawrence's *Cyclopædia* entry was first published in 1814 and so was available to Shelley (see Lawrence 1814). I am grateful to Jessica Evans for bringing this to my attention.
34. A number of critics have fruitfully examined this pairing; see, in particular, Fred Botting (1991) who also considers the 'critical monsters' created by the reception of the novel.
35. Coleridge writes that gothic novels are produced by the 'sickly imagination' of their authors (*Biographia*, II, 211). See also the quotation from Hurd earlier in this chapter.
36. Not all critics have agreed with Butler; for example, editors D.L. Macdonald and Kathleen Scherf write that 'Butler's characterization of the novel as essentially mechanist is a well-intentioned but misguided attempt to align Shelley with the most progressive science of her day' (Shelley 1994, 20).

4 Humphry Davy and the Sublime

1. David Duff also notes the 'chemical poetics' of these passages in Coleridge's *Biographia* (Duff 2009, 176–9). Duff also notes Coleridge's indebtedness to Davy for his chemical knowledge (Duff 2009, 177).
2. From notes for an 'Introductory Lecture to the Chemistry of Nature' to be delivered on 30 January 1807 (quoted in J. Davy 1836, I, 170–1).
3. This research has been aided by the publication of Robert Southey's letters, William Godwin's diaries, and the project currently underway to publish Davy's letters. See the list of abbreviations in the preliminary pages.
4. Johnson published a number of Davy's early works. In the Pforzheimer Collection, at the New York Public Library, there is a letter to Davy recorded in Johnson's Letterbook of 1795–1810 (Pforzheimer Misc. MS 4039) sent to Davy in Bristol and dated 27 February 1800. This sets out the terms for the publication of his 'Physiological Exp^{ts}'. Davy's connection with Johnson continues, with Godwin recording him at dinner at Johnson's on 17 February 1801, 20 October 1802, 29 December 1802, 2 November 1803, 12

December 1804, 20 March 1805, and 25 August 1809 (*Godwin Diary*). Davy's choice of publisher, no doubt influenced by Coleridge and Godwin, further suggests that Davy's politics were rather more radical in his youth than in later years.

5. Coleridge only once notes the date of a particular lecture 'Feb. 6. Lecture on Metals' (Coleridge 1957–2002, I, 1098*f*12ᵛ).
6. *Biographia* (I, 295); Coleridge does continue for a few lines more (Milton 1674, V, 130–1, ll. 469–84).
7. Stuart Peterfreund (2003) uses Davy's sublimation of iodine as a context in which to consider Percy Shelley's use of chemical sublimation as a metaphor.
8. See Ashfield and de Bolla (1996) for the development of the 'sublime' as a historical concept.
9. Anne Janowitz (2005, 469) looks at Adam Smith's description of the sublime, which she finds to be 'in part, a celebration of the Newtonian explanation of the universe'.
10. See Aris Sarafianos (2008) on Burke's medical knowledge, particularly the influence of his father-in-law and doctor, Christopher Nugent.
11. I am grateful to George Rousseau for confirming that Descartes and Thomas Willis are most likely the physiologists referred to here.
12. Cheyne (1724, 91). This text was hugely popular, being republished many times. On Cheyne's influence generally, see the work of Roy Porter and George Rousseau. Sarafianos thinks these passages show the influence of Francis Fuller rather than Cheyne (Sarafianos 2005, 69).
13. I discovered Vermeir and Deckard (2005) late in the writing of this book, but they confirm Cheyne as a source for Burke while adding much more to the subject of Burke's scientific and medical knowledge.
14. Davy refers to Priestley repeatedly in his own scientific writings, demonstrating his familiarity with Priestley's work. John Davy quotes Priestley's assessment of Davy: 'Mr H. Davy's Essays ['on Heat, Light, and the Combinations of Light'] have impressed me with a high opinion of his philosophical acumen' (*Collected Works*, II, 3).
15. Joseph Priestley, 'Of the Sublime' (Priestley 1777, 151–63; see also Townsend 1993).
16. I do take on board Duffy and Howell's (2011, 2–3) concerns about the use of Kant in consideration of the British sublime, but in Davy's case it does seem quite possible that he would have read Kant.
17. See Vickers (1997 and 2004). Monika Class's 2013 book examines Beddoes's review of Kant and its impact on Coleridge's and Wordsworth's constructions of genius. I am grateful to both Neil and Monika for help on these matters.
18. Golinski points out that Davy's use of the sublime changed over his lifetime (Golinski 2009, 539).
19. RI MS HD 20b, 133. Davy wrote this after an experiment dated 26 December 1799.
20. See, in particular, Knight (1992) and Fullmer (2000); both Knight (2005) and Fullmer (1960) have written articles on Davy's poetry. Holmes (2008) includes poetry in his chapters on Davy. Wahida Amin is currently writing a doctoral thesis, 'Science and Poetry: The Case of Humphry Davy' jointly with the University of Salford and the Royal Institution.

21. [John Mitford] (1837). Author identified by Kuist (1982, 103).
22. 'Life' in Baillie (1823, 156–62). John Gibson Lockhart clearly read an early version of this poem: 'for who that has read his sublime quatrains on the doctrine of Spinoza can doubt that he might have united, if he had pleased, in some great didactic poem, the vigorous ratiocination of Dryden and the moral majesty of Wordsworth?' (Lockhart 1839, VI, 245).
23. Davy wrote to Purkis when sending him one of his poems: 'If I thought that people in general would think as favourably of my poetical productions, I would write more verses, and would write them with more care' ([?January 1805] *Davy Letters*; Paris 1831, 123). Of course this could be false modesty; it certainly is the case that Davy continued to write poetry.
24. Holmes compares Davy's poem 'The Tempest' to Thompson's *The Seasons* (Holmes 2008, 243). This poem was published in *Annual Anthology* (Davy 1799a).
25. See Maurice Hindle's forthcoming essay, 'Nature, Power, and the Light of Suns: The Poetry of Humphry Davy' to be published in the *Charles Lamb Bulletin*.
26. Wahida Amin has transcribed hundreds of poems, as well as revisions and re-workings of poems, for her PhD research (see note 20). She intends to publish this as an appendix to her PhD thesis.
27. RI MS HD 20c, pp. 44. 46. 52. This notebook is marked 'Clifton 1800 From August to Novr' in the front cover.
28. This friend may have been Southey; certainly there is a letter dated 3 August 1799 in which Southey tries to persuade Davy to jointly write a heroic epic on 'Mango Capac' the leader of the Incas (*Southey Letters*).
29. Sharrock compares a letter Davy writes to Thomas Underwood in July 1801 with the sentiments of 'Tintern Abbey' as well as the 'sentiment and something of the phrasing and grammatical construction of a stanza of "Hartleap Well"' (Paris 1831, 82; Sharrock 1962, 65). Jenkins compares a number of Davy's poems to 'Tintern Abbey', and more generally states that 'the influence of "Tintern Abbey" on Davy's Clifton poetry is strong' (Jenkins 1998, 144).
30. I am grateful to Lynda Pratt for confirming John Davy's assertion in the *Memoirs* that Davy did this. She pointed me to Southey's preface to *Thalaba* in the last lifetime edition of Southey's *Poetical Works*: 'It was printed at Bristol by Biggs and Cottle, and the task of correcting the press was undertaken for me by Davy and our common friend Danvers, under whose roof it had been begun' (Southey 1837–38, IV, xii–xiii).
31. 'Prologue (*Written by a* FRIEND)', in John Tobin 1805. Elizabeth Benger declares Davy to be the author of these lines (Benger 1820, vii). Paris confirms this (Paris 1831, I, 184).
32. 'Lord Byron, Written Whilst Living' (1823) and 'On the Death of Lord Byron' (*Collected Works*, I, 285–6).
33. Alice Jenkins has also made this connection and finds point of comparison with Wordsworth's 'Tintern Abbey' (Jenkins 1998).
34. Coleridge to Dr Williamson (*Coleridge Letters*, V, 309 (10 [11] November 1823)).
35. Davy (1799b). Hereafter, line numbers are given in the text as is the case for all poetry after the first reference.
36. This letter is held in the Royal Institution of Great Britain.

37. This letter is held in the Royal Institution of Great Britain.
38. This letter is held in the Royal Institution of Great Britain.
39. This letter is held in the Royal Institution of Great Britain.
40. This letter is published in Campbell (1908, I, 281).
41. This letter is held in the Royal Institution of Great Britain.
42. This letter was published in Söderbaum (1912–32, II, 74–5).
43. This letter is held in the Royal Institution of Great Britain.
44. This letter is held in the Royal Institution of Great Britain.
45. This letter is held in the Royal Institution of Great Britain.
46. Letter to John Hamilton Reynolds, 3 February 1818 (Keats, 1970, 60–2).
47. For references to astronomy, see *Collected Works* (II, 314). He describes astronomy as a 'sublime Science' in a letter to H.C. Schumacher (1 March 1825; *Davy Letters*); this letter is held at the Deutsche Staatsbibliothek Berlin. For references to geology see *Collected Works* (VIII).
48. A year after publication, in an essay published in Nicholson's *Journal* in February 1800 Davy qualifies the ideas published in his 'Essay' (*Collected Works*, II, 126). In an essay published in the same journal in December 1800, Davy calls these theories his 'infant chemical speculations' (*Collected Works*, II, 169).
49. 'No more sublime idea can be formed of the motions of matter, than to conceive that the different species are continually changing into each other' (*Collected Works*, II, 29, n.). John Davy notes that his brother intended to strike out this passage, but it is remarkably like other passages published later in Davy's career, which are discussed in this chapter.
50. This letter is held in the Royal Institution.
51. This letter is held in the American Philosophical Society.
52. Fullmer writes that while he gave up those theories in his science, he continued to express them in his poetry and that later in life light became 'synonymous with his personal God' (Fullmer 1960, 108).
53. Letter to Davies Giddy, 10 April 1799 (*Davy Letters*; Paris 1831, 55).
54. He proposes calling the gas nitrous oxide in a letter tentatively dated December 1799 to Nicholson, which is published in his *Journal* in 1800 (Nicholson 1800).
55. There is some evidence that Davy's nitrous oxide research had these aims; for example, Coleridge wrote to Davy on 7 June 1800: 'When you have leisure, you would do me a great service, if you would briefly state your metaphysical system of Impressions, Ideas, Pleasures, & Pains, the laws that govern them, & the reasons which induce you to consider them as essentially distinct from each other' (*Coleridge Letters*, I, 590; see also Holmes 2008, 255).
56. Jan Golinski also makes this comparison (Golinski 2011, 18).
57. Southey also recounts this episode in a letter to Charles Watkin Williams Wynn, 24 September 1799 (*Southey Letters*).
58. Southey to Tom Southey, 12 July 1799 (*Southey Letters*).
59. A number of critics have commented on this aspect of the experiments (see, for example Jay 2009, 180).
60. Noel Jackson also makes the point that Davy is attempting to reconnect language with the senses and that this might be likened to Wordsworth's project in the 'Preface' to the *Lyrical Ballads* (Jackson 2008, 44–5).
61. Holmes notes that one of Davy's earliest known poems, 'My eye is wet with tears' demonstrates 'purely materialist philosophy' (Holmes 2008, 240).

62. This letter is held in the Royal Institution of Cornwall, Truro.
63. Unpublished letter quoted in Levere (1981, 32).
64. For example, Adam Walker, a popular itinerant lecturer believed this (see Ruston 2005, 32) and Golinski writes that Walker influenced Davy's lectures (Golinski 1999, 22).
65. Davy uses the verb 'to trace' a number of times in his poetry, see *Collected Works* (I, 8, 59, 116, 175, 334). This word can have specific scientific meaning, as discussed in the introduction and Chapter 3.

Bibliography

Abernethy, J. (1809) *Surgical Observations on the Constitutional Origin and Treatment of Local Diseases and on Aneurisms* (London: Longman, Hurst, Rees and Orme).

—— (1814) *An Enquiry into the Probability and Rationality of Mr. Hunter's Theory of Life [...]* (London: Longman, Hurst, Rees, Orme and Brown).

—— (1817) *Physiological Lectures [...]* (London: Longman, Hurst, Rees, Orme, and Brown).

Abrams, M.H. (1953) *The Mirror and the Lamp* (Oxford: Oxford University Press).

Addison, J. (1711) *The Spectator*, 161.

Allard, J.R. (2007) *Romanticism, Medicine and the Poet's Body* (Aldershot: Ashgate).

Anon. (1784a) 'Art. 12. *Imogen, a Pastoral Romance; in 2 Vols*', *English Review*, 4, 142.

Anon. (1784b) 'Art. 19. *Italian Letters, or the History of the Count de St. Julian*', *English Review*, 4, 312.

Anon, (1784c) 'Art. 14. *Recherches et Doutes sur le Magnetisme Animal [...]*', *English Review*, 4, 381–90.

Anon. (1784d) 'Art. 15. *Rapport des Commissaires charges par le Roi, de l'Examen du Magnetisme Animal [...]*', *English Review*, 4, 381–90.

Anon. (1785) 'Art. 23. *Report of Dr. Benjamin Franklin and other Commissioners [...]*', *English Review*, 5, 304–5.

Anon. (1788a) *Prospectus of the Analytical Review [...]* (London: J. Johnson).

Anon. (1788b) *Analytical Review [...]*, 1.

Anon. (1791) *A New System of the Natural History of Quadrupeds, Birds, Fishes and Insects*, 3 vols (Edinburgh: Peter Hill; London: Thomas Cadell).

Anon. (1792) *Transactions of a Society for the Improvement of Medical and Chirurgical Knowledge*, 1.

Anon. (1823) 'Compositions of Quack Medicines', *Lancet*, 1:1, 30.

Ansty, C. (1766) *The New Bath Guide; or, Memoirs of the B-r-d Family. In a Series of Poetic Epistles* (Dublin: J. Exshaw).

Appel, T. (1987) *The Cuvier-Geoffroy Debate: French Biology in the Decades before Darwin* (Oxford: Oxford University Press).

Aristotle (1799) *Aristotle's Complete Master-Piece [...]* (London: n.p.).

Aristotle (1970) *History of Animals, Books IV–VI*, trans. A.L. Peck (Cambridge, MA: Harvard University Press).

Ashfield, A. and P. de Bolla (eds) (1996) *The Sublime: A Reader in Eighteenth-Century Aesthetic Theory* (Cambridge: Cambridge University Press).

Asma, S.T. (1996) *Following Form and Function: A Philosophical Archaeology of Life Science* (Illinois: Northwestern University Press).

—— (2009) *On Monsters* (Oxford: Oxford University Press).

[Baillie, J.] (1790) *Poems [...]* (London: J. Johnson).

—— (1798) *A Series of Plays [...]* (London: T. Cadell Jnr and W. Davies).

—— (ed.) (1823) *A Collection of Poems, Chiefly Manuscript, and from Living Authors* (London: Longman, Hurst, Rees, Orme, and Brown).

—— (2000) *Plays on the Passions*, P. Duthie (ed.) (Ontario: Broadview).
Baillie, M. (1793) *The Morbid Anatomy of Some of the Most Important Parts of the Body* (London: J. Johnson).
[Bailly, J.S.] (1784) *Rapport des Commissaires Chargés par le Roi de l'examen du Magnétisme Animal* (Paris: Imprimerie Royale).
Bainbridge, S. (ed.) (2008) *Romanticism: A Sourcebook* (Basingstoke: Palgrave Macmillan).
Baldick, C. (1987) *In Frankenstein's Shadow: Myth, Monstrosity, and Nineteenth-Century Writing* (Oxford: Clarendon Press).
Barker-Benfield, G.J. (1992) *The Culture of Sensibility: Sex and Society in Eighteenth-Century Britain* (Chicago: University of Chicago Press).
Barnard, T. (2009) *Anna Seward: A Constructed Life* (Farnham: Ashgate).
Barrell, J. (1983) *The Dark Side of the Landscape: the Rural Poor in English Painting, 1730–1840* (Cambridge: Cambridge University Press).
—— (2000) *Imagining the King's Death: Figurative Treason, Fantasies of Regicide 1793–1796* (Oxford: Oxford University Press).
Bartram, W. (1792) *Travels Through North and South Carolina, Georgia, East and West Florida [...]* (London: J. Johnson).
Beddoes, T. (1796) 'To the Editor of the Monthly Magazine', *Monthly Magazine and British Register*, 1:4, 265–7.
—— (1799) *Notice of Some Observations Made at the Medical Pneumatic Institution* (Bristol: Biggs and Cottle).
Beer, G. (1993) *Darwin's Plots* (London: Cambridge University Press).
—— (1996) *Open Fields: Science in Cultural Encounter* (Oxford: Clarendon Press).
Benger, E. (1820) *The Memoirs of Mr. John Tobin* (London: Longman, Hurst, Rees, and Orme).
Bennett, A. (2007) *Wordsworth Writing* (Cambridge: Cambridge University Press).
Bennett, J. (1789) *Letters to a Young Lady, on a Variety of Useful and Interesting Subjects* (London: Robinson).
Bewell, A. (1989a) '"Jacobin Plants": Botany as Social Theory in the 1790s', *Wordsworth Circle*, 20:3, 132–9.
—— (1989b) *Wordsworth and the Enlightenment: Nature, Man, and Society in the Experimental Poetry* (New Haven and London: New Haven Press).
Bewick, T. (1871) *Life and Letters*, 2 vols (London: Hurst and Blackett).
Bewick, T. and R. Beilby (1790) *A General History of Quadrupeds* (Newcastle upon Tyne: S. Hodgson, R. Beilby, and T. Bewick).
Bewick, W. (1871) *Life and Letters*, 2 vols (London: Hurst and Blackett).
Blair, K. (2007) *Victorian Poetry and the Culture of the Heart* (Oxford: Oxford University Press).
Blumenbach, J.F. (1792) *An Essay on Generation*, A. Crichton (trans.) (London: T. Cadell).
Botting, F. (1991) *Making Monstrous: Frankenstein, Criticism, Theory* (Manchester: Manchester University Press).
Bour, I. (2005) 'Sensibility as Epistemology in *Caleb Williams, Waverley*, and *Frankenstein*', *Studies in English Literature*, 45:4, 813–27.
Bowler, P.J. (1989) *Evolution: The History of an Idea*, rev. edn (Berkeley: University of California Press).
Braithwaite, H. (2003) *Romanticism, Publishing and Dissent* (Basingstoke: Palgrave).

Brewer, W.D. (1991) 'The Prefaces of Joanna Baillie and William Wordsworth', *The Friend: Comments on Romanticism* 1:2, 34–47.
Brown, J. (1795) *Elements of Medicine: A New Edition*, T. Beddoes (rev. and corr.), 2 vols (London: J. Johnson).
Budge, G. (2007a) 'Erasmus Darwin and the Poetics of William Wordsworth: "Excitement without the Application of Gross and Violent Stimulants"', *British Journal for Eighteenth-Century Studies*, 30:2, 279–308.
—— (2007b) 'Indigestion and Imagination in Coleridge's Critical Thought', in G. Budge (ed.) *Romantic Empiricism* (Lewisburg: Bucknell University Press), pp. 141–81.
Buffon, G.L.L. (1775–76) *The Natural History of Animals, Vegetables, and Minerals; with the theory of the earth in general. Translated from the French of Count de Buffon [...]*,W. Kenrick and J. Murdoch (trans.), 6 vols (London: T. Bell).
—— (1780) *Natural History, General and Particular, by the Count de Buffon, Translated into English* [by W. Smellie], 8 vols (Edinburgh: William Creech).
—— (1792) *Buffon's Natural History, Abridged*, 2 vols (London: C. & G. Kearsley).
Burke, E. (1998) *A Philosophical Enquiry into the Origin of Our Ideas into the Sublime and the Beautiful*, A. Phillips (ed.) (Oxford: Oxford University Press).
Burwick. F. (2004) 'Joanna Baillie, Matthew Baillie, and the Pathology of the Passions', in T. Crochunis (ed.) *Joanna Baillie: Romantic Dramatist* (London: Routledge), pp. 48–69.
Butler, J. (1990) *Gender Trouble: Feminism and the Subversion of Identity* (London and New York: Routledge).
Butler, M. (1995) 'Godwin, Burke and *Caleb Williams*', in D. Wu (ed.) *Romanticism: A Critical Reader* (Cambridge: Blackwell), pp. 343–58.
Bynum, W.F. and R. Porter (eds) (1988) *Brunonianism in Britain and Europe* (London: Wellcome Institute).
Calè, L. (2000) '"A Female Band despising Nature's Law": Botany, Gender and Revolution in the 1790s', *Romanticism on the Net*, 17, <http://www.erudit.org/revue/ron/2000/v/n17/005889ar.html> (accessed 20 February 2013).
Campbell, C. (1908) *Diary of a Lady-in-Waiting*, 2 vols (London: Bodley Head).
Carlisle, A. (1818) *An Essay in the Disorders of Old Age, and on the Means of Prolonging Human Life* (London: Longman, Hurst, Rees, Orme, and Brown).
Castle, T. (1995) *The Female Thermometer: Eighteenth-Century Culture and the Invention of the Uncanny* (Oxford: Oxford University Press).
Chandler, A. (2005) 'The "seeds of order and taste": Wollstonecraft, the *Analytical Review*, and Critical Idiom', *European Romantic Review*, 16:1, 1–21.
Cheyne, G. (1724) *An Essay on Health and Long Life* (London: George Strahan).
Chibka, R.L. (1986) 'The Stranger Within Young's *Conjectures*', *ELH*, 53:3, 541–65.
Christie, J. and S. Shuttleworth (1989) 'Introduction: Between Literature and Science', in J. Christie and S. Shuttleworth (eds) *Nature Transfigured: Science and Literature, 1700–1900* (Manchester: Manchester University Press), pp. 1–12.
Clark, T. (1997) *The Theory of Inspiration: Composition as a Crisis of Subjectivity in Romantic and Post-Romantic Writing* (Manchester: Manchester University Press).
Class, M. (2013) *Coleridge and Kantian Ideas in England, 1796–1817* (London: Bloomsbury-Continuum).
Coleridge, S.T. (1818) *The Friend*, 3.
—— (1848) *Hints Towards the Formation of a More Comprehensive Theory of Life*, S.B. Watson (ed.) (London: John Churchill).

—— (1956–71) *The Collected Letters of Samuel Taylor Coleridge*, E.L. Griggs (ed.), 6 vols (Oxford: Clarendon Press).
—— (1957–2002) *The Notebooks of Samuel Taylor Coleridge*, K. Coburn (ed.), 5 vols (London: Routledge and Kegan Paul).
—— (1969–2002) *The Collected Works of Samuel Taylor Coleridge*, K. Coburn (gen. ed.), 23 vols (Princeton: Princeton University Press).
—— (1983) *Biographia Literaria*, J. Engell and W. Jackson Bate (eds) (Princeton: Princeton University Press).
—— (1985) *Poems*, H.J. Jackson (ed.) (Oxford: Oxford University Press).
—— (1992) *The Collected Works of Samuel Taylor Coleridge*, Vol. 12, Marginalia: Part 3. Irving to Oxlee, H.J. Jackson and George Whalley (eds) (London: Routledge and Keegan Paul, 1992).
—— (1995) *Shorter Works and Fragments*, H.J. Jackson and J.R. de J. Jackson (eds) 2 vols (Princeton: Princeton University Press).
Collini, S. (1993) 'Introduction', in C.P. Snow, *The Two Cultures*, S. Collini (ed.) (Cambridge: Cambridge University Press).
Cooper, M. (2008) 'Monstrous Progeny: The Teratological Tradition in Science and Literature', in C. Knellwolf and J. Goodall (eds) *Frankenstein's Science: Experiment and Discovery in Romantic Culture, 1780–1830* (Farnham: Ashgate), pp. 87–117.
Corfield, P. (1995) *Power and the Professions in Britain, 1700–1850* (London and New York: Routledge).
Craciun, A. (1997) 'Violence Against Difference: Mary Wollstonecraft and Mary Robinson', in G. Clingham (ed.) *Making History: Textuality, and the Forms of Eighteenth-Century Culture, Bucknell Review*, 42.1, 111–41.
Crouch, L.E. (1978) 'Davy's *A Discourse, Introductory to A Course of Lectures on Chemistry*: A Possible Scientific Source of *Frankenstein*', *Keats-Shelley Journal*, 27, 35–44.
Daffron, E. (1995) '"Magnetical sympathy": Strategies of Power and Resistance in Godwin's "Caleb Williams"', *Criticism*, 37:2, 213–32.
Dalton, J. (1808) *A New System of Chemical Philosophy*, 2 vols (London: R. Bickerstaff).
Darnton, R. (1968) *Mesmerism and the End of the Enlightenment in France* (Cambridge, MA: Harvard University Press).
Darwin, C. (1846) *Journal of Researches into the Natural History and Geology of the Countries Visited during the Voyage of the H.M.S. Beagle*, 2 vols (New York: Harper & Brothers).
Darwin, E. (1791) *The Botanic Garden [...]* (London: J. Johnson).
—— (1794–96) *Zoonomia, or the Laws of Organic Life*, 2 vols (London: J. Johnson).
—— (1797) *A Plan for the Conduct of Female Education in Boarding Schools* (Derby: J. Johnson).
—— (2006) *Temple of Nature*, M. Priestman (ed.), Romantic Circles Electronic Edition, October 2006, <http://www.rc.umd.edu/editions/darwin_temple/> (accessed 7 February 2013).
Daston, L. (2001) 'Fear and Loathing of the Imagination in Science', in P.L. Galison, S.R. Graubard, and E. Mendelsohn (eds) *Science in Culture* (New Brunswick: Transaction), pp. 73–93.
Daston, L. and P. Galison (2007) *Objectivity* (New York: Zone Books).
Davies, J. (1599) *Nosce Teipsum [...]* (London: John Standish).

Davis, P. (2002) *The Victorians*, The Oxford Literary History, volume 8: 1830–1880 (Oxford: Oxford University Press).
Davy, H. (1799a) 'The Tempest', *Annual Anthology*, 1, 179–80.
—— (1799b) 'The Sons of Genius', *Annual Anthology* 1, 93–9.
—— (1799c) 'Ode to St Michael's Mount, in Cornwall', *Annual Anthology*, 1, 172–6.
—— (1799d) 'Extract from an Unfinished Poem on Mount's Bay', *Annual Anthology*, 1, 281–6.
—— (1802) *A Syllabus of a Course of Lectures on Chemistry* (London: J. Johnson).
—— (1830) *Consolations in Travel, or the Last Days of a Philosopher* (London: John Murray).
—— (1839) *The Collected Works of Humphry Davy*, John Davy (ed.), 9 vols (London: Smith, Elder, and Co.).
Davy, J. (1836) *Memoirs of the Life of Sir Humphry Davy, Bart.*, 2 vols (London: Longman, Rees, Orme, Brown, Green and Longman).
Dawson, G. and S. Shuttleworth (2003) 'Introduction: Science and Victorian Poetry', *Victorian Poetry*, 41:1, 1–10.
Dawson, P.M.S. (1986) '"A sort of animal magic": Shelley and Animal Magnetism', *Keats-Shelley Review*, 1, 15–34.
de Almeida, H. (1991) *Romantic Medicine and John Keats* (New York and London: Oxford University Press).
[de Quincey, T.] (1834) 'Animal Magnetism', *Tait's Edinburgh Magazine*, 4:22, 456–74.
Desmond, A. (1992) *The Politics of Evolution: Morphology, Medicine, and Reform in Radical London* (Chicago: University of Chicago Press).
Dixon Hunt, J. (1976) *The Figure in the Landscape: Poetry, Painting, and Gardening during the Eighteenth Century* (Baltimore: Johns Hopkins University Press).
Duff, D. (2009) *Romanticism and the Uses of Genre* (Oxford: Oxford University Press).
Duffy, C. (2005) *Shelley and the Revolutionary Sublime* (Cambridge: Cambridge University Press).
—— and P. Howell (eds) (2011) *Cultures of the Sublime: Selected Readings, 1750–1830* (Basingstoke: Palgrave).
Duveen, D.I. and H.S. Klickstein (1955) 'Benjamin Franklin and Antoine Laurent Lavoisier: Joint Investigations', *Annals of Science*, 11, 271–302.
Eagleton, T. (1987) 'Creation', in *A Dictionary of Modern Critical Terms*, R. Fowler (ed.) (London: Routledge), pp. 45–6.
Earl, S. (2010) *Blake, Lavater, and Physiognomy* (London: Maney Publishing).
Edgeworth, M. (1971) *Maria Edgeworth: Letters from England, 1813–1844*, C. Colvin (ed.) (Oxford: Clarendon Press).
Eliot, G. (2003) *Middlemarch*, R. Ashton (ed.) (Harmondsworth: Penguin).
Engell, J. (1981) *The Creative Imagination: Enlightenment to Romanticism* (Cambridge, MA: Harvard University Press).
Ewell, J. (1816) *The Medical Companion [...]* (Philadelphia: Anderson & Meehan).
Fara, P. (1995) 'An Attractive Therapy: Animal Magnetism in Eighteenth-Century England', *History of Science*, 33:2, 127–77.
Ferguson, M. (1993) *Colonialism and Gender from Mary Wollstonecraft to Jamaica Kincaid: East Caribbean Connections* (New York: University of Columbia Press).

Fincher, M. (2007) *Queering Gothic in the Romantic Age: The Penetrating Eye* (Basingstoke: Palgrave Macmillan).
Ford, J. (1998) *Coleridge on Dreaming: Romanticism, Dreams, and the Medical Imagination* (Cambridge: Cambridge University Press).
Fordyce, J. (1765) *Sermons to Young Women* (London: S. Crowder, C. Ware, and T. Payne).
Foucault, M. (1991) *Discipline and Punish*, A. Sheridan (trans.) (Harmondsworth: Penguin).
—— (2001a) *Madness and Civilisation* (London and New York: Routledge).
—— (2001b) *The Order of Things: Archaeology of the Human Science* (London: Routledge).
—— (2003) *The Birth of the Clinic* (London and New York: Routledge).
Franklin, C. (2004) *Mary Wollstonecraft: A Literary Life* (Basingstoke: Palgrave Macmillan).
Fulford, T. (2002) 'The Electrifying Mrs Robinson', *Women's Writing*, 9:1, 23–35.
—— (2004) 'Conducting the Vital Fluid: The Politics and Poetics of Mesmerism in the 1790s', *Studies in Romanticism*, 43:1, 57–78.
Fulford, T., D. Lee, and P. Kitson (2004) *Literature, Science, and Exploration in the Romantic Era: Bodies of Knowledge* (Cambridge: Cambridge University Press).
Fullmer, J.Z. (1960) 'The Poetry of Sir Humphry Davy', *Chymia*, 6, 102–26.
—— (2000) *Young Humphry Davy: The Making of an Experimental Chemist* (Philadelphia: American Philosophical Society).
Furniss, T. (1993) *Edmund Burke's Aesthetic Ideology: Language, Gender, and Political Economy in Revolution* (Cambridge: Cambridge University Press).
Fyfe, A. and B. Lightman (eds) (2007) *Science in the Marketplace: Nineteenth-Century Sites and Experiences* (Chicago: University of Chicago Press).
Genette, G. (1997) *Paratexts: Thresholds of Interpretation*, J.E. Lewin (trans.) (Cambridge: Cambridge University Press).
George, S. (2005) 'Linnaeus in Letters and the Cultivation of the Female Mind: "Botany in an English Dress"', *British Journal for Eighteenth-Century Studies*, 28, 1–18.
—— (2007) *Botany, Sexuality, and Women's Writing, 1760–1830: From Modest Shoot to Forward Plant* (Manchester: Manchester University Press).
Gigante, D. (2009) *Life: Organic Form and Romanticism* (New Haven: Yale University Press).
Gilpin, W. (1768) *Essay on Prints* (London: J. Robson).
[Godwin, W.] (1785) *Report of Dr. Benjamin Franklin, and Other Commissioners, Charged by the King of France, with the Examination of Animal Magnetism, as now Practised at Paris. Translated from the French. With an Historical Introduction* (London: J. Johnson).
Godwin, W. (1805) 'Biographical Sketch of the Late Joseph Ritson, Esq.', *Monthly Mirror*, 19, 291–4.
—— (1834) *Lives of the Necromancers* (London: Frederick J. Mason).
—— (1992) *Collected Novels and Memoirs*, M. Philp (ed.), 8 vols (London: Pickering and Chatto).
—— (1993) *Political and Philosophical Writings*, M. Philp (ed.), 7 vols (London: Pickering and Chatto).
—— (2000) *Caleb Williams*, G. Handwerk and A. Markley (eds) (Ontario: Broadview).

—— (2001) *Fleetwood*, G. Handwerk and A. Markley (eds) (Ontario: Broadview).
—— (2010) *The Diary of William Godwin*, V. Myers, D. O'Shaughnessy, and M. Philp (eds) (Oxford: Oxford Digital Library), <http://godwindiary.bodleian.ox.ac.uk> (accessed 7 February 2013).
—— (2011) *The Letters of William Godwin*, P. Clemit (ed.), 6 vols (Oxford: Oxford University Press).
Golinski, J. (1992) *Science as Public Culture: Chemistry and Enlightenment in Britain, 1760–1820* (Cambridge: Cambridge University Press).
—— (1999) 'Humphry Davy's Sexual Chemistry', *Configurations*, 7:1, 15–41.
—— (2003) 'Chemistry', *Eighteenth-Century Science*, in R. Porter (ed.) *The Cambridge History of Science*, 8 vols (Cambridge: Cambridge University Press), IV, 375–96.
—— (2007) *British Weather and the Climate of Enlightenment* (Chicago: University of Chicago Press).
—— (2009) 'The Literature of the New Sciences', in J. Chandler (ed.) *The Cambridge History of English Romantic Literature* (Cambridge: Cambridge University Press), pp. 527–52.
—— (2011) 'Humphry Davy: The Experimental Self', *Eighteenth-Century Studies*, 45:1, 15–28.
Goodridge, J. (ed.) (2006) *A Biographical & Bibliographical Database of British and Irish Labouring-Class Poets 1700–1900*, Version 6.2, <http://human.ntu.ac.uk/research/labouringclasswriters/elsie1.htm> (accessed 7 February 2013).
Gordon, L. (2005) *Vindication: A Life of Mary Wollstonecraft* (London: Virago).
Gregory, J. (1765) *A Comparative View of the State and Faculties of Man, with those of the Animal World* (London: J. Dodsley).
—— (1774) *A Father's Legacy to his Daughters* (Edinburgh: W. Strahan, T. Cadell, J. Balfour, W. Creech).
Hawkins, A.R. (ed.) (2011) 'The Seward-Weston Debate', *Romantic Women Writers Reviewed*, 3 vols (London: Pickering and Chatto).
Hetherington, N. (1997) 'Creator and Created in Mary Shelley's *Frankenstein*', *Keats-Shelley Review*, 11, 1–36.
Heringman, N. (ed.) (2003) *Romantic Science: The Literary Forms of Natural History* (New York: SUNY Press, 2003).
—— (2004) *Romantic Rocks: Aesthetic Geology* (Ithaca: Cornell University Press).
Higgins, D. (2005) *Romantic Genius and the Literary Magazine: Biography, Celebrity, Politics* (London and New York: Routledge).
Hindle, M. (2012) 'Humphry Davy and William Wordsworth: A Mutual Influence', *Romanticism*, 18:1, 16–29.
—— (forthcoming) 'Nature, Power, and the Light of Suns: The Poetry of Humphry Davy', *Charles Lamb Bulletin*.
Holmes, R. (2008) *The Age of Wonder: How the Romantic Generation Discovered the Beauty and Terror of Science* (London: HarperPress).
Hone, W. (1839) *Everyday Book [...]*, 3 vols (London: T. Tegg).
Huet, M.H. (1993) *Monstrous Imagination* (Cambridge, MA: Harvard University Press).
Hunter, A. (2009) *The Life and Times of Anne Hunter: Hadyn's Tuneful Voice*, C. Grigson (ed.) (Liverpool: Liverpool University Press).
Hurd, R. (1766) *A Dissertation on the Idea of Universal Poetry* (London: A. Millar).

Hutton, J. (1795) *Theory of the Earth [...]*, 2 vols (Edinburgh: Cadell, Junior, and Davies).
Jackson, N. (2008) *Science and Sensation in Romantic Poetry* (Cambridge: Cambridge University Press).
Jackson-Houlston, C. (2006) '"Queen Lilies"? The Interpenetration of Scientific, Religious and Gender Discourses in Victorian Representations of Plants', *Journal of Victorian Culture*, 11:1, 84–110.
Janowitz, A. (2005) '"What a rich fund of Images is treasured up here": Poetic Commonplaces of the Sublime Universe', *Studies in Romanticism*, 44:4, 469–92.
Jardine, N., J.A. Secord, and E.C. Spary (eds) (1996) *Cultures of Natural History*, (Cambridge: Cambridge University Press).
Jay, M. (2009) *The Atmosphere of Heaven: The Unnatural Experiments of Dr Beddoes and his Sons of Genius* (New Haven and London: Yale University Press).
Rousseau, J.J. (1783) *Emilius and Sophia*, W. Kenrick (trans.), 3 vols, 3rd edn (London: H. Baldwin).
Jenkins, A. (1998) 'Humphry Davy: Poetry, Science, and the Love of Light', in R. Cronin (ed.) *1798: The Year of the Lyrical Ballads* (Basingstoke: Palgrave Macmillan), pp. 133–50.
Johnson, C. (1995) *Equivocal Bodies: Politics, Gender, and Sentimentality in the 1790s* (Chicago: University of Chicago Press).
Johnson, S. (1752) *The Rambler*, 6 vols (London: printed for J. Payne).
—— (1765) *Plays of Shakespeare [...]*, 8 vols (London: J. and R. Tonson et al.).
—— (1781) *The Lives of the Eminent English Poets*, 4 vols (London: printed for C. Bathurst et al.).
Jones, V. (1997) 'The Death of Mary Wollstonecraft', *British Journal of Eighteenth-Century Studies*, 20:2, 187–205.
—— (2002) Mary Wollstonecraft and the Literature of Advice and Instruction', in C.L. Johnson (ed.) *The Cambridge Companion to Mary Wollstonecraft* (Cambridge: Cambridge University Press), pp. 119–40.
—— (2005) 'Advice and Enlightenment: Mary Wollstonecraft and Sex Education', in S. Knott and B. Taylor (eds) *Women, Gender and Enlightenment* (Basingstoke: Palgrave Macmillan), pp. 140–55.
Juengel, S. (2001) 'Countenancing History: Mary Wollstonecraft, Samuel Stanhope Smith, and Enlightenment Racial Science', *ELH*, 68, 897–927.
Kant, I. (1987) *Critique of Judgement*, W.S. Pluhar (trans.) (Indianapolis: Hackett).
Keats, J. (1970) *Letters of John Keats*, R. Gittings (ed.) (Oxford: Oxford University Press, 1970).
—— (2002) *Selected Letters*, R. Gittings (ed.), J. Mee (rev. edn) (Oxford: Oxford University Press).
Keen, P. (1999) *The Crisis of Literature in the 1790s: Print Culture and the Public Sphere* (Cambridge: Cambridge University Press).
Kelley, T. (1988) *Wordsworth's Revisionary Aesthetics* (Cambridge: Cambridge University Press).
—— (2003) 'Romantic Exemplarity: Botany and "Material Culture"', in N. Heringman (ed.) *Romantic Science: The Literary Forms of Natural History*, Studies in the Long Nineteenth Century (New York: SUNY Press), pp. 223–54.
Kelly, G. (1992) *Revolutionary Feminism* (Basingstoke: Macmillan).
Kenyon-Jones, C. (2001) *Kindred Brutes: Animals in Romantic-Period Writing* (Aldershot: Ashgate).

Kerr, R. (1811) *Memoirs of the Life, Writings, and Correspondence of William Smellie*, 2 vols (Edinburgh: John Anderson).
Kilner, D. (1790) *The Life and Perambulation of a Mouse* (London: John Marshall).
King-Hele, D. (1986) *Erasmus Darwin and the Romantic Poets* (Basingstoke: Macmillan).
Kitson, P. (2007) *Romantic Literature, Race and Colonial Encounter* (Basingstoke: Palgrave Macmillan).
Klancher, J. (1987) *The Making of English Reading Audiences, 1790–1832* (Madison, Wisconsin: University of Wisconsin Press).
Knight, D.K. (1990) 'Romanticism and the Sciences', in A. Cunningham and N. Jardine (eds) *Romanticism and the Sciences* (Cambridge: Cambridge University Press), pp. 13–24.
—— (1992) *Humphry Davy: Science and Power* (Oxford: Blackwell).
—— (2005) 'Humphry Davy, the Poet', *Interdisciplinary Science Reviews*, 30:4, 356–72.
Kuist, J.M. (1982) *The Nichol's File of The Gentleman's Magazine: Attributions of Authorship and Other Documentation in Editorial Papers at the Folger Library* (Madison, Wisconsin: University of Wisconsin Press).
Labbe, J.M. (2011) *Writing Romanticism* (Basingstoke: Palgrave Macmillan).
Laplace, Marquis de (Pierre Simon) (1830) *The System of the World*, H.H. Harte (trans.), 2 vols (Dublin: Rees, Orme, Brown and Green).
Laqueur, T. (1990) *Making Sex: Body and Gender from the Greeks to Freud* (London: Harvard University Press).
Lawlor, C. (2006) *Consumption and Literature: The Making of the Romantic Disease* (Basingstoke: Palgrave Macmillan).
Lawrence, W. (1814) 'Account of a Child Born Without a Brain', *Medico-Chirurgical Transactions*, 5, 165–224.
—— (1819a) *Lectures on Physiology, Zoology, and the Natural History of Man* (London: J. Callow).
[Lawrence, W.] (1819b) 'Monster', in A. Rees (ed.) *Cyclopædia*, 39 vols (London: Longman, Hurst, Rees, Orme and Browne), vol. XXIV 'MON-NEW' (n.p.).
Leask, N. (1991) 'Shelley's "Magnetic Ladies": Romantic Mesmerism and the Politics of the Body', in S. Copley and J. Whale (eds), *Beyond Romanticism: New Approaches to Texts and Contexts, 1780–1832* (Syracuse: Syracuse University Press), pp. 53–78.
—— (2007) '"The Shadow Line": James Currie's "Life of Burns" and British Romanticism', in C. Lamont and M. Rossington (eds) *Romanticism's Debatable Lands* (Basingstoke: Palgrave Macmillan), pp. 64–79.
Lee, D. (2006) *Romantic Liars: Obscure Women who became Impostors and Challenged an Empire* (Basingstoke: Palgrave Macmillan).
Levere, T. (1980) 'S.T. Coleridge and the Human Sciences: Anthropology, Phrenology, and Mesmerism', in Marsha P. Hanen, Margaret J. Osler, and Robert G. Weyant (eds) *Science, Pseudo-Science and Society* (Waterloo, Ontario: Wilfred Laurier University Press), pp. 171–92.
—— (1981) *Poetry Realized in Nature* (Cambridge: Cambridge University Press).
Locke, L. (1989) *Some Thoughts Concerning Education*, J.W. and J.S. Yolton (eds) (Oxford: Clarendon Press).
Lockhart, J.G. (1839), *Memoirs of the Life of Sir Walter Scott, Bart*, 10 vols (Edinburgh: R. Cadell).

Logan, P.M. (1996) 'Narrating Hysteria: "Caleb Williams" and the Cultural History of Nerves', *NOVEL: A Forum on Fiction*, 29:2, 206–22.

Lovat, S. (1797) *Memoirs of the Life of Simon, Lord Lovat, Written by Himself in the French Language; and now first translated from the original language*, trans. W. Godwin (London: J. Nicol).

Lovejoy, A.O. (1936) *The Great Chain of Being: A Study of the History of an Idea* (Cambridge, MA: Harvard University Press).

Lussier, M. (2000) *Romantic Dynamics: The Poetics of Physicality* (Basingstoke: Macmillan).

Macaulay Graham, C. (1790) *Letters on Education: With Observations on Religious and Metaphysical Subjects* (London: Dilly).

Mackenzie, H. (1808) *Works*, 8 vols (Edinburgh: A. Constable).

Manly, S. (2004) *Language, Custom and Nation in the 1790s* (Cambridge: Cambridge University Press).

Matlak, R. (1990) 'Wordsworth's Reading of *Zoonomia* in Early Spring', *Wordsworth Circle*, 21:2, 76–80.

McGrath, R. (2002) *Seeing her Sex: Medical Archives and the Female Body* (Manchester: Manchester University Press).

McMillan, D. (1998) '"Dr Baillie"', in R. Cronin (ed.) *1798: The Year of the Lyrical Ballads* (Basingstoke: Macmillan), pp. 68–93.

McNeil, M. (1987) *Under the Banner of Science: Erasmus Darwin and his Age* (Manchester: Manchester University Press).

Mee, J. (2003) *Romanticism, Enthusiasm, and Regulation: Poetics and the Policing of Culture in the Romantic Period* (Oxford: Oxford University Press).

Mellor, A.K. (1988) *Mary Shelley: Her Life, Her Fiction, Her Monsters* (London: Routledge).

Mill, J.S. (1981) *Autobiography and Literary Essays*, J.M. Robson and J. Stillinger (eds) (Toronto: University of Toronto Press).

Milton, J. (1674) *Paradise Lost* (London: Samuel Simmons).

—— (2009) *Complete Shorter Poems*, S.P. Revard (ed.) (Oxford: Wiley-Blackwell).

Mitchell, R. (2007) *Sympathy and the State in the Romantic Era: Systems, State Finance, and the Shadows of Futurity* (London: Routledge).

[Mitford, J.] (1837) 'On the Poetry of Sir Humphry Davy', *Gentleman's Magazine*, 339–53.

Moers, E. (1976) *Literary Women* (New York: Doubleday).

Monsam, A. (2008) 'Biography as Autopsy in William Godwin's *Memoirs of the Author of "A Vindication of the Rights of Woman"*', *Eighteenth-Century Fiction*, 21:1, 109–30.

Moore, W. (2005) *The Knife Man: Blood, Body-Snatching, and the Birth of Modern Surgery* (London: Bantam Books).

Moorman, M. (1957) *William Wordsworth: A Biography*, 2 vols (Oxford: Oxford University Press).

Moran, M.C. (2007) 'Between the Savage and the Civil: Dr John Gregory's Natural History of Femininity', in S. Knott and B. Taylor (eds) *Women, Gender and Enlightenment* (Basingstoke: Palgrave Macmillan), pp. 8–29.

Moretti, F. (2005) *Signs Taken for Wonders: On the Sociology of Literary Forms* (New York: Verso).

Morfitt, J. (1788) *Philotoxi Ardenae: The Woodmen of Arden*, trans. by J. Weston (Birmingham: printed by M. Swinney).

Morris, R.J. (1972) 'Lavoisier and the Caloric Theory', *British Journal for the History of Science*, 6, 1–38.
Morton, T. (1994) *Shelley and the Revolution in Taste* (Cambridge: Cambridge University Press).
Ni Chonaill, S. (2007) '"Why may not man one day be immortal?" Population, Perfectibility, and the Immortality Question in Godwin's *Political Justice*', *History of European Ideas*, 33, 25–39.
[Nicholson, W.] (1781) *The Doubts of the Infidels; or, Queries relative to Scriptural inconsistencies and contradictions ... By a Weak Christian* (London: printed for the author).
Nicholson, W. (1782) *An Introduction to Natural Philosophy*, 2 vols (London: J. Johnson).
—— (1790) *The First Principles of Chemistry* (London: G.G.J. and J. Robinson).
—— (1800) *Journal of Natural Philosophy, Chemistry, and the Arts* (London: for William Nicholson and W. Stratford).
O'Connor, R. (2007) *The Earth on Show: Fossils and the Poetics of Popular Science, 1802–1856* (London and Chicago: University of Chicago Press).
O'Neill, D.I. (2007) *The Burke-Wollstonecraft Debate: Savagery, Civilization, and Democracy* (University Park: Penn State Press).
O'Shaughnessy, D. (2007) '"The vehicle he has chosen": Pointing out the Theatricality of *Caleb Williams*', *History of European Ideas*, 33, 54–71.
—— (2010) *William Godwin and the Theatre* (London: Pickering and Chatto).
Paley, W. (1881) *Natural Theology* (New York: American Tract Society).
Paris, J.A. (1831) *The Life of Sir Humphry Davy* (London: H. Colburn and R. Bentley).
Park, K. and L.J. Daston (1981) 'Unnatural Conceptions: The Study of Monsters in Sixteenth- and Seventeenth-Century France and England', *Past and Present*, 92, 20–54.
Parkinson, J. (1820) *Organic Remains of a Former World [...]*, 3 vols (London: Sherwood, Neely, and Jones).
Pennant, T. (1781) *History of Quadrupeds*, 2 vols (London: B. White).
Perkins, D. (2007) *Romanticism and Animal Rights* (Cambridge: Cambridge University Press).
Peterfreund, S. (2003) 'The Color Violaceous, or, Chemistry and the Romance of Dematerialization: The Subliming of Iodine and Shelley's *Adonais*', *Studies in Romanticism*, 42:1, 45–54.
Playfair, J. (1956) *Illustrations of the Huttonian Theory of the Earth* (New York: Dover).
Pomata, G. and N.G. Siraisi (eds) (2005) *Historia* (Cambridge, MA: MIT Press).
Pope, A. (1711) *An Essay on Criticism* (London: W. Lewis).
Pope, R. (2005) *Creativity: Theory, History, Practice* (London: Routledge).
Porter, R. (1989) *Health for Sale: Quackery in England* (Manchester: Manchester University Press).
—— (2004) 'Erasmus Darwin: Doctor of Evolution?' in J.R. Moore (ed.) *History, Humanity and Evolution: Essays for John C. Greene* (Cambridge: Cambridge University Press), pp. 39–70.
Priestley, J. (1767) *The History and Present State of Electricity, with Original Experiments* (London: J. Dodsley, J. Johnson, B. Davenport, and T. Cadell).
—— (1775) 'An Account of Further Discoveries in Air', *Philosophical Transactions*, 65, 384–94.

—— (1777) *A Course of Lectures on Oratory and Criticism* (London: J. Johnson).
—— (1794) *Head of Lectures on a Course of Experimental Philosophy* (London: J. Johnson).
Priestman, M. (2006) 'Introduction', Erasmus Darwin, *Temple of Nature*, in M. Priestman (ed.), Romantic Circles Electronic Edition, October 2006, http://www.rc.umd.edu/editions/darwin_temple/ (accessed 7 February 2013).
—— (2007) 'Lucretius in Romantic and Victorian Britain', in S. Gillespie and P. Hardie (eds) *The Cambridge Companion to Lucretius* (Cambridge: Cambridge University Press), pp. 289–305.
Reid, I. (2004) *Wordsworth and the Formation of English Studies* (Aldershot: Ashgate).
Richards, R.J. (2002) *The Romantic Conception of Life: Science and Philosophy in the Age of Goethe* (Chicago: University of Chicago Press).
Richardson, A. (2001) *British Romanticism and the Science of the Mind* (Cambridge: Cambridge University Press).
—— (2004) 'A Neural Theatre: Joanna Baillie's *Plays on the Passions*', in T. Crochunis (ed.) *Joanna Baillie: Romantic Dramatist* (London: Routledge), pp. 130–45.
—— (2010) *The Neural Sublime: Cognitive Theories and Romantic Texts* (Baltimore: Johns Hopkins University Press).
Rix, R.W. (2002) 'Healing the Spirit: William Blake and Magnetic Religion', *Romanticism on the* Net, 25, http://www.erudit.org/revue/ron/2002/v/n25/006011ar.html?vue=resume (accessed 20 February 2013).
Roberts, D.S. (2003) 'Literature, Medicine and Politics, 1795–1800: *Lyrical Ballads* and Currie's *Life of Burns*', in C. Barfoot (ed.) *A Natural Delineation of the Passions: The Historic Moment of the Lyrical Ballads* (Amsterdam: Rodopi), pp. 115–28.
Roe, N. (ed.) (2001) *Samuel Taylor Coleridge and the Sciences of Life* (Oxford: Oxford University Press).
—— (2002) *The Politics of Nature: William Wordsworth and Some Contemporaries*, rev. edn (Basingstoke: Macmillan).
Roe, S.A. (2003) 'The Life Sciences', in R. Porter (ed.) *Eighteenth-Century Science*, The Cambridge History of Science, 8 vols (Cambridge: Cambridge University Press), IV, 397–416.
Roger, J. (1997) *Buffon*, trans. S.L. Bonnefoi (Ithaca, New York: Cornell University Press).
Rose, M. (1993) *Authors and Owners: The Invention of Copyright* (Cambridge, MA: Harvard University Press).
Ross, C.E. (2003) '"Twin Labourers and Heirs of the Same Hopes": The Professional Rivalry of Humphry Davy and William Wordsworth', in N. Heringman (ed.) *Romantic Science: The Literary Forms of Natural History*, Studies in the Long Nineteenth Century (New York: State University of New York Press), pp. 23–52.
Rousseau, G.S. (1991) *Enlightenment Borders: Pre- and Post-Modern Discourses, Medical, Scientific* (Manchester and New York: Manchester University Press).
Rousseau, J. (1979) *Emile, or on Education*. Allan Bloom (ed.) (Harmondsworth: Penguin).
Rudwick, M.J.S. (1985) *The Meaning of Fossils: Episodes in the History of Paleontology*, 2nd edn (Chicago: University of Chicago Press).
Rumford, Count (Benjamin Thompson) (1798) 'An Inquiry concerning the Source of the Heat which is excited by Friction', *Philosophical Transactions*, 88, 80–102.

Russett, C.E. (1991) *Sexual Science: The Victorian Construction of Womanhood* (Cambridge, MA and London: Harvard University Press).
Ruston, S. (2005) *Shelley and Vitality* (Basingstoke: Palgrave Macmillan).
—— (2007) *Romanticism: An Introduction* (London: Continuum).
—— (2008a) 'Introduction', in S. Ruston (ed.) *Essays and Studies*, 61, 1–13.
—— (2008b) 'Natural Rights and Natural History in Anna Barbauld and Mary Wollstonecraft', in S. Ruston (ed.) *Essays and Studies*, 61, 53–71.
—— (2012) '"What was I?": *Frankenstein*, Natural History, and the Question of What it Means to be Human', *La Questione Romantica – Nuova Serie*, 3:1, 81–92.
Ryan, V. (2001) 'The Physiological Sublime: Burke's Critique of Reason', *Journal of the History of Ideas*, 62:2, 265–79.
Rzepka, C.J. (1986) *The Self as Mind: Vision and Identity in Wordsworth, Coleridge and Keats* (Cambridge, MA: Harvard University Press).
Sapiro, V. (1992) *A Vindication of Political Virtue: The Political Theory of Mary Wollstonecraft* (Chicago and London: University of Chicago Press).
Sarafianos, A. (2005) 'Pain, Labour and the Sublime: Medical Gymnastics and Burke's Aesthetics', *Representations*, 91, 58–83.
—— (2008) 'The Contractility of Burke's Sublime and Heterodoxies in Medicine and Art', *Journal of the History of Ideas*, 69:1, 23–48.
Schaffer, S. (1992) 'Self Evidence', *Critical Inquiry*, 18:2, 327–62.
—— (2010) 'The Astrological Roots of Mesmerism', *Studies in History and Philosophy of Science, Part C: Studies in History and Philosophy of Biological and Biomedical Sciences*, 41: 2, 158–68.
Schiebinger, L. (1986) 'Skeletons in the Closet: The First Illustrations of the Female Skeleton in Eighteenth-Century Anatomy', *Representations* 14: *The Making of the Modern Body: Sexuality and Society in the Nineteenth Century*, 42–82.
—— (1989) *The Mind Has No Sex? Women in the Origins of Modern Science* (Cambridge, MA: Harvard University Press).
Seward, A. (1789a) 'Letter', *Gentleman's Magazine*, 59:4 (Part One), 291–2.
—— (1789b) 'Miss Seward's Strictures on the Preface to the Woodmen of Arden', *Gentleman's Magazine*, 59:6, 510–12.
—— (1811) *Letters: Written Between the Years 1784 and 1807*, 6 vols (London: A. Constable).
Sha, R. (2009a) *Perverse Romanticism: Aesthetics and Sexuality in Britain, 1750–1832* (Baltimore: Johns Hopkins University Press).
—— (2009b) 'Toward a Physiology of the Romantic Imagination', *Configurations* 17, 197–226.
Shakespeare, W. (1994a) *Hamlet*, G.R. Hibberd (ed.) (Oxford: Oxford University Press).
—— (1994b) *A Midsummer Night's Dream*, P. Holland (ed.) (Oxford: Oxford University Press).
—— (2007) *A Winter's Tale*, S. Synder and D.T. Curren-Aquino (eds) (Cambridge: Cambridge University Press).
Sharrock, R. (1962) 'The Chemist and the Poet: Sir Humphry Davy and the Preface to *Lyrical Ballads*', *Notes and Records of the Royal Society*, 17:1, 57–76.
Shaw, P. (2006) *The Sublime* (London: Routledge).
Shelley, M. (1993) *Frankenstein: 1818 Text*, M. Butler (ed.) (Oxford: Oxford University Press).

—— (1994) *Frankenstein*, D.L. Macdonald and K. Scherf (eds) (Ontario: Broadview Press, 1994).

Shelley, P.B. (1964) *The Letters of Percy Bysshe Shelley*, F.L. Jones (ed.), 2 vols (Oxford: Clarendon Press).

—— (1986–2002) *Bodleian Shelley Manuscripts* D. Reiman (gen. ed.), 23 vols (New York and London: Garland Publishing).

—— (2003) *The Major Works*, Z. Leader and M. O'Neill (eds) (Oxford: Oxford University Press).

Shelton, D. (2009) 'Sir Anthony Carlisle and Mrs Carver', *Romantic Textualities: Literature and Print Culture, 1780–1840*, 19, <http://www.cf.ac.uk/encap/romtext/reports/rt19_n04.pdf> (accessed 7 February 2013).

Shteir, A.B. (1996) *Cultivating Women, Cultivating Science* (Baltimore and London: Johns Hopkins University Press).

Shuttleton, D. (2007) *Smallpox and the Literary Imagination, 1660–1820* (Cambridge: Cambridge University Press).

Sidney, P. (1989) *Selected Poems*, K. Duncan-Jones (ed.) (Oxford: Oxford University Press).

Siskin, C. (2011) 'Afterword', *Journal for Eighteenth-Century Studies*, 34:2, 281–90.

Sleigh, C. (2011) *Literature and Science* (Basingstoke: Palgrave Macmillan).

[Smellie, W.] (1771) *Encyclopaedia Britannica; or, a Dictionary of Arts and Sciences, Compiled upon a New Plan*, 3 vols (Edinburgh: A. Bell and C. Macfarquhar).

Smellie, W. (1790) *The Philosophy of Natural History* (Edinburgh and London: printed for the heirs of Charles Elliot; and C. Elliot and T. Kay, T. Cadell, and G.G.J. & J. Robinsons).

—— (1800) *Literary and Characteristical Lives of John Gregory, M.D. Henry Home, Lord Kames. David Hume, Esq. and Adam Smith, L.L.D. [...]* (Edinburgh: Alex. Smellie, Bell and Bradfute, J. Dickson, W. Creech, E. Balfour).

Smith, O. (1984) *The Politics of Language, 1791–1819* (Oxford: Clarendon Press).

Snow, C.P. (1993) *The Two Cultures*, S. Collini (ed.) (Cambridge: Cambridge University Press).

Snow, S. (2006) *Operations Without Pain: The Practice and Science of Anaesthesia in Victorian Britain* (Basingstoke: Palgrave Macmillan).

—— (2008) *Blessed Days of Anaesthesia: How Anaesthetics Changed the World* (Oxford: Oxford University Press).

Söderbaum, H.G. (ed.) (1912–32) *Jac. Berzelius Bref.*, 6 vols (Uppsala: Almqvist and Wiksells).

Southcott, J. ([1814]) *A letter from Joanna Southcott to Dr. Richard Reece: containing a circumstantial exposition of her present situation, as given by nine medical gentlemen* [...] (London: John Fairburn).

Southey, R. (1837–38) *The Poetical Works of Robert Southey*, 10 vols (London: Longman, Brown, Green, Longman, and Roberts).

—— (1951) *Letters from England*, J. Simmons (ed.) (London: Cresset Press).

—— (1965) *New Letters of Robert Southey*, K. Curry (ed.), 2 vols (New York and London: Columbia University Press).

—— (2009–11) *The Collected Letters of Robert Southey*, I. Packer and L. Pratt (eds), 8 Parts, A Romantic Circles Electronic Edition, Part One: 1791–1797 and Part Two: 1798–1803 <http://www.rc.umd.edu/editions/southey_letters/> (accessed 20 February 2013).

Sperry, S. (1973) *Keats the Poet* (Princeton: Princeton University Press).
Sprat, T. (1667) *The History of the Royal Society of London [...]* (London: J. Martyn and J. Allestry).
St Clair, W. (1989) *The Godwins and the Shelleys: The Biography of a Family* (London: Faber and Faber).
Stafford, W. (2002) *English Feminists and their Opponents in the 1790s: Unsex'd and Proper Females* (Manchester: Manchester University Press).
Stanhope Smith, S. (1788) *An Essay on the Causes and Variety of Complexion and Figure in the Human Species [...]* (Edinburgh: C. Elliot).
Syson, L. (2008) *Doctor of Love* (London: Alma Books).
Tasso, T. (1987) *Jerusalem Delivered*, R. Nash (trans. and ed.) (Detroit: Wayne State University Press).
Taylor, B. (2003) *Mary Wollstonecraft and the Feminist Imagination* (Cambridge: Cambridge University Press).
Thelwall, J. (1793) *An Essay towards a Definition of Animal Vitality [...]* (London: T. Rickaby).
Thouret, M.A. (1784) *Recherches et Doutes sur le Magnétisme Animal* (Paris: Chez Prault).
Tobin, J. (1805) *The Honey Moon: A Comedy, in Five Acts [...]* (London: Longman, Hurst, Rees, and Orme).
Todd, D. (1995) *Imagining Monsters: Miscreations of the Self in Eighteenth-Century England* (Chicago: University of Chicago Press).
Toor, K. (2007) '"Offspring of his Genius": Coleridge's Pregnant Metaphors and Metamorphic Pregnancies', *Romanticism*, 13:3, 257–70.
Townsend, D. (1993) 'The Aesthetics of Joseph Priestley', *Journal of Aesthetics and Art Criticism*, 51:4, 561–72.
Tydahl, B. (1962) 'Edward Young and Wordsworth's "Intimations Ode"', *English Studies*, 2, 127–32.
Tyson, G.P. (1979) *Joseph Johnson: A Liberal Publisher* (Iowa City: University of Iowa Press).
Underwood, T. (2003) 'Skepticism and Surmise in Humphry Davy', *Wordsworth Circle*, 34, 95–103.
Vermeir, K. and M.F. Deckard (2005) *The Science of Sensibility: Reading Burke's Philosophical Enquiry* (New York: Springer).
Vickers, N. (1997) 'Coleridge, Thomas Beddoes and Brunonian Medicine', *European Romantic Review*, 8:1, 47–94.
—— (2004) *Coleridge and the Doctors 1795–1806* (Oxford: Oxford University Press).
Wakley, T. (1823) 'Preface', *Lancet*, 1:1, 1–2.
Wallen, M. (2004) *City of Health, Fields of Disease: Revolutions in the Poetry, Medicine, and Philosophy of Romanticism* (Aldershot: Ashgate).
Walpole, H. (1961) *Horace Walpole's Correspondence with Hannah More, et al.*, W.S. Lewis, R.A. Smith, and C.H. Bennett (eds), Vol. 31 (New Haven: Yale University Press).
Warton, J. (1756) *An Essay on the Writings and Genius of Pope* (London: M. Cooper).
Weston, J. (1788) 'Preface', in J. Morfitt, *Philotoxi Ardenae: The Woodmen of Arden*, trans. by J. Weston (Birmingham: printed by M. Swinney).
Whale, J. (2000) *Imagination under Pressure, 1789–1832: Aesthetics, Politics, and Utility* (Cambridge: Cambridge University Press).

Whewell, W. (1834) 'Review of Mary Somerville', *Quarterly Review*, 51:101, 54–68.
White, D.E. (2006) *Early Romanticism and Religious Dissent* (Cambridge: Cambridge University Press).
White, R.S. (2005) *Natural Rights and the Birth of Romanticism in the 1790s* (Basingstoke: Palgrave Macmillan).
Wickman, M. (1998) 'Imitating Eve Imitating Echo Imitating Originality: The Critical Reverberations of Sentimental Genius in the "Conjectures on Original Composition"', *ELH*, 65:4, 899–928.
Williams, J. (2001) 'Displacing Romanticism: Anna Seward, Joseph Weston, and the Unschooled Sons of Genius', in P. Kitson (ed.) *Placing and Displacing Romanticism* (Aldershot: Ashgate), pp. 146–56.
Williams, R. (1976) *Keywords: A Vocbulary of Culture and Society* (London: Croom Helm; rev. edn (1983) London: Fontana).
Willis, M. (2006) *Mesmerists, Monsters, and Machines: Science Fiction and the Cultures of Science in the Nineteenth Century* (Kent, OH: Kent State University Press).
Willis, M. and C. Wynne (eds) (2006) *Victorian Literary Mesmerism* (Amsterdam: Rodopi).
Wilson, C. (2003) 'Astronomy and Cosmology', in R. Porter (ed.) *Eighteenth-Century Science*, The Cambridge History of Science, 8 vols (Cambridge: Cambridge University Press), IV, 328–53.
Wilson, E. (2003) *The Spiritual History of Ice: Romanticism, Science, and the Imagination* (Basingstoke: Palgrave).
—— (2006) 'Matter and Spirit in the Age of Animal Magnetism', *Philosophy and Literature*, 30:2, 329–45.
Wilson, P.K. (2005) 'Erasmus Darwin on Human Reproductive Generation: Placing Heredity within Historical and *Zoonomian* Contexts', in C.U. Murray Smith and R. Arnott (eds) *The Genius of Erasmus Darwin* (Aldershot: Ashgate), pp. 113–32.
Winters, A. (1998) *Mesmerized: Powers of Mind in Victorian Britain* (Chicago and London: University of Chicago Press).
Wollstonecraft, M. (1989) *The Works of Mary Wollstonecraft*, J. Todd and M. Butler (eds), 7 vols (London: William Pickering).
—— (1997) *The Vindications*, D.L. Macdonald and K. Scherf (eds) (Ontario: Broadview).
—— (2004) *The Collected Letters of Mary Wollstonecraft*, J. Todd (ed.) (Harmondsworth: Penguin).
Wood, P. (ed.) (2004) *Science and Dissent in England, 1688–1945* (Aldershot: Ashgate).
Wordsworth, W. (1967) *The Letters of William and Dorothy Wordsworth*, E. de Selincourt (ed.), 8 vols, 2nd edn (Oxford: Clarendon Press).
—— (1974) *Prose Works*, W.J.B. Owen and J.W. Smyser (eds), 3 vols (Oxford: Clarendon Press).
—— (1990) *Poetical Works*, T. Hutchinson (ed.), E. de Selincourt (rev. edn) (Oxford: Oxford University Press).
—— (1992) *Lyrical Ballads and Other Poems 1797–1800*, J. Butler and K. Green (eds) (Ithaca and London: Cornell University Press).
Wu, D. (1995) *Wordsworth's Reading, 1800–1815* (Cambridge: Cambridge University Press).

Wunder, J.N. (2008) *Keats, Hermeticism, and the Secret Societies* (Farnham: Ashgate).
Wyatt, J. (1995) *Wordsworth and the Geologists* (Cambridge: Cambridge University Press).
Wylie, I. (1989) *Young Coleridge and the Philosophers of Nature* (Oxford: Clarendon Press).
Yeo, R. (1993) *Defining Science: William Whewell, Natural Knowledge and Public Debate in Early Victorian Britain* (Cambridge: Cambridge University Press).
[Young, E.] (1759) *Conjectures on Original Composition. In a Letter to the Author of Sir Charles Grandison* (London: A. Millar and R. and J. Dodsley).
Youngquist, P. (2003) *Monstrosities: Bodies and British Romanticism* (Minneapolis: University of Minnesota Press).
Yudin, M. (1994) 'Joanna Baillie's Introductory Discourse as a Precursor to Wordsworth's Preface to *Lyrical Ballads*', *Compar(a)ison*, 1, 101–12.

Index

Printed by Printforce, United Kingdom